CW00428941

THE FINAL HOUR

A DUBLIN NIGHTS NOVEL

BRITTNEY SAHIN

The Final Hour

A Dublin Nights Novel

By: Brittney Sahin

Published by: EmKo Media, LLC

Copyright © 2020 EmKo Media, LLC

This book is an original publication of Brittney Sahin.

In accordance with the U.S. Copyright Act of 1976, the scanning, uploading, and electronic sharing of any part of this book without permission of the publisher constitute unlawful piracy and theft of the author's intellectual property. If you would like to use material from the book (other than for review purposes), prior written permission must be obtained by contacting brittneysahin@emkomedia.net Thank you for your support of the author's rights.

This book is a work of fiction. Names, characters, places, and incidents either are products of the author's imagination or are used fictitiously. Any resemblance to actual persons, living or dead, business establishments, events, or locales is entirely coincidental. The author acknowledges the trademarked status and trademark owners of various products, brands, and/or restaurants referenced in this work of fiction, which have been used without permission. The publication/use of these trademarks is not authorized, associated with, or sponsored by the trademark owners.

Chief Editor: Deb Markanton

Editor: Arielle Brubaker

Proofreader: Judy Zweifel, Judy's Proofreading

Cover Design: LJ, Mayhem Cover Creations

Ebook ISBN: 9781947717299

Paperback ISBN: 9798574539965

❀ Created with Vellum

For Annette Reavis

A kind, caring, and amazing lady. I am honored to call you a friend. Thank you for everything.

ALSO BY BRITTNEY SAHIN

Stealth Ops: Bravo Team

Finding His Mark - Bravo One, Luke
Finding Justice - Bravo Two, Owen
Finding the Fight - Bravo Three, Asher
Finding Her Chance - Bravo Four, Liam
Finding the Way Back - Bravo Five, Knox

Stealth Ops: Echo Team

Chasing the Knight - Echo One, Wyatt
Chasing Daylight - Echo Two, A.J.
Chasing Fortune - Echo Three, Chris
Chasing Shadows - Echo Four, Roman (3/25/21)
Book 10 - Echo Five, Finn

Becoming Us: Stealth Ops spin-off series

Someone Like You
My Every Breath

Dublin Nights

On the Edge
On the Line
The Real Deal

PROLOGUE

EMILIA

LAS VEGAS, NEVADA (TEN YEARS AGO)

"Would you stop worrying?" Chanel yelled in my ear as the audience roared, many on their feet, pumping their arms as if they, too, wanted to be inside the Octagon and fighting at the MGM Grand Garden Arena. "I promise, hanging out with me won't land you on Santa's naughty list. Too late, anyway. Christmas was last week," she teased, poking me in the side with her elbow.

"I'm not worried," I finally responded, the protest bubbling from my lips like a hot drop of acid.

I caught Chanel's brown eyes as she fingered strands of honey-brown bangs away from her face. "Liar."

Maybe I was lying, but if our fathers ever found out we were friends, I couldn't imagine the consequences. Our families were sworn enemies. The good-versus-evil kind.

So, I couldn't stop myself from constantly looking around and searching the crowd. Ensuring no one was spying on us. Or hell, checking for snipers in the wings. A two-for-one special. Take out the daughters of two of the most powerful men in the world with two quick pops.

I forced my focus back on the ring just as one of the fighters slammed his fist hard into the other guy's jaw. Chanel turned my way, stealing her eyes from the view of the scene. For the daughter of a killer, she sure hated blood.

We were sitting in the second row back from the cage. It was round three between Nate Diaz and Donald Cerrone. From the looks of it, the fight would go to a decision.

It was much less exciting when judges chose a victor. Selecting a winner based on strikes and takedowns still felt too subjective. Too open to personal biases. I wanted a clear result. Let the fighters go at it until someone tapped out or was knocked out. That's how the underground fights were handled back home in Italy, at least.

Chanel crossed her long legs, much more comfortable now that the fight was over. "Just remind me why I flew halfway around the world to hang out with you for your birthday, yet instead of partying, we're watching men beat the shit out of each other?"

I checked my skinny silver watch as we waited for the winner to be declared. "Not my birthday for thirty minutes. And how can you not love this? Two people inside a cage going at it. It's primitive and raw. And it's also controlled, so you don't need to worry. No one is dying tonight."

"We have a lot in common, Ems, except this." She smiled. "But you're the birthday girl, so I'm here for you and whatever you want to do."

A friend of mine managed the shows at the MGM Garden Arena, and he helped me get tickets the second they were available. Thankfully, he had no connection to my father or Chanel's, which meant our attendance together shouldn't raise any flags if he spotted us. Not that he'd recognize Chanel. We were in the States, and most Americans were unfamiliar with our families. And that meant Chanel was most likely right. I needed to cut the worrying. Damn the strange nagging feeling in my gut, though.

My attention abruptly swung to four men in casual business attire. Dark trousers and jackets, crisp dress shirts with the top buttons left undone. They headed down our row toward the empty seats next to us. Many of the VIPs showed up at the last minute to watch the evening's main event, which was up next, so I shouldn't assume they were secretly sent as assassins to take one of us out.

I shifted closer to Chanel when one of the nicely dressed men filled the chair next to mine, his arm bumping into my bare one.

"Pardon," he commented, but I offered a tight "no worries" nod without casting a look his way. I didn't need to put a face to the suit. I'd met a lot of businessmen in my two years thus far in Vegas, and none had ever been worth a minute of my time.

"You sure you want to be here?" I overheard him speak. "There are other events I'd be happy to take you all to."

Apparently, the suit disliked fighting as much as Chanel.

The Irish lilt of his voice was an interesting surprise, though.

Plot twist.

I did have a weakness for an Irish accent—who didn't?

I glanced at Chanel while I continued to eavesdrop on the suit, contemplating the odds of his looks being as sexy as the sound of that deep, baritone voice. A sexy businessman was preferable to a sexy hitman, at least.

"You don't like fighting?" a different voice chimed in,

American from the sounds of it. "You're Irish. Isn't an affinity for a good fight a requirement if you're from Dublin?"

Yeah, not a hitman. Unless he's a really good actor.

"Just not a fan of fighting. I have my reasons," the Irishman responded, a glib tone to his voice.

I had the sudden urge to lure an answer out of him. Uncover the truth. Apply a little pressure and discover whatever it was that had this Irishman probably wishing he were anywhere else.

"Fighting is cathartic. Watching it. Doing it. Trust me." A raspy, flirtatious edge sounded through my tone. "You don't know what you're missing." Why did I just say that?

The Irishman didn't respond. Maybe he assumed I'd been speaking to Chanel.

A few moments passed before he shifted in his seat, inadvertently bumping his leg into mine, and the movement sent my black clutch sliding off my lap.

With lightning-quick reflexes, he snatched the clutch before it hit the ground. I was somewhat shocked to realize he'd been faster than me.

And hitman was back on the table.

My gaze followed the line of his suit jacket down to his strong hand that now offered my clutch. "Thank you," I said softly. Dragging my eyes up his white pressed shirt, sans tie, and along the tan column of his throat, I paused to appreciate his handsome face. A clean-shaven, not-quite-chiseled jawline. Full lips that begged to be kissed. To be tasted. A perfectly straight blade of a nose. Short blond hair, the top a touch unruly, above brilliant blue eyes that now held mine. He couldn't be but a few years older than me. And the looks did indeed match the sexy voice.

I kept my hand on top of his as he remained holding my clutch between us.

I wasn't one to get starstruck or become speechless. No tingling sensations because of a man unless I was mid-orgasm. And butterflies? The only kind I'd experienced were the ones that flitted around in our yard while I practiced archery when I was younger.

Of course, my life was unique, and maybe that meant my responses to normal situations were also different.

Papà loved me like a daughter but treated me like a man preparing to wage war starting at a young age. I was shooting arrows and learning to fight with knives before I got my period.

And yet, right now, my heart beat harder. Faster. Not its normal steady rhythm. And a wicked slash of desire cut sharply down my belly and between my legs.

All that from just one look piqued my curiosity. It had me wondering what this Irishman would be like in bed.

It'd honestly be my kind of luck if this hot guy was sent to kill me, though. *You're just jumpy because Chanel is here. He's a guy in a suit. A freaking hot Irish guy in a suit. That's it.*

I couldn't form words as I partook in this staring contest that felt more like a battle. But for the first time in my life, I didn't know if I was strong enough to prevail.

I blinked. Folded. Lost the round.

I quickly looked away from those startling eyes. Eyes that seemed as if they might hold all the answers to the universe. As I took the clutch, I focused on catching my breath while attempting to explain away the bizarre sensations ransacking my body.

Unlike Chanel, I'd gone head-to-head with more than one billionaire businessman before I could even drive. I'd sparred with men twice my size. Her father treated her like a glass doll to be shelved and observed. My father taught me to inspect dolls for listening devices.

But this life was the price that came with being the daughter of the Italian leader of *La Lega dei Fratelli*, The League of Brothers. Our family took down bad guys for a living, and as a result, we had a lot of enemies.

So, for being so tough, it was hard to believe my heart was stuttering and my breathing suspended all due to this man and his bold, blue eyes beneath slanted brows, pinning me with a curious look.

I closed my eyes and sucked in a breath, finding myself pleasantly gathering in the Irishman's masculine cologne, a contrast to the perfume I wore. White petals, honey, and ivory wrapped my limbs like a blanket. The only sweet and pure thing about me tonight was my scent, as I was dressed in all black save for my red heels and lips.

The man's cologne and my perfume clashed in the air. Masculine versus feminine. And now, I was longing for a stranger to touch me.

"I'd like to get laid tonight."

Chanel's abrupt statement had the Irishman clearing his throat. It was loud in the arena, but his surprised reaction made it clear he'd heard.

"Oh, really?" I eyed Chanel, amused by her bluntness. She'd also offered me a reprieve from my confused feelings about the stranger off to my left.

"I think you should, too. Birthday sex. Or at least, a midnight kiss when you turn twenty-one. You know, something sexy and romantic. Very fairy tale-esque. That's what I want when it's my big day," Chanel went on, oblivious to the ogre off to her right staring at her like he might throw her over his shoulder and hightail it to his suite if she kept it up.

I lifted my chin and snarled on instinct, a warning to back off. He quickly returned his gaze to the fight as if he knew I was dangerous just by looking at me.

And hell, I was dangerous, wasn't I?

Papà was a good man, fighting for justice, but there was still blood on his hands. Eventually, there'd be blood on my hands, too.

As Papà's only child, I was expected to take the path he'd designed for me. It was meant to happen the day I turned twenty-one, too.

But for tonight, I wanted to follow Chanel's advice and stop worrying. Stop assuming the hot Irish guy was sent to kill me. I wanted to momentarily forget the shackles of my family name.

"Honestly, you should be having a minimum of two orgasms a day, and preferably not by your own hand," Chanel continued her sex lecture since I'd yet to respond. "I'm worried your uptight look means you haven't even been getting yourself off." She twirled a pink-tipped fingernail my way, swiveling on her seat to face me.

I rolled my eyes at her attempt to draw natural color to my cheeks when she knew damn well I was like her. We didn't get embarrassed.

A flash of light had me turning on my seat and finding the man who'd taken a snapshot of the audience as he stood near a camerawoman panning her lens on the crowd.

I lowered my head and lifted the clutch in front of my face until the lens pointed another way.

That camera was probably more dangerous than the Irish guy or anyone else in the arena, for that matter. We were way too close to the action, and the last thing we needed was to wind up on television. Wow, I had not thought this night through.

Chanel whispered a mishmash of her mother's native Greek and her father's French beneath her breath, her assessment of my "situation" evident by the concerned expression on her face, and I remembered what we'd been talking about before my thoughts had taken a sharp turn.

Right. I need to get laid.

She dropped her eyes to my outfit and her mouth tightened in disapproval. "You're too intimidating. I think you scare men off. That black halter top dips into a sharp V and shows your cleavage, but men are too damn afraid of you to actually check out your tits. Probably fear you'll break their neck for looking." She grinned, knowing I could and would hurt a man if he were to bother me. "And those tight-fitting black trousers paired with that 'stay the fuck away' smoky eye makeup scares them off. I'm just saying—"

"I'm not wearing all black." I had to raise my voice over the music as Brock Lesnar, one of the main fighters, made his entrance, his theme song blasting.

"You should've gone with pink like I suggested. The red heels and lipstick are killer, but they scream that you'll gladly grab a man by the balls and not in a good kind of way."

"I'm not that intimidating." Only when someone knew of my father did they back away. Well, usually. "Also, we can't all have your flair." I pointed to Chanel's bright gold sequin top and matching gold shorts. Her boots were the show stealer, though. A mix of cowboy and porn star.

She popped up one shoulder and said first in French and then in English, "'*In order to be irreplaceable, one must always be different.*'"

"Mm." I smiled. "You and your Coco Chanel quotes."

"What? Mama named me after her favorite designer.

8

Coco's an icon, and . . ." Her words faded as a frown formed on her lips. "Sorry." Chanel was unnecessarily sensitive when she talked about her mother since she knew I didn't have one, and she always felt guilty when she mentioned her.

I shook off the shitstorm that attempted to grab hold of me and let it drift away.

I chanced a look at the Irishman, still deciding whether or not we should stay for the main event or if we ought to make a quick exit.

He had a hand gripping the nape of his neck, his jaw clenched in obvious discomfort as he viewed the cage.

He must have sensed my gaze because he quickly lowered his hand to his lap, brushing against me in the process.

A quick, barely there touch of our pinky fingers, but that little shock of something—we'll call it static electricity—zipped up my finger, and I hurriedly set my hand atop my clutch.

I'd seen and witnessed a lot in my almost twenty-one years, but this truly was the first time skin-to-skin contact and a pair of blue eyes had me feeling caught in the middle of some cataclysmic event.

His lips slowly parted, as if hesitant to break the spell of this strange moment between us, and then he spoke. "Hi."

There was so much packed into that little word. I couldn't quite determine what it was exactly, but I felt as though I'd just been KO'd in that Octagon. A quick punch, and I was down. Didn't even see it coming. Blindsided.

I'm a fighter. A winner. A damn Calibrisi, I scolded myself to try and get my head on straight. I was only on edge like this whenever I risked hanging out with my best friend, which had to explain my reactions to this man.

The smile that crossed his lips was slow, somehow caught

between surprised and intrigued. And that hot-as-hell smile transformed to a sexy, wolfish, take-no-prisoners grin.

He was about to speak again. Maybe offer his name. His lips were poised and ready to go, and then the strangest thing happened—goose bumps peppered my skin as though a sudden chill had coated my body.

Time to go. I tore my gaze away from him and over to Chanel as I stood. "Let's go dancing."

"Oh." Chanel beamed. "Great." I grabbed her hand and all but yanked her out of her seat and pulled her along behind me without so much as one last look at Mr. Irish.

No more eye contact with that man. He may not have been a killer, but my sudden and very intense response to him had me uneasy.

"I need a drink," I announced once Chanel and I were out of the noise and chaos of the arena, my heels loudly clicking as I fast-tracked us farther away. "Champagne?"

"'*I only drink champagne on two occasions, when I am in love and when I am not,*'" Chanel teased, pulling out another Coco Chanel quote.

Chanel was nineteen, but her ID had her at twenty-three, so we'd be good at the clubs.

"And what are you now?" I asked with a smile.

"Looking to get laid. So, I'll need something stronger." She began speaking in her own special language—that mix of French and Greek, which I jokingly called "Freek"—that she assumed I understood.

I checked the time. Fourteen minutes until my birthday. I was on the cusp of turning twenty-one.

I was born at 12:01a.m., so technically my birthday was the 31st, but I liked to straddle the two days and celebrate right smack between the 30th and 31st. My last birthday as a free woman. *Who am I kidding? Was I ever really free?*

A free woman wouldn't have to turn off her phone because her friend was visiting. She wouldn't have to avoid the hotel desk messages and detach the hotel phone from the wall because that red blinking light, indicating Papà had called, made her stomach hurt.

For such a strong woman, I was . . . weak when it came to him.

I abruptly stopped walking near the lobby of the hotel when I could have sworn I saw a League fixer turn down the hall up ahead, on his way for the main casino.

League fixers worked for League leaders, their job as straightforward and self-explanatory as it sounded. They did a whole slew of tasks for the men in charge.

Had Papà sent someone to bring me home?

When I was in Sicily for Christmas last week, I'd begged for more time, asked for one more week—just until the end of the year. I'd lied to Papà and told him it was about spending my twenty-first birthday in Vegas. I couldn't have told him the truth, that I wasn't ready to join The League, to become a killer.

And on top of that, I'd officially be obligated to partake in the feud between my family and Chanel's. Her father was a notorious criminal and one of the leaders of an enemy group known as The Alliance, but I'd always felt that the hate between our families went beyond who our fathers were.

I wasn't even allowed to breathe the same air as Chanel. When our families discovered she attended boarding school in London while I was at Oxford for university, Papà forced me to transfer out of England. He didn't want us living in the same city. Out of anger, I simply dropped out of school and took off to Vegas at nineteen. I had a feeling I'd never bother to finish my degree. I had plenty of real world experience that couldn't be taught in a classroom, anyway.

"What, you see a ghost?" Chanel joked as I stole a careful glimpse around the corner to where I'd thought Sebastian Renaud had disappeared.

"No, more like Sebastian."

"*The* Sebastian? That super hot but total badass League fixer feared by even my father?"

Sebastian was gorgeous, but he treated me like a sister, as did most League fixers. Only one fixer, Luca Moreau, had ever come on to me, and that had been a drunken mistake. Luca was the nephew of the French League leader. He was also Sebastian's best friend, but he was a master manipulator, and I didn't trust him. Sex with that man was one of my biggest regrets.

I turned back to face her. "I thought it was him, but I think my mind is playing tricks on me." I was overreacting. A big, fat checkmark in the column of strange tonight since that was also not my style. "Alcohol. I need it." I hooked my arm around Chanel's waist. "Let's go dancing."

Ten minutes later, I found myself alone at the bar while Chanel danced with a guy probably twice her age.

The bartender closest to me, Jason, knew me well. He was one of the few men I trusted in Vegas, probably because he never hit on me since he played for the other team.

"Birthday girl," Jason announced and leaned over the counter to plant a kiss on my left, then right cheek.

"Almost," I said while surveying the crowd dancing to a song that was a throwback to the '90s and electronic dance music. I was pretty sure it was *Confusion* by New Order, made famous by the movie *Blade.* The good-versus-evil theme of the Wesley Snipes vampire movie reminded me of my own life. Well, minus the vampires. I was forever caught between the two worlds.

"You here to celebrate?" Jason asked after delivering a cocktail to the woman on the stool next to me.

"Yes," I said over the pounding music pulsating through my body. It was time to relax and enjoy the evening, push my worries aside for one last night. "Whip me up something special, will you? But let's make it official and wait until midnight since we're in the States."

"Ridiculous, right? Not allowed to drink until twenty-one, but you can die for your country at eighteen."

I stilled at the sound of the deep voice behind me, that sexy Irish brogue wrapped around me like a warm caress. The man radiated "confident alpha" without the slightest hint of arrogance and had my nipples standing at attention. Good thing I was wearing sticky nipple pads beneath my halter.

"I would have to agree." At least my voice worked this time. I slowly turned and faced the Irishman with the incredible eyes from the arena. "Did you follow me here?"

"I'm torn about how to answer." He didn't set a hand on the bar and lean in like most men probably would have. He kept his distance as though sensing I was a woman who liked my space. But he was close enough that the smell of his cologne fluttered to my nose. "If I say no, then it appears fate brought us together again, but I hate lying. If I say yes, then I look like a stalker."

Or a hitman, but I quickly shelved that idea as being paranoid because the man had me smiling right now. "I happen to value honesty."

"Then I ditched the boring businessmen and searched all the clubs at the hotel in hopes you'd be in one." The booming surround sound muffled his gorgeous accent. "Because it's not every day a woman knocks the breath out of me without actually doing anything other than look my way."

It was just as hard to see in the club as it had been in the arena, the darkness fractured only by intermittent flashes of colored lights. But we were facing each other now, so I took a tour of his body with my eyes, drinking in the sight of him.

Black trousers encased his long legs. A crisp, white dress shirt, top two buttons popped, with an open jacket. A casual business look.

He had money, but he didn't flaunt it. I'd been around plenty of wealthy men in my life, and there was definitely a stereotype out there, but he didn't fall into that category. But I liked what I saw. My body responded, electricity zipping to every erogenous zone. I grew even hotter whenever our gazes collided.

"Your accent, I'm guessing Italian. Have you been here a long time?" he asked when I'd yet to summon a response to his confession. "I'm—"

"No names." *Safer for us both.* Besides, being a Calibrisi wouldn't tether me to the ground tonight. I wasn't the daughter of a feared and powerful man. "Can we be two strangers who happen to share a moment and leave it at that?"

His brows tightened, and his bottom lip rolled inward for a brief moment. "So, you felt that, too, huh?"

"Hard not to," I admitted.

"Hey, here's your birthday drink," Jason called from behind the bar, and I mentally willed him not to give away my name.

The Irishman checked his watch. "Ten more seconds until midnight."

"Well, technically I was born a minute after twelve." My lips twitched into a smile, which caught me by surprise since the subject of my birth never usually resulted in happy thoughts—no mother and all that. But I didn't avoid celebrating my birthday because that would mean I had . . . well, feelings about it, but . . .

"Fairy tales. You a fan?"

I set my drink down alongside my clutch, momentarily confused about his question until I remembered he'd probably overheard Chanel's words back at the arena. "Do I look like a woman who buys into fairy-tale nonsense? Am I a damsel in distress in need of a hero?"

"No, you look like a woman who can handle herself." Nevertheless, he took one step forward and banded a hand around my waist, evidently deciding to throw caution to the wind.

I could have easily twisted his arm behind his back and brought him to his knees in an instant for setting a hand on me.

But I didn't want to. No, I wanted his hands all freaking over me.

Ah, the midnight kiss. Now I recalled Chanel's earlier words and realized that's what he was suggesting. I nodded, permitting him to do exactly that.

Bright lights danced all around us in time with the bass as he palmed my cheek, clearly waiting for 12:01, wanting it to be official.

Drawing nearer to me, his lips gently pressed to mine, and when I placed my hand on the hard planes of his chest, a rumble of appreciation vibrated through from our connection.

It was soft and sensual, nothing too naughty, as though he were the prince waking Sleeping Beauty. Just enough to draw my attention, yet reserved enough to declare respect, acknowledging that the next move was mine to make. Essentially, it was perfect.

His lips lingered close to mine once our mouths broke apart, but his eyes remained closed as he released a quiet sigh. It was almost as if he were processing a storm of emotions created by our downright sinfully chaste kiss. It felt that way for me, at least.

"Do it again," I commanded, rooted in place, the loud music fading away to the distant background. "But put your tongue in my mouth and taste me this time."

"I'll need a name for that, love." His breath tickled my lips as our bodies remained close but not touching. The beats of our hearts nearly mingling. *Who am I now? A poet?*

"How about we choose names from a book?" For some reason, Charles Dickens popped into my head. "*Great Expectations.*" I was stuck on the ride of pleasure from that kiss, and I didn't want to get off. Well, retract that line. I *did* want to get off. Very, very much.

"I'm not a Pip," he said with a laugh, and God, he had a gorgeous smile, and he probably won a lot of hearts with it. He was currently winning mine over. Well, he was winning over my body. Still, it wasn't an easy feat. "What about *Romeo and Juliet?*"

"Unless you think a good time ends with someone stabbing themselves or drinking poison—"

"Point taken." He smiled. "Favorite Vegas movie, then?"

"You pick," I prompted.

"*Ocean's Eleven.* I'll be Clooney." He certainly had the grace and charm of that actor. They didn't look alike, and he was probably half the man's age, but it would work.

"I guess that makes me Brad Pitt." I smirked, drawing a chuckle out of him as he pressed his forehead to mine.

"I think you're more of a Julia," he countered, though I looked nothing like the redheaded actress.

Julia Roberts and George Clooney. Two strangers, eschewing the confines of our true identities, who desperately needed another kiss.

But damn it, he stepped back, and his hands disappeared

into his pockets. That was the opposite of what I wanted. "Do you want to go somewhere and talk? Take a walk? I'd like to get to know you, *Julia*."

"I don't talk about myself," I warned, reaching for my drink. "Besides, doesn't that defeat the purpose of an alias?" I shifted to the side, accidentally touching some big guy next to me, drawing his immediate attention.

"Hello, hello." The man's eyes became laser-focused on my cleavage. "How much are you?"

Yeah, wrong movie, asshole. I wasn't playing Julia Roberts in *Pretty Woman*, and this guy was two seconds away from meeting my fist, but Clooney reprieved his role of the prince, setting a hand to the big guy's arm as he stepped alongside me.

"Apologize and back off," Clooney growled, eyeing the guy with sharp confidence even though the man looked to be a professional weightlifter.

"Thank you," I said to Clooney, "but I can handle myself." *Remember?* I lifted my chin and pinned my gaze to the idiot. "How about you take the cash you saved up for this little trip to Vegas that you were probably planning to spend on blow or poker, maybe both, and—"

"I'd rather fuck you." The stupid asshat kissed the air and circled his hand around my wrist.

I closed my eyes, warning myself not to strike him and draw attention. *Chanel is in town.*

But at the sound of a thud and the Irishman rasping a curse, my eyes flew open as Clooney drew his fist back from the man's jaw.

Jason had security on us in a flash before the scene turned into a brawl.

"I need air." Snatching my clutch from the bar top, I strode in search of Chanel, who was now making out with the man she'd been dancing with earlier, clueless to what had just happened.

"Be right back," I told her after she came up for air.

"You didn't have to do that," I informed Clooney once we were in the hall outside the club. "Let me see your hand." I turned and faced him. "I thought you weren't a fan of fighting." I held his clenched fist between my palms. His knuckles were red, but the skin wasn't broken.

"You heard me say that?"

I lifted my eyes to meet his, and his intense blue gaze had me forgetting why we were standing out in the hall. The memory of his lips on mine spontaneously painted a picture in my mind of all the other places on my body I'd like to feel his mouth.

"If you don't like fighting, why'd you nearly start one back there?" I let go of his hand and took a few slow steps forward, tucking my clutch under my arm.

"My brother." He surprised me with a response after a few quiet minutes of taking in the scene as we strolled through the massive hotel and casino. When MGM first opened its doors, it was the largest hotel complex in the world. It was also originally decorated in an Emerald City à la *Wizard of Oz* theme. The hotel was going through another round of renovations, but for the most part, the newest Hollywood theme was draped in Christmas from end to end.

My heels came to an abrupt stop in front of the famous MGM lion, who wore a Santa hat and was surrounded by a bed of red poinsettias.

Clooney pinched the bridge of his nose with his thumb and forefinger. "My brother likes to fight. Underground stuff back in Dublin. He doesn't do it for the money. He just likes that MMA shite, I don't know." He released a ragged breath. It was obviously a sore subject.

"And you're worried he'll get hurt?"

"More like I'm worried he'll kill someone."

His words stung more than he could possibly know. Because someday, I would be a killer.

Sure, The League had its own prisons for the scum of the earth. Lowlife human traffickers, murderers—people The League couldn't trust in a regular prison, worried their ability to commit crimes would happen even from behind regular prison bars.

But there were times when death was the only option. I didn't know how many lives Sebastian had taken in the name of my father, or other billionaire League leaders, or how many deaths I'd rack up when it was time.

His eyes dropped to the hand he'd used to clock that guy when he'd saved me the trouble.

"For a second in that club, you understood your brother's desire to strike, didn't you?" I whispered the realization.

He immediately looked at me as if I'd caught him naked.

I stepped closer, drawing the distance between us to barely a whisper of space. "It felt good to hurt that man." My attention skated to the movement of his Adam's apple as he swallowed hard. "There's something inside you," I began, pointing to his hard chest, "something innate that made you respond like that. And if you're beating yourself up for despising your brother's life choices all the while wishing you could track that asshole down and do more damage to his face—"

Lips fused to mine in a hot second, cutting me off.

This was not soft or gentle. It was raw and intense. Fierce. Exactly what I needed.

Pleasure rolled and wrapped around every part of me as my chest tightened and need grabbed hold of me—spectators be damned.

19

I groaned against his mouth when his tongue slipped between my lips.

Yes. This. This was what I needed for my birthday. A moment of truth only found in the honesty of such a passionate kiss. You can't hide from a kiss like that.

"You're . . . different," he said after easing his lips from mine a few heartbeats later. "There's something about you."

Yeah, you have no idea.

Our eyes connected, our faces still close enough to lean in for another one of those delicious kisses.

I looked left and then right, realizing we were too out in the open. Sebastian may not have been in the casino, but that didn't mean my father hadn't sent one of his men to watch over me. "You want to go to my suite? We can have a drink and talk there." *And hopefully I didn't read you wrong, and you were sent to kill me.*

"I don't normally hesitate to go to a beautiful woman's room . . ." He shook his head and briefly closed one eye. "Well, that came out bloody wrong."

"Are you turning me down?" A surprised but playful smile touched my mouth.

He scratched the back of his head, another wave of discomfort crossing his face. "I just—"

"You just what?" I asked, captivated by this handsome man becoming tongue-tied.

"Like I said," he began while reaching for my hand, "you're different, and I think you deserve more than whatever I can give you."

I splayed my palm on his firm chest, noticing how my short, blood-red nails stood out against the stark white of his dress shirt. "And what can you give me, *Clooney*?"

His hand reached around my body and landed on the small of my back. "Multiple orgasms."

I wet my lips. "What's wrong with that?" I was a bit dizzy from the bright lights, the way-too-cheerful holiday music, and the heady desire pouring through me.

"I'm heading to Dublin in the morning. And I have the distinct feeling that if I go to your room, I won't want to leave. And I'll want a name and number. And I don't do the after stuff or the numbers."

I didn't even care that he'd just admitted he was a player. Wasn't I one, too? I didn't have boyfriends, and I certainly didn't draw hearts around men's names while waiting for them to send me flowers and chocolates.

I scared him, didn't I?

He felt the same thing I was feeling. That strange, hypnotic lure I couldn't explain.

And it terrified him because it chipped away at his fear of intimacy and attachment.

I wasn't so much afraid of those things as I knew they weren't in the cards for me anytime soon, especially since I was about to follow in my father's footsteps and own my birthright, but I could understand his desire for walls. After all, I was the one who didn't want to share my name.

"I promise you I won't give you my number even if you ask." Why would I? Why subject anyone to the darkness of my world? Once that door opened, once someone saw what really went on in the world, they'd never be able to unsee it. Sometimes ignorance was bliss. Papà made sacrifices, along with other League members, so men like Clooney wouldn't be subjected to the true darkness of the world. It was a powerfully heavy burden and one I was destined to carry.

His attention went to the floor, his jaw tightening. He was fighting an internal war, one I knew so well. When he redirected those gorgeous blue eyes back on me, I realized he was going to give in to desire. "Julia and Clooney, huh?"

"Yes," I mouthed, wishing for one night where I could close that door and forget everything I'd witnessed in my life. Shut it all out. Just tonight.

In one fast movement, he pulled me against him and crushed his mouth to mine as if the Titans or gods themselves couldn't keep him away.

We broke apart at the ding from the nearby lift doors opening. And thank God it was empty because he pulled me inside and had my back to the wall in an instant. I let go of my clutch when Clooney took hold of my wrists, raised my arms, and trapped them above my head. Holding both wrists with one large hand, he used the other to cup my chin, then moved in for another searing kiss.

Once we arrived at my floor and exited the lift, I sputtered in a hurry while snatching my clutch, "My suite is this way." Our clasped palms felt somehow as intimate as when our bodies had been fitted together moments ago.

He released my hand when I stopped in front of my door and indicated I needed to search for my keycard. But as soon as I retrieved it, he hoisted me up and had my legs wrapped around his hips, my back to the wall next to the door, and he held me there as our tongues dueled.

The need had taken over.

It was otherworldly.

I felt it, too.

But . . .

Something was wrong. That knot of concern in the pit of my stomach that'd bothered me in the arena earlier came back, and when I shifted my ear to the wall, I heard indistinct sounds coming from within my suite. And it sure as hell didn't sound like Chanel having sex, either.

I lowered my red heels to the floor. "One second," I told

him as he brought a hand over his mouth, covering my smeared lipstick around his lips.

I swiped the card as quietly as possible, then slowly peeked my head into the room.

Oh God. My eyes connected with a man towering over a motionless body lying on the floor, a knife in his hand, blood dripping onto the tan and maroon patterned carpet. He looked up, relief in his eyes at the sight of me.

Sebastian *was* in Vegas. And now there was a dead guy in my hotel room.

A hitman? I quickly slammed the door shut and spun around to face Clooney in the hall. "You have to go. Now." Fear constricted my throat.

"Oh." He stepped back, blinking in surprise.

"The, um, person I was with tonight, she's inside and sick, and I-I need to be with her." The lie rolled clumsily from my tongue. I was worried Sebastian would open the door any second. "I'm sorry. But maybe you were right—this shouldn't happen."

I wanted to grab his shirt. Fist the material and kiss him goodbye. But the dead body inside stopped me. The fact Papà had sent Sebastian, the most dangerous of all League fixers to Vegas, stopped me.

"Goodbye, Clooney," I said, the words feeling like shards of glass and sounding painfully broken as they caught in my throat. "Thank you for the birthday kiss." It would have been a perfect night.

His fingers twitched at his sides as if he were itching to reach for me. "I guess it's goodbye, then, Julia." His brows dipped inward, and it had my stomach sinking. He was a stranger. It shouldn't feel this sad to walk away from him.

But what choice did I have? A dead body and a powerful League fixer waited on the other side of the door.

I finally willed myself to turn away so I could confront another Irishman.

My shoulders collapsed in defeat once I was inside my suite, not finding Sebastian anywhere in sight. I tossed my clutch and maneuvered around the dead body staining the carpet. We'd need to call a special team to remove it and all evidence of what happened.

Sebastian exited the downstairs bedroom and stalked my way with purposeful strides.

"What's going on? Who is this guy?" I pointed to the dead man ruining the carpets.

Sebastian reached for my shoulders when my focus moved to the bedroom door he'd closed. "Your father and I have been trying to reach you all day. We got word there'd be an attempt on your life tonight." He kept hold of my shoulders but sealed his eyes tight. "Why were you with the daughter of Simon Laurent tonight? Her family is Alliance, Emilia," he seethed. "What were you thinking? And why in God's name was she in your suite?"

"*Was*?" My stomach roiled when pain stabbed me every which way. Terror clawed and scratched. "Where's Chanel?" I tried to move around him to get to the bedroom, but he was tall and a dominating force. When his eyes met mine once again, I saw the kind of worry there a man like Sebastian didn't often display.

"Don't make me drop you to your ass," I warned.

Sebastian may have helped train me, but I would get around him one way or another.

"I can't let you go in there," he said in a throaty voice as he continued restraining me.

I stopped fighting him, knowing the horrible truth as to why he didn't want me in that room. Chanel must have come back to the suite while I was off with Clooney.

"No." Tears welled in my eyes, and I sank to my knees. "No, no, no."

"I'm so sorry. I think they assumed it was you in the room, and then I showed up." He lowered to his knees before me and urged me to look his way. "Emilia, it's time to come home."

CHAPTER ONE

SEAN

DUBLIN, IRELAND – PRESENT DAY (DECEMBER 2021)

LEAVE IT TO EMILIA TO RETURN TO THE CITY BY MAKING AN entrance impressive enough for an action film. Her black hair, pulled into a ponytail, whipped behind her as she ran, chasing down the target. It looked like she planned on "hunting" tonight based on the quiver of arrows strapped to her back. Most likely, a sidearm and knife on her as well.

Lamp posts dotted the park emitting their hazy yellow glow in the late hour, lighting up my path and allowing me to see clearly.

She was ridiculously fast. I was on my Ducati, a gift I bought myself a few weeks ago, tearing up the dirt trails in the old park, and yet, Emilia was running. Well, now, she was jumping. She stepped up onto a worn-out wrought-iron bench and leaped over a spread of tall bushes.

"Get on," I yelled, keeping pace with her as she pumped her arms, continuing her pursuit of the two men who were

27

racing toward the middle of the park on their bikes. Did she really think she could outrun motorcycles?

"About time you showed up." She veered my way, and I stopped only long enough for her to climb on behind me.

I hated how much I loved the feel of her pressed tight to me, one arm slung around my chest over my black leather jacket and the other most likely reaching for some type of weapon.

"You didn't give me much warning," I hollered over the noise of the engine as we chased down the two men.

"What? Too busy having sex with some petite blonde at two in the morning?"

Blonde, huh? "Not funny," I bit out, doing my best not to let the past two years of craving this woman to no avail crowd my head and distract me from the task at hand. "I didn't even know you were in town." Not until she called me about twenty minutes ago sounding a bit out of breath as she quickly asked if I had time to assist her in taking down some gun runners who were making a swap in the park about five kilometers from my flat. Based on the sound of painful groaning in the background, it'd been clear she'd already gotten into it with them. By the time I'd arrived, the men had split up, and she couldn't cover all of the park on her own.

"Well, you know now." She pointed with her free hand, and by free, I meant the one now holding a bow. They made everything small and travel size these days, didn't they?

The men on bikes did a one-eighty and swerved around to face us.

Thankfully, the park appeared empty except for us. Most people out here at this hour were either homeless or not on the up-and-up. Otherwise, the noise we were making tearing through the place would have had the police there by now.

"Oh, they want to play chicken," Emilia said, a hint of excitement in her tone. The woman got off on this, didn't she? And maybe I didn't blame her. After diving into action during the last twenty-plus months, I was beginning to live off the adrenaline, the rush of such vigilante-type moments, too.

Most League leaders didn't handle business themselves, much less go after criminals at two in the morning.

Emilia was more hands-on than her father had been as leader of *La Lega dei Fratelli* in Italy. When she took over for him after his death, she'd become the first woman leader in its history. And *La Lega dei Fratelli,* The League of Brothers, officially became known as *La Lega,* The League. There was no question she was qualified for the powerful position—this woman was hell on wheels. Literally.

I stopped and set my booted feet on the ground on each side of the Ducati as I waited for the men to charge us. This was a fight they wouldn't win.

We were closing in on two years since I joined the Irish League. I'd trained with the best in The League, Emilia included, ever since. Fifteen families from fifteen different countries, each set to share equal power within the organization.

I took over as leader, along with my cousin Cole, his wife, Alessia, and Alessia's brother, Sebastian Renaud. Sebastian had once been the only leader of Ireland after swapping his role as a fixer for more power when he'd inherited money from Alessia and a wealthy father he'd never known. To be a leader, you had to be rich. Billionaire-type wealth.

My family members were businessmen and women, not crime fighters. But when my twin, Adam, got himself mixed up in underground fighting for a man with ties to The

Alliance, we found ourselves in the middle of a feud between two powerful organizations. To put it simply, The League was on the side of good, and The Alliance was on the side of evil. The League had worked tirelessly to protect its cities from their criminal activities while attempting to take them down permanently.

And now here I was, a bike between my legs and a sword-like dagger sheathed at my back while helping a gorgeous and strong woman do just that. Adam and I had pretended to be pirates as kids in the halls at Trinity College while Ma was a professor there, but never in my wildest dreams did I picture this life was in my future. It was insane.

CEO of a multibillion-dollar company by day, and by night . . . *this*.

A few years back, the French League leader arbitrated a truce between the two organizations in hopes The Alliance would back down some. Sebastian had insisted a group like The Alliance couldn't be trusted, and he was correct. Their offenses became even more egregious. And now we were bringing war to The Alliance—they just didn't know it yet.

I focused back on Emilia as she hopped off the bike as the two men came speeding toward us, their bright headlights in our eyes.

I'd seen her in action a few times, and I never grew any less spellbound or impressed witnessing her up close and personal as she did her thing. I'd barely seen her since October, though, when we fought side by side to take down a criminal known as The Italian.

During that battle, she'd defeated multiple enemy targets while her castle-like home in Sicily was riddled with bullets.

Emilia pushed the nock of the arrow onto the string, preparing herself for the shot. I moved the bike alongside her, readying myself as the men rushed us.

"You set?" she asked, her voice calm and casual.

"Yeah." I revved the engine, reached for the sword at my back, and then moved like lightning toward target two. I kept the wicked gleam of the blade low as Emilia's arrow took flight, nailing the first man in the chest. The man opposite me must've spotted the danger because he took a too-sharp turn to veer away and slid on the damp dirt path, careening into a nearby bench.

I parked my bike, sheathed the weapon, and went for the 9mm at my side. The second man pulled his leg out from beneath the bike, but he'd gone for his gun while cursing in another language as I stalked his way.

Emilia appeared before I had a chance to react. I glanced over as she drew back the bow with her index finger. She snapped out a shot, sending the arrow into the man's shoulder. He yelled out, letting go of his gun.

"You're welcome," she tossed out while brushing past me and toward the man she'd just shot, her bow now stowed.

"I had it," I grumbled.

"Who are you?" he asked, eyes pinned on Emilia as she crouched before him.

"I'm Emilia Calibrisi, daughter of the late Signore Calibrisi, and now leader of The League of Italy." Her voice was smooth like silk, confidence flowing through her words. "Go back to your boss and tell him I'm coming for him." Emilia pushed back up to her booted feet and brought a mobile to her ear. "I need a cleanup crew." She turned to face the man she'd first shot in the chest, now groaning on the ground and scrambling to get up. "And transit for prisoners. Four wounded."

The guy with the shoulder injury moaned and tried to stand while the other man hopped back onto a bike after removing the arrow.

"I guess your friend will be the messenger," Emilia responded, letting the man leave on his motorcycle. "You'll go to one of our prisons with your friends who are hanging by a thread back there."

Emilia had already tied up three men before I'd arrived. All unconscious, but they had pulses. Clearly, they'd put up a fight.

The man cursed in his native tongue, maybe Dutch, as I walked around to secure him to his downed bike.

"Welcome back to Dublin," I said once back on my feet, my gaze positioned on Emilia standing in her black jeans, boots, and dark jacket, looking every bit as fierce as I'm sure she intended.

She had her back to me, her eyes on the dark, cloudy sky.

I strode to stand next to her since we'd have to wait for the crew to clean up the mess and handle the men. But she didn't turn to look at me as I expected her to. She was always so damn distant when we were alone together, and it was rare we were ever alone these days. If we weren't working together or training, she was out of sight. The woman made me absolutely crazy, though, so maybe it was better this way.

Feck. What was I thinking? I was crazy *because* I couldn't have her. And only for that reason.

I'd swear, balancing board meetings and vigilantism was easier than dealing with this woman at times.

"Please, don't."

"Don't what?" I tore my hands through my hair, not much to claw at since it was short on the sides and only slightly longer on the top.

Also, I had *not* been sleeping with anyone when she'd called, but I wasn't about to tell her that since she only said shite like that to get under my skin. It'd become an art form for her. Ways to piss off Sean McGregor was probably a to-do list saved in her mobile.

"Don't start with me. Don't do the thing with your eyes." Emilia was looking at me now, her dark gaze transfixed on my lips before she allowed her attention to wander up. "You always give me that look, but you know nothing can happen, so—"

"Yeah, I know," I snapped. "I remember the damn rule." How could I possibly forget?

March of last year, The League leaders had gathered at Emilia's home in Sicily for an unprecedented vote, which established me as a joint leader of Ireland.

But before that fateful vote, Emilia and I had managed a few moments of privacy. We'd kissed like we were starved for each other. She'd torn my shirt off in a rush, her nails clawing at my back, nearly drawing blood during our shared lust.

Then my cousin Cole and Sebastian's sister, Alessia, walked in on us, preventing us from having sex. And our mouths never touched again after that night.

Because after the vote, Emilia had pulled me aside and told me the shittiest fecking news ever. Rule one of The League: *romantic relationships between League families of other countries are strictly forbidden, and that includes sex.*

That rule had been a gut shot. A left punch from my brother—whose fighting was notorious for causing significant damage.

I couldn't believe Emilia hadn't warned me about the rule before the vote. She'd placed The League above her own feelings, believing it was more important I join than for us to discover if we might have a future together.

"You'd think if we can have more than one leader in Ireland, then—"

"That's different. Same country," she cut me off, like she always did whenever we argued about the so-called sacred first rule of The League.

I understood The League's reasoning for the rule, but that didn't mean I had to like it.

"And you may act like the king of one-night stands, but you'll want more from me. More than I can give."

And there it was. Had she rehearsed and memorized those lines word for word? She never missed a beat in her delivery, same as the last five times when we did our little back-and-forth like this.

Emilia sure as hell didn't lack confidence. But her words always hurt more than I'd cared to admit. She could handle sex without growing attached, but apparently, I was too soft. I'd be a bloody "victim" to love.

"Sean." Emilia palmed my cheek, a contrast to her cold words.

"This arrangement with me as one of the leaders is most likely temporary. When I signed on, I thought we'd take down The Alliance within a year, and I'd be done. So, why can't we—"

"Your family is still connected. Even if you left, it wouldn't change the rules," she interrupted, and it also felt like a blow to the balls. But it also sounded as though she'd considered the idea. "You won't want to get out, though. Your eyes are now open to the darkness. Do you think you will be able to just forget and ignore everything you've seen?"

I dragged my palm down my face, frustrated with that bit of truth. Hell, she was right. I wouldn't be able to turn a blind eye to what I now knew. Alliance or not.

It was late. And maybe I was too exhausted to tangle with her anymore tonight. "Why is it that I only see you when you need my help, or you need to release tension by training?" There went my mouth.

I had other ideas on how to release tension. And the longer I stood directly in front of Emilia, the closer I'd get to opening my big mouth again and describing in vivid detail how great our bodies would feel together, tangled between the sheets.

"You wouldn't avoid me so much, otherwise, if you didn't want to—"

"Tonight *was* about releasing tension." Her crisp words were a flat line to my heart.

"Taking down those gun runners?" Why was I surprised that was how she chose to wind down? Some women did yoga. Others stress cleaned or shopped. Emilia took down bad guys to work loose the knots in her body.

And now that I'd joined her world, one I had no clue existed two years ago, I understood that. I'd watched my cousin Cole transform into someone tougher and stronger when he'd been forced to step in as leader, and I felt those changes happening to me now as well.

I'd first blamed Sebastian for bringing the danger into our lives, and then my brother blamed himself since his issues with a now deceased crime boss had placed us in the crosshairs of The Alliance in the first place. But the deeper I became entrenched in League affairs, the more I just blamed criminals for everything. So many people were tainted by greed and power, and the world needed cleansing from the sins of the likes of The Alliance.

Yeah, she was right. My eyes were almost *too* open.

Emilia peeked at the guy squirming against his bike before focusing back on me, her hand no longer on my chest and feeling the intense beats. "I'm sorry this has taken so long, though," she said, catching me off guard. "Sebastian and I had hoped we'd wrap up everything before his daughter was born last year."

"Holly and Sebastian's baby is now a year old," I said under my breath. "And Luca Moreau is still living free after everything he did."

"Trust me, the idea that Luca of all people is out there and not dead or inside a League prison bothers me more than it troubles you." She folded her arms and lifted her chin, her red lips taunting me. Screaming for me. I wanted to suck that bottom lip. Watch those lips wrap around my cock while my hand tangled in her hair.

Bloody hell. I couldn't think straight around this woman. I couldn't separate work from desire.

"Luca will pay for his sins. He'll pay for what he did to Alessia. But he's the reason we have so much intel on The Alliance. The plan for him to weasel his way into the depths of their organization is working."

"You're more trusting of him than I am." I turned away, no longer able to look at her beautiful face.

Luca Moreau had been a fixer for The League. He'd betrayed his uncle, France's leader, and he'd especially fecked over his best friend, Sebastian. Luca had faked Sebastian's sister's death and locked Alessia away in his League-controlled prison in Russia.

But Alessia was free now and married to Cole. And my sister, Holly, was a mother and happily married to Sebastian. And as for my brother, Adam, he was married with a son, and I'd never seen my twin so happy.

We'd managed to keep our younger brother, Ethan, out of League business by placing him in our company's New York office, but I was worried if we didn't wrap up everything soon, the claws of evil would reach for him, too. And it had a vicious bite. I didn't want his eyes open. Nor Cole's sister, Bree, an actress in the States, either.

Somehow, everyone around me managed to be happy even though we were facing the belly of hell regularly, all the while trying to keep our business up and running. Well, everyone except me.

No, I can't be happy because the only woman I want is off-feckin'-limits.

"How long are you staying in Dublin this time?" I firmly tamped down my frustrations and realized purchasing expensive toys and fighting, things I'd thought alleviated my tension, wasn't working.

"Holly and Sebastian invited me to spend Christmas here since I don't have any family."

We're your family. And wow, was Christmas around the corner? I was losing track of the days. "Holly didn't tell me." How on earth would I survive the holidays with Emilia without fantasizing about shedding her clothes and dragging my tongue along her body? "Feck."

"What?"

Had I cursed aloud? I willed my thoughts to swirl around the drain and vanish. I needed a clear head for the next few weeks if she'd be staying in town. "You plan on working while you're here? Or should I say, continue working?" I jerked a thumb toward the guy out of earshot from us tied to his bike. "I assume they're not Alliance or you wouldn't be so openly going after them."

Dismantling The Alliance was complicated. Slowly moving the pieces into place without Alliance leaders knowing we were responsible. Positioning people or teams we trusted in Alliance stronghold positions worldwide for when we were ready to advance on the leaders. Take them down simultaneously in one fell swoop before they had a chance to react.

Emilia began to turn away without answering me, and I captured her wrist on instinct. "What is it you haven't told me? Or all of us? You have secrets, and I get the feeling at least one of those secrets might get someone killed." It wasn't just about me wanting to know all of her secrets. I had my family to protect.

Her gaze cut down to where I held her wrist. Was she contemplating dropping me to the ground right there? She could. But I wasn't the same man she'd kissed last year, and that was thanks to her and The League. I could easily flip her over and pin her beneath me, too. I was sort of hoping for that to happen.

"We all have secrets," she countered in a soft, almost seductive voice.

I only had one secret. And it wasn't dangerous.

I remembered her from Las Vegas ten years ago. I remembered our kiss just as vividly as though it were yesterday. But I never told her for reasons I have yet to understand. And since she never brought it up, I had to assume she didn't remember me.

Years later, when I saw her in Dublin for the first time since Vegas, I'd been gobsmacked. My sister thought I'd had the wind knocked out of me because of attraction. But no, how could I ever forget "Julia"? How could I forget a woman like Emilia?

Over the years, I'd searched for someone to make me feel even a fraction of what "Julia" had made me feel that night. I was a prince trying to find his Cinderella.

I'd tried and failed, and as a result, had developed a reputation as a playboy. I'd slipped my cock into vaginas the way the prince had slipped the glass slipper on women's feet in that damn fairy tale. None were a match.

And wow, was I a feckin' arsehole before joining The League? Even my analogy made me want to go back in time and slap the shite out of myself.

I had hoped fate had brought "Julia" back into my life for a reason.

And the first League rule closed the door in my face.

Slammed it the feck shut.

CHAPTER TWO

EMILIA

"This should be your job. I mean it. Just make babies."
I handed Holly's daughter back to her, not all that comfortable holding a child, especially one so small. Her daughter had Holly's green eyes and a head of dark hair the same as her parents.

Siobhan Colleen Ryan. The Irish name Siobhan, pronounced "Shih-von," meant "God is gracious," and it was rather fitting for their daughter.

Sebastian still went by his fake last name, Renaud, for business purposes, but Holly had taken on his family's surname, Ryan, once they were married. And Holly had insisted they use Colleen as their daughter's middle name in honor of Sebastian's late mother.

Thinking about Siobhan had me remembering Papà's words before he died.

"Emilia Tessa Calibrisi. My only child," he'd whispered before dying, clutching my hand between his palms. *"Our name and legacy cannot die with me. You must carry it on. Do not die alone like me."* His eyes had closed, breath

stuttering. *"But I beg of you, marry an Italian. Do not fall in love with anyone else. Promise me."*

I'd considered reminding him of his arranged marriage to my Italian mother, who left not long after I was born to escape the life she'd never wanted. But I couldn't bring myself to do it. Would it have caused him pain to mention it? Doubtful, since he hadn't loved her, but I didn't dare take the chance.

The pain that had seeped through his voice while he delivered his dying words to me wasn't because of my mother, and I was sure of it. His reasoning behind wanting me to marry an Italian had nothing to do with the woman who'd walked away from us and everything to do with the woman he'd loved and couldn't have.

Tears had filled my eyes, knowing I was losing the man who'd shaped me in every possible way—the good and the bad. And I loved him so much. My love outweighed any resentment I'd once had for him while growing up, knowing I would be forced to join his world. But everything changed when I turned twenty-one. I'd finally embraced my path and understood who I needed to become.

"Please, my red rose," he'd whispered to me in Italian and then in English. *"Promise me you will find a good Italian man. One who is not afraid of your strength, but who is also strong enough to be your equal."*

I'd quickly brushed away the tears with my free hand, knowing he wouldn't want to see me weep for him. *"I promise, Papà."*

"The Calibrisi legacy will live on through you, then," he'd answered around a cough.

"I can't believe she's already one." Holly's words brought me back to Dublin.

Siobhan was born in November of last year, and the plan

41

had originally been to dismantle The Alliance before then so Sebastian wouldn't have to worry about endangering his child. But the task proved too great to handle so quickly, and an unexpected curveball delayed the plan further.

Three months before her birth, a plane crash over the Alps killed Milos Castellanos and his son-in-law, Simon Laurent. They'd been the leaders of the Greek and French families for The Alliance. Their deaths meant that at twenty-seven years old, Atlas Castellanos-Laurent was in a unique position to lead two of the most powerful families in the criminal organization since his mother, Penelope, wasn't allowed to lead, not that she'd wanted to. The Alliance now viewed Atlas as an overlord of sorts of the entire organization.

How would I explain to Sean, to the others, why I'd been procrastinating going after our primary target, Atlas Castellanos-Laurent? Sebastian knew, but he'd respect my privacy. He'd let me explain the truth when I was ready.

Bad guys were bad guys. Usually. But this bad guy was Chanel's brother. And I couldn't wash the stain of her blood from my hands no matter how much I scrubbed and scrubbed.

Having Chanel with me the night of my twenty-first birthday got my only real friend outside The League killed.

I killed her by disobeying Papà's orders. By selfishly allowing her to be in my life.

And after that, what choice did I have but to take my place in The League and find those responsible for what happened that night? I'd vowed the first life I'd take would be that of the person sent to murder me but accidentally killed Chanel instead.

I'd never even met Atlas, but . . . how could I kill the brother of the closest friend I'd ever had? And what if Penelope Castellanos-Laurent was caught in the crossfires?

I'd never be able to live with myself if anything happened to her either.

"Hey, you okay? You seem pale, and you don't, um, get pale." Holly set Siobhan in the playpen in her living room and offered me a glass of whiskey.

Anything but red wine. I didn't want to stare into the glass and see the color of blood. I was there to visit Holly and her daughter, to savor that small semblance of normality they made me feel when I was around them.

Holly was bold and confident like Chanel, but there were other sides to her I admired. She wasn't one-dimensional. She was a reminder that a woman could be soft without being weak. Strong without being intimidating.

I couldn't help but admire her. Often, from afar. I was intrigued by the woman who had turned a fierce man like Sebastian into a husband and a father.

I swished the drink around and sipped it. "You and your love for Proper Twelve."

A smile played on her lips. "Sebastian and I have some fond memories associated with this drink."

"And where is the man of the hour?" I went to the window and looked out at her front yard, where a heavy downpour had flattened the grass.

"He's at the club with Alessia."

"It's Wednesday. Aren't they closed today?" I turned to face her.

"Yeah, but that's when they get most of their business stuff done." Holly sat on the couch and stretched her long, jean-clad legs out in front of her.

Sebastian and his sister ran a trendy nightclub in the heart of Dublin. When Alessia "came back from the dead," I'd ridiculously hoped that maybe, just maybe, Chanel might be granted the same luck. But no, I'd seen her motionless body ten years ago. She'd been beneath the guy she'd met at the club that night. Both shot and killed.

"You're pale again." Holly's brows tightened, concern cutting across her face. "What's going on?"

"Oh, I was just remembering something." I faked a smile and strode around the playpen to sit in the chair by the couch.

Siobhan was looking at a book on her lap as if she were actually reading it. Babies couldn't do that yet, right? Shit. I had no clue about anything, but yeah, they couldn't read at one. And was she still a baby, or was she considered a toddler? Hell if I knew the first thing about kids.

"I assume you're staying at our hotel in the city. How long will you be in town? I'd love to see you stay through the new year. Celebrate your birthday in Dublin."

I hadn't celebrated a birthday since Chanel died. Not a single one.

"Maybe we girls can even get away for a spa weekend," she went on when I didn't answer. "I haven't taken a vacation since Siobhan was born. And I know Anna is the same. Adam watches her like a hawk, especially—"

"After she was kidnapped on their wedding day?" I interrupted, and she frowned at the reminder. Maybe that's not what she'd planned on saying, but I'd gone straight for the typical gloom and doom. "A night or two away might be nice," I tried to recover. "I'll be here for a few weeks or more. I'd planned on coming after Christmas, but your invite sped up my timeline. Business to handle and all."

"Right. The Alliance." Her long lashes fluttered as her eyes fixated on her glass of whiskey. Her thoughts probably drifting to the imminent battle that she knew would transpire at some point.

I couldn't hold off going against Atlas forever, could I?

"I know what has to be done. I just wish no one had to

die." Holly carried her focus to me, and I was fairly confident she was thinking about the fact her husband broke his promise to her in October at my home in Sicily. "Did you know we fought after he went all Punisher at your house? That night you all worked with those military guys?" She paused for a breath, a touch of red meandering up the column of her throat. "I was hormonal since I was in the middle of weaning Siobhan off breastfeeding. But he'd promised me he'd never kill again, and I was upset that he did, so he slept at the hotel a few nights. I just worry about what killing does to him, though. The aftereffects of such a decision to take a human life."

"We were up against a lot of armed men. He was trying really damn hard not to kill anyone," I defended him.

A criminal, known as The Italian, practically sent an army to my house to get to the woman I was helping, along with a group of American Navy SEALs.

"Sebastian said those SEALs told him it'd be easier to ask forgiveness later and just . . ." She let go of her words as if talking about it only upset her again. "You know they told him killing again was like riding a bike? Their humor is a bit grim." She grimaced. "Sorry if I'm insulting you since you, um, still kill."

"It's not exactly easy to insult me." I set the tumbler on the coffee table before me and placed my hands on the arms of the chair. "Killing is never the goal." We'd explained that to Holly before, but she was from a different world than Sebastian and me. And I was glad about that. I wouldn't wish my life experiences on her. Not ever. "Defend ourselves or die. That's usually what it comes down to. And if it's Sebastian or the other guy . . ." I trailed off. She got the idea.

Holly placed her glass on the side table, then lifted her hand and applied pressure to her forehead as if the topic was giving her a headache. Her green eyes disappeared behind her lids, and her long, dark lashes were on display. "Isn't it ironic that Adam was the one I'd always been worried would end up killing someone, and yet, he doesn't have blood on his hands?"

I glimpsed at my red fingernails and flipped my palms up, studying them as if they held the answer to how many men had died by my hands.

"I know Cole had to but has Sean killed anyone?"

I wasn't about to reveal to his younger sister whether or not Sean had a body count. "I, um, think you should talk to Sean about that."

"I knew who I was marrying with Sebastian, and I love that man, even if he considers firing a weapon like riding a bike . . . but I had this image of Sean in my head and now—"

"Sean is still that man." I stood and went over to sit next to her and hesitantly set a hand on Holly's forearm. "He just sees the world a bit differently now. And your husband and brothers are doing their best to shield you from that world."

Based on her downturned lips, I was failing to alleviate her worries.

"I mean, your brother has changed in the sense that he's very ripped now. Perfectly carved, like Michelangelo's *David*," I said with a smile, trying to lighten the mood, to get a laugh out of her. But all my words did was flood my thoughts with images of Sean's toned body.

Don't go there, Ems. People you care about die. I died. It was Chanel's voice in my head instead of mine, something that only happened whenever guilt rose its ugly head to trip me up. *And he's not Italian. Don't forget your promise.* That voice was all me.

My hand went back to my lap, and I stole a look at Siobhan as she rolled to her side, her eyes getting sleepy.

"Sean was always more like Adam than he'd admit. He tried to be the son Ma and Da didn't have to worry about. They had too much on their plates with Adam. Sean was the balance. The yin to Adam's yang or whatever you want to call it." Holly was on her feet, rubbing her arms as if chasing away chills. "But now Sean doesn't share his feelings much with me. He keeps everything bottled up inside, which worries me. He's harder, and I'm not referring to his body, Emilia."

She was definitely the yin to Sebastian's yang or whatever Holly had meant by that about Adam and Sean.

"You can't be together because of League rules. Sean told me."

At some point, I had to admit to Sean that it was more than just League rules as to why we couldn't be together. "Why do you think Sean's like Adam?" I asked, curious to try and better understand the man from his sister's point of view since my judgment was tainted by the feelings I refused to allow myself to feel.

Holly added more whiskey to her glass, checked on Siobhan, now asleep, and then focused on me. "In high school, my boyfriend got too handsy. Didn't like the word no."

I didn't tolerate assholes who set their hands on a woman without permission.

She must have noticed my face or body tense up because she gave me a moment to let go of an angry breath through my nostrils.

"Sean happened to come into our house, and my boyfriend backed off. Adam was outside on his mobile, but if he'd been the one to come in and witness for himself my arsehole boyfriend making an uninvited move on me, he'd have killed him without hesitation. And Sean did have to stop him from attempting to do exactly that when he'd come inside and heard what happened." Her shoulders relaxed, and I sensed the boyfriend never got too far and that her worries had more to do with protecting her brothers right now. "Adam's temper is very out front. He's worked on it over the years, and his marriage to Anna has calmed him down. But Sean was always careful about masking his. He lets his anger simmer beneath the surface."

"Sean went after your ex, didn't he? After the fact."

Holly nodded. "Went to his house and broke his arm and threatened him. I didn't know about it at the time."

And I would've done the same thing if I'd been Sean.

"That's one incident, though. Maybe there are a few more, but he's careful from what I've seen of Sean. Cautious and in control." *Unless he's dealing with me and his frustrations about the fact we can't be together.* "I don't think you need to worry he'll unnecessarily take things too far."

She studied me, taking in my assessment, but I wasn't so sure if I'd convinced her to stop worrying about her brother.

I expelled a deep breath. "He's never killed anyone." I allowed the confession to slip free, deciding Holly didn't need any unwarranted stress. If my words could help her, then so be it.

He'd shot people. Stabbed them. So on and so on. But he'd always stopped short of killing.

"You were afraid to ask him that, and so there, you have the answer. Neither Adam nor Sean are killers."

Holly's chest fell from relief, and she tucked her bottom lip inward.

Oh no, not tears.

"But I can't promise there won't be a day that his zero-kills statistic doesn't change." I stood and zipped my brown leather jacket that matched my tall boots. "The last person you need to worry about is Sean, though." *You're the unstable one, Emilia. How many people did you kill in the name of revenge for me, for a friend you weren't supposed to have?* Chanel's voice loomed in the back of my head, leaving me unsettled.

"You're leaving. I'm sorry."

Oh, I was, wasn't I? My boots had taken me to the door on autopilot. "I have some business to attend to."

"I didn't mean to make you uncomfortable."

I looked back at Holly, her hand on her chest as she drew in a deep breath.

"You had questions, and you're a parent now, so I can understand how that may make you leery." Well, I understood the way a daughter raised without a mother could.

"How long until you think The League will shut down The Alliance once and for all? I always ask Sebastian, but he never gives me a straight answer."

That's because there isn't one. "I don't know. Maybe in January."

Holly's bottom lip lowered as if contemplating her words before she let them free. "And the main guys, the main players in charge—what about them? January, too?" She circled the playpen, giving me no choice but to face her.

I squeezed my eyes closed as Chanel's lifeless body came to mind. *You can't kill Atlas. He's my brother,* Chanel whispered in my head.

"The Alliance falls when the leaders fall," I whispered and drew in a shallow breath, shaking Chanel from my mind as I found Holly's green eyes on me when my lids parted. "I'm sorry. I have to go." I turned away and opened the door before she had a chance to ask more questions I wasn't prepared to answer.

Once in the red BMW M5 I'd rented for my time in

Dublin, I grabbed my mobile and scrolled to Sean's number. Stupid idea, but perhaps I had an addiction to pain since I kept finding ways to spend time with the man even when I didn't have a valid reason.

"Emilia," he said upon picking up two rings later.

"I need to release some tension again."

CHAPTER THREE

EMILIA

"Not what I had in mind when you called," Sean said in a low, raspy voice as he eyed me on the blue mat inside the MMA-style gym Adam owned. It was after hours, so we had the place to ourselves.

"It was this or finish what we started last night in the park." I tossed him a bokken, which was a Japanese wooden sword used for training in martial arts.

"What *you* started, you mean. Those gun runners were your targets, not mine. Hell, they hadn't been on my radar." Sean's Irish lilt tended to thicken whenever he was aroused or angry. I couldn't always tell the difference between when he was upset or turned on. Passion and frustration often went hand in hand and fueled the other. And right now, I was fairly certain both of our accents were deeper than normal and for both reasons.

"And maybe they should've been on your radar since this is your city." I went straight for him with the bokken, and his instincts kicked in. He blocked my strike, deflecting a jab to his torso.

The arc of his blade stayed pointed above our heads, and

he surprised me by stepping back, a smirk on his face, to create what would've been a vertical slash across my body had it been a real blade.

And did I just lose my focus because of rippling abs? Damn it, and he noticed, too.

I used my foot to kick up a second bokken from the mat and captured his weapon between my wooden swords when he came at me with another strike. I held him there, but he was stronger than me now. He'd become more defined and powerful this year, and his strength had my limbs trembling as I tried to maintain my position.

Change of plans. I relaxed my arms and shifted to his right, released my weapons, and ducked to the side while simultaneously tripping him and circling my arm around his neck to take him down.

He fell with a hard thud, and I straddled him, forcing him beneath me.

"If you wanted to be on top, you could've just asked." His husky voice sailed to my ears and had me pressing my palms to his biceps and pinning his arms at his sides out of frustration.

I felt the strength in his corded arms. Admired the raw power in his taut body. I wouldn't be able to hold him down much longer unless he allowed it to happen, and that would irritate me more. I'd take a loss rather than have a win handed to me.

I was panting harder than I should've been, and it wasn't because I was out of breath from our short fight.

His cock stirred beneath his sweats, perilously close to my center as I sat on top of him. His lips twitched into a small, knowing smile—that playboy charm he loved to toss my way to get a rise out of me.

He knew I was desperate for him to fill me. Stretch me

with his hard length. I'd violate the rule and have sex with him if this thing between us was merely about desire. I'd happily surrender to him if an orgasm would fix our problems.

Dragging my gaze from his mouth, I let my eyes travel purposefully down his chest and onto the tattoo, a requirement upon joining The League. He'd chosen a lion on its hind legs, paws up, with an Irish League shield in front of it.

When my focus fell to his well-defined abs, his breathing sped up, and I caught a whiff of his heady masculine scent. Why did he always have to smell so good? Not even trying to be discreet, I pulled in a deep breath of *man* and dropped my gaze to the light trail of blond hair that disappeared under the waistband of his gray sweats.

Move, I willed him, our eyes locked. When he failed to follow my silent command, I slowly lowered myself to an awkward plank so that my breasts touched his chest. My lips hovered over his mouth, and his warm breath fanned across my face. His eyes remained riveted on mine, waiting for me to make the first move and do what we both wanted.

We were dangerously close to kissing in this intimate position with him trapped beneath me.

I was more like Papà than ever, wasn't I? Caring for someone off-limits.

And so, I had to kill the moment. Stop this from going any further. I couldn't let my need for someone nearly destroy me as I was convinced had happened to my father. He'd never moved on from the only woman he wanted and couldn't have. He died alone.

I'd survived more than twenty months without giving in to my attraction to Sean, so why in the hell was I becoming weak now?

I blinked and stole my focus from him, forcing myself to back off. "I'm sorry I made you leave your date to come train. You could've said no."

I started to push off from him, my hands moving to his chest for leverage, but in one fast movement, he had me on my back before I realized what happened.

His eyes dropped to my breasts, nearly spilling out of the tight black tank top as I pulled in gulps of air. Maybe I should've gone topless so he'd be the distracted one.

"I wasn't on a date," he announced tightly, continuing to restrain me between his strong, muscled thighs. He also had my wrists secured to the mat alongside my head, and the dominance he exuded only served to fuel my lust.

God, how many times had I envisioned this exact moment sans clothes? But in my daydream, he was thrusting his cock inside me instead of murdering me with his stare.

Those blue eyes were not only captivating, they provoked a frenzy of emotions to stir inside me.

Even if he were Italian, you'd find another excuse to push him away. And Chanel was back in my head again. I was turning into an actual crazy person. *You're afraid his blood will end up on your hands, just like mine did. That he'll die and you'll be forever alone. Or maybe it's something else. Do you fear he'll abandon you the way your mother left you?*

"I heard a woman in the background," I countered, lamely trying to fortify my walls with utter nonsense. I was also desperate to get my subconscious, aka Chanel, to stop wreaking havoc on my mental stability and shut the hell up. "She sounded blonde."

He rolled his eyes. "And how does a blonde sound?" He kept our bodies ridiculously close, the bulge in his sweats distracting me.

"You have a thing for blondes, from what I can tell. Birds

54

of a feather and all that." Complete bullshit. I had no idea what type of woman Sean was attracted to. Well, aside from me. I was only trying to push his buttons and drive him away. I was acting like a child to protect both of us from getting hurt. I didn't need Chanel's voice in my head to understand why I did what I did. I knew it. Understood it. And I hated it.

He scrutinized me with a stare that could melt the wax from a candle. "That *brunette* was a client I had to take out to dinner for work."

Client? Yeah, sure. "You don't owe me an explanation."

"*You* brought it up. I was clarifying," he grumbled, his tone a hairsbreadth from angry. There was no mistaking his thicker Irish brogue as anything but frustration with me this time.

He rolled off me and to the side, which was what I'd wanted but now felt . . . alone.

Sean pushed the bokkens out of his way but remained flat on his back. His face was tipped toward the ceiling, and he covered his eyes with his palm.

I stood and contemplated grabbing the weapons for another go. We'd probably end up back on the ground.

"People need to screw, Sean. It's human. You should enjoy yourself."

He lowered his hand and shifted onto his elbows to sit up a little. His intense gaze raked over my body before landing on my face. "Does that mean you're enjoying yourself?" He tried to hide it, but I heard the nerves slicing through his tone as he waited for my answer.

What I needed to do was say yes. Lie and tell him I'd been having sex—plenty of it. Hurt him and force him to move on. I just couldn't seem to do it. "I'm just saying I want you to be happy. And if blondes are your thing, then good for you. Find one to marry, and I'll come to your wedding."

The time we were required to spend in each other's company would be a lot easier if he weren't so handsome, smart, and caring. Any of the things most women surely included on their checklist for the perfect mate. I wasn't most women, though. So why was my heart racing right now while he peered at me like I was his whole world?

It was unnerving, so I looked away as I said, "You're stronger than I remember."

"What choice did I have? A woman of your strength and intelligence would never look twice at a weaker man." Sean was behind me in a moment, his breath a warm caress at the nape of my neck as he gently pushed my fishtail braid to the side. "I needed to become a fighter so that I could fight for you."

He wasn't referring to physically protecting me. He knew I was capable of taking care of myself in that regard within The League as well as outside of it. No, Sean meant that he'd been working toward fighting for an "us," on being the equal my father wanted for me.

And that hurt, made my heart hurt. So many parts of me were aching at his admission, and I didn't have a clue how to handle it right now.

I banded an arm across my midsection. Physical pain I could handle. Emotional pain . . . not so much.

I spun around to find him close enough to lean in, press up on my toes, and kiss him if I dared.

"We can't," I repeated the standard answer I gave him every time he brought up the idea there was something more between us.

"I know the rules, Emilia. But the leaders voted unanimously to change the name of the organization, specifically for you. You don't think they'd make this exception?" This was the first time he'd suggested that.

His gaze went to my mouth and took a tortuously slow journey down my body once again before returning to meet my eyes. My nipples betrayed me by poking through the thin material of the sports bra and tank top I wore, clearly on board with his plan.

"Sex, then," he said gruffly. "Screw that part of the rule. The League doesn't control your body." Sean crossed his arms over his chest, defiance in his stance. "You're okay with casual sex, right? Problem solved."

"That's not . . ." He cut me off by moving back into my space and bringing us nose to nose, then lowered his head to find my eyes.

"You slept with Luca Moreau. Well, you fucked him, so why not me?" He backed up, his words like calloused hands scraping over my skin. "I'll tell you why. The men from your past didn't make you feel a damn thing, and that's your safe place."

Low fucking blow. An intentionally painful one meant as payback for the many times my rejections must have burned him. "How dare you throw my past with Luca in my face. You know nothing about it," I responded, rage bubbling to the surface. "You wouldn't even know had he not mentioned it in front of you."

"Right. You'd never open up and tell me shite, would you?" He waved a dismissive hand in the air, but he was far from done talking. From unleashing whatever he'd kept buried beneath his walls of muscles for who knew how long. "What you feel for me scares the bloody hell out of you."

I was stunned into silence at his accurate assessment but damned if I was going to give in. I couldn't do that to another person I cared for. So I said nothing. And my heart broke a little at the defeated look on his face.

"Emilia, just admit you're scared of what you feel. At

least give me that. And I'll stop fighting for you. I'll give up and walk away. Fuck a blonde or two like you seem to want me to," he hissed, his eyes laser-focused on mine, challenging me, daring me to say it.

"Sean, we only gave in to lust and shared a kiss moments before you became a leader. We never even slept together," I added in a low voice.

He pulled his head back a fraction as if I'd slapped him. "Not everything is about sex."

"Says the notorious Irish player." I'd allowed my anger to answer for me once again instead of facing the truth of his words.

He leaned so close the scruff on his jaw nearly touched my skin. "I'm not that man anymore," he responded between barely parted lips. "And after two years of spending time with you, I don't believe for one bloody minute I'm alone in my feelings."

Of course I had feelings. Those feelings were why I was at this gym, hoping to knock them out of me.

But the only love I'd ever borne witness to was my father's love for me and his screwed-up love for a married woman.

I didn't know how to do love. How to comprehend what I felt for Sean and make sense of it because I'd never experienced such emotions before.

"How about we stick to why we're both here at the gym?" I bowed out of one fight and launched myself into another one. One I was better equipped to handle. I tossed an elbow, and he allowed it to hit him square in the face.

His mouth tightened as he pinned me with narrowed eyes, and damn if my desire reached for me like a long-lost lover. Angry, I tossed out another shot, but he blocked this one.

And the sparring began. We went at it hard. Fast. Rough

without him ever actually inflicting pain. Damn him for finding a way to be gentle when I just wanted . . . well, I wanted to punish myself. But the pain in my heart, I couldn't seem to punch that away.

I dropped onto a folding chair by the mat about twenty or thirty minutes later. We were both sweaty and breathless.

"I can't change," I said in a defeated tone, hating myself for that. But he needed to hear this. Clearly, he did, because he kept pushing the conversation of there being an us whenever we had two minutes alone ever since that kiss at my house last year. "You can't expect me to. I made my father a promise, and that promise can't include you. League rules or not."

He was quiet for a moment, silently processing my words. "What promise?" he asked, his tone soft this time.

I shook my head, opting to ignore his question. "And I don't want you to change for me. You can stop fighting for . . . us." If somehow I'd been stringing him along, allowing him to believe there was hope because a part of me wasn't ready to let go, it had to end. We had to focus on defeating The Alliance.

His long legs closed the space between us in three quick strides. "Emilia, I've been changing every second of every day since you walked into my life." The deep timbre of his voice rolled over my skin, but at least I'd distracted him from pushing for answers about my promise to Papà.

"That's different." My protest sounded pathetic. It felt weak.

"Everything I've done has been to protect my family and to protect you. To be with you." He stretched out his arms, palms up. "But you want me to fuck some blonde, huh? That's what you want? You want me to officially turn my back on the fact that when we're in the same room together,

I can barely breathe because you steal the air from my lungs?"

I slowly rose to confront him. In as steady a voice as I could manage, I said, "I want you to be happy. But you won't find happiness with me. It's not possible."

He shook his head, frustration clinging to his expression. "Fine." He nodded as if finally coming to terms with the conditions I'd set out since he took over as a leader in March of last year. "Find someone else when you want to fight. Just call me if you have League business to discuss." He went for his white tee and pulled it over his head, rolling the material over his slick abs. "I'm done. You think I should date? Screw around? Fine, you win." His tone was eerily low. Distant.

"Sean, wait," I hurriedly called out, and hell, I even threw a hand in the air to try and stop him as he lifted his bag, preparing to walk away.

He stopped moving but remained turned to the side, offering only his profile.

I wanted so badly to explain. Tell him I wasn't simply afraid of the feelings he evoked in me. I was petrified.

But . . . "Tomorrow. We all need to have a meeting. It's time we move forward with the next stage of our plans."

His shoulders flinched, the slightest hint of disappointment evident. His bicep holding his black duffel bag flexed and tightened.

Maybe Holly was right. There *was* a lot he kept buried beneath the surface, but would he eventually lose control? Would the calm and controlled Sean McGregor snap?

I didn't want to be the cause of that.

"I can't be like Sebastian." No amount of observing Holly and Sebastian's love for each other would teach me. I'd been naïve—a fool. "I can't fall in love," I whispered, shocked by what felt like tears pricking the corners of my eyes. "I don't believe in—"

"Fairy tales?" he asked while quickly glancing at me, his eyes cold. A disappointed expression pointed my way. "You don't need a hero to save you. I got it."

I closed my eyes and brought my hands to my hips.

Fairy tales?

My twenty-first birthday . . . Vegas.

I'd subconsciously blocked out much of that night, redacted all of the events prior to the trauma of Chanel's death. Those details I remembered vividly, and I'd spent years blaming myself for my friend's murder.

But more had happened the night she died. More I hadn't let myself remember until now.

My hand went to my stomach, and I closed my eyes.

Clooney.

Oh fuck.

CHAPTER FOUR

SEAN

BLONDES. WHAT THE HELL WAS WITH EMILIA'S DELUSION that I preferred blondes?

I slapped my MacBook closed on my desk at the headquarters of McGregor Enterprises and loosened the knot of my navy-blue tie.

Her words last night had been pinging around in my head all day like one of those little metal balls inside a pinball machine.

And knowing I'd have to see her for League business tonight had me on edge.

I leaned back in my black leather reclining chair and closed my eyes, trying to force myself to relax. There was a mental transition I always tried to make, to shift my mindset from CEO to League leader before I left the office. Scotch usually helped, but my assistant had forgotten to refill my decanter, and I'd been too busy to do it myself. It hadn't been long since it was full, so apparently, I was drinking too much as well.

I left the gym last night feeling like a beaten man. Even though I'd been tired, both from physical and emotional workouts, adrenaline still coursed through my system. I was wound up, and rather than get myself into any more trouble, I went straight to my flat in the city and directly into the shower. I figured maybe a session with my hand might take off the edge, but of course, all I could think about was Emilia's luscious red lips wrapped around my cock as I jerked off. Considering she was the core of my problem, not even blowing my load had calmed me down.

A knock at my office door had me growling out, "What do you want?"

I cursed at my arsehole-ness when I spotted Anna in the hall through the narrow window by the door, then quickly rose and waved her in. "Sorry. Bad day." I felt more like a gobshite when I saw she had my nephew with her.

As Braden came running in, I circled the desk to get to him. He was going on two. Time had flown by since The League, and well, The Alliance, had entered our lives.

"Hey." I scooped Braden into my arms and balanced him on my hip. Thank God for the little squirt. Finally, someone to help get my head back on straight. "I wasn't expecting you two."

Anna closed the door behind her and brushed her strawberry-blonde locks off her shoulders and to her back. "I'm meeting Holly for dinner. Sort of a kid date while y'all have your meeting." She hadn't lost her American Southern drawl during her time in Dublin, and I knew my brother loved it.

My thoughts unexpectedly whirred back to the Italian League leader and the meeting later.

What promises had Emilia made to her father before he died?

I set Braden down on my chair and carefully spun him around a few times while he clapped and cried, "Again,

again." It sounded more like "arghhh-gen," which actually got a laugh out of me.

"So." I set my palms on the top of the chair to steady it as Braden rose to his knees and started pounding on the wireless keyboard with his fists.

The laptop was shut, so he wouldn't accidentally be sending an email to our distributors in Asia to cancel some big shipment.

"Oh shit." Anna hurried to the desk chair.

"No worries." I smiled when Anna scooped him into her arms and away from trouble. She gently set him down on the floor in front of my desk after blowing a raspberry on his cheek, making him wriggle and shriek. She was a great mother and had a kind heart. My brother said it was Anna who'd pulled him away from the edge of darkness and into the light.

I'd witnessed the transformation firsthand, and once Adam had become a father, those changes were even more pronounced.

His hands, once used primarily for fighting, tenderly cradled his baby and changed nappies, or diapers as Anna called them. And as gentle as he was with his son, becoming a father had also managed to make him harder. Tougher. A fierce need to protect his family radiated from him, especially once Cole and I joined The League. The threat of danger striking close to home was a real possibility.

Anna and Braden were the exact reasons we hadn't wanted Adam involved, but he'd asked more and more questions about League affairs over the months. Went so far as to offer ideas on how to handle The Alliance. He became so insistent that we allowed him to join our meetings, thereby making him sort of an honorary silent member.

"Can I ask you something?" Anna set a Matchbox car in

front of Braden, and he immediately began rolling it around and making vroom vroom noises. Once she was sure he was busy, she settled in the chair on the other side of my desk.

Feeling as though I ought to sit too, I removed my tie, tossed it onto my desk, and sank into my chair. "Sure. I might be able to provide an answer." I winked, trying to lighten the mood and wipe away the concerned look on her face.

Anna's emerald-green eyes studied me for a moment. "Adam doesn't talk about League stuff. Like ever. He wants to keep it as far away from me as humanly possible."

Yeah, just like we tried to keep him away. "I wholeheartedly agree with my brother's decision," I said without hesitation.

Anna and Braden were his life. His reason for existing. I didn't want to picture what would become of my twin if anything were to happen to them.

We weren't identical, and I'd always believed we had different personalities, but in the last few years, I wasn't so sure about that anymore. Maybe we were far more alike than I would have admitted in the past.

"And I appreciate that, truly, I do, but—"

"You're curious." I had no idea what, if anything, my brother had confided in her, and if she had questions, why didn't she ask him?

"When I bring it up, Adam gets pissy," she responded as if she could sense my question. "Then he likes to go and beat up his punching bag at our home gym. I think it stresses him out when he considers the idea that League affairs might bleed into our lives." She frowned. "Bleed. Shitty choice of words." She combed her fingers through her hair, adjusting it away from her face again. "When you and I first met when I moved to Dublin as an intern here, I'd always thought of you as this polished, sort of pretty boy." She circled a hand in the air, closing one eye. "Like you walked off the pages of a Banana Republic or J.Crew catalog."

"Tell me how you really feel," I responded with a laugh, not sure how the conversation had veered this direction.

Her glossy pink lips parted, a match to the soft pink of her cheeks. "You've changed, is all. You're more like—"

"Adam?"

She shook her head. "Sebastian."

Oh. I shifted uncomfortably in my seat, unsure whether she was complimenting me or had concerns about my new lifestyle. "So, what'd you want to know about The Alliance?" I'd rather talk about that than myself, I supposed.

The way the corners of her eyes creased had me wondering if she'd thrown me off on purpose to get me to open up. Well played.

Sitting up taller, Anna brought her green gaze to me and said, "I tried researching The Alliance, but I couldn't find anything about them online."

"Secret societies do their best to stay hidden," I said with a small smile. "Adam hasn't told you anything about The Alliance?"

"Alliance bad. League good," she said in her best Tarzan impression.

I laughed. Yup, that was Adam. A man of few words. But he would also go to any lengths necessary to protect his wife and son.

"I've been totally fine not knowing anything. Mostly. But I overheard him talking to you last night. Upcoming plans for The Alliance or something like that. And now I'm nervous."

"Did you tell him you're nervous?" I stood, not sure how to handle the fact Anna was coming to me with this instead of Adam. "You should talk to him. He can take you and Braden out of Ireland."

She held a hand up and patted the air. "Slow down, Sean. No need for us to flee the country in the middle of the night." Anna shook her head. "But, could you just help me understand?"

My shoulders slumped. Maybe I was overreacting. I peeked at Braden, who was now pushing the car up the wall by the windows and sat down. "You ever heard of the Bavarian Illuminati or the Freemasons?"

She nodded. "In movies."

"Well, those organizations were founded to combat injustices and corruption. And some secret societies were also created to plant agents in corporations or within governments to gain power and influence over world order. The Alliance has had different names in the last few hundred years, but they, too, started like the Freemasons and Illuminati."

"So, what changed?"

"Too much power. Too much greed." A direct result of powerful families merging. My impromptu history lesson for Anna suddenly had rule number one of The League circling in my head like a racehorse stuck on go. "Heads of their business enterprises began taking shortcuts to increase their bottom line. They bribed elected officials to obtain government contracts and bypass labor laws. Eventually, they dug themselves into a deeper and deeper hole of illegal activities to the point they saw no difference between trafficking women and producing cars. Money was money. Power was power."

"Oh." She frowned. "And what if that happens to The League?"

Good question. "There are specific rules in place to prevent that. And The League is not nearly as large as The Alliance, so it's more controlled."

"And once The Alliance is taken down, do you think The

League will still be needed? Can't law enforcement handle everyday criminals?"

"I honestly don't know." And that was the truth.

Before I could say more, I cleared my throat and tipped my head toward the door, signaling to her that I spied Adam about to enter.

She startled as if he'd caught her cheating and quickly rose. I fastened my lips to hide a humorless chuckle at the idea anything would ever happen between us.

"Braden," Adam said, and his son raced toward him like a miniature Olympic sprinter. Adam took him into his arms, lifted him over his head, and spun him around.

He was in jeans and a long-sleeved tee beneath a black leather jacket. I was a bit envious of the casual dress code Adam was allowed to get away with. It looked damn comfortable. Even though he worked for the family business, he no longer wore a suit and tie since he handled our nonprofit organization in addition to running his fighting studio.

"You two driving to the meeting together?" Anna asked after Adam greeted her with a kiss, still holding Braden, who was patting his cheeks and demanding attention.

"I thought it'd be easier," Adam answered, looking to me for an okay, and I nodded.

"Holly should be here any second to pick me up," Anna said. "Wait with us downstairs?"

In the building's lobby, Adam and I stood on each side of Braden, holding his little hands, swinging him forward before making a dramatic whoosh back, which had him laughing and begging for more.

I peered over as Holly pulled her SUV up in front of the building a minute later, and Adam buckled his son into the back car seat next to Siobhan.

I'd never have predicted Sebastian would be such an excellent father. He and Holly had an amazing relationship and were also great parents. Part of me wondered if I'd ever have kids. Have a family and the kind of love that my siblings experienced with their spouses.

"Love ya, babe. Don't have too much fun." Adam leaned in and kissed Anna in a hot, fierce kiss that had Holly playfully whistling.

"Get a room, will ya?" I teased. Anna shot me a smile, her cheeks blushing a rosy pink before getting into the passenger seat.

Adam ducked in for one last kiss, then shut the door, patted the side twice as if sending them on their way and faced me. His mood changed the moment they were gone. The shift from father and husband to "honorary League member."

We walked in silence to my new black Maserati GranTurismo. It was a sophisticated sedan with a race car engine, which was probably why the vehicle's slogan was, "Rarely seen. Always Heard." Beautifully packaged power with a hot red interior.

Red. The bold color reminded me of Emilia and her sensuous red-painted lips. Sleek, classy, and a total badass. I wasn't one to compare a car to a woman, but . . . had I subconsciously chosen this Italian car because of her?

I pushed the thought away and pulled onto the road. The Maserati was yet another toy I'd bought to get a handle on my tension. Dropping far too much money on a performance car seemed like a wiser choice than fucking my way through half of Dublin. Just because I couldn't be with the woman I wanted, didn't mean I should resort to random hookups to ease my frustration.

"You're turning into the me I was seven years ago. The

pre-Anna me," Adam casually commented. "Remember when I went through that phase of buying fancy, expensive toys?"

"How could I forget? Although I have no plans to buy a chopper."

"Hey, it came in handy for that op back in October with those Navy SEALs in Italy." Adam shook his head. "Did I just say op? We Special Forces guys now?"

"I don't think Spec Ops guys are vigilantes."

"You and I both know those guys weren't typical military. Hell, they even persuaded Sebastian to kill again."

"You shouldn't have even gone with us to Italy for that. Just because you've decided to partake in League meetings doesn't mean I want you putting your neck on the line. You have a family."

He grumbled something under his breath. A few cheap shots, most likely. "Sebastian has a family."

"That's different. Sebastian has been League since he was eighteen." He'd been pulled into the organization by the French League leader, Édouard Moreau, which was how Sebastian met and became friends with Édouard's nephew, Luca. It wasn't until years later that Sebastian and Édouard discovered the extent of Luca's disloyalty. "Don't want anything happening to you. I'm the one with the least to lose. I don't have a wife and kids."

"You're not expendable. Don't piss me off with that shite," Adam said, his tone dipping lower.

"Anyway." Out of my peripheral view, I caught my twin closing his eyes and resting his head back.

"Long day?" I asked, wondering if his sudden mood swing was a result of something else.

He rolled his head to the side to glance at me. "A couple of the kids at the youth center got into some trouble." He muttered a string of curses under his breath. "New drug dealer in town pushing dope on them."

My grip on the wheel tightened. "Give me the details. I'll handle it," I said, thinking back to Anna's concerns. Adam needed to keep his hands clean of our late-night activities as part of The League. "Cole can come with me."

"This is my problem. I'd like to look the man in the eyes who is getting fourteen-year-olds high on my streets," he seethed.

"Adam, Anna has concerns about your involvement with The League. Or maybe more so fears. I don't think—"

I glimpsed at him as he sat taller. "She told you that?"

What else could I do but nod? I didn't want to cause an issue between them, but I also didn't want Braden losing his father or Anna losing her husband.

The grimace on his lips faded as he said, "Fine. You and Cole handle the drug dealer."

"I got it. Don't worry."

"Can't believe this is your life," Adam spoke up a few minutes later as we neared Grafton Street in the city. "Or Cole's. Still feels like my fault that you're in this mess."

"Don't start with that. I thought we were over this bullshite of you blaming yourself for everything."

"We wouldn't be caught up in this fecking dilemma if not for my fighting," he said, and out of the corner of my eye, I could see him flexing his hands.

"You can't blame yourself for what happened. You fought to save Anna. You went up against a criminal instead of bowing down in defeat like most would have in your position. No way could you have known that the crime lord you were dealing with was connected to some evil criminal organization." When he didn't speak up, I added, "I have a feeling this mess would have found us one way or another." I twisted in my seat and faced him while waiting for the pedestrians to cross at the next light. "And honestly, I'm fairly convinced it's fate."

"Fate," Adam scoffed, as if not convinced.

"All of it." I let go of a deep, pent-up breath. "Hell, it has to be. Because ten years ago I was sitting ringside at a fight in Vegas right alongside Emilia, I just didn't know her name at the time."

"Say what?"

I scratched at my jaw, the week-old beard suddenly annoying. "Da sent me to the States after we bought some American company. I was to wine and dine the CEO and a few others . . . entertain them. They chose Vegas. Big fans of the UFC stuff you like," I explained while pulling through the green light.

"What fight? Who was on the main card?"

"I don't remember." I shot him a pointed look. "But anyway, I almost slept with Emilia that night. We talked. Kissed. But then, at the last minute, she backed out." I gave him a few seconds to process the details.

"She's the woman you couldn't stop talking about for weeks when you came back from the trip. I remember now. I'd thought you'd lost your bloody mind. You never talked about a woman you slept with, let alone one you didn't."

Eerily, he was right about that.

"You must've been feckin' surprised when she showed up at your flat in Dublin a few years back. Did she mention anything to you about Vegas? To be honest, I'm not sure if I'd remember a woman I made out with ten years ago."

"You would if that woman had been Anna, even if you didn't see her again for years."

"True." He was quiet for a second.

"And I haven't exactly brought it up."

"Because?" Before I could answer, he added, "You worried you're wrong, and it wasn't her? Or are you afraid she'll think you're nuts for remembering when she didn't?"

"Maybe both," I confessed as I parked near the club owned by Sebastian and his sister. Anytime I considered bringing up Vegas, I couldn't get the bloody words out for some reason. "But last night I alluded to something about that night while we were arguing, and—"

"Why were you arguing?"

I hadn't had a conversation like this with my brother in a long time. We were close, but we didn't talk about our love life or lack thereof in my case. I needed someone to talk to, though. I'd normally open up to Holly, but I didn't want her repeating any of this to her husband.

"Rule number one of The League." *Among other reasons that we can't be together.*

"Oh." His mouth rounded, and he nodded in understanding.

"I mentioned something from our conversation in Vegas, though, and her face . . . she had a reaction. A spark of a memory, maybe. If she didn't remember before, maybe she does now."

"And what does that mean?"

"Shite." I dragged a palm down my face, then turned off the car. "Probably nothing because she's stubborn. Emilia is practically pushing me to be the man I was before I became League."

"A playboy?" His brows slanted in confusion for a moment, and I shrugged. I still wasn't buying what Emilia was trying to sell.

"No offense, brother, but you've never been a one-woman kind of guy." He set a hand over my shoulder. "And if this woman has you messed up like this, well, that has to mean something. I've seen the chemistry between you two whenever she's around. It's not something you should ignore." He paused. "And like you said, maybe it's fate she's back in your life. Screw the rules."

"I want what you have," I admitted aloud for the first time in my life. "I just don't think Emilia does." At least not with me.

"Only one way to find out. And you're more like me than you think, which means you're not a quitter."

CHAPTER FIVE

SEAN

"MᴄGʀᴇɢᴏʀ?"

"Which one?" I asked as Adam and I turned to match the voice to a face. We were just outside the club, a few minutes before our meeting was to start.

A woman in a red jumper and black fitted trousers stood before us. Long, flowing blonde hair down past her breasts. *Shite.* I knew her, didn't I?

Adam nudged me, letting me know he was heading inside. He nodded goodbye to the blonde and walked around her to get to the club entrance. "See you in there."

Great, thanks for leaving me. I'd get in a few cheap shots at the gym next time we sparred for that. "Hey." A lame response, but I was coming up short on a name.

The blonde set a hand to my chest like she felt it belonged there. And of fecking course, Emilia would arrive with Cole and Alessia while I was standing out front with a *blonde.*

"Sean," Cole greeted me, but I was too busy following Emilia's gaze as it swept over the blonde before she strode past me, leaving a cold chill in her wake.

And hell, maybe there was a way to get Emilia to open up and stop hiding her feelings. To stop hiding behind League rules.

Make her jealous?

But I hated games. Hated the idea of resorting to that kind of shite. I'd told myself, well, more accurately, Emilia, that I'd do as she'd asked and give up. But Adam was right about me. I wasn't exactly a quitter.

"Be in soon," I told Cole and sent a smile Alessia's way. Emilia, on the other hand, had already disappeared inside the club.

"How are you?" The blonde's glossy lips pursed, and she lifted her palm from my chest, suddenly seeming to register the fact I didn't have a damn clue who in the hell she was.

I hid my hands in my trouser pockets. "I'm sorry. I don't remember you," I admitted sheepishly.

Her sultry expression softened into one of disappointment. Had I upset her?

"If we slept together and I ghosted you after, I apologize." Being League leader meant it was time I started owning my past transgressions. "I assume it was years ago, though." *Because I've changed.*

"Wow. Okay." She threaded her pink-painted nails through her long locks. "We, um, didn't have a one-night stand. We dated for a few months while we were getting our MBAs at Trinity."

Her definition of dating and mine were clearly different. As far as I could remember, I'd never dated anyone. Back then, my flat was considered a revolving door for random women I'd screwed.

Feck. I'd been more of an arsehole in the old days than I'd realized. "Sara," I said as the memory hit me. Yeah, she was more like a friend with benefits in college than a girlfriend, but why split hairs now? "Been a long time."

"It has." Sara reached into her purse and handed me a business card. "I'm putting that MBA of mine to good use now."

"You own a lingerie store?" I examined the address. Grafton Street. Must have been a hell of a business to score that location.

"A few, actually. Here in Dublin. London. New York. We carry some of the best brands in the world." She smiled, clearly proud, as she should be. "I rotate between locations to make sure everything is running smoothly."

"That's amazing. Congratulations."

"You should come by. I mean, if you have a special someone in your life to shop for."

Someone special, huh? I'd love nothing more than to buy lingerie for Emilia. "Thanks. Maybe." I stood awkwardly, not sure what else to say. "Well, it was good seeing you. Congrats on the store." I turned to the side, my attention moving to the club.

"Sean?"

"Yeah?" I pivoted around to face her.

"I, um." Her lips slammed shut and tightened into a smile before she said, "See you around, McGregor."

"Take care, Sara." I nodded and pocketed her business card. For a split second, as I watched her fire-red heels click down the street, I considered asking Sara out on a date. Get back at Emilia and make her jealous. But I quickly dismissed the idea. *You hate those kinds of games, remember?* I shook my head at my stupidity and then went inside the club to face the music.

Sebastian, Cole, Alessia, and Adam were seated in a

lounge area not far from the main bar, but Emilia was nowhere in sight. It was always strange being at the club when the place wasn't open, and I didn't have to yell over booming music.

My sister celebrated her twenty-first birthday here years ago, and little did we know that same night Sebastian and Alessia were upstairs purchasing the club. Sebastian told Holly he'd seen her that night, too. The man's obsession for Holly was about on par with whatever I felt for Emilia. I'd never admit that to him, though.

Sebastian was once known as a devil among men in our city, but I still liked to poke fun and make a Batman jibe here and there, completely ignoring the fact I was now a billionaire vigilante as well. My sister loved to tease me that I looked like the Green Arrow character on TV. But I didn't wear green or carry a bow. No, that was Emilia with the bow. Of course, Emilia had always joined in on the joking and countered Holly's claim that I reminded her of some actor who fought paranormal beings. Jenson something? I disagreed with everyone, especially since they were trying to get a rise out of me. *But . . . shite, where the hell is my head right now?*

I squeezed my temples and got my feet moving, circling the long length of the bar to spot Emilia crouching to grab the stash of whiskey we kept hidden for our meetings. Everyone who worked the bar knew not to touch the Glendalough 25-Year-Old single malt Irish whiskey in that cabinet. Sebastian was a bit of a whiskey expert, and he'd often bring out different brands for us to taste test.

Emilia slowly rose, meeting my eyes in the process.

She'd already removed her overcoat, and I was surprised by her look this evening. Dark skinny jeans, gray running shoes, and an oversized gray Oxford jumper—not how she normally dressed, but she was just as stunning. And now that I was standing right in front of her, I realized she wasn't wearing any makeup.

Emilia's lashes were naturally dark, and her long black hair hung in soft waves, framing her face and highlighting her big, brown eyes. *Gorgeous* was a seriously inadequate description of this woman. I'd need to consult a few love poems to find something that would do her justice. Maybe Pablo Neruda. My sister was a big fan of his poetry. Whenever she had a crush on some bloke in her teenage years, she'd go around reading Pablo's love poems.

No makeup needed, but I was fairly certain I'd never seen Emilia like this before. So exposed.

"Hi." She kept hold of the whiskey bottle as her eyes fixed on my pocket like she had X-ray vision and knew I had Sara's number there.

I set a hand to the bar top at my side. "Hi." Seeing her without makeup and not all dressed up had me picturing her wearing only my tee, spending a lazy Sunday lounging around my flat.

"I was in London. Just got back from the airport. I didn't want to be noticed," she casually said and went for a circular cocktail tray.

I caught a whiff of her perfume when she reached across me for some glasses. It was the only scent she ever wore, and it seemed to be a sharp contrast to her personality. At least, the side of herself she let us all see.

Her gentle flowery fragrance floated to my nose before she stepped back, setting the glasses on the tray. Holly had once asked her about the perfume she wore. Chanel No. 5. Always.

"You didn't mention you'd be going to London." Our hands brushed when I went for the tray, and she stilled and regarded me with an apologetic pair of beautiful eyes.

"Vegas," she mouthed, blindsiding me with a single word. And then she doubled down. "I'm sorry."

I hardly knew what to make of the words she chose to hit me with tonight. Here of all places. *You're sorry?* For what exactly? For forgetting? I removed my hand from the tray, a bit off guard, and she walked past me without another word.

I set both palms to the bar top and bowed my head, reeling from that moment.

I had to gather my fecking wits. I took a shot from the closest bottle of whiskey I could find with my back turned to the group, then one more, before I allowed myself to join everyone.

Emilia had her focus on the floor as I approached, and there was a vulnerability present I hadn't expected. Maybe it was the fact she'd stripped herself of her leather and red lipstick or the way she'd whispered sorry in such a quick, confusing way. Or, hell, I was grasping at straws. Looking for meaning in anything and everything when it came to this woman who did her best to shield her emotions.

Sebastian poured two fingers of whiskey in each glass, and Emilia handed out the drinks. I took a seat next to my brother, and when Emilia offered the tumbler, I swept my gaze up to her face to find her eyes meeting mine. But in one fast movement, whatever touch of emotion I'd sworn I witnessed vanished. Her thoughts now unreadable to me in every possible way. Her body language. Eyes. Everything. She'd perfected the ability to block me out.

I shifted my focus to Cole's wife on the couch opposite me. It'd been two years since Sebastian had learned Alessia was not only alive but that it was his best friend Luca who'd faked her death. Every so often, I caught him eyeing his sister as though she were a ghost, worried she wasn't really there.

I couldn't imagine losing my sister. Conversely, mourning her for four years only to discover she'd been locked away in a League prison in Russia.

Luca.

Feck that man.

My loathing for him wasn't limited to what he'd done to Alessia. I was jealous he'd tasted Emilia's lips. Had her body. Her time and attention. I especially hated that he was currently living as a free man while helping us gain intel on The Alliance. He'd engineered that deal not too long after we'd rescued Alessia, only for Luca to have turned a Russian mob on us. Luca offered to go undercover within The Alliance in exchange for his life. We'd all hated the idea, but in the end, the arsehole had won.

I couldn't help but secretly hope I'd get the privilege of taking him down after he outlived his usefulness. He could be my first kill, but I had a feeling I wouldn't be so lucky. A guy could hope, though.

"How'd it go?" Sebastian was the first to break the silence, eyes set on Emilia. It was clear he'd been clued in as to her whereabouts today.

I crossed my ankle over my knee, rested the tumbler on my thigh, and did my best to keep my emotions in check. Being a League leader meant I had to be tough, not fixated on a woman. Not obsessed, a word I was beginning to hate.

Obsession was dangerous.

Da had been obsessed with work, driving Ma away to the point they nearly divorced. Not to mention his heart attack that had forced Adam and Anna to postpone their original wedding date.

Sebastian's obsession with Holly had painted a target on

her head two years ago as well.

So, I'd be smart to end this obsession with Emilia. We weren't meant to be, despite all my talk of fate throwing us together again. Besides, if I didn't get a handle on my feelings, it could end up destroying me as well as hurting people I cared about.

"I got as close to him as possible without drawing attention to myself." Emilia's words stole my focus her way as she remained standing, her back to one of the black poles separating the large room into sections.

"Him?" Cole's hand went to Alessia's thigh, and he leaned back on the couch.

"I went to London because Luca gave me the heads-up that Atlas Castellanos-Laurent was in town for meetings and told me I ought to drop by today. More specifically, to be there at three in the afternoon. He said I wouldn't want to miss out on the photoshoot taking place in the park across the street from Atlas's hotel."

At the mention of Luca's name, my attention veered to Cole. He clenched his jaw and fisted the hand on his wife's thigh. Alessia placed her hand atop his in a gesture I was sure was meant to calm him.

"And?" Sebastian spat out like he'd tasted something foul with Luca's name mentioned.

"Clearly, Luca wanted me to see that it appears as though Atlas is having an affair with Bridgette Krause, the twenty-six-year-old German model, or he's hoping to start one, at least. Bridgette was part of the fashion shoot for a commercial in the park, and Atlas observed from a nearby bench. Never took his eyes off her. And every free moment she had, she stared at him. There was definitely *something* between them."

"Why can't Luca ever just be feckin' straightforward?

Him and his damn antics these past months when providing intel makes my skin bloody crawl." Just thinking about Emilia talking to that smarmy bastard had me itchy.

"I gave him shit for purposefully withholding that important detail," Emilia quickly responded. "Luca said he had a hunch they were having an affair, but he hadn't managed to get any proof, and he didn't think I'd believe him without checking for myself."

"Well, that's probably the truest thing that man has said," Cole tossed out bitterly. "I wouldn't have believed him."

"When I pressed Luca, he did manage to obtain Atlas's schedule for the last few weeks for me. Atlas made four trips between November and now. I can also confirm Bridgette had fashion meetings or events in three of those four cities at the same time Atlas was there."

Alessia stood at Emilia's news. "Bridgette Krause is married to The Alliance leader of Germany, right? Peter Krause. And her husband is, what, fifty?"

And now things just got a lot more interesting.

Emilia pinned her eyes on Alessia, a smile crossing her lips.

"Bridgette's father was the German leader until two years ago. When Bridgette and Peter married, the position passed to him," Sebastian added the reminder. "The Krauses happen to be the wealthiest Alliance family in Germany, so the union made sense to Bridgette's father."

"No one ever gives a damn about what the daughter wants," Emilia said in a soft voice, then appeared to physically shake off whatever was going on in her head.

"So, if something is going on between Bridgette and Atlas, are you thinking about using that information to pit the German Alliance branch against Atlas?" Adam asked.

"Start a little civil war within the organization?" Cole added, but I remained quiet, taking it all in.

Emilia folded her arms and surveyed our group, her eyes landing on me last. "Exactly. I was hoping the affair could help us turn Peter and Atlas against each other. Peter already doesn't like Atlas and finding out about Bridgette's affair will tip him over the edge. They'll be distracted dealing with each other. More vulnerable. And then we make our move."

"We're listening," Alessia said, poised and ready to learn more. When Alessia returned from years of captivity, Emilia had stepped in and helped her cope with the trauma and PTSD of the hell she'd endured. She'd also helped Alessia hone the fighting skills she'd learned in that prison—working to bring down The Alliance was a form of therapy.

"Let's start with what we know of both the German branch and Atlas's family," Sebastian said, and it had me wondering how much he and Emilia had already discussed before our meeting. Of course, Sebastian had his finger on the pulse of The League as well as a sharp eye on The Alliance, and he kept Emilia in the know. At times, it made me feel like an outsider watching the two of them. "As Emilia mentioned, Peter Krause holds a grudge against Atlas's family for several reasons," Sebastian went on. "The main one being that when Atlas's father and grandfather died in that plane crash last year, Atlas inherited control of not just one, but two Alliance countries. Peter resents the fact that Atlas is only twenty-seven and relatively inexperienced, yet he's required to go to him for permission for certain deals. In Peter's mind, Atlas should never have been in a position to inherit such power. And Peter's father was against the marriage of Penelope Castellanos and Simon Laurent. Like The League, he took issue with two powerful families merging."

"Peter's father went so far as calling on one of The Alliance's rituals they'd borrowed and modified from ancient Rome. He'd hoped to prevent the powerful union from happening," Emilia added, her expression blank.

"I'm all ears. What is it?" Adam asked, setting his elbows on his thighs, leaning forward with interest.

"It's called *L'ultima ora*," Emilia said, her tone cool and detached. "The Final Hour. The ritual is invoked when two families from different countries attempt to unite."

Alessia grimaced. "And why do I get the feeling this is going to be a 'Russell Crowe in *Gladiator* on steroids' kind of challenge?"

"Because it is." Sebastian looked at his sister apologetically, probably remembering what Luca Moreau had done to her in that Russian prison, forcing her to fight against men twice her size—including having her kill the son of the most powerful Russian crime boss in the world. "Simon had to prove himself worthy of such a powerful position. One hour of fighting. Within that hour, he went up against the best of the best fighters. Or anyone in The Alliance looking to challenge him for his power instead. Simon had to knock the assassins unconscious or kill them. But the goal for him was survival."

"Wow. So, it would have been game over for him if he'd failed," Alessia mused, "which obviously, he didn't."

"He killed two men and severely wounded three more that night," Sebastian told her.

"And did Penelope even have a choice, or was she forced into the wedding by her father, Milos?" Alessia asked, sounding almost concerned for the man's daughter.

"Arranged marriage," Emilia answered. "Simon barely survived the hour, but he earned himself the blood right, as

The Alliance called it, to be the one to unite the Greek and French houses of the organization."

"With the assumption that his heirs would one day take over," Emilia pointed out, her tone easing out of the semi-hollow state it'd wandered into, taking on more depth. More emotion.

"Atlas had a sister as well, right?" Cole asked, and he clearly had a better memory than me on such details. I'd been focused on training to ensure I didn't die going up against a criminal, and he had a bit more time in the so-called ring of League life than me before I'd joined. "Chanel?"

Emilia's spine stiffened ever so slightly at the same time she cast her dark gaze to the floor. Something about Cole's question had her either on edge or uncomfortable. Maybe both.

Sebastian cleared his throat rather loudly and put a fist to his mouth. His actions were about as subtle as a gun. It was obvious the two of them knew something we didn't.

But would they share? Jury was out.

And also, would I press?

Emilia had learned from Sebastian—the master. Getting either of them to open up was near impossible. They were like two seemingly impenetrable fortresses. Just because my sister got through to Sebastian didn't mean Emilia's defenses would come crumbling down.

"Yes, Atlas had a sister, but even if she hadn't died, she wouldn't have been allowed to lead. So, Atlas was Simon's only heir." Based on Emilia's lack of eye contact with anyone but Sebastian, she was done with that part of the conversation.

"So, we know Peter isn't a fan of Atlas. And I'm betting Atlas feels the same toward him," Adam spoke up. He knew even less about Alliance and League dynamics than me. He probably felt like he was playing catch-up every time we had a meeting. "As for Atlas, on a scale of one to ten, how bad of a bloke are we dealing with?"

"Now? A five. But he has the potential to be an eleven," Sebastian commented in a low voice.

"Great," I grumbled under my breath.

"So, we take him out before that happens. That's the plan," Alessia said as if serving a reminder to a group of disheartened people who'd lost their way.

Emilia nodded, her posture suddenly more relaxed. "According to Luca, Atlas will be attending a special New Year's Eve event in Monaco, and I did some checking, and Bridgette will be there as well. That's where we can get evidence of their affair. And even if her husband is there, I have a feeling Atlas may still try and chance a moment alone with her."

"Are we really trusting Luca, though? What if he's playing us somehow, and this intel is a trap?" Cole bit out. He was now on his feet, hands diving through his dark hair.

"He knows if he lies or his intel is bad, he's done. Everything he's offered us thus far has only helped," Emilia said with a confident nod. "Don't worry."

How could we not worry?

"The man double-crossed The League. He locked Alessia away in a prison in Russia," Cole said in a dark voice as if we'd forgotten. "He forced Alessia to kill the son of the leader of a powerful mob organization to try and turn the Petrovs against The League. Luca can't be trusted."

Sebastian was the next to stand, his voice gravelly and low as anger pierced his words. "All of that is true, but we also can't deny that every piece of intel he's provided us thus far has been helpful. So, like Emilia said, we keep using him until he's no longer useful."

Alessia peered at her brother and gave him a tight nod. The woman was tough. "How will we get into this event in Monaco?" Alessia asked Emilia. "Won't that raise some eyebrows if we show up? Unless you mean for one of us to sneak around and not actually get on the invite list."

"The event is for the ultra-wealthy. And it's not sponsored by The Alliance, so if one of us happens to show up, it won't appear all that suspicious." I had a feeling Emilia still had more to reveal.

"Monaco, of course. Nicknamed the billionaires' playground," Adam said, drawing our eyes. "What?" He shrugged. "I went there often in my pre-Anna days."

Emilia's smile was resurrected for a brief moment at my brother's playful grin before returning to business-mode. "I think it'd be smart for one of us to make a move on Bridgette before Monaco and plant a listening device on her. She might meet up with Atlas before New Year's Eve, which would get us the proof we need that much sooner. We might even be able to gather intel on Peter in that time as well. And if neither of those things happen, we still have our original plan. No downside risk here."

"What do you propose?" I asked.

"I did some digging, and the designer she models for rotates Bridgette's everyday seasonal looks, including her bag. For the next few weeks, she should be carrying the same purse with her. That's our target," Emilia explained.

"And how will one of us get close to her?" Adam scratched his jaw, now covered in a few days' worth of scruff.

"Me," I said under my breath. "And let me guess, she's blonde, right?" I stood and jammed my hands in my trouser pockets, finding Sara's business card there.

The look Emilia gave me was downright frigid, but I was likely the only one who noticed. "You'll need to get her alone. Maybe in her room. A place without any cameras to spot you slipping a device into her bag," Emilia added after allowing the icy moment between us to dissipate. "She'll be in Edinburgh this Saturday. Bridgette's in a lingerie runway event, and there's a private after-party. You're single. I'm sure watching mostly naked women strut down a runway won't be a hardship for you."

Damn this woman. She was really trying to get a rise out of me at every opportunity. Her words, coupled with whatever angry look I was probably sporting, drew a few throat clears around us.

"And how am I landing a last-minute invite to this lingerie event and after-party?" I asked, but then my thoughts drifted to Sara. Surely, she had connections in the industry. She'd said she carried some of the best lines, so maybe.

Was it fate I'd bumped into her?

I was growing tired of that word since it never seemed to work in my favor.

"I'd prefer not to flash your name around as a way in because I want you flying under the radar, but I'll think of something," Emilia said with confidence.

"Will Bridgette's husband be at this event?" Sebastian asked, directing his attention to Emilia, saving me from her icy glare. "Atlas?"

"No. Peter rarely attends her fashion shows. And according to the schedule Luca provided me, Atlas is staying in London through Sunday," Emilia answered, then turned her gaze back to me. "So, you'll have the all-clear to do what you do best."

What I do best, huh? "And what makes you think Bridgette will take me to her room? What if she recognizes me as League?"

Emilia's eyes raked over me as if the answer was obvious.

"Oh, I don't think you'll have a problem garnering her attention." She wet her lips, and I was fairly certain she hadn't realized she was doing it because a second later, she blinked and turned away from me. "As for being an enemy of her husband, looks like that didn't stop her with Atlas. Might thrill her that much more if she knows you're League."

"You're not actually going to sleep with her, right? We want her husband hating Atlas not focusing his attention on you," Alessia asked, and this conversation had me wanting to go blow money on something ridiculous. Maybe one-up Da and get a newer model Ferrari than the one he had.

I cupped the back of my head. "Of course not," I snapped, letting everyone know up front there were lengths I wouldn't go to, not even for our war with The Alliance. Maybe before Emilia and my League position, the old Sean wouldn't have fecking cared, but The League had turned me into a better man. A confused man, at times, but a better one. I saw the darkness now that I was in The League, but looking at Emilia, even right now, I also saw the light. And it was so bright it hurt at times to look at it.

"I'll be in Edinburgh with you at the fashion show," Emilia said without looking at me. "I'll make sure the device is properly working once you place it in her bag. Plus, it wouldn't hurt to snap a few photos of you two together. If things don't pan out in Monaco for some reason, we can use those to blackmail her for intel on her husband and Atlas. She wouldn't want either man finding out about you." Her gaze cut to me. "Make sure to get the curtains open. I can use a long-range lens from the building across from the hotel to get the shots. A kiss should be sufficient." Her tone was a touch weak. Barely noticeable to probably everyone but me.

I tried not to cling to the hope that Emilia was jealous

because, despite her quips about blondes, I didn't think she had it in her.

"What kind of tech do we have for a listening device?" Adam asked. "I assume her husband is cautious and does routine sweeps."

"A friend of mine who creates gadgets for MI6 gave me a few small devices while I was in London today. He promised me they would go undetected." Emilia turned to the side, offering her profile.

"Why not send someone in The League to Edinburgh instead? Why chance going yourselves?" Adam proposed.

"Honestly? The only people I trust with the plan are in this room," Sebastian answered, then looked to the rest of us for our opinion, and we all nodded in agreement.

"So, we get the backup blackmail photos of Sean and Bridgette. Plant the device. Listen and wait for Monaco. Then we get the proof we need of her and Atlas and share the photos with her husband," Alessia summarized. "The two territorial alphas will go at each other, and that's when we make our move, the one we've spent twenty months preparing for."

"The final takedown," Cole said in awe like we'd all been chasing this elusive unicorn, and now it was finally within our reach. Cole was also eager because I knew my cousin was ready to have kids with Alessia, but he was holding off until we destroyed The Alliance.

"The Russian Petrov family is ready to help," Emilia began. "Our American allies. And more. They're all waiting for our call. I think it's time."

"But are we okay with sacrificing a potentially innocent woman in the process?" Adam lifted his palms as if he were on the verge of surrendering a fight. "We good with that?"

"Bridgette is in bed with the enemy," Alessia spoke up in

defense of Emilia's plan. "That makes her as guilty as her father, husband, and her lover."

"You can't sleep with a killer without getting a little of the blood they've shed on your hands." Emilia directed her words my way. I felt them in my bones.

And why the hell did those words feel like a warning?

CHAPTER SIX

EMILIA

"I'D NEVER TELL YOU HOW TO DO YOUR JOB, BUT—"

"Sounds like you're about to," I cut off Sebastian, mentally prepping for some type of lecture from him as we talked over the phone.

The valet standing outside the hotel was patiently waiting for me to exit my vehicle, but I needed to finish this call with Sebastian. His name popped up on my mobile just as I pulled into the *porte cochére*, and I had a feeling this was a call I didn't want to take while walking through the lobby.

"Just maybe call for backup next time. The team said there was a lot of blood," Sebastian spoke in a low but steady voice, clearly doing his best to tiptoe around his "not telling me what to do" declaration.

"Not my blood." *Mostly not.* I set my free hand to the fresh cut on my side and winced in pain.

"Mmhm." He was quiet for a moment, and I was waiting for the real reason he called. "When are we telling the others about your connection to Atlas?"

Ever since our meeting Wednesday night, I'd been

wondering when he was going to ask that. "I don't have a connection to Atlas."

"You know what I mean." The man sounded borderline broody just now, and I doubted it was because of me.

"Where are you?"

"Late night working at the club. I missed dinner again and—"

"Hoping you don't get banished to the couch?" I attempted a laugh, but it came out more like a coyote moaning from pain. "Anyway, we'll tell them about Chanel. Maybe after Christmas. I know I can't keep my past a secret from them if we're going to go after Atlas." I grabbed the weapons bag on the passenger seat and exited the BMW. "I have to go. Talk soon." I ended the call before Sebastian had a chance to say more.

He'd been overly patient with me once I'd learned Chanel's father and grandfather had died, passing on the leader role to her brother. I owed him a lot for that.

"Good evening," the valet said while taking my keys. He had on a festive but hideous Christmas jumper, something I doubted I'd be able to pull off even in a do-or-die moment.

I smiled at him, then did my best to hide my pain and not hobble my way through the lobby of Sebastian's hotel. I stayed in one of the two penthouses on the top level whenever in town, and I didn't need anyone calling him up to confirm his suspicions—that I *was* bleeding.

I had a thick gauze bandage covering the wound beneath my clothes, but I could feel the blood beginning to seep through, and it'd be a matter of minutes before a trail of evidence followed me.

Thankfully, no one appeared to notice so far, and I made it safely inside the lift.

When a big guy wearing a cowboy hat and brown leather

jacket attempted to enter the lift with me, I stepped forward forcefully, swallowing a wince. "Back off, cowboy. I'm riding alone." I'm pretty sure I snarled.

He retreated two steps and tipped his hat. The man didn't deserve that, especially because he respected a woman enough to take a hint, but I also needed a moment alone.

After the doors closed, I faced the mirrored walls and peeled the waistband of my trousers down to eye the gauze, confirming it was soaked in blood.

I was out of the lift in a hurry once I reached the top level, barely managing to open the door to my suite because my hands were so shaky.

My clothes came off as I walked to the bathroom. Jacket gone. Boots tossed. My top a flash of black material over my shoulder. Getting out of my skinny jeans was the greatest challenge because of my injury and the wriggling necessary to get the damn things off.

I backed into the shower and gasped when the cold water hit my back, then made quick work of washing my body, taking care to clean around the wound thoroughly. I needed to get a good look, determine the damage, and decide whether I'd have to fix myself up.

Another thing Papà had taught me was to patch myself up. I didn't have any official medical training, but my life required me to be a jack-of-all-trades.

I bit down on my back teeth when the water turned hot and burned my skin. Blood circled the drain beneath my bare feet, and my hand became a fist as I rested it against the tiled wall and hissed.

I'd been distracted tonight. When the leader of the Dutch gun runners Sean and I had encountered in the park the other night made a surprising appearance in the city looking for me, I'd gone after him alone. Not my best idea.

The man in charge managed to swipe me before I rendered him unconscious and called in a team to escort him and his two "colleagues" to a League prison. I'd been tempted to let the local police come and pick the men up since they were alive, but I didn't need anyone tossing around my description to detectives. Sebastian had a few guys on the inside at the police station, but I didn't want to take a chance.

Both Sean and I had kept ourselves busy the last two days, dealing with separate issues.

Sean and Cole had handled a local drug dealer after our meeting ended on Wednesday, so he'd been tied up and couldn't pin me down with questions about my Vegas comment that night.

But tomorrow was our trip to Scotland, and we'd have no choice but to spend time together, especially since we had to stay in the same suite. He'd be my date to the fashion show after all.

I stepped out of the shower, wondering what Chanel would have to say about all of this, including the woman I'd become. As well as Papà. I knew why he'd never gone after his rivals as fiercely as his father had in the past. But how would he feel about my plans now?

I won't let Atlas or Penelope die, I told Papà and Chanel in my head as if they'd hear me, hoping I'd be able to keep that promise. Hoping when the time came, Atlas wouldn't put me in a position to force my hand.

I toweled off and stepped in front of the floor-to-ceiling mirror attached to the walk-in closet door to get a closer look.

Idiota. The bastard who cut me nearly destroyed the tattoo I'd received the day I'd taken over as League leader. My League ink was just below my hip bone, only visible when I wore a swimsuit or was naked.

I reached for a tube of antibiotic cream but nearly

dropped it when incessant banging on the main door of my suite startled me.

I slapped a piece of gauze over the wound and secured it with medical tape, then pulled on a pair of cotton drawstring shorts and a tee.

"Who is it?" I asked while hurrying through the living room, doing my best not to yelp in pain with each step.

"Sean," he barked out loudly, then dropped his voice to a low hiss. "Why is there blood out here?"

I set a palm next to the door and took a breath before swinging it open. Sebastian must've told him I'd called in a League team after facing off with the Dutch criminals tonight. His flat was only five minutes away, which meant he came here immediately after Sebastian had snitched.

Sean stood before me wearing dark denim jeans and a cream-colored pullover. His hair was slightly damp as if he'd hopped out of the shower and raced right over.

"Why is there blood?" he repeated, pointing to the small spot on the carpet in the hall. "Are you okay?"

"A scratch. I'm fine." With one hand grasping the edge of the door and the other still planted on the wall, I sank into the doorframe a bit, going for casual and trying like hell to keep him from barging into my suite. I prayed Sean wouldn't notice how much pain I was in, though it was my pride that hurt more than anything.

His brows slanted. Worry still cutting across his face while his eyes searched my body, obviously looking for the source of the blood. After a quick once-over, his eyes lingered on my T-shirt.

Right. No bra. And I was wearing a light gray top. If I looked down, I'd most likely find my nipples poking through the fabric. No panties, either. Should I let him know that, too? Make things even more awkward between us?

"So, you're okay?" He slowly guided his focus to my face, and my heart nearly skipped a beat at the lust burning in his gaze.

"I'm okay. Sebastian didn't need to call you. Just had to handle the boss of those assholes we dealt with earlier in the week. Everything worked out."

"I'd like to see. Can you let me in?" He wasn't buying my act. Why was I surprised? He was one of the few people in my life who had the uncanny ability to see right through me.

"Ethan back? You picked him up at the airport earlier, right?" I made a lame attempt to derail his focus from my injury.

"Yeah, he's home." He jerked his chin, motioning for me to let him in.

My shoulders sagged, but I relented and moved out of the way. If I needed stitches, it'd probably be easier if I had help.

"You should have called me," he said while following me to the ensuite, maneuvering around my discarded clothes.

"I had it handled." *I would've been fine if you weren't in my head, distracting me to no end. Or Chanel, for that matter.*

"A scratch, huh?" he tossed out sarcastically, pointing to the bloody gauze on the vanity counter.

"I bleed easily." But what was the point in lying when he was about to have a look himself?

"Sure." He surprised me by pulling the jumper over his head, and he carelessly tossed it into the bedroom, revealing a plain white tee that showed off his corded forearms and tight triceps. Too hot in here for him?

When I was at Holly's on Tuesday, I'd mentioned her brother had physically changed since joining The League, and now that my memories from Vegas were surfacing, those words couldn't be truer.

He'd been handsome back then, a decade ago, but the man he'd become, the man standing before me now was absolutely stunning.

His jawline was more chiseled, and his once lean body was cut and defined in a way only fighting and rigorous League training could produce.

But it was his eyes that had undergone the most noticeable changes. Their alluring blue color had reeled me in that night in Vegas, but it was more than just their hue. They expressed a genuine curiosity and love for life. Maybe even a touch of innocence. Now, whatever innocence had been present ten years ago was long gone. Replaced with wisdom and experience and hardened by the realities from which he'd been shielded. For Sean, joining The League was like getting pulled from the matrix, and he finally saw the true pain and suffering in our cities. Sometimes, looking at him was like looking into a mirror.

"You're not invincible, you know?" He advanced closer. "I know you think you are, but everyone bleeds." His tone was rough, like he wanted to yell at me but was holding back. Pissed that I could have gotten myself killed. And if I was being honest with myself, angry for a lot more than that.

I blinked a few times, then backed up against the vanity as if my body knew he was a force not to be taken lightly and sought a reprieve from the fallout.

Heat radiated from him, saturating the air as he grew closer with slow decisive steps. A lion stalking his prey. And was it strange that this growly, fierce side of him turned me on? He set both hands on the counter on either side of where I gripped and leaned in, not giving me much room to show him the injury.

But . . . what injury? The only pain I could focus on was

between my thighs. A dull, achy unfulfilled need that grew stronger with each passing second.

I lifted my chin, challenging his dominant stance. He didn't afford me much space to do more than breathe. And even then, his masculine scent crowded my senses, dizzying my mind and crumbling my resolve with every inhalation.

"Where's. The. Scratch?" I could almost feel the rumble of his chest as he gritted out the words, and damn if that didn't send a thrill of excitement to my core.

Tuesday night after our fight, Sean had told me he'd back off. That he'd fuck a blonde to get me out of his system. This was the opposite of backing off. This was pushing me to want to reach for his buckle and shove down his jeans. To stroke his length and bury him inside me.

Suddenly, he lifted his palms and stepped back, and I followed his silent command and brushed my shirt aside to reveal the gauze covering my wound.

He lowered himself to one knee and leaned in so close I felt his warm breath caress my exposed skin.

If I moved a fraction to the right, his mouth would be perfectly positioned between my legs.

"More than a scratch," he mumbled after gently removing the tape and gauze. The low, raspy quality still clung to his tone.

I couldn't deny the hold he had on me. And being alone with him in my suite, his mouth within licking distance to my wet center, was more than I could handle.

It was a coin toss as to what I'd do next.

Peel off my tee and give myself to him, or push him away and demand he leave?

Sean lifted my shirt to get a better view of my injury. Not too far from where his hand lay was a scar I'd gotten at a wedding years ago—stabbed by a corkscrew of all things.

Interestingly enough, that was what led to my friendship with Roman, one of the Navy SEALs we helped out in October. He'd saved me that night, and we kept in touch over the years, developing a platonic friendship along the way. And now Roman was one of the closest friends outside of The League I'd allowed myself to have since Chanel. He had walls and barriers and issues like me, so we understood each other.

"I need your shirt and shorts off to fix you up. Can you change into a bikini or something?"

"It's December in Dublin. No bikini."

He lifted his chin to find my eyes and returned the ghost of a smile on my lips. He repositioned his hands on my outer thighs and held me in place. Whether it was to keep me from running or simply to hold me, I wasn't sure. Logic told me it was option one, but I desperately wanted it to be option two.

"What do you Irish call them? Knickers?"

"That's more of an English or Northern Ireland term." He managed a smile. "Pants are panties to us, but that can be a wee bit confusing to non-Dubliners, so we can go with whatever you'd like. Your *panties* and bra are fine." Sean stood, carefully smoothing his hands up the sides of my torso in the process.

The fact we were discussing the semantics of undergarments meant we were both crazy. I was sure of it.

"Then I'll need to go put them on since I'm not wearing any."

His hands froze beside my breasts, and that lustful gaze of his returned even brighter. It couldn't have been more than a few seconds, but it felt so much longer.

"Why are you still holding me?" I finally asked, breaking our silence, a slight tilt to my lips.

His blue eyes gleamed as he studied me. Such wicked thoughts mirroring my own, no doubt, going on in his head.

He didn't answer, and I followed the tan column of his throat to witness the movement of his Adam's apple. He unhanded me, then unexpectedly brought his knuckles over my cheek before catching my lower lip with his thumb.

The movement sent shivers down my spine, and I tipped up my chin and closed my eyes. "I truly wish you were capable of no-strings sex." It took all of my strength to remain composed and to keep my tone steady as I spoke. And after that, I did an about-face and left.

I shut the ensuite door to be alone in the bedroom and alone with my thoughts. I took my time going through the dresser, shuffling around through panties and bras in search of something plain. The most boring pair I could find. More of a safety precaution for me. Red or black lace would scream, *I want you to take me here and now.* On the vanity counter. No protection. Just raw and primitive.

My fingers skimmed over a matching bra and panty set in beige. Boring beige. Perfect. Plus, full coverage up top.

I shook my head and stole a few breaths, collecting myself.

I whipped my wet hair into a messy bun at the top of my head, took an unsettling look at myself in the mirror over the dresser, then went back to the ensuite.

When I opened the door, Sean's head was bowed, his palms positioned on the vanity counter.

"Ready," I announced, feeling like a virgin about to have sex. But with this man, I had so many firsts in regard to my emotions, so . . .

I caught his reflection in the mirror and saw his eyes screwed tight as if *he* wasn't ready.

"You can't help me with your eyes closed, Sean.

Doubtful, at least." Calling up a page from the playbook I'd been using for the last twenty months, I kept my tone teasing and coy. Well, I suppose one could say I was throwing flags on the field to prevent a touchdown. I always did love American football.

Sean's blue eyes found mine a beat later in the mirror, and he kept them locked on my face instead of dipping lower to take in my lingerie.

"Got these from a place on Grafton. Sara-Grace's or something like that." Not sure why I said that. It wasn't like Sean was staring at me and wondering where he might buy the same pair for someone he loved.

Regret that I couldn't be that someone for him bloomed inside my chest.

His mouth rounded as if surprised about something other than my choice in lingerie, and he muttered, "Of course you did."

"And that means?"

"Sara happens to be the blonde you saw me talking to outside the club Wednesday." His expression hardened. "And no, I'm not sleeping with her."

Ohh. "Well, I didn't ask."

"I was clarifying," he answered, drawing out the words for emphasis. He then knelt before me and focused on the wound, all methodical and doctor-like. "I'd always wondered where your League tattoo was," he said as he fixed me up, and I chanced a look his way to find his thumb tracing the lines of the Doberman inside a warrior's shield standing as a guardian with *Fedeltà* in script above my last name. Ironically, my family hadn't owned a pet in decades.

"Fidelity?" he took a guess.

"Loyalty. Faithfulness." I swallowed. "And *sì,* fidelity."

"You rarely speak Italian around me. Not even a simple,

sì." His Irish accent remained thick, wrapping tight around the word for yes in Italian.

Sean's League ink of a lion, for bravery or courage, was perfect for this man. And I was normally courageous, but right now, I wasn't sure what I was.

"I had a British nanny and British tutors," I offered instead of confessing he was making me nervous. His hands on my body had my pulse racing. "I was surrounded by people speaking English more than Italian most of my life. Plus, I spent two years at Oxford."

"And time in Vegas." A frown touched his lips for a brief moment before he focused back on my wound.

A vision of the MGM Grand in Vegas floated across my mind. The lion wearing a Santa hat surrounded by poinsettias. *A lion, of course. How fitting.*

I would never have forgotten those memories with Sean had Chanel not been murdered.

"Are you really willing to break the rule about sex?" he tossed out casually as if discussing something trivial. My heart stuttered as I let his question replay in my head.

Sean was right about what he said at the gym earlier in the week. *The League ought to stay out of my sex life.*

"I've been having casual sex my whole life, you know," he added.

"Ah, but with me, you'd want a name and number afterward, remember?"

"Looks like you do remember that night," he said while continuing to scrutinize the wound. "I don't think you need stitches. It's mostly superficial. Antibiotic cream and a bandage should be fine." He applied the cream and taped the gauze to the injury, but he remained on his knees.

I stiffened at the feel of his fingers skirting toward the old injury from a corkscrew. "This one was from the night you met that SEAL, Roman, right?"

Without thinking, I set a hand to his shoulder for balance instead of pushing him away. "Yes."

"And this one here?" he asked while finally rising, forcing my hand away from his shoulder. He traced a line over the faded scar below my collarbone near my breast.

I did my best to crush the rise of anger the memory of that scar prompted. I was still pissed I'd ever let someone fool me. Trick me into trusting them only to have them physically hurt me instead. "Machete. Don't ask," I forced out and turned to place my hands on the vanity counter. If there was ever a time to slip away and get dressed, it was now. But instead, my gaze climbed up the length of the mirror to find him standing behind me.

"What if I could do casual sex without expecting more?" He angled his head, studying me for a response in the reflection of the mirror. When I didn't deliver one, he added, "Your father wanted you to marry an Italian, am I right? It's the only thing I can think he'd ask. Maintain some type of bloodline or something."

It sounded ridiculous when Sean said it. Blood was blood, wasn't it? I understood Papà's reasoning, but it had more to do with the fact he'd fallen in love with an enemy and less to do with that woman's heritage.

I reached for my bottle of perfume on the counter. Chanel No. 5. I brought it to my nose and closed my eyes. "In 1921, Coco Chanel said this was a revolution in a bottle. Most scents were single-notes at the time, and she wanted a perfume with layers of complexity. No one ingredient overpowering the other. A perfume for a woman in motion, and on each woman, the scent would smell differently." I inhaled a pull of orange blossom, followed by notes of jasmine unfolding beneath my nose.

"Why are we talking about perfume?" Sean asked as his hands settled on the outside of my arms.

"Because the night you and I met in Vegas was obscured in my mind for ten years by a tragic incident. My friend Chanel, named after Coco Chanel, was murdered in my hotel room." The words fell almost emotionless and flat from my mouth.

He released me, and when I opened my eyes, his head was turned, eyes looking off to the side of the room, most likely wrapping his thoughts around my admission. "That's why you grew uncomfortable at the club Wednesday at the mention of her name," he said, his gaze reconnecting with mine in the mirror.

Wow. And the man could read me well.

I nodded. "I didn't remember you because my best friend died that night. She'd come to Vegas to celebrate my birthday and was murdered by the assassin sent to kill *me*." I set the bottle down and drew a hand around my neck, feeling like I was suffocating. But it was by my own making. I'd allowed her death to haunt me for years. "I was with you when it happened. It should have been me."

"Emilia." Sean placed a warm hand on my waist and gently guided my body toward him.

"When I opened the door to bring you inside my suite, I saw Sebastian standing over a dead body. The assassin sent to kill me," I explained and turned to face him.

His palm went to my cheek, and his thumb moved in small circles over my flushed skin. "I'm so sorry."

"And then Sebastian did something I'll never be able to forget. He cleaned up the mess in my room as if Chanel had never been there. And he had to hide her body and . . ." My knees unexpectedly buckled, but Sean caught me by the arms and held me upright.

He motioned for me to head into the bedroom and handed me the plush white hotel robe. I took it as if on autopilot, which was uncharacteristic of me, but this man had me doing all kinds of uncharacteristic things. And maybe I needed someone to help me through this moment.

Forget sex *or* running. I was about to open up instead.

Sean sat next to me on the king-sized bed and quietly waited for me to continue.

"Sebastian relocated Chanel's body and the man she'd been with to another hotel and hid all evidence that we'd been hanging out that night." My stomach tucked in at the memory of her body being transferred from my room like a piece of luggage. "Sebastian was under Papà's orders. He had no choice." I slowly looked over at him. "With Chanel being the daughter of Simon Laurent, well, you can imagine what would have happened if they discovered we were friends and that she was killed accidentally because she was mistaken for me."

"There'd be war," Sean said, his voice grave.

There was more to the story, but I wasn't sure those words were mine to tell. Because in reality, it wasn't really my story. It was Papà's, and he was gone.

"I went back to Italy after that, and I took my place in The League as I was destined to do. And I spent my time seeking revenge for Chanel."

"Did you find who sent the assassin?"

"Yes. A criminal faction in Naples that hated Papà and his power. My father had killed the leader's brother, and in retaliation, they sent someone to kill me." I closed my eyes. "Things were a bit different back then. Every so often, my father's power would be challenged. Sometimes those he'd taken down sought their revenge." League power and presence had grown over the years. "Most don't dare try to come after us now. Far too afraid." I swallowed. "But the first life I took was the man who hired the assassin that killed Chanel."

Sebastian was the only one in The League, aside from Papà, to know the truth about what happened. And for the first time, I was sharing the painful memories. I was opening up, surprising myself. That didn't change League rules or the promise I'd made to Papà. And it didn't diminish my fear of being incapable of loving someone romantically, but . . .

I'd avoided being alone with Sean since our sparring session Tuesday because I was trying to come to grips with the fact he'd been with me the night Chanel died. And what that signified, if anything. Maybe I was overthinking.

"Why didn't you tell me you were Clooney?"

"In part, I was afraid I was wrong. That you weren't Julia, and I so badly wanted you to be." I started to look away, but he brought a fist beneath my chin, guiding my focus back. "I wanted you to be her because I'm pretty sure I've been looking for her—you—ever since that night."

Like a fairy tale. I never let myself believe in fairy tales. Tragedies, yes. But happily-ever-afters were far and few between, weren't they? I couldn't hope to replicate what Sebastian and Holly had.

"Also, I didn't bring it up because you never did. I figured if you were Julia, you'd say something, so I had to believe I was mistaken. Or I wasn't as memorable to you as you were for me." His lips crooked at the edges. A frown or a smile? I wasn't sure which way it'd go. "That reason sounds a lot like pride now that I say it out loud." He lowered his hand to his lap, his lips going flat instead. "I guess now that you know I was with you that night while Chanel was killed, that's another—"

"Another reason not to be together?" I finished for him since those thoughts had pushed into my mind upon realizing he was Clooney.

I lost sight of his stunning blue eyes when he looked away, seeming to find the open doorway more interesting. His eyes were more turquoise on a regular day, but when passion or anger cut through, they intensified. A dark, stormy blue. Tonight, they were a clash of the two.

"I did promise Papà I'd carry on his name and marry an Italian. And although League rules clearly can be changed since I'm a woman in charge, I fear they won't change rule one, especially after seeing how much power Chanel's brother has as a result of the two families uniting. The Castellanoses and Laurents joining together serve as an example to League leaders as to why they believe the rules should be kept intact."

He stood and held the back of his head. "I'd leave The League if that would make a difference. You know I'd do that for you, right?" His shoulders fell when he faced me. "But that would also make me a quitter, and I have a feeling that's not an attribute you admire." His eyes softened a bit. "But then there's the promise you made to your father, and I don't know if I could live with myself if I pushed you into going against a dying man's wishes."

"What are you saying?" I was on my feet now, too.

I'd told Sean to move on. Tried to drive him crazy with comments about blondes. I'd done everything I could to get to this exact moment. The moment when he stopped pursuing me and gave up.

And here I was feeling as though I was drowning in a sea of lost possibilities.

"Fate did bring you into my life, Emilia. But I guess it was for other reasons than I'd hoped." His expression hardened as though he were working to build a barrier of his own making instead of dealing with the one I'd spent a lifetime crafting. "I promise I'll respect your wishes and back off." He extended his hand.

A handshake?

God help me.

"Friends?" His eyes traveled up to meet mine. But the heated flame of desire couldn't be tamped down despite the word he'd most likely forced out of his mouth.

His warm palm slid against mine as he united our hands as if we'd just made a business deal. "Friends," I repeated.

"Will going after Atlas be a problem since he's Chanel's brother? And what of her mother?" he asked while easing his touch free of mine. That was more painful than the Dutch gangster slicing me earlier.

"They're still the enemy. But I don't want Atlas or Penelope dying. And can we wait to let the others know about this? I need more time."

"Of course." He nodded and started for his jumper, pulled it over his head, then went for the door. But I wasn't ready for him to leave. To be . . . alone.

It was absurd because I'd pretty much been alone since the day Papà died.

"Do you want to stay for a bit?"

He pivoted to look at me as if I'd lost my mind. Maybe I had.

Sex with no strings? Perhaps it needed to be on the table for discussion? It may be the only way to remove the tight fist in my chest that squeezed relentlessly.

His focus dipped to the V of my robe. The knot had

loosened, and when I looked down, I spied my bra partially on display.

He was contemplating. Reading my thoughts. Reading my body language that said I wanted to give myself to him in the only way I could, sexually.

"I need to think. Tonight might not be the best night to . . . hang out." He pried his eyes free of me and turned for the door.

I followed him into the living room of the suite, and he nearly bumped into me when he halted and did a one-eighty to face me. I followed his pointing finger toward the window.

"What?"

He raised a brow. "No Christmas tree? I thought the penthouses had a tree."

"Oh, I told the front desk not to bother decorating."

"Hm." He lowered his hand back to his side, but the grim look on his face remained. He wasn't satisfied with my answer?

"I guess it's goodnight, then," I whispered.

His brow scrunched, and he let go of a deep breath. "Goodnight, *Julia*."

CHAPTER SEVEN

SEAN

HOW COULD I ASK A WOMAN LIKE EMILIA TO DISREGARD HER father's dying wish and choose me? When I suggested she challenge League rules, specifically the first rule . . . that was one thing. But asking her to go against her father was a line I refused to cross.

She'd offered up the idea of casual sex between us shortly before I left her suite, hadn't she? It didn't take much reading between the lines to figure that out when she'd said, *I really wish you were capable of no-strings sex*. Feck if I didn't want to take her up on the offer, but this gut punch I dealt with whenever I was around her made me so bloody miserable. Wouldn't that feeling intensify if we slept together only to have her walk away afterward like it was nothing?

I wasn't some pussy who couldn't handle his game. Never had been. But it was also the first time in my life that the shoe was on the other foot. I was the one wanting more with little hope of getting it.

I probably deserved whatever I had coming to me after all the shite I'd done over the years. Forgetting women's names. Leaving before sunrise. Bailing on a date for another woman who I found more interesting. I never cheated, but I was never really with anyone long enough for that to happen, which said a lot in and of itself.

Yeah, I was a bloody arsehole. A gobshite of the highest order.

I should've written an apology to every woman whose heart I broke because now I knew what it felt like, and it bloody sucked.

"Your car, sir?" the valet asked when I exited the hotel. He had on one of those ugly Christmas jumpers that were still all the rage. It was an alarming shade of green with Will Ferrell's character Buddy on the front, smiling like a lunatic beneath the quote, "Smiling is my favorite." Not that I spent my time memorizing Christmas movies, but my cousin Bree's son, Jack, loved it.

Before Alessia came back into Sebastian's life, and before he married my sister, I doubted Sebastian would have allowed an employee at one of his hotels to dress in such a manner. I wouldn't call that man soft, but love had undoubtedly changed him.

"Gonna get some air. Be back for it later." I pushed my already chilled hands into my pockets to warm them as I began to walk, aimlessly heading for I had no idea where.

I just had to get away.

If I got behind the wheel of my car, I'd be reckless.

So, I kept walking.

Traditional Irish and folk Christmas music strummed through the air as I walked the cobblestone paths alongside the lit-up street. Christmas lights hung like sheets along the fronts of buildings in an array of colors. Chandelier-like Christmas lights were overhead in the middle of the street, and green garlands wrapped around lamp posts.

I'd always loved Christmas. Ma was a big fan, so she

made the holiday a huge deal while we were growing up. I missed those times, to be honest. The simpler times. The less dangerous ones, too.

My arms tightened as I shoved my hands deeper into my pockets when a bluster of chilled air greeted me. It was five Celsius out, not too bad, but I'd left my jacket in the Maserati.

I turned a corner, approaching the illuminated blue and gold **Grafton Quarter** sign hanging between buildings on my left and right. It'd always be Grafton Street to me.

I bumped into people as I walked, passing pub after pub with blokes partaking in the 12 Pubs of Christmas. You had to visit twelve pubs in one day while following silly rules. Adam and I hadn't done that in at least six years.

Maybe I ought to get drunk?

But shite, I was a lousy drunk when down and didn't want to do something stupid.

When a cover band outside on the patio of one pub began playing a familiar song, *Too Much to Ask*, by Niall Horan, I stopped walking and listened. My heart lodged in my throat as Emilia immediately came to mind.

The words were like a dagger to the chest.

Thoughts of Emilia standing before me in nothing but her "knickers," as she'd assumed I called them, had a flood of warmth chasing up my spine and heating my body. She'd looked so damn beautiful I'd wanted to run my calloused palms over her soft, tan flesh all night. Steal her into my arms and never let go.

I'd had to fight to keep my composure as she confidently faced me, her back pinned against the vanity counter. It was hard to be so close to her without wanting to kiss her everywhere. Discover her taste.

And, of course, her tattoo included the Italian word for

loyalty. She was loyal to her father. To the Calibrisi family name. She was the last living Calibrisi, and that in itself had to be a huge burden to carry.

I'd done my best to focus on the task of examining her wound, one she should never have gotten, but the woman was not only stubborn, she was a lone wolf. She may have been tough, but if she didn't slow down, she'd wind up getting herself killed. And I couldn't handle the idea of anything ever happening to her.

Fate would be cruel like that. Bring Emilia to me only to take her away.

I'd come close to losing loved ones before but, thankfully, I'd been spared that heartache so far.

Da's heart attack. Anna nearly dying during labor, which would have been the death of Adam.

I spun in a three-sixty, feeling a wee bit crazy. I wasn't sure which way to bloody go, but I had to get away from the music. It made me feel way too damn much.

I started walking, more like fleeing the music, but slowed a minute later at the sight of a storefront. Blue letters wrapped in red Christmas lights read **Sara-Grace's Place.**

A lone light appeared to be on in the store, but the place was closed. I'd planned on walking by, just going on my merry feckin' way, but the sound of a scream from inside jolted me.

I whipped my focus to the door and hurried to grab the handle. Unlocked, thank God.

Another cry from farther inside had me moving quickly, navigating around Santa's sleigh full of mannequins in lingerie.

"Please, just wait. He'll be here," a woman begged, her voice full of fear.

It was Sara or one of her employees. But who was she pleading with?

"No," she screamed as I followed the gruff, distinctive sounds of a scuffle coming from the back room.

I hung back around the corner of the hallway, then stole a look into the office. A big guy in all black had Sara up against the wall, her arms pinned over her head with one large hand as she struggled against him. In his other hand was a blade, pushed against her hip. The same damn spot Emilia had just been cut.

Sara shifted her head to the side as if sensing another presence. Her eyes connected with mine, and I brought my finger to my lips while stalking closer to the man as quietly as possible.

He bit out a word I was fairly certain was German for bitch.

Before I had a chance to surprise him, he spun around.

The man snarled and lunged at me, but my League training kicked into gear without a thought. I sprang back and out of reach of the blade he swiped through the air.

At least Sara was free. "Run," I yelled, but she remained frozen against the wall, most likely terrified by the scene unfolding.

"You're the wrong McGregor," the man hissed when his eyes met mine.

How the hell did he know me? Then again, my face was relatively recognizable throughout the city. And most lowlifes were beginning to fear the McGregor name now that we'd aligned with The League.

But why the *wrong* McGregor? It had me off guard, and the punch I sent after blocking his next jab of the knife missed my intended target, his jaw.

He stepped back and cocked his head as if I had a bloody

clue what was going on right now. Tall, dark hair. A jagged scar along his right cheek. Gnarly teeth. Yeah, I would've remembered him if we'd met before.

I charged him, ignoring the crazy look in his eyes, and shoved him against the wall, knocking a picture to the floor. I quickly snapped his arm around behind his back, not able to break it because he had tree trunks for arms, but he dropped the knife as a result.

A body shot, then elbow next. An uppercut to his abdomen followed.

It was like hitting steel. I'd needed to go harder. Faster. Use my speed to outmaneuver him before I lost control and things went arseways.

I ducked under a wild swing to get behind him. Then I brought my forearm around his thick throat, thankful I was the taller man and threw all my strength into trying to cut off his circulation.

I brought my back to the wall for support and kept him in a headlock.

Sara surprised me by approaching us with a lamp and bashing it across his face, then backed away quickly when it crashed to the floor.

It took a minute, but I got the bloke to the ground like I was Adam inside the ring. Once on top of him, I served punch after punch.

I unleashed. Taking all of my pent-up frustrations out on this guy.

"Sean."

The sound of my name pushed past the buzzing in my ears, but just barely.

"Sean." It was louder this time. "You're going to kill him." It was Sara, and she was yelling now.

I stopped my hand before connecting with his jaw again and left it hovering over his face.

"Are you okay?" I tossed a look back to find her covering her mouth with both palms, her features twisted in disgust as she looked at the damage I'd done to the man's face.

I'd most likely broken his nose as well as his jaw. And there was blood staining the once polished beige floors.

I had two options: Garda or a League cleanup crew. The police would ask me too many questions, but I doubted I'd be able to convince Sara to keep this night to herself if League members arrived to clean up this garbage.

I checked for a pulse. Thankfully, I found one. And that's when I noticed my hands were covered in blood.

I slowly rose and looked over at Sara. Her pink lips were rounded in shock, matching her wide eyes.

With a sob, she abruptly threw herself at me, flinging her arms around my neck, whispering a tearful *thank you* alongside muffled cries. "What . . . are you . . . doing here? Did Ethan . . . send you?"

I ran a hand up and down her back to soothe her.

If I hadn't been too angry to drive, well, I didn't want to think about what this arsehole might have done to her.

"Ethan? My brother?" I asked once her comment registered.

"I meant to tell you on the street Wednesday, but it felt awkward at the time," she said, remaining attached to me, her face buried against my chest.

"Tell me what?"

"You're my hero, Sean," she said instead of answering me.

I was no hero.

But what was her connection to my younger brother? And what was the practically dead guy's connection to my family?

"Sara, oh God. Sara."

The familiar sound of my brother's voice had me peeling Sara away from my body and looking up to see Ethan hurrying toward us. "What-what are you doing here?" he asked me when she turned toward him. He circled his hands around her waist and held on to her as if they were . . . a couple?

As she sobbed once again, this time into Ethan's chest, he rested his chin on top of her head and stared in shock at the motionless body on the floor.

My brother's time in New York City had changed him somewhat. Hardened him. His green eyes were sharper. His once lean frame had more muscle on it based on how his trousers and black jumper fit.

He'd been thrust into Cole's old position, which came with a lot more responsibility than he wanted, but he'd done a good job. He wasn't happy doing the corporate thing, though. I could feel it in his calls and texts. Ethan would rather be singing in a pub than wearing a suit.

I blinked a few times, trying to wrap my head around the fact that a few minutes ago, I'd been having my own pathetic pity party while walking down the street, and now I was looking at a thug I'd nearly killed.

"I was walking by and heard a scream," I explained. "What are *you* doing here?"

I'd picked Ethan up from the airport this afternoon. Home for the holidays since he worked out of our New York office with my uncle. He wasn't due in until Monday, but he'd called me up last night and said he was coming home early and asked if I could pick him up.

Now I understood why.

"I don't know what to say. Thank you. I was scared I wouldn't get here in time after Sara called. She was freaking out." It was obvious Ethan feared he was on the verge of losing her the way he'd lost his music. Taken away. Stripped from him because of his duties as a McGregor.

"Why'd she phone you and not the Garda? Clearly, you're dating, but if some guy breaks into your store, you call the police." I crouched to check the man's pockets, searching for his mobile and ID. Nothing.

If Sara was in danger, and she was dating my brother, that meant Ethan was at risk, too.

"I-I can't call the Garda," Sara said in a shaky voice. Strands of hair had strayed from her blonde ponytail. Her eye makeup was smeared beneath her blue eyes. Her skin pale as if she might toss her dinner. She kept her focus on Ethan, avoiding eye contact with me.

"I think you both need to come clean and tell me what's going on. I can help. And I have people who can clean this mess up. Give me a second."

"Don't worry," I overheard Ethan tell her as I went into the hall.

I rinsed the blood from my hands in the employee bathroom before making the call to the city's local League cleanup crew member.

"You should have let me help you. I don't know why you kept this from me," Ethan said, his tone soft.

After ending the call, I stayed in the hall, feeling bad about eavesdropping on Ethan and Sara, but in case they didn't open up to me, I needed to know what was going on.

"I didn't want to put you in danger," she responded around quick breaths, fear hanging on with a death grip in her tone.

"You asked me to change my flight and come back early. Was this why?" Ethan asked her, and I decided to go ahead and join them.

"Someone will be here soon to remove this guy," I promised them. *And interrogate him.*

"How'd you do that to him?" Sara pointed to the man on the ground, still motionless. "And who did you just call?"

"He recognized me. He knew I wasn't you," I said to Ethan, then turned to Sara. "What kind of trouble are you in?" I held up a palm, sensing she was about to lie. "This wasn't a robbery. Or an attempted assault."

I stepped around the body and perched a hip against her desk as I studied them across from me. Ethan hooked his arm around her waist and held her tight to his side.

"First of all, I planned on telling you that Sara and I are dating. But since you two used to date, I wasn't sure how you'd feel about it," my brother said, and now I realized what it was that Sara had started to tell me on the street the other day.

"Sean didn't even remember me when we bumped into each other earlier this week," Sara informed Ethan as if I weren't in the room, then turned her attention to me. "Ethan and I met in a bar in New York four months ago. Ethan remembered me from when you and I were together, and we sort of hit it off."

This was so damn strange.

"No offense," I began, "but I don't need the details about your love life. I approve. Happy for you both." I pointed to the man on the floor, his eyes still shut. "What I do need to know is why he's here? And why'd he expect Ethan?"

"After he showed up, I phoned Ethan. He listened to the call. I couldn't tell the Garda because I owe his boss money. He was here to collect it, said he'd kill me if I didn't give it to him." She turned toward Ethan and took hold of his hands. "I'm sorry I didn't tell you, but things haven't been easy. I needed financial help."

"And let me guess, you didn't go the bank route?" I tensed at the news I suspected she was about to lay on us.

"The banks turned me down." She faced me, tears in her eyes. "A designer I know connected me with one of her models she said would be able to help. Her husband is uber-wealthy, like you all, and he helps out other models and designers from time to time."

"Why do I get the feeling you're about to tell me the model was Bridgette Krause?" I gritted out.

Sara's eyebrows rose on her forehead as if someone had just yanked on her ponytail.

Well . . . feck. Another instance of fate screwing with me? "Why'd they come looking for the money tonight?" I demanded, assuming in her stunned silence I'd been right about Bridgette. "What happened?"

"I'm really behind on payments." She frowned. "I asked until the weekend to come up with the money. Since, um, Bridgette would be at an event in Scotland this weekend, I offered to hand it off to her there. I was told to skip the show, though, and then this guy showed up tonight," Sara finished her ramble with a shaky breath.

"He's probably one of Krause's people," I said. "You never did get the money, I assume?"

"I was . . ." Sara peered at Ethan. "I was going to ask you for it. I know we haven't been dating too long, and I have no right to ask, but I was worried they'd kill me. And then when this guy showed up tonight, I told him Ethan would pay back my debt."

My jaw tightened, and I closed my eyes. "Did you tell anyone Ethan's name before tonight? Is there a chance Peter Krause knows you two are together?"

The Alliance. The damn Alliance. I'd wanted my kid brother as far away from those cocksuckers as possible, but despite all of our efforts to protect him, he was being pulled in.

"I didn't mention Ethan until tonight. And that guy," she said while motioning to the man on the floor, "didn't have a chance to make any calls before you showed up."

"Good." I let a deep breath escape through my nose and opened my eyes. "How much do you owe?"

"Three hundred thousand U.S. dollars," she responded.

"That was what you owed tonight, I'm guessing. What is the total to get you debt-free from these guys?" I had to assume Sara had no idea she'd gotten into bed with one of the worst criminal groups in the world. And yet, I was struggling to believe this was all a coincidence.

"Nine hundred thousand U.S. dollars." Her lips pinched with disappointment, and Ethan unhanded her as if he'd been burned. Was he feeling used? Had she targeted him because of his name?

I'd have to figure that out later. For now, I needed to get The Alliance off Sara's back and my brother out of harm's way.

"I'm going to the show tomorrow in Edinburgh. I'll need your tickets." I held a hand up to keep her from protesting. "I don't want you near either of the Krauses. Peter or his wife. You have no idea the kind of people you're dealing with," I said, stepping closer to them. Frustration burning through me.

"You won't tell her about tonight, will you? That you were here, and I mentioned her?" She worried her lip between her teeth.

"Why would I talk to her?" I asked, unsure if I caught a flash of hesitation in her eyes. "No, I don't want to endanger you further. Or Ethan." I grimaced. "And I'll give you the money. All of it. Don't tell them where you got it, okay?" I tried to get a read on her, but all I saw was a terrified woman.

"You transfer the money to your contact and tell them you're done." I'd be tracing the funds to verify the story, but she didn't need to know that. "Understood?"

She nodded and brushed the tears from her cheeks. "I don't know how to thank you."

"I need a word with my brother." I waited for her to leave, checked to make sure the man on the floor had no chance of getting up anytime soon, then approached my brother. "What the feck, Ethan?"

"I'm sorry." His hands darted through his dark hair, his green eyes pinned on me.

"What were you going to do when you got here? Take the guy to the bank in the middle of the night and withdraw three hundred grand?"

"I-I didn't know I was coming here to help pay her debt. She just called and said I had to come alone, and she was in trouble."

I set a finger on his chest. "You call me first. You got it? If something is wrong, you call me. Or Cole. You don't get involved in shite like this. We're trying to keep you safe. Don't you get that?"

"I had no clue," he said, his tone rife with confusion.

"And if she's using you?" I whispered, leaning in closer in case Sara was out in the hall.

"She's not. I love her. And if anyone is giving her the money, it's me."

Love? Sure. I whirled away from him, wanting to deck the love right out of my little brother. "It's family money, Ethan. What's the difference?" I cursed. "I want you to stay away from her. The people she got herself involved with are dangerous."

"You can't ask me to do that. When Anna was in trouble, Adam protected her."

"Adam put her in danger. This is different."

"Sara has no family. I won't abandon her, and if you really think I'd just walk away to protect myself, you're out of your bloody mind." He turned to make a hasty exit, but I grabbed him by the arm, redirecting his focus.

"Ethan," I seethed, my muscles locking tight. Every part of me on edge. "The people she owes money to . . . this man on the ground," I said while angling my head, "they're Alliance."

"All the more reason I watch out for her, then." He jerked out of my grasp.

"Damn it, then at least stay at Sebastian's hotel. You'll be safe there."

He gave a hesitant nod, then left, and I reached for my mobile and called up Sebastian.

"Hey," I began straight away when he answered, "we've got a problem."

CHAPTER EIGHT

SEAN

EDINBURGH, SCOTLAND

A STUNNING BLUE SKY HUNG OVER THE LIMO AS THE DRIVER circled a roundabout, heading for the hotel. I hadn't spent all that much time in Scotland over the years, even though Ma's grandfather was Scottish—born in Glasgow and moved to Dublin as a child. We did have some distant cousins still in the country, the Kincaids, but I'd only met them once on a family vacation as a kid.

According to my great-grandfather, we were actually related to Mary, Queen of Scots, same as Queen Elizabeth the second, but I doubted the royal family would be inviting us for the holidays anytime soon.

"Down that way is the Palace of Holyroodhouse," my driver said, his Scottish brogue much thicker than my Irish. He pointed out his window in the direction of the royal palace, too far away for me to get a clear view of the place.

"Did Mary, Queen of Scots, live there?"

"Aye," he answered. "Such a shame what happened to her. Beheaded by her cousin."

Rivalries. They were complicated. I understood them now. "But hadn't Mary been plotting to murder Elizabeth?" I did my best to remember the stories passed down to us from Ma's grandfather.

"Ah, maybe the historians lied. Ya never know with those bloody Brits." A hearty laugh met my ears. "Kidding. Kidding."

Sure you are. There was no official League leader in Scotland, but Adam had joked once or twice that one of us ought to do it with our familial connection to the country. I wasn't sure how that'd play out in the handbook of power. And I had no intention of moving away from Ireland unless it was to go to . . .

I sheared the word Italy from my thoughts, not allowing myself to continue down that road again.

When Emilia had told me about Chanel, I wanted to ask how the daughters of rival families had come to be friends, but my impression of Emilia from ten years ago told me that she probably lived outside the rules, or at the very least skirted them.

Maybe she would've ignored League rules once upon a time, but she wouldn't do it now, although sex might be the exception, I supposed. And she had her father's wishes to consider as well. Emilia partially opening up to me and sharing her story didn't erase her promise, but it did make me painfully aware that there would never be an "us."

As surprising as the evening in Emilia's hotel room had been, the second part of the night, dealing with Sara's attacker, had been more shocking. A complete blow to my system.

Because of Ethan's girlfriend, he was now possibly entangled with The Alliance. And I didn't have a fecking clue whether it was a coincidence or not, and not being able to get a read on Sara left me feeling twitchy.

Adam and Cole were supposed to keep an eye on Ethan to make sure he didn't do anything crazy in the name of love. According to Ethan, Sara paid off her debt today, though I hadn't yet been able to confirm the transfer since I'd been traveling. But apparently, her contact said Krause wanted another two hundred and fifty thousand since the man he'd sent to collect the money last night mysteriously disappeared in Dublin.

I'd begrudgingly told my brother to pay, hating that any of our money was going into Alliance hands, but what choice did I have? I needed to get them off Sara's back and keep my brother out of the line of fire. Thankfully, Ethan wasn't like Adam or me, and he wouldn't track down Krause and go swinging in the name of revenge for what happened to Sara.

Well, I bloody hoped not. I had to believe Adam and Cole would make sure of that, at least.

I sent a quick text to Cole, and he immediately responded.

Cole: *No, the guy is still unconscious. You did a number on him, cuz. Let you know when he wakes.*

I wanted to hear the other side of Sara's story, even if it was from the guy who showed up to collect from her last night.

I stowed my mobile as my driver pulled up in front of the hotel. After checking in and walking through what felt like a tunnel of Christmas with the decorations exploding all over the place, I took the stairs to the fourth floor and opened my suite to find Emilia waiting for me on the couch sipping champagne.

Well, a *blonde* Emilia was there. "Blonde? Really?"

I let go of the handle of my luggage but kept the garment bag draped over my arm.

She lowered the crystal flute, uncrossed her legs, and stood. "I'm your plus-one tonight, and I'd prefer no one recognize me. Red hair wouldn't look good with this dress, so I had no choice. I wasn't trying to give you a hard time." She actually came across as sincere, her tone soft. "Chanel used to quote Coco all the time." Her eyes moved to the flute. "The night she died, she said, '*I only drink champagne on two occasions, when I am in love and when I am not.*'" A small, sad smile touched her red lips.

Interpreting her words was like trying to understand the lines in *Hamlet* or *Macbeth*. *Stars, hide your fires; Let not light see my black and deep desires.* The *Macbeth* quote popped into my head, and Ma would be proud I'd remembered. Her love for literature was about the same as my father's love for the family business.

I bought myself some time to think about how to react to Emilia's radiant presence and discarded my garment bag in the hall closet.

"And I guess you're drinking champagne because you're not in love," I finally interpreted her words, not a damn clue if I was right or not.

She strode toward me in a red and black dress that hugged her curves and stopped just above her knees. Although the neckline rose to slightly below her clavicle, a section of sheer black material plunged down the front in a V shape, revealing a hint of cleavage.

Black strappy heels showed off her long, tan legs, and I did my best not to allow my gaze to linger too long on her shapely body.

Eyes up top, Romeo.

Great. Another tragedy I didn't want to compare my life to. And yet, Mercutio's line from *Romeo and Juliet, A plague o' both your houses*, now sat in my head. Maybe that was more fitting.

"You okay, Clooney?"

. . . *And* she went there. She couldn't have been reading my thoughts because who thinks about Shakespeare in a moment like this? Who other than me, that is. But I'm sure the expression on my face was a clear indication that I was back in Vegas, crushing my mouth to hers with fierce intensity.

"Take off the wig," I rasped, my voice dropping lower. The words probably came out like a command, but I loved her natural, dark waves that normally hung to her breasts.

"Excuse me?"

Her body was stunning, but her face was the showstopper for me. Her delicately shaped oval face, tan skin, dark slanted brows atop gorgeous brown eyes all combined to make her an exquisite beauty. And those full lips . . . plump and begging to be kissed. When she graced me with a smile, I was done.

"We're not in public, and I want to see you. The real you."

"Too many bobby pins." She ate up the remaining space between us since I'd yet to budge. I was too distracted with committing the vision of her in this dress to memory for when I was alone later.

"You're beautiful." It dawned on me that I never said as much despite thinking it every time I looked at her.

Her white teeth were but a quick gift as she flashed a fleeting smile.

"How's the wound?" I focused my gaze on her hip. Damn woman, stubbornly going against a bunch of criminals on her own as if she had superpowers.

"Nothing a little ibuprofen and champagne can't fix." Her mouth briefly tightened. "Cole told me what happened last night. Do you buy Sara's story? If the banks wouldn't lend her the money, she's either naïve or ignorant to believe someone like Krause would fork over that kind of cash without some major strings attached. And that makes me wonder if she knows more about the Krause family than she let on. Plus, she's now dating your brother and called him for the last-minute save. And Sara said her attacker was waiting for Ethan. If that's true, why'd he let you get the jump on him? Wouldn't you think he would have been in a less compromising position, say, with his back *not* to the door?"

"You suggesting she might work for The Alliance?" I had my concerns but using my brother as a means to infiltrate our family as a spy for Peter Krause hadn't been one of them. I may not have remembered dating Sara until she reminded me since it felt like an eternity ago, even before I met Emilia in Vegas, but she didn't seem like a master manipulator.

Although, I did find it interesting I hadn't remembered Sara, but less than an hour with Emilia in Vegas ten years ago, and every moment was stitched into my mind like it'd happened yesterday.

"I have someone checking into her story, but I just think it's highly suspicious that we happen to be targeting the very people who helped her with a loan. Don't you?"

I stroked my jaw, unsure of what to think. Women like Sara didn't involve themselves with criminals, did they? She may have been desperate to save her stores, believing a model she trusted could help her. Naïve was more probable.

"You're a League leader now, Sean. You have to be able to look at situations objectively, cut emotion out of the equation completely." A look of annoyance I had no clue how to interpret crossed her face. "But I can tell you still trust her. Okay, let's say she did get a proper loan from Krause, but then he added some new terms to the deal when he discovered she was dating Ethan. Such as requiring her to infiltrate your family and feed The Alliance information. What if we're attempting to make a play on Peter, and he's doing the same to us?"

"And what if she hadn't met Ethan yet?"

"Then they instructed her to target him." Emilia folded her arms across her chest, clutching her glass of champagne to her bare arms.

"Why not choose me as the target if that was the case? We have a history and—"

"So," Emilia began around an uncomfortable swallow, "you did sleep together."

"In college," I grumbled. "And the point is, I'm single and living in Dublin, and Ethan is younger and in New York. He's also not League. Going directly after me would be the more obvious play."

"Which is why they wouldn't do it," she pointed out. "Too obvious."

I didn't want to see my brother hurt, but she was right, we had to be cautious. "Alright, then let's figure out why they sent someone after her last night to collect if she was using Ethan."

Her mouth pinched, her thoughts whirling. Calculating possibilities. "Where is Sara now? Ethan?" she asked instead of answering, and maybe it was because she didn't have one.

She spun on her heels and moved to the window overlooking the industrial building across the way where she'd planned to set up later while I attempted to flirt my way into Bridgette's hotel room.

"Sebastian has Ethan and Sara staying at the hotel. The second penthouse on your floor. They'll be safe there if Krause isn't finished with her yet." I couldn't stomach the idea of anything happening to my brother.

"Well, there's our answer."

I drew my hands to my hips. "Sara is now closer to The League. Under our protection. Feels a little too much like a Trojan horse to me."

Emilia was brilliant. And entirely too suspect of everyone.

"We'll look into her," I agreed. "Cole is also watching over the guy who showed up to collect the money from Sara last night. As soon as he regains consciousness, he'll question him."

"And you paid Sara's debt, right?" she asked, still looking out the window.

I cringed at the thought, and I was half waiting for her to tell me how that was a bloody stupid idea. "Yes." I crossed the room to join her.

"I assume you traced the transfer?"

"Of course." I was offended she'd even asked. I pulled out my mobile to confirm Ethan's information. "Money is sitting in an account in Germany. No name in the bank's system."

"We can have the account monitored in case someone shows up to make a withdrawal."

"Already on it."

"And why didn't you call and tell me what happened last night?" she asked, her tone slightly strained. And maybe this was why her mood was foul about the subject. Less to do with Sara and more to do with feeling betrayed because I didn't call her up. "Why'd I hear about it from Sebastian? You spoke to everyone but me."

I did my best not to guffaw or huff out a heavy breath of *Are you kidding?*

Her shoulders betrayed the slightest hint of disappointment that I narrowly picked up on. Emilia was a pro at hiding her emotions, but I was beginning to wonder if my ability to read her every so often had less to do with League training and more to do with the fact she was letting her guard down a bit, allowing herself to be more vulnerable around me lately. Whether she meant for it to happen or not. A guy could hope, at least. "We're still partners, Sean. We need to work together. No secrets."

"I knew Sebastian would tell you. I'm not the one keeping secrets." I shook my head. This wasn't the time or place to get into round two of last night's standoff. Quarrel? Misunderstanding? Feck if I knew what it was.

We may have officially closed the chapter on "more" happening between us, but we'd yet to rule out the possibility of no-strings sex, and that unanswered question lingered in the air between us.

"I don't want things to be awkward."

"Kind of late for that, don't you think? Plus, why do I get the feeling Emilia Calibrisi doesn't do awkward?" Damn it. I'd told myself to let the anger I was harboring about our situation go. It wasn't her fault. "I'm sorry. This isn't easy for me. But I do need to get ready."

She sent a curt nod my way. The type of nod you'd give a commanding officer. "I'll wait out here."

I grabbed my luggage and started for the bedroom before tossing a look at her from over my shoulder. "By the way, how'd you get in here?"

She lifted the hem of her dress, revealing a key card strapped to her outer thigh and a knife on the inside. "I got my hands on a universal key for all rooms here."

"Of course you did." I disappeared into my room, quietly shut the door behind me, and let go of my bag.

Once in the shower, I kept the water cold. It felt good on my flushed skin. Cooled off my temper. Prevented my dick from getting hard so that I didn't give in to the urge to jack off to thoughts of Emilia while she was in the other room.

But then my carefully placed mental snapshots of her in that dress circled front and center in my mind.

One hand went to the tiled wall beneath the spray as I bowed my head and closed my eyes. I ran my fingers along the length of my rigid cock as it came to life with thoughts of what was under that dress she had on. I had a feeling it wouldn't be nude "knickers" tonight.

No, something red or black. Lacy and see-through. Sexy as feck.

And before I knew it, I was fisting my cock.

Beating off.

Blowing my load in the shower and grunting while she sat in the other room.

And my inability to let this woman go meant only one thing—sex with no strings was back on the table for me. Screw the pain of what would happen after. Maybe I deserved the pain.

Because I had to have her.

Tonight.

CHAPTER NINE

EMILIA

I GRITTED MY TEETH EVERY TIME A RUNWAY MODEL STRUTTED in front of us. They didn't have angel wings on their backs like at Victoria's Secret shows, but the models were dolled up like walking Barbies in lingerie. They left a trail of sequins and glitter with every stride, too. The plus side to this show? The designers actually had models that represented women of all sizes.

The hotel ballroom had been transformed to accommodate the event—rows of white chairs along each side of the silver platform runway and chairs at the end as well. The lights overhead were bright enough to illuminate the event without giving you a headache, house music played over speakers, and I'd swear each model managed to time her walk perfectly to the beats.

I crossed my legs, noticing Sean's gaze zero in on my bare skin for a brief moment, and I elbowed him as a reminder to keep his focus on the models and, when the time came, Bridgette.

Despite months of rejecting the idea there could ever be an us, I'd opened the door for sex.

I'd once believed our demarcation zone was permanently set. Unmovable.

But all it took was being alone with him last night for my walls to begin crumbling when I shared what happened in Vegas.

Something had officially changed between us. Last night, he'd left my suite with uncertainty in his eyes. But this afternoon when he entered the living room after his shower, wearing only a towel, his decision was clear.

I'd mentally willed that towel to slip, which was sadly not a superpower I possessed. But with his wet hair slicked back and droplets of water clinging to his powerful chest, he looked like a veritable Adonis. Although, in my opinion, Sean rivaled the Greek god's beauty. And now he had me waxing poetic about Greek gods.

That kiss of ours over twenty months ago had been heated. I'd torn off his shirt. Felt his hard length press against me, so I knew he was impressive in size.

Tonight, I'd wanted nothing more than to skip the fashion show and lick the water from his skin. Drop to my knees and take him in my mouth.

Hear the words fall gruffly from his lips—*I'll take whatever you'll give me. If that's no-strings sex, then yes. Just sex.*

Of course, those stuffy old League leaders who predated the likes of Sebastian and myself had to be dicks when they wrote rule number one. In addition to prohibiting marriage between League families, even straight-up sex was forbidden. Maybe they had the right to determine who could marry whom, but my sex life? No, I wouldn't let a group of men tell me who I could sleep with.

And like Papà, I was unable to resist the lure of the

forbidden. The apple didn't fall far from the tree in that regard.

Nevertheless, there was work to be done, and work had to come first. That was my life. I'd been born into the role.

"She's coming out," I said, leaning closer to Sean as Bridgette stepped onto the runway from behind two silky blue curtains. I reached for his palm and set it on my exposed thigh just below the hem of my dress to establish we were there together. The Tag Heuer on his wrist moved into sight when the fabric of his jacket sleeve shifted. I recognized the watch as an automatic chronograph, almost the exact one I gave Papà at Christmas the year before he died. The only difference was that Sean's lacked the bezel made of yellow gold. I didn't take Sean for a man who wore gold jewelry.

I pulled my focus back to the reason we were there.

Bridgette Krause.

She was tall and blonde, with a voluptuous figure, now walking the runway wearing what appeared to be two tiny white scraps of cloth as if we were in the caveman days. Was this high fashion? Really?

Sean managed to draw Bridgette's eyes, no surprise there, when he reached up and slowly raked his free hand through his thick, sexy hair as she walked in front of us. I was more shocked by the fact my heart stuttered at the sight of him blatantly flirting with her. But that was why we were here, wasn't it?

I truly hadn't known what jealousy felt like until that moment. And it pretty much knocked the wind out of me. My chest was so tight it felt as if someone had reached inside, grabbed hold of my heart, and separated my soul from my body.

I may have also envisioned myself punching Bridgette in the face. Right smack between her blonde brows. Knocking free that sexy look she'd sent Sean in response to his very convincing adoring gaze.

He was doing what I'd asked, garnering Bridgette's attention, and I was acting irrationally.

And on her second, then third, walk during the show, I was certain it made Bridgette feel all that much better to have captured his attention when it was clear I was his date by his possessive hold on my thigh. She loved the idea of stealing someone that wasn't hers.

Oh yeah, this plan would work. Bridgette would take him to her room. No doubt in my mind.

Sean's palm was big and warm on my skin. And his intention was clear. What he wanted to do to me later with that rough palm was unmistakable, and it lit a fire inside of me.

When his fingers flexed as though itching to claim me, I tightened my thighs and imagined his hand trailing over my curves. Seeking. Exploring.

Thankfully, the staff kept the champagne flowing, and I accepted every glass of the rather mediocre stuff in an attempt to dull the want coursing through my body. To crush the ridiculous jealousy. But the thought that Sean would someday belong to another woman nearly sent me over the edge. And somewhere in the back of my mind, I knew I was drinking more than I should.

"It's working," I whispered into his ear as Bridgette exited and another model took to the runway. Sean shifted to face me and tightened his grip on my leg.

The blue of his eyes had darkened to the color of a turbulent sea, and the look he pinned me with was borderline feral. I wanted him to lean in and let the animal loose, take my mouth in a searing kiss and make his claim on me more obvious than a hand on my knee.

His broad chest lifted, and a deep exhalation followed.

"She's coming back. Let's wrap this up," I said ten minutes later, catching sight of her again.

Bridgette was the type of woman who was accustomed to winning over powerful men with the crook of a finger. Maybe cheating was even like a sport to her.

Sean was a taken man. And I had the feeling she rejoiced in the fact he appeared to be stripping her naked with his eyes while his hand rested on my thigh.

And in one, two, three. I flicked Sean's hand off my leg when Bridgette strode close to our seats for the last time of the evening, wearing black lace thigh-highs and a black see-through lace bra that showed her nipples. *Oh, for fuck's sake . . .*

After my blatant rebuff, purely for her benefit, Sean settled his hand back on his lap—a sign to Bridgette he didn't give a damn I'd caught him eye-fucking her, too focused on her to care. I spotted the wry smile at the edges of her mouth.

After the show concluded, Sean set a hand to my back, and we walked out of the ballroom, doing our best to avoid conversation with anyone else. "I guess you were right. It worked," he said, not sounding all that enthusiastic about it.

"You're an excellent actor," I told him as we made our way to the party.

"You, too. You almost looked jealous."

Because I was. No way would I confess that. "On our way here, didn't you say you have Scottish relatives? Any chance you could introduce yourself as one of them?"

He politely nodded at a couple that went by us. "And at the club you made it sound like she might get a kick out of screwing one of her husband's enemies."

"Then Sara happened, and I got to thinking . . . if Bridgette accidentally lets the name 'Sean McGregor' slip around her husband or Atlas, it could derail our plans for Monaco."

"And what if she knows I'm giving her a fake name? What if she's more involved in Alliance affairs than we thought? Or hell, she could know who I am simply because I'm a McGregor. We own a fecking football team, Emilia. If she knows me at all, and I lie to her, I'll lose my chance to plant the bug."

"I doubt she follows your family business. And sports? Don't make me laugh. We can't risk her knowing your real name. If she already does, which I highly doubt, well, then, we'll cross that bridge when we get there. But I'm not willing to risk you or Ethan or any other McGregor for a bug. We'll find another way."

We stared at each other for a few moments before he finally said, "I have some distant cousins that live in Scotland. I can use one of their names. I doubt she'd have met any of them," he offered. "You know the type," he said with a smile, his mood lightening again, "recluse and rich."

"Of course they are." I copied his smirk. "And how's your Scottish accent, *Macbeth*?"

"I've got it covered." He winked and took my hand.

We showed our passes and entered the room where the party was being held, and I snatched a new flute of champagne upon entry.

The cocktail servers all wore designs from the fashion show. Lacy numbers. And barely there all-black pieces.

The servers managed to keep my flute full of champagne —the good stuff this time—as we waited for Bridgette to make her move. I needed to stop drinking soon. If all went according to plan and Sean was invited to Bridgette's suite later, I'd wind up taking a photo of the wrong room.

Sean had me by the elbow twenty minutes later, a gentle

but dominating touch that would indicate to anyone with their eyes on us that I was his in every way. It also felt that way to me. But still no sign of Bridgette. "You okay?"

I gulped down some of the Dom Pérignon I'd planned not to drink more of and focused on his blue eyes. They weren't a stormy or turquoise blue right now. They were a soft shade of concern.

Yeah, I'd most definitely had one too many. *Soft shade of concern?* A humorless chuckle fell from my lips, and I slapped my free hand to my mouth as a hiccup escaped.

"Are you drunk?" I couldn't tell if he was amused or upset.

"I become a poet around you, so it would seem." He had no clue what I was talking about, but from the sounds of my voice, I was sliding into tipsy-slash-drunk territory.

"I can relate. I've had Shakespeare lines running through my head tonight."

"*Macbeth*," I teased, and he crooked a smile. Maybe we were a pair? "The only time I've ever been drunk was when I was sixteen." The champagne was talking, and I didn't feel like stopping it. "Chanel and I were bonding over the fact her mother and my father were having an affair."

Sean nearly choked on the swallow of champagne he'd taken. When the coughing subsided, he pulled me off to the side of the room. Even in my tipsy state, or perhaps because of it, I noticed there was no sign of Christmas anywhere. That was surprising, considering the rest of the hotel looked like someone from Hallmark was filming three holiday films there at once.

"Papà took me to Bali to celebrate my sixteenth birthday in style. Well, that's what he told me. And Chanel was there with her mother having a mother-daughter trip. Or so she was told," I went on, hoping my words were clean and crisp and not as wayward as they sounded to me.

"You're saying Penelope and your father . . .?"

I nodded and then hiccupped again. This wasn't me.

No, that was Emilia at sixteen. Drunk after having just walked into her father's room to find him with Penelope, our sworn enemy. *That* Emilia bumped into Chanel in the hotel hallway as she searched for her mother that same night.

Right now, I wasn't even acting like the current version of myself—on the verge of turning thirty-one with a few years of experience as a League leader under my belt.

Here I was in Scotland at a lingerie party to help take down The Alliance, and I was divulging my secrets because of some gold-hued liquid.

"That's how you met Chanel. And you became friends because of it?" His expression was blank, as if my shocking admission had dulled his thoughts to nothing.

"Yeah. Our parents said it was a one-time thing, and if anyone found out, we'd all be in danger," I quickly explained. "But we knew they were lying. And we chose to keep our friendship a secret. Chanel and I . . . we instantly clicked. She understood me, and I felt the same about her."

Sean reached out and moved strands of my blonde wig off my shoulder before racing the back of his hand over my cheek and down the side of my neck.

"And now she's dead," I whispered, then broke away from him to mindlessly snatch another flute.

"Maybe we call this night off?" His hand went to my wrist before sliding up my arm.

"Don't be ridiculous." I sipped more champagne, and he reached for the flute, deciding I was done. This time I didn't protest. He was right. We were there for work.

"Emilia." He spoke my name like he was biting into it.

Getting a feel for how it'd taste when he called it out during sex.

My body was hot. Almost feverish.

I wanted to rip the uncomfortable blonde wig off and toss it into the fountain of overpriced champagne pouring from the mouth of . . . *is that a vagina?*

I peered back at Sean as he turned me toward him. "You have the most incredible eyes." My palm landed on his chest, and my fingers slowly walked up the buttons of his dress shirt to reach his black bow tie.

"You sure you took ibuprofen and not something else with that champagne?" His brows became defined lines of worry.

After I was born, my mother left my father, but the woman he'd spent years longing for was the one who'd done the most damage to his heart. Penelope had made the deepest cut.

"What, do you think I carry a bottle of Xanax around in my purse and mistakenly took one?" I asked around another hiccup.

"Did you leave your drink unattended?" he probed. "Set it down for a second?"

"I'm drunk, McGregor," I blurted, then retracted my hand from his bow tie at the sight of Bridgette approaching us. *This should be interesting.*

Bridgette had changed into a long, tight black dress that wrapped around her torso like a corset, making her boobs look like the cork in a champagne bottle about to pop.

"Mrs. Krause." As if on cue, Sean brought his attention to her, and voilà, I was a distant memory. "I'm an admirer of yours."

Maybe now I'd puke.

"And you are?" she purred. "You seem extremely familiar to me."

And here we go.

"I have one of those faces." Sean dazzled her with a smile. "Landon Kincaid," he offered her one of his cousin's names.

"Mm." Bridgette raised a curious brow. Was she not buying it? Did Sara give Bridgette's husband a heads-up we'd be coming? "Of the Scottish Kincaid Group?"

She was either also a great actress and hiding the fact she knew who Sean really was and was equally playing us. *Or* she wasn't part of her husband's master plan and saw Sean as another handsome conquest. Or hell, there was the possibility Sara was innocent, and there was no plan.

"You know your companies," Sean went on with the act. The man really did have skills, and his Scottish brogue was on point.

"No, Landon, I know money." Well, at least Bridgette was honest there.

Bridgett's eyes flitted over me, sizing up her competition. "I'd love to show you our private collection reserved for only those who attend this party." Her icy glare melted when it switched from me to Sean. "Maybe pick something out for your"—she paused to check Sean's ring finger—"girlfriend?" Her English was polished and perfect like mine despite German being her native tongue. "Surprise her later."

"Sounds like a grand idea." Sean curved his hand around to my ass and brought his mouth to the shell of my ear. "Are we still on?"

"Of course." I responded to his touch of my derrière by leaning in, my eyes meeting Bridgette in a competitive stare from over Sean's shoulder, and I grabbed his ass. Very, very firm ass, too.

Bridgette's eyes lowered to my hand, her eyes drawing into slits as she dragged her gaze back to my face like a challenge. And wow, was the woman competitive. It wasn't enough that she had a husband and possibly a lover, but she was upset with me for fondling my boyfriend. Okay, well, he wasn't my boyfriend, but Bridgette didn't know that.

She lifted her chin and shot me a fierce, this-is-game-on kind of look. It was also a sobering gut check. Her lips would soon touch Sean's and it had me wanting to kill her.

"See you later, love." Sean nodded goodbye, discarded my glass of champagne he'd been holding, and walked off. Each step he took farther away should have served as a painful reminder I had a job to do, but the damn alcohol had created a green monster inside me. I was on the brink of face-planting this woman into the vagina fountain.

I'm a Calibrisi. A fierce League leader. I mentally pinched myself and snatched a bottle of water. *Maybe you're also a woman in love? Too scared, though. Too obedient to your dead father.*

"Not now, Chanel," I muttered under my breath like a crazy person before sucking the bottle dry to prepare for what was to happen next.

I grabbed my bag from the hotel room, then went to the industrial building across from the hotel to set up. I'd bypassed the building security system to break in. It was the weekend, and thankfully, no one was on the fourth floor where the offices were located.

It took a mere fifteen minutes for Bridgette to "lure" Sean into her suite. The drapes were still drawn, but the light in the living room had turned on.

First step, Sean needed to find Bridgette's purse and plant the listening device without her noticing. Be extra careful in case she suspected Sean had ill intentions.

Second step, open the curtains and kiss her so I could get a shot of the action.

Third step, maybe I really would vomit.

I reached for my long-range camera, the kind paparazzi loved to use, and waited.

After meeting Bridgette, I honestly didn't feel so bad for dismissing Adam's concern we might be ruining her life. There was no doubt in my mind, despite being slightly under the influence, that she knew exactly what her husband and Atlas were up to. She was as guilty as they were for every one of their sins.

Part of me always wondered if Chanel would have wound up sucked into her family's affairs when she was older, same as me. She'd never wanted anything to do with their illegal activities, like her mom, but I doubted her father or brother would have offered her much of a choice.

Thinking about Chanel was like a bucket full of heartache and regrets dumped on my head. I was now fully sober.

And the moment the curtains parted, and Sean had Bridgette in his arms in front of the window, I wished for an entire bottle of Dom Pérignon. Forget the glass.

Looking through the camera lens, it was as if I could reach out and touch them.

The fact he was about to kiss her meant he'd already planted the device. That was my cue.

Sean slowly leaned in, and my stomach clenched at the sight of his mouth touching Bridgette's. She had one hand on his chest and the other on the back of his black trousers.

Her dress swiftly and unexpectedly fell to the floor, leaving her in absolutely nothing. Not even a stitch of the lingerie she'd modeled.

Sean gripped her hip and pulled her tight to his body and kissed her again.

I snapped shot after shot, pieces of me dying a small death with every click of the camera.

I had plenty, so I set the camera down and checked to ensure the listening device worked. Opening the app on my tablet, I reluctantly listened.

"I don't think I can do this," I heard Sean speak up as planned.

"Oh, come on." Bridgette began speaking in German before shifting back to English. "I'm a model. That woman you're with is not one."

"That woman I'm with is *everything*," he growled out, but before she could respond, the device picked up on a loud knock, followed by someone calling out Bridgette's name.

"It's me. Atlas."

You're supposed to be in London. I peered through the camera lens to see Bridgette scrambling to get dressed, whispering too low for me to pick up on the device.

The next thing I knew, she motioned for Sean to go out onto the small terrace off the bedroom.

I had to think fast. We had proof of the affair now with Atlas there, which we hadn't expected to get, but if Atlas caught Sean with Bridgette, our plans would not only be ruined, he'd probably shoot him. While Sean's defensive skills were excellent, it was still hard to block a bullet.

I hurriedly grabbed my things, knowing I only had one choice. I reached for the edge of my dress at the side and ripped the fabric, so I'd be able to move faster.

Once on the street, I peered up to see Sean had stepped off the patio and was now balancing on the thin ledge that ran parallel with the building.

He was going to try and make it to the balcony one room over.

I didn't have time to wait for the lift. Once in the stairwell, I hurried up the steps to Bridgette's floor.

Praying no one was inside the suite next to hers, I grabbed the universal keycard strapped to my thigh and opened the door.

Silence. It was empty.

I ran to the terrace and unlocked the door just as Sean threw his leg over the railing.

"Hey." The word floated on a pant. I was out of breath.

He swung his other leg over, and I fisted the material of his lapels, urging him to get out of sight and inside in case Atlas had his suspicions and looked outside.

"Thanks," he said as I locked up.

I lifted the strap over my shoulder to remove my bag and dug inside to listen in to Bridgette's room.

"I wasn't expecting you. What a nice surprise. I thought you were swamped with meetings in London for the rest of the weekend," Bridgette said in English. Perhaps Atlas didn't know German. Or maybe she didn't know French or Greek.

French and Greek. Freek. And now I was thinking of Chanel. And why wouldn't I be? Her brother was in the room next to me.

"I had a meeting get canceled at the last minute and decided to sneak over since your husband wasn't going to be here tonight," Atlas told Bridgette.

"Guess they are having an affair." Sean motioned for us to get the hell out of there, but I halted at the sight of a travel bag on the floor by the couch in the living room. Attached to the zipper was a large metal charm of a perfume bottle. Chanel No. 5.

"We're in Atlas's room," I whispered to Sean.

And Atlas . . . he's sentimental? I didn't know what to think about that.

149

I reached into my bag and grabbed the second listening and tracking device, which was like a small black sticker the size of a coin. This night turned out to be a hell of a lot better than I'd anticipated, minus Sean potentially falling to his death on the ledge.

Sean took hold of my arm a moment later, urging me to move after I planted the device inside his bag. "They're coming. We have to go." He pointed with his free hand toward a connecting door, which led to Bridgette's suite, joining the two rooms together. A quick beep sounded, alerting us to the fact they'd unlocked the door.

Unable to make our escape, Sean pulled me into a nearby closet in one swift movement.

He carefully clicked the door shut and lowered my bag to the floor.

The space was tight and cramped, and our bodies were pinned together.

"Mm. I missed you." Atlas's words were followed by sounds of kissing. "I need you now."

I was going to be sick. Between too much champagne, seeing a naked Bridgette kissing Sean, and now this, heaven help me, I'd need to wash these memories from my mind with Clorox.

Sean wrapped his hand around my waist as my palms skated up his chest with no room for my elbows. We were trapped until they finished screwing.

Why couldn't they have stayed in her room, damn it?

"I need you in my mouth," Bridgette said, her voice raspy. There was a thud, maybe her falling to her knees. This was not how I'd planned to spend my evening. Listening to Bridgette suck off the most powerful Alliance leader.

After my gaze had adjusted to the dark, I lifted my chin to see Sean peering down at me. The adrenaline, the close call of nearly being caught, and the sexual energy between us . . . it had me out of sorts. Confused. A little light-headed.

And despite the sounds of sex not far away, I found myself remembering Sean's words to Bridgette back in her room.

Everything. I'm everything?

"Bedroom," Atlas commanded.

Relief soared through me at the sound of a door shutting. Sean nodded, letting me know we ought to take the chance and make a run for it.

I slowly opened the closet, stole a look toward the bedroom to see the door was shut, then we crept out of the suite.

"Holy shite," Sean said while blowing out a breath once we were safely away and in the lift, heading for our room. "Dress malfunction?"

I shrugged. "My dress was slowing me down."

His lips went from a smirk to a frown in one quick blink of an eye. "About Bridgette's dress . . . she unzipped it, not me. I wouldn't have done that. I didn't even want to kiss her. And with you watching—"

"You don't need to explain." I flicked my wrist as the lift doors parted. "Made for great photos."

"I know I don't need to explain." His voice chased after me once I'd quickly fled the cramped space of the lift. "Emilia, would you stop walking away from me?"

His plea had me walking faster, and I flung the door open, but Sean was on my heels, and his presence loomed large, stealing my breath before I'd yet to confront him.

When the door clicked shut, I swung around to face him, the bag still hanging from my shoulder and nearly hitting him in the process.

"That's what I do, Sean. I see a problem, I fix it, and then

I walk away." I let go of the bag and set my hands to my hips. "Tonight was a close call," I deflected. "I'm sorry, I shouldn't have gotten drunk earlier or started talking about my father and Penelope. It isn't like me to be so irresponsible." I tensed, my body on fire. My thoughts wild and chaotic. "But we got way more than we bargained for tonight. Now we have evidence of the affair from the listening device, photos of you with her, and now maybe we can even move up our timetable. Adjust the Monaco plans."

"New Year's Eve. Your birthday." He squinted as if the sun was in his eyes.

"I don't celebrate my birthday anymore."

He stepped around the bag, whittling the space between us to almost nothing. "Maybe you ought to."

"I don't want to," I said, fighting like hell to inject a touch of stubborn sass into my tone to keep from letting my emotions loose.

I worked the blonde wig and pins free from my hair, unleashing my black locks.

Sean's focus followed the wig to the floor as I tossed it on top of the bobby pins.

"I thought we might . . ."

"Have sex?" I finished for him, breathy and confused. Not a feeling I liked. "I admit, I was ready to go. I had it all mapped out in my head. And you—" I dropped my words as he had me stumbling back to the wall, his strong body framing mine.

"What changed?" he asked, hooded eyes searching my face for answers while he leaned in and set a hand to the wall over my shoulder.

He was so close I felt his hard cock desperate to plunge inside me.

I squeezed my eyes tight, unable to look at him and turn him down. "You weren't acting with Bridgette."

"Of course I was, what are you talking about?" he hissed, and I felt his absence. I didn't have to look to know he'd backed away as if I'd slapped him.

"When you told her I was everything. You weren't acting." My voice was shaky. My words trembling like the aftershocks from a quake still felt hundreds of kilometers away. "I want to be with you," I confessed, my voice sounding like a strangled cry. "I've never wanted anyone or anything so much."

His expression hardened. He clamped down on his teeth as if restraining himself from tossing me over his shoulder and carrying me straight to bed.

"But—"

"I think Adam has the right idea about that word. It should be off-feckin'-limits." He grabbed hold of me and gathered me into his arms before I could protest.

My elbows were bent, my hands trapped between our bodies while he held me. And strangely, this feeling of being cocooned in his embrace was comforting. Like being swaddled in love, something I'd lacked growing up without a mother.

"We can't be together aside from sex. Okay?" I needed to hear him confirm it before this moved forward. Before I gave him a piece of myself that I knew I'd never be able to take back.

A line cut across his forehead, but he nodded. "We can't be together."

"We can't be together," I repeated, surprised when my eyes became damp and my vision blurry.

"I hear you, Emilia." He set his forehead to mine, and I freed my arms to encircle his hips. "But for tonight, we can."

CHAPTER TEN

EMILIA

I CAN'T. THAT WAS THE BRILLIANT RESPONSE I'D MUTTERED before ripping myself out of Sean's embrace, racing into the second bedroom of the suite, and slamming the door shut a minute ago.

The dress was too tight. I couldn't breathe. I did my best to finish the job I'd started earlier and desperately tore at the fabric. My hands trembled as I fumbled to get it off, my thoughts mangled and unclear. It wasn't until my fingers touched the small metal pull that I remembered the hidden side zipper. When I finally yanked myself free, a huge whoosh of air left my lungs.

No longer constricted by the dress, I took several deep, calming breaths, the effects of which were ruined when I caught sight of my reflection in the mirror over the dresser.

My hair and my flushed cheeks had the post-sex look without the benefit of an orgasm, and I shoved the wispy strands away from my face and willed away the color from my cheeks.

Shoulders back, I heard my nanny's voice, my pseudo-mother, repeating what she said to me every day from age five to six whenever I let them slump. I unhooked my bra, tossed it back, and let my shoulders dramatically droop.

"Screw you," I whispered under my breath. Screw her and that sharp fingernail she jabbed in my back when I wanted to be a normal kid for five minutes.

I traced my finger over the faint line near my breast. Another bad memory in a sea of dozens and dozens.

Sean felt like the life raft meant to save me.

And I was the stubborn woman too afraid to jump to safety. To take a chance that it'd be better on the other side. Somehow. Someway. It was supposed to be, right?

But the grass was never greener.

The grass was always fucking dead.

"Emilia, you okay?" Sean's voice floated through the door, the longing he had for me still kicking around in his tone.

My eyes fell shut, and the only thing I could see was his mouth claiming Bridgette's. Another ridiculous stir of jealousy had my palms landing on the dresser, my head bowing. "I'm . . ."

What am I? Oh, I was lots of things right now, but *fine* wasn't one of them. That was for sure.

Sean had agreed to my terms, accepted that the only thing I could offer was sex. And then I freaked out. Decided the price of us being together was still too high, too dangerous, and I walked away.

What the hell, Emilia? This time, it wasn't clear whose voice was in my head, mine, the nanny's, or Chanel's.

"May I come in?" he asked softly, interrupting my mental break from reality.

"There's nothing to say." Damn the crack in my voice.

"I disagree. Let me in," he responded, his words like a

calloused palm dragging over my skin, designed to hurt me where it would the most—my heart.

If I let him in, I knew what was sure to happen. There'd be nowhere left to run but into his arms.

"I'm naked. One second." Apparently, my body had taken over, opting to ignore the precautions of my mind to wave a white flag because the words came tumbling out on their own accord.

I unstrapped my heels and retrieved a fuzzy white cotton robe from the closet. After securing the belt around my waist, I steadied my breath and swung open the door before I changed my mind.

He was leaning against the wall, one hand on the doorframe and the other hand in the pocket of his black sweats. No shirt or shoes. He'd changed, same as me. The lines of his chest were as hard as the tight draw of his mouth as he studied me.

His gaze lingered on the robe before sliding up. "Now that we're both more comfortable, maybe we can start over?" Those vivid blue eyes were a window to all that was the beauty of Ireland, and they were my weakness. Sean knew how to weaponize them. Dismantle my defenses. Conquer me.

And was it wrong I wanted him to do exactly that? For it to be my lips that he kissed and my body that he pulled tight to his, not Bridgette's? The memory of their brief moment together was torturing my thoughts, and I was desperate to erase it.

I angrily slapped a hand to my chest, attempting to claw at the pain building there. "It hurts. Like a heart attack." *Whenever I think of you not being in my life.* That's what I needed to say, but I chickened out and chose a half-truth instead, murmuring, "Thinking of you and Bridgette . . ." I whirled away, but he tightened a hand around my wrist and abruptly spun me back and into his arms.

"That's the pain I feel knowing you're right here in front of me, and I can't have you," he rasped, clutching my arms, willing me with his touch and commanding blue eyes not to run again. To be with him. "A deep, throbbing feckin' pain," he added, his Irish accent growing thicker with each word. That familiar blend of arousal and anger I now knew well coloring his words. When he spoke like this, it was as though he were reaching out and transferring his emotions inside me, willing our souls together. I felt every nuance of what he was feeling.

And it hurt.

Why did it have to hurt so much?

Slowly, my hands went to his abdomen and up over the hard ridges of his chest. His heart was thrashing wildly beneath my palm, and yet, he stood steady before me. A dominating force that appeared capable of weathering any storm. Unflappable. Powerful and focused. Determined to have his way, and his way was to be with me.

And I wanted that power and that force to wrap me up tight because I was tired. So, so tired of being strong every second of every day. Of pinning my shoulders back every moment when sometimes I just wanted to let them fall, if only for an hour.

"I'm scared of you," I whispered, hating the wobble in my lower lip that I think he noticed because his gaze cut straight to my mouth. His brows slanted, and he brought both palms to my face.

"Then let me show you there's nothing to be afraid of." His rough tone skated over my skin and had me shivering.

"I can't do more," I protested, my tone weak and not all that convincing, not even to me. *I can't jump.*

With his hands still caressing my face, Sean brushed his thumbs over my cheeks as he brought his lips closer to mine.

"Can't you just be the Irish guy with swagger and charm? A playboy? Why do you have to be so much more?" Could he feel the tremble in my body as he held me? Did he see the battle in my eyes I was fighting?

His jaw clenched, a hint of restraint there. "Tonight, I'll be whoever you need me to be." He slanted his mouth over mine, and this time, my knees did buckle.

I felt weightless, completely lost to our kiss. The endless worrying of my mind stilled. But I quickly pushed away from his chest and set a hand to mine, trying to recover the breath he stole from my lungs with that kiss.

Sean was breathing hard. Quick twitches of his abdominal wall. He dragged his thumb along the bottom of his lip as if trying to taste me again. Or sear the memory there forever.

His kiss was imprinted. On my lips. My body. In my mind.

"Emilia." My name rolled from his tongue, but the command was clear, *Don't run.*

Determined to meet his silent order, I wet my lips and brought my fingers to the knot of my robe, unfastening it and never breaking eye contact. And he didn't look away either. Didn't follow the slow movements of my hands. His eyes remained on mine. Bold. Beautiful. Making a statement.

With the belt free, I hooked my fingers beneath the lapels of the robe and slowly peeled the thick fabric back, letting it fall and pool at my feet.

"I'm not running." *Not tonight, at least.* I lifted my chin like a warrior who knew she'd be leaving the battlefield on top of her shield instead of walking behind it.

Wearing only my lacy thong, I stepped around the robe,

flung my arms over his shoulders, and linked my wrists behind his neck, bringing his lips back to mine.

His warm palms gripped my waist as we kissed again with more fervor and intensity than before. That achy throb in my chest slid down and settled between my legs as heat bloomed throughout my body.

I kissed him like it was my first time. Like it was my last.

Like the sky was falling, and there was only this moment left.

And just as in *Cinderella*, when the world reset at the stroke of midnight, we were also short on time.

His tongue matched mine stroke for stroke, and when his hand slid between my thighs and cupped my sex atop the panties, a soft moan of surrender left my mouth—a yearning for more.

"You're soaking these things. I ought to take them off," he said into my ear, his warm breath feathering lightly over my skin.

My nipples felt amazing pressed to his muscular chest, the sensations of skin-on-skin contact with him driving me wild. So wild I barely recognized he was ridding me of the thong.

Setting my hands to his hips, I trailed my fingertips just beneath the waistband of his sweats, happy to feel he wasn't wearing anything underneath. I shoved them down, and he took over, freeing his legs completely and kicking the sweats away, giving me a mouthwatering view. His cock was hard. Thick and veiny with precum glistening the tip.

I licked my lips, envisioning taking him between my lips, but he crooked a finger beneath my chin, stealing my focus back to his lust-darkened eyes.

"Tonight is about you. I need . . ." The movement in his

throat was a signal he was working through his emotions, same as me.

This wasn't the playboy I'd requested, the one who'd leave before the sun came up. But was he ever that man? Even in Vegas, he'd admitted he'd want my name and number before parting ways.

I couldn't think about that now. Instead of getting lost inside my head, I needed to get lost in his body. Be in the moment without fear of tomorrow. Or the consequences.

I set a finger to his lips and shook my head.

Sex with no strings. No *amore.*

But hell, if I wasn't a ball of yarn all tangled up right now.

"You drive me crazy, woman," he seethed in a sexy growl before retaking my mouth. He gently fisted my hair, urging my chin up in the process, taking command of the situation.

And it felt good to give him the control.

Before I knew it, we were standing in front of the mirror. His chest to my back, one hand cupping my wet sex and the other teasing my nipple between his fingers. His eyes captured mine in the reflection. "This is about sex. Just two people getting off." Sean's voice was flat. He was working to disguise his emotions, to hide the lie. "But I need you to look at us. See how beautiful you are as you clench around my fingers when you come," he said just as his thick finger pushed inside, drawing a gasp from me. "Keep your eyes open. Watch," he ordered before I had a chance to close them.

As he slowly fucked his finger in and out of me, he changed the angle and added a second, rubbing against all the sensitive parts of my sex. I couldn't speak. I could barely breathe. And all the while, he played with my nipple with his other hand.

His gaze wandered from where he fingered me, then

moved up my tight abdomen and to my full breasts, avoiding my eyes as if he were afraid *he'd* break down and demand more from me.

A jolt of pleasure shot through my body as he moved his thumb over my clit. I rotated my hips, desperate for more friction, and gasped at the feel of his hard length behind me, wishing he'd take me and ease the pain in my sex.

I bit down on my lower lip, growing dizzy as I stared at his strong hands gripping me, fucking me, demanding my pleasure. I turned my cheek, drawing his attention, and his mouth met mine in a bruising kiss. Like he was punishing me for refusing to give him more than my body.

"Come for me," he said against my mouth before pulling away. I looked back into the mirror, my gaze going to his hand on my pussy, and I obeyed, unable to stop myself even if I wanted to.

I cried out his name as I fell forward, setting a hand to the dresser, little tremors shooting through my body. I clamped my legs together when he kept at it, rubbing harder and faster.

At the loss of his heated touch, I splayed both hands on the dresser and leaned over farther, revealing more of his naked perfection in the reflection. Taut skin and hard muscles and eyes burning for more.

He palmed my ass cheeks with both hands, then gripped my hips and thrust his cock against my flesh, just below my sex, and I responded by pushing my ass into him.

"Sean. I need you inside me," I pleaded, not even ashamed that I was begging.

He flipped me around and set me on top of the dresser in one quick movement, the mirror at my back rattling with the force of it. He guided my legs around his waist, hooking my ankles behind him. "Right here?" he rasped, a dark look in his eyes.

He'd been holding back for months, and so had I. Ravenous for each other but refusing to act on it. Tonight he let the beast out, which was required if we were to keep it to sex without those frustrating strings. To remain as emotionless as possible.

"You wanna fuck like this?" His hands landed on the dresser on either side of me as he leaned in, his eyes harsh and piercing, testing me. That strong jaw locked tight. I was desperate to have his beard scratch up the length of my inner thigh before setting that handsome mouth on my pussy to lap at the wet mess he'd made between my legs. "Is this what you want, Emilia?" He was trying to hang on, to remain detached, but the Sean I knew, the one I couldn't help but care about, was breaking through.

And that scared me.

So, I cried out, "Yes. Like this."

He wrapped a hand around my lower back and pulled me to the edge of the dresser, then wordlessly buried himself inside me. My spine arched, and the back of my head hit the mirror. He never lost hold of my eyes, though.

With one hand still on my back, his other moved to my hip to hold me in place as he took me hard. And deep. All the way to my core.

I bit down on my back teeth as the dresser shook with each thrust.

He kept our bodies tight and dragged me into his arms before either of us came. "No, not like this," he said in a strained voice. "You deserve better." Picking me up, he walked us to the bed, and I was powerless to protest. I didn't just want the beast I'd tried to let free. I wanted his heart, too.

Our bodies disconnected as he laid me down on the bed and crawled up my body. He shifted to his forearms and softly brushed the wild strands of hair away from my face, finally capturing my eyes and stealing my breath once again.

"This is how," was all he said before sinking inside me, and I was overwhelmed with an explosion of emotions. So much so I was on the verge of tears as we moved together, our bodies effortlessly in sync as I held his arms and stared deep into his eyes.

No condom. And that was a jump if I'd ever taken one, wasn't it?

But it was . . . incredible.

That feeling in my chest earlier had nothing on whatever was happening to me now.

"You're mine, Emilia Calibrisi," he said huskily. "For a lot longer than tonight."

CHAPTER ELEVEN

SEAN

Waking up to the sight of Emilia standing naked, coffee in hand, and staring at the slit between the curtains was a sight I wanted to wake to for the rest of my life.

"*Buongiorno*," I said, murmuring the Italian word for good morning and hoping it was the right one. I had no idea what today would be like. How she would act or respond to me.

We'd had sex last night. *Unprotected* sex. That was a first for me, but I wouldn't change anything about it.

Afterward, part of me assumed she'd slip out of bed or turn into a pumpkin or something.

Instead, she woke me in the middle of the night, her mouth wrapped around my cock, and worked me over until I couldn't see straight. Before I was able to gather my wits, she'd climbed on top and rode the living hell out of me. Poised and confident, her hands on my chest, back straight, glossy black hair swinging over her breasts.

And a few hours ago, it was me waking her. The sheet had slipped from her torso as she slept, so I took a few moments and watched her in that relaxed state of slumber.

Her tits rising and falling with each soft breath was erotic, and I couldn't resist taking turns sucking each nipple while strumming her clit. Eventually, my mouth eased down on her pussy where I devoured her like she was my favorite dessert. She'd fisted the bedspread and cursed in several languages.

But now that the sun was awake, I had no clue if I'd get Emilia the Lover or Emilia the League Leader. Would there ever be a world in which this beautiful, strong woman allowed herself to just live her life without feeling the need to choose one or the other?

Maybe I was blind to our ending, and we were living some tragic love story, but for now, at least there was a story. Emilia was still here. She hadn't run. *Yet.* I wanted to knock that word from my head.

When she released the curtains and faced me, I braced myself to hear what she'd most likely been overthinking.

Not a hint of shyness in her nakedness as she strode my way, sipping her coffee.

I propped my head up with my elbow, doing my best not to allow my eyes to linger on any of her scars, knowing she wouldn't like that.

She yanked at the white sheet, allowing it to slide off the bed and expose my naked body. That was actually my first time sleeping in the nude. I hoped there'd be a next time. Hugging her sensational body as I fell asleep was something I could get used to.

"I like you like this." She continued to sip her coffee, her brown eyes, a shade similar to espresso beans, eyeing my cock.

I wrapped a hand around the base, fully aroused and ready to go. Although, if I were an artist, I'd be tempted to paint her in the nude instead, blue balls be damned.

From the looks of it, Emilia was still in lover-mode, ready for sex. And I'd be happy to oblige.

"About last night."

Scratch that, then. I sat taller, releasing my shaft, and set my back to the headboard.

She smiled. "I was hoping for more before we head back to Dublin. More of what we did."

What we did? Sex? Fuck? Make love? I'd expected a number of descriptors from her, and "what we did" wasn't one of them.

"And as for the no-condom thing," she began, "I'm safe. And on the pill. I know we should have discussed that before, but I also know you, and you'd never be with me if you weren't safe," she said, her tone borderline businesslike.

"I'm safe. I always wrap up." I cleared my throat. "With you, my one head took a back seat to the other, and I forgot. I'm sorry."

"It was *our* decision," she responded with a small nod. "Don't apologize."

I reached out for her, and to my surprise, she came closer. I encircled her wrist and urged her to sit on the edge of the bed next to me.

She discarded the mug on the bedside table and twisted to view me.

I did my best to resist scooping her up and setting her right on my dick. She was naked and tempting, and if the look in her eyes was any indication, I was betting she was wet. I'd slide right into her.

Emilia took my hands and placed them at her waist before leaning into me, bringing her back to my chest and settling between my legs.

My cock was now trapped against my stomach, but when she set her hands on my thighs and shimmied her arse, I was two seconds from flipping her onto her knees and ramming into her from behind.

"You keep moving like that, and my cock might just find a way inside you even from this position," I promised, my voice deep, desire pounding through my veins.

I wanted more of her.

More here.

More everywhere.

Just more.

It was cold outside. Cooler in Scotland than back home, and I'd love nothing more than to stay in the hotel in bed all day. I didn't even want to spoil this moment by providing an update to the others about how last night went down, which we really should've already done had we not been distracted.

Instead, I found myself blurting, "Come to dinner tonight."

She stilled her hips.

Mood killer?

"I promised my parents I'd come home tonight. Everyone will be there. I mean, you said Holly invited you to Dublin for the holidays and starting tonight our holiday festivities begin." The office was closed now through January seventh, even. Sure, we had The Alliance to defeat, but it was also Christmas on Saturday. We'd been waiting forever to go after the sons of bitches. Did we really need to get a jump start this week? The bad guys would be around after the holidays.

"We have the listening device and tracker now for Bridgette and Atlas. What we hear might alter our plans." Emilia shifted out of my arms and sat on the bed next to me. "Although, the device in Atlas's bag may be useless. But if a lead turns up . . ."

Yup, I killed the mood. Just grand.

She turned to face me and combed her fingers through her

sexy, tangled hair. But it was her plump lips, slightly swollen from hours of kissing and bare of all traces of her red lipstick, that drew my eyes.

"If a lead turns up, we'll follow it. But for now, we can listen in and see what they say. Wait until New Year's Eve. Use that night to turn Peter and Atlas on each other since we already have the proof of the affair."

"And the thug who was sent after Sara? What of him? We need to get him talking to see what he knows," Emilia reminded me.

"Sure, we'll add 'torture the thug' to Ma's schedule of holiday festivities." I grinned. "But in all seriousness, what happened with Bridgette should clear up our concerns about Sara working for The Alliance, right? Bridgette didn't seem to recognize me. And if Peter did pay Sara to worm her way into my family and spy on us, Sara would have given him the heads-up I took her tickets for the event last night. Bridgette didn't look the least bit suspect of me, I promise." I paused to consider everything. "And would Peter really use his wife to sleep with me to gain more intel? Gotta be some lines even bad guys draw, right?"

Emilia's raised eyebrows and dubious expression had me realizing there must have been a hole or two in my theory. "There's no telling what a man like Peter would do for power. Hell, I wouldn't put it past him to ask her to sleep with Atlas to try and take him down, too."

Now there was an idea. A terrible fecking idea. I wasn't an arsehole criminal that could ever do such a thing, but Emilia was right. Anything was possible where Peter Krause was concerned. "Feck. You're so good at this it's almost scary."

"A lifetime of experience." She shrugged.

"And if Bridgette is screwing Atlas because her husband asked her to, won't that mess up our plans?"

"Hopefully, the listening devices we planted can change some of our theories to facts before then so we know what we're up against."

"See, you proved my point. We can't rush into things." It'd be nice to have some semblance of normalcy amid our chaotic, hunting-down-bad-guys life. "Spend the holidays with me," I pleaded again and reached for her hands. "An Irish Christmas." I hated what I was about to say next, but— "Even if 'what we did' doesn't happen again, I'd love to spend the week with you."

At that, Emilia closed her eyes, effectively hiding any reaction I might see there. But she didn't pull her hands back. I'd take the small wins with this woman when I could.

Hopefully, she was measuring the possibilities and would choose . . . well, me.

"We're in Scotland now. Dublin could be dangerous if anyone saw us together as more than colleagues or friends."

"We don't have to walk around holding hands or kissing on the streets," I reminded her. "People are used to seeing us together because of our jobs."

She opened her eyes. "I always loved the holidays as a kid. I think my father overcompensated because we didn't have family. Usually just us. But still, he made it special."

Was this a roundabout way of saying yes? Or was she saying no?

"Your mother. What happened to her?" Why was I going out on that limb? *Why, fecking, why?*

We still hadn't gotten around to discussing that tipsy admission she'd made about her father and Penelope at the lingerie party last night, either.

Emilia swung her legs over the side of the bed and

dropped her feet to the plush carpet. Standing, she quickly plucked up her coffee and took a sip, then turned to face me. I rose as well, not sure if I'd royally screwed this all up.

Mastering how to talk to Emilia about her past, or her emotions attached to those events, was like toeing a very fine line. One step in the wrong direction could cause her to shut down or shut me out. I was a tightrope walker without much experience and no net.

But I had to push every once in a while if I wanted to get to know her more. And I did want to know her. All of her.

"Arranged marriage." She leaned her back to the window by the bed. "Another Sicilian family. Sophia didn't love my father. And vice versa. After she had me, a few months later, she ran away with one of our bodyguards. Like a thing from the movies."

Her words stole my breath and had me tensing. Not because of what she said, but the fact she told me the truth. I didn't know what to say or do. I honestly hadn't expected an answer.

"I decided to try and find her when I was fifteen. Close to my sixteenth birthday. I wanted to yell at her. Tell her off. I left without my father's permission. Ditched my guards." Her eyes fell closed again, and she allowed the empty mug to dangle from her hand, the coffee now gone. "I made it to her home in Tuscany. But Sophia refused to see me. Her guard slash lover for fifteen years slammed the door in my face. I went so far as to climb the fence but found myself facing off with Dobermans. And I never looked her up again after that." She peered at me, unable to hide the glossy look of her eyes. The threat of tears she'd most likely resisted for God knew how long. "The irony in it being Dobermans that sent me on my way, the same watchdog on the Calibrisi family crest, wasn't lost on me," she added in a tentative voice.

"I'm so sorry."

"There's nothing to be sorry about."

"Surprised your dad didn't kill the bodyguard," I mused.

This produced a surprising smile. "Me, too. But Papà didn't love her. If he wanted her back, he could have easily taken her back." She shrugged, the emotion in her eyes vanishing as fast as it'd come. "I guess it's interesting Papà wants the same for me, though. To marry someone who I may not love just because of my family name."

I reached for her hand and laced our fingers together, unable to stop myself. I wanted her to know I supported her decisions. If I could travel back in time, I would beg her father not to force her to make that promise.

I could find a way around League rules, but changing the past?

I'd take as much of her as she'd give me for as long as possible.

"I don't know when Papà began to sleep with Chanel's mother, but she was the only woman he ever truly loved. And I think after Chanel died, Penelope must have blamed my father, because I'm fairly certain they didn't see each other again."

I tightened my grip on her hand and raised our clasped palms between us, gently kissing her knuckles, and I'd swear I felt a shift between us. Her walls were slightly lowering.

The only problem? When it came to this woman, I didn't have a bloody clue how to get them to crumble.

CHAPTER TWELVE

EMILIA

DUBLIN, IRELAND

"I WASN'T EXPECTING COUNTRY MUSIC IN AN IRISH household," I said to Anna, who was sitting on the couch inside Sean's parents' house. She was trying to rock her growing boy to sleep on her lap, the travel playpen ready nearby for when he fell asleep.

We were eating a late dinner, so she'd fed him before arriving. Same with Sebastian and Holly, though Sebastian was some sort of baby whisperer and managed to get Siobhan to sleep in under two minutes. But Holly probably wouldn't let him keep telling their daughter tales of taking down bad guys for much longer. It was most likely his deep voice that soothed her and not the stories, but for now, it worked.

Anna's bold green eyes tracked my movement as she switched her son into a new position. "Nothing like a little Garth Brooks to get Braden down."

My fingers feathered over the spines of the books on the tall mahogany shelf closest to me. Sean's mother had a love of literature akin to my father's, and her collection was extensive.

"What song is this? I like it." I removed *Romeo and Juliet* from the shelf and held it to my chest. Rival families. A great love ending in death. Why I held on to it like it was a book of revelations into my own life was beyond me.

"Um." Anna stealthily reached for her mobile from where the music played without dropping Braden. "It's called, *'Ask me how I know.'* It sounds crazy, but I'm pretty sure Braden's taste in music is genetic. He's got some Kentucky in him for sure."

I barely heard her, stilling when the lyrics finally clicked with me. The music resonated on a level I wasn't ready to accept, and it was as if I were the singer, and the song was about Sean and me. *Stubborn. Afraid to settle down. Falling for someone.* Chills erupted over my skin as the meaning of the song hit me.

"You okay?"

The book nearly slipped from my grasp, and I quickly shelved it. "Of course." *Polished smile? Yes. Shoulders back? Check.*

"I think I'm close to transforming Adam into a cowboy as well as a country music fan." I shot her a more than shocked look, and Anna wrinkled her nose and lightly laughed. "Alright, probably not."

Seeing her so carefree and chuckling about the man she loved had me surprisingly loosening up a bit, especially when she pointed to a little sign nailed between the two bookshelves. "'*Sometimes I laugh so hard the tears run down my leg.*'" Sean's mother had a sense of humor. I liked that.

"Cara loves proverbs," Anna said softly. "Obviously, literature. She works a good proverb into a lot of our conversations."

Cara and Ronan McGregor. Two loving parents. They'd nearly divorced in the months leading up to Holly and Sebastian's wedding. Through Sebastian, I'd been aware of how it had affected all of their kids, as well as what a gift it was for Holly when her parents announced they'd gotten back together the night she married the love of her life.

Anna stood and gently set Braden into the travel playpen, and he rolled to his side, already asleep.

"*Brava*," I commented, turning to look through the open doorway to spy on Sean and Ethan talking down the hall. Ethan had brought Sara to dinner, and Sean was giving him some type of big-brother lecture from the looks of it.

I'd already begun working to corroborate her story. I wasn't prepared to trust her intentions, especially not after Sean paid off her debt to the German Alliance leader.

"What do you think of her?" Anna stood next to me, reading my thoughts. "My mother always says there's not a pot too crooked that a lid won't fit, but I'm getting the vibe that lid isn't for Ethan."

I stole a look at Anna and smiled. "You're going to have to translate that for me."

She went back to the couch and turned off the music on her mobile. Anna had curled her strawberry-blonde hair and was wearing a classy, red knee-length dress with capped sleeves and a gold belt around her waist. She was a classic Southern beauty.

I shifted my gaze away from the hall and peered down at my ensemble. Black, high-waisted trousers cinched with a sash at my waist, paired with gold pointed-toe pumps and a gold silk long-sleeved blouse. Dangly gold earrings. For the first time in my life, I'd agonized over what to wear, finally settling on what I thought was an appropriate outfit for a McGregor family holiday dinner. I hoped, at least.

I'd met Sean's parents before, but I had the sudden urge to make a good impression.

When Sean picked me up at the hotel an hour ago, his gaze had swept over me with as much desire as if I'd been naked. And yet, I was still unsure about where we stood.

We'd stayed in Scotland later than planned. Even though a source had informed us that Atlas had checked out of the hotel before dawn, eliminating the chance of bumping into him in the lobby, I hadn't been ready to break free of the cocoon Sean and I had spun around ourselves. Plus, I was worried I might never let it happen again.

"I swear when I listen to country music, I start talking like my sisters."

I shook my thoughts free and pulled my focus back to Anna.

"I get the feeling that Adam enjoys your Southern accent." I peeked back into the hall, but Sean and Ethan were gone.

"I was just saying there's a match for everyone, but I don't get a good vibe about Sara. Not sure she's the match for Ethan," Anna explained, and it took me a second to remember she was obliging me with a translation of her mother's Southern proverb.

"I'm looking into her." I hadn't meant to be so bold, but Anna knew who I was, unlike Sean's parents, so I had nothing to hide from her. "Anna?" I faced her. "When you look at Sean, what do you see, for, um, a lid?" *What am I saying?*

Anna set a hand to my shoulder, her green eyes brimming with sincerity. I could almost visualize the rolling green hills of Kentucky as she observed me. "I'm pretty sure that man has already found the perfect lid." She lightly squeezed my shoulder, then started for the hall.

You're mine, Emilia Calibrisi. Sean's words to me right before he came the first time we'd had sex kept spinning around my head.

I lifted my eyes to the ceiling. *Why'd you do this to me?* But Papà didn't answer back. He never did.

"You have a second?" Cole slipped into the study and gently shut the French doors. Well, that couldn't be good.

"What's wrong?" I cut straight to the point and closed the space between us.

Cole cupped his mouth for a moment.

"That asshole not talking yet?" I whispered.

He lowered his palm, eyes growing dark. "The arsehole is still not awake yet. The doctor we brought in said he's in a coma."

My stomach dropped. "Did you tell Sean?"

Cole grimaced. "What, right before our happy family dinner, tell my cousin he may have killed a guy?"

"Don't tell him that." I circled his wrist with a tight grip, my thoughts flying. "He may wake up. Just tell Sean he's awake but not talking yet."

"You want me to lie?" His brows rose.

"Yes," I said without hesitation. "And people wake up from comas all the time," I added in a steady tone. "No sense in ruining Sean's Christmas when we don't know the outcome yet."

"Emilia—" Cole let go of his words at the sound of the doors opening.

I quickly retracted my hand from Cole's wrist as Sean entered.

"Everything okay?" Sean asked, eyes darting between us.

Cole gave me an *oh, shit* look before turning toward his cousin. "She's trying to figure out what to buy a man who has everything." He strode toward him, tipped his head, then left Sean and me alone in the study.

Don't let that man die, I pleaded, sending up a silent prayer. Sean hadn't killed anyone yet, and I knew he'd hate himself if the man he punched—maybe to death—never woke.

My eyes cut back to Sean, and I put on as real of a smile as possible, choosing to push thoughts of what Cole told me to the back burner.

"I know something only you can give me," Sean teased in a seductive voice. And there went my negative thoughts.

He looked devilishly handsome in casual clothes. Dark denim jeans with black loafers. A lightweight black jumper with a zipper pulled down a bit to show a hint of his black tee beneath. His hair was styled with a touch of gel, and that dashing smile I adored was surrounded by a light growth of beard. But those stunning blue eyes of his were a lasso around my heart. Pulling me closer every time I saw him.

Lasso? Maybe Anna's country music was getting to me.

"You good?" He approached Braden in his playpen and stole a look, then came back over to me.

During the few seconds that it took Sean to check on his nephew, I quickly established my guard. What I really wanted to do was spin that cocoon around us again and repeat the intimacy we shared in Scotland. Sean was an adventure I wasn't allowed to have, though, so I crossed my arms over my chest and wiped all emotion from my face.

"Emilia?" He gently gripped my bicep.

"Dinner almost ready?" I deflected. It was for the best. Besides, I was unsure of where we were headed after last night. And this morning. And the two orgasms in the hotel before we left this afternoon.

"Five minutes." He released me and pocketed his hands.

"I'm sorry I couldn't help in the kitchen." I left his side to read a few more spines on the bookshelf.

"It's no worry at all."

"Your mother must be shocked that I'm Italian and don't know how to cook." I stopped at the sight of *Great Expectations*. "You were right. You're no Pip," I said at the memory from our night in Vegas.

"Most certainly not," he responded with a light laugh.

I continued walking around the room, eyeing the shelves, and he kept up with me while maintaining a little space between us. "My nonna, my grandmother on Papà's side, died when I was seven, but Papà said she was an excellent cook." I swallowed and turned, surprised to find he'd moved closer.

He angled his head, his gaze growing heated. "You have many other talents, so your lack of cooking prowess shouldn't bother you too much."

"I can make pasta. The box kind. And you know, use sauce from a jar." *Shut up, Emilia. You're babbling.*

His brows scrunched as he leaned in even closer, and I gathered a whiff of his cologne. "Are you nervous?" One hand went to the bookshelf over my shoulder.

I set a palm on his chest. "I don't do—"

"Everyone gets nervous." His eyes zeroed in on my mouth as if he were imagining the kiss he wished to set upon my lips.

"We should get to dinner," I rushed out.

Sean pushed away from the bookshelf and placed his hands behind his back. "If that's what you want." A challenge cut through his tone. I heard it loud and clear.

Oh, I wanted to rip the jumper over his head and rake my fingernails down his washboard abs. Smooth my palms over his taut body and sink them lower into his trousers.

But this wasn't the time or place. His family was down the hall prepping for a holiday dinner, and the last thing I needed was his mother walking in on her son doing naughty things to me against her shelf of Shakespeare and Dickens.

I didn't worry much about other people's opinions, but I found myself caring a hell of a lot about what Sean's mother would think of me.

When I didn't respond, Sean turned and held out a hand, motioning for us to move on.

We walked in silence, side by side, down the long hallway, the walls of which were lined with family photos as well as quotes from literature and proverbs, beautifully penned and framed like works of art. Before making a turn into the dining room, I paused at the sight of the last frame, a quote by Oscar Wilde. *Keep love in your heart. A life without it is like a sunless garden when the flowers are all dead.*

"It's true," Sean spoke up, and I peeked at him, my heartbeat gaining momentum.

"And if I'm already dead on the inside?" I whispered, lifting my face as if he'd hooked his finger beneath my chin to guide my eyes his way.

"Not possible." He brought his face close to mine, clearly not caring if anyone saw us. "You're the most alive person I've ever met," he added in a husky voice, then tapped the wall with a closed hand and entered the dining room.

I was startled when a single tear began to slide down my cheek before I realized what was happening. I dismissed it, dismissed whatever truth was trying to get free, pulled myself together, and followed him into the room.

"Aw, too bad your sister and her son couldn't join us for the holidays," I overheard Sean's mother say as I entered. She was off to the side of the table, talking to Cole.

"Her idiot ex wouldn't let her bring Jack here this year. At least my parents can spend the holidays with Bree and Jack in New York, though," Cole answered, then pulled out the chair for Alessia.

A table for twenty stretched the length of the enormous room. Gleaming hardwood floors reflected the crackling fire roaring in a large brick fireplace flanked by floor-to-ceiling windows that overlooked the backyard.

A festive arrangement of holly and garland decorated the center of the table on top of a red tablecloth. And the food looked and smelled delicious.

"Thank you so much for having me," I said when Cara set her sights on me, the last to join the table.

I sat opposite Sean, finding myself between Alessia and Holly, which I would normally find comfortable, but this seat afforded Sean the chance to confirm just how nervous I really was whenever he looked directly into my eyes.

My plan also included avoiding looking at Cole as much as possible since I could tell he was uncomfortable with my request, but if he loved his cousin, he'd protect him. And that meant lying to Sean.

"We're so happy to have you, dear." Cara patted my back and sat at the end of the table while Sean's dad, Ronan, occupied the other end.

Sean stood, lifted a bottle of wine, and leaned across the table to fill my glass.

"Such a gentleman," Ethan joked, and then Sara not-so-subtly elbowed Ethan, a hint to do the same for her.

Sara looked as polished as Anna in a similar dress but the color of holly. Her hair was in a chignon with two big pearls decorating her ears.

Holly and Alessia also played up the holidays in their ensembles. Red trousers and white silk shirts. They'd accidentally dressed alike.

Adam, Cole, and Ethan all went for the casual look like Sean. And Sebastian was the only one in black trousers with a black dress shirt. Sometimes I wondered if the man knew the meaning of casual.

Ethan raised his glass once everyone had theirs filled, and we all did the same. "To quote my favorite saying, '*May your glass be ever full. May the roof over your head be always strong. And may you be in heaven a half an hour before the devil knows you're dead.*'"

"That's horrible," Sara remarked, then took a modest sip of her red wine.

"I much prefer the proverb, '*A good laugh and a long sleep are the two best cures for anything,*'" Cara said and clinked glasses with Anna sitting next to her.

"You got something that ails ya, Ma?" Ethan asked, and Cara playfully waved away his question with a smile.

"Any Italian sayings you'd like to share?" Cara's dark lashes framed her crystal blue eyes as she turned her attention on me. Her hair was a match to Adam's dark instead of Sean's light hair. I had to assume Sean's father had once had light hair before he'd gone gray, or somehow, it'd skipped a generation.

I thought for a moment, then spoke in Italian first before repeating the line by Dante in English, "'*We cannot have a perfect life without friends.*'" And as I sat there, observing everyone so full of love at the table, I wondered if Dante should have added family, too.

"Mm. I'm framing that quote." Cara opened her palms, inviting us to link hands, and then she said an Irish blessing and told us to all eat.

Spiced beef, boiled potatoes, Brussels sprouts, and a variety of other foods were the main meal. I'd had my eye on the soda bread since I'd first smelled it baking when we arrived.

"This is delicious," I said a few bites later. "Thank you to everyone who cooked."

"My only contribution was the Brussels sprouts," Anna said between bites.

"As kids, we hated Brussels sprouts before even trying them. It was the foul smell. And they are bloody terrible. Well, they were." Adam added some of the veggie to his plate. "But then this woman came into my life and kindly explained we've been making them wrong all these years, the mistake being that we boiled them."

"The secret to Southern foods is frying," Anna added with a light laugh, and I had to wonder if the two lovebirds were playing footsies under the table. You wouldn't think they'd been together for years.

For a brief moment, I contemplated lifting my heel to skim the point along Sean's leg, and then I realized that was an insane thought, so I focused on my meal.

"Emilia, how is business? It must be a lot to juggle after your father died," Ronan asked after some light banter went back and forth between Sean and his family. He'd dressed more casually than his wife this evening. A beige jumper with khakis compared to his wife's white cashmere dress matched with brown boots.

"Oh, when my father died, he left CEOs in charge to handle his various business holdings. I only run one business, so my schedule is more flexible."

"Which one?" Ronan reached for a bottle of whiskey, swapping his wine for something with more kick.

Sean cleared his throat, eyes lifting to mine.

"We're sort of in the peacekeeping business," I said, hoping I didn't sound crazy.

"Yeah, the company manufactures weapons," Sean noted. "Bows." He coughed into his fist. "Arrows." Watching this man stumble through explaining my work was somehow adorable.

"Maybe I'm missing something, but how does manufacturing weapons contribute to keeping the peace?" Sara asked. I shifted her way, deciding that I really didn't like this woman, and it had nothing to do with the fact she'd once dated Sean.

"That's a good question," Sebastian spoke up as he eyed the bottle of whiskey. Ronan must've read his thoughts because he passed it down the table to his son-in-law. "The weapons are meant more as a deterrent."

Likely story. And we were botching this lie, weren't we? "About this soda bread," I began while pointing to the slice I now had on my plate, "where did you learn to make it?"

"My mother," Cara said with a smile, and she went on to explain the recipe.

Sean nodded at me, his eyes saying, *Nice save*.

"I was discussing with Emilia that we ladies might take a little holiday together soon," Holly said a few minutes later. "What about we go on the sixth? Women's Christmas Day?"

"Women's Christmas Day?" This was new to me.

"January sixth is considered the last day of Christmas festivities," Cara began, her face lighting up. "It represents the Epiphany, the day the three wise men visited the baby Jesus. It's celebrated differently around the world and goes by a variety of names, but in Ireland, women take the day off to rest after all our hard work from the holidays."

"Sounds nice." But go on a girls' trip that day? I highly doubted that'd be possible. "I'll probably be working then. Maybe we can get away another time?"

"Your peacekeeping work?" Ronan asked, his lips

twitching into a smile that told me he suspected we were all telling some white lies at the table.

"With the bows and the arrows?" Sara arched a blonde brow.

The first thing I'd be doing at the hotel was tossing the lingerie I bought at her store.

But what struck me as odd, as well as somewhat suspicious, was that Sara didn't act like a woman who feared for her life after being manhandled on Friday night.

"Instead of a girls' trip," Ethan began as if realizing Sara's intent, "how about we all do something fun together this week? Maybe take part in the shenanigans of the Twelve Pubs of Christmas."

Why was it Sara shifted her focus to Sean whenever I glimpsed her way? Was she jealous of whatever she thought was happening between—

"I'm too old for that," Ronan said with a close-mouthed smile, interrupting my thoughts.

Sean playfully rolled his eyes. "Funny, Da."

"Besides, you're the babysitter," Adam added. "But yeah, I'm in."

"Well, before *I* commit, what is it?" Anna asked. "I mean, I can guess."

Ethan and Adam took turns explaining rules that basically involved getting drunk while having some laughs at twelve pubs. It wasn't something I'd normally say yes to, but part of me liked the appeal of breaking out of my norm.

"I don't know if that's such a grand idea," Cole said in a low voice, and based on the way Alessia was now looking at me, he'd told her about our conversation before dinner. Her eyes were soft and filled with understanding. We were on the same page. She'd struggled with the burden of taking a life, and I had a feeling she wasn't ready for Sean to experience the same emotions. At least not at Christmas.

I was born into this life. Alessia and the McGregors were thrust into it. Alessia by way of Sebastian—a brother she only discovered existed when she was twenty. The McGregors by way of Adam's involvement with a Dublin crime boss. It was different for them. *I* was different from them.

"I think we could use some fun." Alessia looked to her husband, sending him some sort of message with her eyes, and he grumbled and relented.

"Will you be busy, Emilia? With all that work of yours?" Sara asked, her smug tone and insincere comments driving me nuts.

"I'm free this week. That's the luxury of owning a profitable business," I responded, taking a sip of my wine and never breaking eye contact with her. But it wasn't a complete lie. I would be digging into Sara's story. Eavesdropping on Bridgette and Atlas. And hoping a man who probably deserved to die didn't actually croak, but otherwise, my calendar was open. "I'm in."

Sean let go of his fork, eyes zipping to my face. Total surprise there.

"Well, just no punching anyone for looking at your wife the wrong way, okay?" Cara stood and began heaping seconds onto her sons' plates without asking them first.

"I've only done that once. Or twice," Adam said.

And Ethan coughed out the word, "Bullshite."

"I wasn't referring to you." Cara dipped her chin down, her head pointing Sebastian's way.

Ah. Yeah, the man had a temper when it came to anyone bothering Holly. Clearly, there'd been an incident or two while I was back home in Italy.

"He'll be on his best behavior." Holly looked to her husband for confirmation.

"I don't make promises I can't keep." Ohhh. Wrong words from Sebastian because Holly shot him a death stare, a reminder he'd promised not to kill again, and then did exactly that at my home in Sicily in October.

"If you'll excuse me." Holly set her red linen napkin on her plate and abruptly stood. The room had gone completely silent, and the sound of her chair's legs scraping across the floor was almost deafening.

Sebastian was on his feet and following her a hot second later, and I could see his jaw working as he moved. He no doubt wanted to kick his own ass for that slip-up.

"Well, the make-up sex will be grand," Cara said in a cheerful voice, and I almost spit out the sip of wine I'd taken.

Adam grimaced. "Ma."

"What, dear?" She opened her palms to the table. "Sex is good. It's natural." Her focus shot to her husband at the end of the table, and I was certain her sons were going to lose their stomachs soon. "Healthy, too."

Well, it seemed their marriage was doing just fine. That was good. And honestly, I liked Cara that much more for being so candid.

Cole attempted to change the mood at the table by sharing a few funny encounters he'd had with his sister's celebrity friends over the years. Cole's sister, Bree, was an actress in the States.

I barely heard what Cole talked about, though, too entranced by this night. The humor. The feeling of family. The look in Sean's eyes when our gazes collided.

Cara's attention fixed on me a few minutes later, and it had me drawing in a nervous breath. She had questions. I doubted I had answers.

"Emilia, such a beautiful name," Cara spoke up, and I'd been right. She'd set her sights on wanting to get to know me more. "What is your middle name?"

My lips were dry. Throat parched. I finished my wine and slid my tongue between the seam of my lips. "Tessa," I answered.

"A Greek name," Cara said as if that should have meant something to me. "Tessa has a few meanings from what I remember, but the one I prefer is 'huntress.'" She angled her head, the rest of the room falling into silence, and I'd swear this woman was reading me. Seeing something inside me that I wasn't so sure if even I saw. "Emilia is Latin for 'rival,' yes?"

"I-I honestly don't know." *I just know my last name means I can't be with your son.* "I never asked my parents why they picked those names." Maybe because I was fairly certain my mother chose those names, and she abandoned me without a second thought.

"And what of your mother?" Cara asked. I should have seen that coming.

"Ma," Sean hissed, eyes tight on her. I'd swear they were having a telepathic conversation as he viewed her in silence. Had he warned her of some off-limits topics she was blatantly ignoring?

"What?" Cara dramatically lifted her shoulders and refilled her wineglass.

"It's okay." I didn't want him mad at her because of me. "My mother's not in my life." I resisted the impulse to stand and walk away from the table. That'd be rude. But my instincts were begging to kick in. Every part of me screamed to run.

It was Sean's soft gaze that calmed me down.

"I don't have any family left," I whispered and took a

breath, but then Alessia set a hand on top of mine between our plates.

"That's not true. We're your family now," Alessia told me, and when I gathered my attention to look at her, I found myself wishing it were that simple.

CHAPTER THIRTEEN

EMILIA

"Sorry about my mother." Sean collapsed on the queen-sized bed. He'd taken me upstairs to see his childhood bedroom, which was so well preserved I was sure it hadn't been touched except for a bit of dusting over the years. He shoved his sleeves to his elbows and leaned forward, setting his forearms to his thighs, eyes on the hardwoods as my heels clicked around the room, taking in the accolades and photos he'd received over the years hanging on the wall.

I smiled at the photo of Sean standing in the center of a cast for a play. Probably a sixteen-year-old Sean. "Now your superb acting last night makes that much more sense. You are quite the thespian after all."

"That was for *Macbeth*. And that was Ma's doing," he grumbled.

Macbeth, of course.

"I should have taken up fighting like Adam instead." I could hear the blush in his tone. I didn't have to check for confirmation. "And she put all that stuff up after I went to Trinity."

"I like your mother, by the way. No need to apologize." I

was happy he had such a caring, intelligent, and free-spirited woman in his life.

Sean's mother had kept her teaching job at Trinity despite the empire her husband had built over the years, but from what I had learned, she now focused on charity foundations in her retirement. In my opinion, she didn't fit the stereotypical wife of a billionaire.

"Looks like Holly is still sore about what happened in October." I changed the subject, preferring not to think about mothers or my lack of one.

"You mean when your Navy SEAL buddies convinced Sebastian to break his promise to her?" The Irish lilt of his voice almost hid the hint of sarcasm infusing his tone.

"Roman's only a friend, you know. We were never together." Maybe Sean and I weren't allowed to have a future, but I wanted him to know I wasn't off screwing around.

The old floors creaked beneath his footsteps. "And have you ever been in a relationship?"

I tracked his movement in the reflection of the mirror over his dresser, finding him an arm's length away. "Once. Although, I'm not sure if you could call it that." I fingered the collar of my blouse and shifted it to show the scar that was aging with time. "It didn't work out so well."

His eyes turned dark, anger eclipsing the beautiful blue. "*He* did that to you?" Flared nostrils. Shoulders rounding back and a broad-barreled chest rising. Clear indicators Sean wanted to inflict damage.

"I was backpacking in South America when we met. He was one of my hired guides. Someone to teach me life lessons and survival skills—the things Papà felt were important for me to learn." I paused, letting him fill in the details himself. "After about a month of traveling, and him gaining my trust, getting close to me, he made his move. It turned out 'Paulo' had been sent to try and draw out family secrets. He'd murdered the real Paulo. And when he made his move against me . . ."

Sean held on to my shoulder, encouraging me to face him. I didn't cry. I couldn't remember crying aside from when Chanel and Papà died.

"I guess he suspected I was onto him, but I wasn't quite as skilled at reading people, so he surprised me with a machete one day." I let go of my shirt, allowing the memories of that asshole to wash away. "I killed him. Kicked his body into the Amazon, then kept on with my hike as if nothing had happened. Shocked, I supposed." I finally gave in to face him, checking to see if he'd look at me differently. "Not everyone is capable of being with someone who takes lives. Outside of the law, I should say. Holly loves Sebastian enough to overlook his past, but it's not easy for her to handle him killing anyone in the present," I noted, attempting to bring the conversation back to where we'd started.

"There's a difference between a killer and what The League stands for. What you, Sebastian, and the others do in the name of justice." The back of his hand caressed my cheek, an intimate and forgiving touch I struggled to admit, even to myself, I needed.

Would he feel the same if he knew he'd put that German thug in a coma?

I set my palms to his chest, planning to push away, but I was trapped in place by the warmth of his gaze. "I could have sent the man who hired Chanel's murderer to jail instead of to his death. And I didn't have to kill the fake Paulo." I was intent on punishing Sean with the truth. I also wanted him to know the kind of woman I was.

"I know what you're doing," he responded in a low voice. "It won't work."

"There's no penance for me. I'm not in the military. Nor a police officer. I take the law into my own hands and choose who lives and who dies. But my sins are mine alone. I won't burden anyone else with them." My shaky voice reminded me to drop my hands from the hard planes of his chest. "Sebastian has a chance at redemption with Holly. His daughter. I-I don't see that happening for me."

"And is that true for me when I take a life?" he probed.

"*If*," I reminded him.

A line creased his forehead as he was no doubt working on grasping the underlying issues holding me back from him. Hell, I'd yet to figure that out myself. "Us not being together, it's not just about League rules or your promise to your father, is it?"

"Does it matter?" I tried to dodge his focus by turning, but he spun me back around with a firm hand on the hip.

"I'm not a psychologist, but it sounds to me like you're scared to fall in love."

I gently set my hands on his chest again, tipped my chin up, and stared into his blue eyes that held so much sincerity it was unnerving.

Before I knew what I was doing, I rose to my toes, slid my hand up the back of his neck, and kissed him. The whiskey on his tongue mingled with the wine on mine, making for a heady combination as we tasted each other in a rough, almost angry kiss.

I nearly fell into his tall frame. I was off-balance and out of my damn mind.

Firm hands chased over my body before he cupped my ass and pulled my hips to his.

Sean continued the kiss as his hands roamed freely,

tugging on my clothes here and there yet managing to hold on to his restraint. This level of reserve was no doubt costing him if his grunts of frustration were anything to go by.

I hooked one leg around his hip, needing to get even closer to his hard shaft, to grind against him and take pleasure in the only thing I was allowing myself to feel—desire.

Reaching between us, I quickly unzipped his jeans and dipped my hand into his boxers, taking hold of his cock. He lightly bit my lip as I slid my thumb through the precum and circled it around the head. With both heels back on the floor, I lowered to my knees, my hands dragging down along the sides of his frame.

Was this a distraction from reality? Yes.

Did I care? No.

Sean placed his hand on top of my head as I took him into my mouth and teasingly circled his crown with my tongue. With a grunt, he grabbed hold of my hair and urged me to take all of him.

"Feck," he bit out, his voice low and strained as I sucked and sucked. "Emilia." Strings of curses continued under his breath, and I was fairly sure only the Pope walking in would stop me from getting this man to the finish line. And maybe not even then. I was going to hell anyway, wasn't I?

I sucked down every last drop of cum as Sean released into my mouth, then wiped my lip and slowly rose with his helping hand.

"That'd be a first in my bedroom here," he said while zipping his fly. "Thank God my ma didn't walk in since I didn't lock the door."

"Judging by your mother's views on sex, she'd never open a closed door while her son and a woman are inside." I traced my bottom lip with my thumb, desire still thrumming through me as I clenched my sex, wishing he could plunge into me. Alleviate the pain between my thighs that had managed to build despite all of the orgasms he'd delivered since last night.

Sean had my back to the door a moment later. Our bodies pressed together. One strong hand propped over my shoulder, his other hand working the sash loose from my waist.

He angled his head and dipped in to give me a surprisingly tender kiss, not caring in the least that he released in my mouth only moments ago. Torturous sweeps of his tongue parted my lips like a tease as he unzipped my trousers and palmed my sex over my panties, no doubt feeling how wet he made me.

When his mouth went to my ear, I shuddered. The feel of his hot breath gliding over my skin was almost more erotic than sex. I tilted my head back, my eyes on the ceiling as he dipped his hand beneath my panties and plunged two fingers inside me, covering himself in my wetness before gliding his fingers over my sensitive and swollen bud. "I could touch you all day and never tire of it."

My eyes closed as he stroked me, touching me in just the right way. My trousers managed to stay up with our bodies only separated by his hand between us. What I wouldn't give to be back in our hotel room so I could feel his skin against mine.

I arched into the heel of his hand and moved my hips, desperate for relief from this intense need building between my legs. A need I was certain now more than ever only Sean would ever be able to satiate.

I came hard, biting into his shoulder to keep from moaning my ecstasy out loud, which I knew this man loved every second of.

"We ought not to leave Ma waiting on us for dessert, I suppose," he said a moment later, a playful air to his tone.

Dessert. Right. We were still in his parents' house. And did I manage to table our conversation about my apparent commitment issues with orgasms?

"It's not fair." I tightened the sash around my waist and checked myself in his mirror. "You don't smell like sex, but now I do. My panties are soaked."

He set both hands at the sides of my arms and met my eyes in the mirror, a devious twinkle in those bold blues of his. "Well, you could always take them off."

* * *

"ARE YOU RESPONSIBLE FOR THIS?" I ASKED AFTER THE DOOR to my penthouse suite swung closed. A Christmas tree covered in strings of gold twinkle lights and decorated with colorful ornaments now sat in front of the living room windows.

"I may have arranged for your suite to be decorated while we were at dinner." He stroked a hand over the scruff covering his jaw. "I know you opted out of the decorations when you arrived, but it doesn't feel like Christmas without a tree, and you did agree to have an Irish Christmas this week."

I set my jacket down on one of the stools in front of the island that separated the kitchen and living room, then approached the pretty tree, its lights seeming to dance before my eyes. "And you have one in your flat?"

"I was planning on putting one up this week. Been preoccupied."

"Hm." I offered him my profile, keeping sight of both him and the tree. "I like it. Thank you."

"You sound unsure."

"I'm unsure of a lot of things, but I can handle a

Christmas tree." I forced a smile and faced him. "It was a nice gesture. I appreciate it."

Instead of advancing closer, like a small part of me wanted him to, he said, "Will you come shopping with me tomorrow? The office is closed, and I haven't bought anything for my family yet."

"Shopping," I repeated as if I'd never heard the word. "I guess since I'm spending Christmas with your family, I should buy some gifts as well. I take it Adam might frown upon me gifting Braden with a bow and arrow, though. Perhaps a Robin Hood jumper instead."

That comment produced one of his more charming smiles. "Good to hear your experience at my folks' house tonight isn't keeping you from coming back."

The fact he was still wearing his overcoat suggested he'd be leaving soon and that he'd truly only meant to walk me to my door like he stubbornly insisted on doing. "Pick me up at ten? I'd like to get a workout in first." I needed to run off my stress. Get rid of the nagging feeling clawing at me about asking Cole to lie to Sean.

"Want me to join you for that?"

Thoughts of sparring with him transformed into images of rough, wild, and incredible sex on those blue mats at the gym. It'd help with stress, but . . . "Just going to run a few kilometers. I think it's best if I go alone."

He nodded, his lips drawing together. "Okay." He hooked a thumb over his shoulder. "I guess I ought to let you get some rest. Lots of stuff planned this week."

True. I was going to have more Christmas in one week than I'd had in a decade.

We also needed to monitor Bridgette and Atlas's listening devices and stay apprised of their activity, if any. So far, it appeared Atlas's bag was parked somewhere in France and too far away to pick up any noise. As for Bridgette, nothing of use had transpired.

My friend Roman was checking out Sara's story. Hopefully, he'd have news soon. It was hard to believe she'd managed to date two McGregors by mere chance. And without being able to question the unconscious German, we were relying on only her side of the story. "Sara was a bit too relaxed tonight, don't you think?"

He nodded. "I was thinking the same. I also wasn't a fan of her attitude toward you."

Comes with the territory when dating you. Women now hate me.

Wait.

Dating?

"A penny for your thoughts," he said softly. His playful, endearing smile lifted my spirits and managed to save me from falling into the dark abyss in which my mind often trapped me.

"Do you think Atlas is redeemable?" *Where did that come from, Ems?* No, I didn't need my inner Chanel talking to me right now. Atlas is nothing like her from the little I knew about him. And what I did know was all bad.

Sean folded his arms as he worked through my question.

"There was a charm attached to his travel bag—a miniature bottle of Chanel perfume. I wouldn't have expected a man in his position as leader of a dangerous organization to have a sentimental bone in his body," I went on to explain.

"I suppose even monsters are capable of love. But as for if he's redeemable? I don't know." His attention moved swiftly to the Christmas tree and remained there for a beat. "We're not murderers," he said, reminding me of our earlier conversation in his bedroom. "Unless he gives us no other choice, he won't die by our hands."

My gaze fell to the floor. "Atlas was only seventeen when Chanel died. She told me he was more interested in girls at school than learning the workings of The Alliance. I had hoped he'd remain free of his father's influence, but I can't help but wonder if her death changed him like it changed me. Made him cynical, callous. Turned him into a killer." When I looked up, Sean was standing before me, and without a word, he wrapped me in his arms and held me tight. As though he was afraid that the wind would carry me away.

"No blaming yourself. His choices are on him."

"But were they? Look at my life." Why was there a tremble in my voice? "Look what being denied choices and control over my life has done to me. To the possibility of us."

His brows quirked together. "Possibility?"

I blinked. "Impossibility," I whispered, suddenly feeling frazzled. I worked my hand up between our bodies to catch a tear that'd broken free, quickly dismissing it from existence, as I'd done at his parents' home earlier.

Where were these emotional tears coming from? These signs of weakness.

"Emilia, I—" Sean let go of his words at the sound of the distinct ring from my burner mobile in my jacket pocket.

"That's my burner. I've been waiting for that call." I eased out of his grasp, happy for the save. "Sorry."

He cupped his mouth before turning and walking to the window by the Christmas tree.

"Hey," I answered after retrieving the iPhone. Only one person had the number, so I knew it was Roman, my American SEAL friend.

"Am I catching you at a bad time?" Roman asked.

Yes and no. I swallowed, trying to pull myself back into work-mode, not needing to guess why Roman was calling. "No, the time is good. Sean is with me." I felt Sean turn at my words, felt his disappointment. It made my skin sting with regret and my chest ache with sadness. "What'd you find out?"

"Sara did receive a large cash infusion into her bank account three months ago. But she never applied for a bank loan. That part is a lie," Roman said.

I'd placed the mobile on speakerphone so Sean could listen.

"Honestly, she probably could have survived without the cash. Not as comfortably, but she didn't need that extra money to stay afloat," Roman went on. "Also, that deposit was made three weeks after she met your brother."

"So, she was already dating Ethan." Sean's shoulders slumped. I wasn't sure if that made him feel better or worse.

"It doesn't rule out whether or not they targeted her because she was dating Ethan. Getting close to your family could have been a stipulation for the loan . . . she gives them info along with her loan payment," I pointed out.

"Our facial recognition software also scoured the available CCTV footage the week before her deposit in hopes we'd find her hanging out with anyone of interest," Roman explained. "Sara met with two men at her store in New York City after hours three nights before the money was deposited into her account. It may be nothing, but I'm texting you the photos now. One man was German, Hans Frederick. Most likely an alias from what we can tell. Possibly hired by Krause off-the-books. No ID for the other man."

I tapped my mobile screen to switch to the app, waiting for his message to come through.

"Either of them look familiar?" Roman asked.

As Sean and I stared at the pictures, my stomach dropped because the nameless guy sure as hell was familiar. The black wig and fake nose were classic Luca Moreau.

"Luca?" Sean asked in surprise, and I nodded.

"His name is Luca Moreau," I told Roman. "And if he was in New York, that means he somehow temporarily removed the tracker we planted in his body."

Sean cursed and grabbed his mobile, probably calling Sebastian or Cole as he walked toward the window.

We exchanged a few more words, and Roman promised another update after I sent him some additional information on Luca to help his search. "Sounds good. Talk soon." Roman ended the call.

"Luca would've informed us about that trip if he was undercover per our agreement with him. He wouldn't have removed the tracker we planted in him," I said after Sean explained the little we knew to Sebastian from the sounds of it and hung up. "Luca is doing what he does best. Manipulating everyone. And we need to figure out what his game plan is before it's too late."

"Emilia." Sean blinked a few times as if an idea had just come to him. "It was Luca's intel that sent you to London. What if he wanted you there that day for a reason? To discover Atlas's affair with Bridgette and bring that to The League. I think we can now confidently say that Luca's working with Krause since it appears he met with Sara in New York. I think he wants us on this road, whatever road it is, and his reasons sure as hell can't be good."

My stomach knotted at his words. At the realization of what this all meant. We were being played again by the son of a bitch. Luca was supposed to help us take down The Alliance in exchange for not killing him, but now it looked like he was masterminding a plan to take us down instead.

I hastily put on my jacket and started for the door, but Sean quickly closed the space between us.

"Where are you going?"

"I'm taking him into custody now. I'll get him to talk before I kill him."

He grabbed my wrist on top of my jacket sleeve. "You know Luca better than me. If he's planned all this out already, then he absolutely has a contingency plan in place if you do that. An ace up his sleeve like he's had every feckin' time. Pieces will already be set in motion, ones we won't be able to stop without his help. He'll have the upper hand again."

"What are you suggesting?" I asked bitterly, sensing he was about to take away the revenge I was more than ready for.

"We figure out his endgame, let him believe he's winning. Then we take down The Alliance as planned and kill that fecker, too."

I cursed in Italian and took a deep breath. Maybe I'd been thinking with my heart instead of my head, which wasn't like me. "I can put in a call to some of our League members to confirm his location and inform them to keep him in their sights. We can't rely on the tracker anymore."

"Sebastian is already on it."

I wasn't used to being behind the eight ball. But it was nice to have an assist. Not be the only steady hand. In this case, I wasn't even all that steady.

"We need to keep a close eye on Sara this week as well. She'll already be with us for almost every holiday activity because of Ethan, and this might be our best chance to find out if she's in on whatever game Luca is playing or if he's simply pulling her strings without her knowledge." He walked behind me and wordlessly removed my jacket, letting me know I wasn't going anywhere. "And hopefully, Cole gets that German to talk. Maybe he knows more than what Sara told us."

"Yeah," I mused. "Okay. So, we stick to our plan this week."

"Aye." He paused and circled me. "But if I discover Luca is behind dragging Ethan into our mess," Sean began, his tone rough and fierce, "I'll kill him myself. It'll be a bloody fecking Christmas this year."

CHAPTER FOURTEEN

SEAN

Not only was it too early for this conversation, but the morning light streaming through the windows felt like laser beams focused on my retinas. Worrying about Ethan possibly mixed up in League business had kept me up last night, and I'd drunk too much bourbon to try and turn off my racing thoughts. Now I was suffering the painful aftereffects.

But here I was, after maybe an hour of sleep, at Adam's gym. Adam, Cole, Sebastian, and I were in the midst of a conversation about Luca, our nemesis. The bane of my existence, as well as everyone else's. So, yeah, the dull, achy throb that had taken residence in my head coupled with the why-the-feck-was-it-so-sunny-in-Ireland-today-of-all-days had me on edge.

"That son of a bitch." Cole paced the length of the blue gym mat, his hands tearing through his hair and pulling at the ends. "I want first dibs when it's time. Luca locked Alessia in prison for years. Forced her into killing a friend. If anyone takes his life, it needs to be me."

"I already fecked up and broke my promise to Holly," Sebastian remarked, hands set to the wall near one of the empty fighting cages off to our left. He was shirtless, the cross tattoo on his back drawing my eye. The whole *Thou shalt not kill* idea of our Catholic religion seemed more like a suggestion than a rule given our work with The League. "Strangling the life from the bastard who made me believe my sister was dead should be my honor."

Adam moved to the center of the room and stretched his arms out like a ref trying to separate two fighters. "Are we really arguing about who gets to kill this guy?"

"Yes," Cole, Sebastian, and I all hissed at the same time, then simultaneously broke out into laughter, which managed to diffuse some of the tension hanging in the air.

We'd come to Adam's gym early that morning to train as well as discuss the wrench in our plans that was Luca. Fecking Luca Moreau. The bastard was like dog shite on the bottom of your shoe—no matter how hard you scrubbed, the stink never went away. But despite our intentions, we hadn't thrown one punch, lifted one weight, or done anything aside from plot how we'd drain every last drop of blood from the man.

"But really." Adam slipped his hands into a pair of thin black gloves. "I don't think you ought to be pissing off my sister again and so close to Christmas. Your dumb-arse slip last night at the dinner table revived her anger."

Sebastian faced him, but his eyes were on the ceiling as if working through a problem. Or maybe trying to restrain himself from punching my brother.

"And what of a divorce?" I pressed when Sebastian had yet to answer Adam. "You want that?" It was an exaggerated stretch, but I didn't like seeing my little sister unhappy, and I was prepared to knock the shite out of anyone who made her that way. Even if that someone was her husband.

In my mind, Sebastian was the true League leader of

Ireland, and as such, decided the fate of scum like Luca. It was within Sebastian's right to end the man's life any way he chose.

But there were plenty of us itching to finish Luca when the time came. No sense in breaking my sister's heart over that piece of garbage.

Sebastian froze and swung his gaze my way, an angry glint in his eyes at the mention of the word "divorce."

My parents had once separated, and it'd killed us to learn Da had seen another woman during that time, but Ma and Da were now back together. Their problems were much different than what we were dealing with, though. I had a feeling Sebastian would burn down the world if he ever lost my sister.

Sebastian stalked closer and set a palm on my chest as though he meant to shove me away. I'd once watched this man throw my cousin through a glass wall at his club. Times had changed. We were all on the same side now, but it wasn't wise to poke a bear.

"Easy, man." Adam stepped alongside us, his gloved hand wrapping over Sebastian's shoulder.

Sebastian kept his gaze fixed on me, his jaw muscles clenched. Maybe my sister was holding out on him, and he was on the verge of hulking out from lack of sex.

I could relate. The more I wanted Emilia, the harder I trained. But the fact was I couldn't have her. I had to find a better way to channel my frustrations.

"We all want the fecker dead, but Holly's more important." I let go of a deep breath.

"You think I don't know your sister is more important than that arse?" Sebastian's low timbre was eerily calm, like the quiet before the storm.

Damn, we needed another laugh to cut through the thick

air. "Of course, but my sister is stubborn, and you know that." I stepped back and held my hands in the air in surrender. "And selfishly, I want to kill the guy myself. He'd be my first, and who better to pop my cherry?" My lame attempt at a joke had Cole eyeing me with a strange expression. All the fight seemed to have gone out of him, and in its place was sadness. What the hell was that all about?

Before I could ask him if my crude humor bothered him, Cole surprised me by saying, "How about none of us do it? Emilia can kill Luca."

Sebastian expelled a deep breath as if this solution relaxed him, and Adam released his hold of him.

Emilia already thought of herself as a killer. No need for that useless piece of shite to add to her negative thinking. "Emilia is as tough as any of us in this room," I began, "but I refuse to give Luca the chance to hurt her."

"Maybe we table this topic for another day," Adam spoke up, the voice of reason today. "We're taking our kids to see Santa later," he began while pointing at Sebastian, "so I suggest you get rid of your aggressions inside the ring before then. Put on a nice smile, maybe surprise my sister with something pretty while you're at it, and we'll have a merry good time later, okay?"

A gruff, bullish sound left Sebastian. The only McGregor that Sebastian tolerated putting him in his place was Holly. I had a feeling his "aggression," as my brother put it, was going to damn well hurt a few of us inside that ring, too.

"I think Adam should go in the ring with Sebastian first," Cole said as if reading my thoughts. "Ya know, since it's your idea to let the beast out before he goes to see jolly old St. Nick with his kid." Cole was working hard to fight back a laugh, and when he couldn't hide it any longer, I cracked a smile as well.

"I'd rather face you, brother," Adam said, turning his attention on me a minute later after Sebastian appeared to calm down. "See how your training has been progressing."

"Oh, it's like that, huh?" I teased him back and grabbed a pair of gloves. "It's on." I ducked under the rope of the closest ring and slid on the thin black gloves.

Cole and Sebastian circled the ring, resting their forearms on the rope to watch as Adam and I squared off.

My twin knew he was a better fighter inside the ring. He'd also spent nearly half his life fighting outside of it, and I didn't even have two years yet. But hell, I'd throw down with him to the best of my ability.

Adam rotated his left shoulder, loosening up.

"Hey now, don't forget family photos," Cole reminded us. "Your parents will kill you if the both of ya show up for Mass on Christmas Eve with bruises."

Adam smiled. "Oh, no worries. It'll only be one of us." He flicked his wrists, and I went toward him, ducked to his left, and swung, catching him with a right to the cheek. He stepped back, touching his face in surprise. "So, it's gonna be like that, I see," he said with a laugh, then came back at me swinging.

CHAPTER FIFTEEN

SEAN

"YOU'RE REALLY NOT GOING TO TELL ME WHY YOU'VE BEEN clutching your side every few steps we take?" Emilia stole a look at me from the corner of her eye, and I immediately let my arm fall.

We'd spent hours shopping and strolling down the streets decorated in Christmas finery. From O'Connell to Henry and Grafton. We'd started at the Dublin Castle Christmas Market, where Emilia had lit up nearly as bright as the fairy lights strung throughout the place, as well as covering the hundreds of trees lining the grounds. The look in her eyes as we rode the vintage carousel, a first for her, had been priceless. We sat side by side, and as our horses seesawed up and down and the carousel sailed round and round, I almost felt like I was inside some holiday movie where the ending was a guaranteed happily-ever-after.

Mistletown Christmas Market had been another success, and we both found a few toys for Braden and Siobhan while there. And I'd convinced Emilia to play some carnival games. Of course, Emilia won a bigger stuffed teddy bear than I did at one of the shooting booths. But we gave our prizes to two random kids before leaving the market, which, judging by the looks on their faces, made their day.

We were at our final stop, Dun Laoghaire Christmas Market. Our shopping bags were packed into the Maserati, and we probably didn't need to buy anything else, but I wanted to take her to one of my favorite places at Christmas. It'd been nice spending a day with Emilia without the weight of The League and our worries hanging over our heads. In fact, I'd made a rule when picking her up: no work talk.

Her friend Roman was looking into Luca's whereabouts over the past few months, presumably while he'd been cooking up a plan against us, so there wasn't much for us to do at the moment but wait for his call. And tomorrow evening, we planned to meet with Sebastian at his club to discuss options.

So, today, we shopped. Acted as though we were two normal people.

But damn, after shopping all day, my body was truly feeling the effects of my session in the ring with Adam that morning.

I'd swallowed a handful of ibuprofen afterward—having learned my lesson ages ago—but the pain was kicking into high gear again, and I was apparently doing a shite job of hiding it. I'd hoped the waning daylight as evening approached would help mask my efforts to lightly massage my side every so often, but Emilia was too observant.

"Tell me what's wrong, and maybe I'll go on that thing with you like you asked." Emilia stopped walking and pointed to that "thing," a Ferris wheel. Not just any Ferris wheel. This one had been featured in the movie *Grease*. Emilia was fearless, but something about the Ferris wheel made her nervous as hell. Maybe it was the idea of not being in control? Or perhaps getting stuck in one of those boxes with me? Probably the latter.

I rubbed my jaw, about the only spot not aching on my bruised body. A minute into our fight, Adam and I had agreed to heed Cole's advice and not mess up our faces so that Ma didn't kill us.

A group of carolers dressed like they'd escaped a scene out of Charles Dickens's *Christmas Carol* stopped near us and began singing *O Come All Ye Faithful.* We gave them our attention, and I was grateful for the chance to stand still for a few minutes and buy myself time before answering Emilia.

We applauded the group, a mix of ages, but once they were gone, Emilia's gaze turned back on me. The woman had a wicked *Don't bullshite me* look on her face.

And that only made me want to play around that much more. "I'm just full from all the hot chocolate, pints of beer, and sweets you've been pushing me to eat all day. Got a cramp," I joked and clutched my stomach. "Gonna lose this amazing figure I've worked so hard to get."

When Emilia playfully slapped my chest, I made a show of twisting my face into a wince, doubled over theatrically, and cried out, *Ouch,* as though she had indeed hurt me. Which she damn well had. Kudos to me for calling up my brief acting career at school to turn the tables—act as though I was in pain to hide the fact I *was* in pain.

The smell of roasted chestnuts wafted through the air, another Christmastime favorite of mine. I was shocked when Emilia admitted she'd never tried them. And even though I'd love to see her reaction—in my experience, people either loved them or despised them, no in-between—I really was too full to eat another bite of food today.

Before I had a chance to convince her to try the chestnuts,

she crooked a finger, beckoning me closer. "Out with it, McGregor. I want the truth."

I gave in with a caveman-like grunt of protest and dropped my shoulders in defeat. "Adam and I went a few rounds inside the ring this morning." With the truth out there, I clutched where she'd poked my chest and rubbed.

"You've sparred before," she said casually, not convinced. "You don't normally walk away as if you'd been in a car accident."

"We treated it like an actual fight. But at Cole's insistence, no screwing up our faces. Body shots only." Although, I did get in one blow to his cheek before we made up our minds not to piss off Ma.

"You're really hurt." She frowned and scanned my body as if the woman could see beneath my jacket. "He shouldn't have been that hard on you."

I smirked. "Oh, you assume I got my arse handed to me, do ya?"

There was mischief in her eyes when Emilia pursed her lips, crossed her arms in a haughty stance, and said, "You didn't?" Good God, this woman turned me on. Even bundled up in a black wool coat, she pulled off chic and sexy.

"Believe it or not, we ended in a decision. Sebastian was pissed at the both of us, more so at me, so he chose Adam. Cole went with me. So, it was a tie." I held a black-gloved palm up. "Before you make the assumption, he didn't take it easy on me."

"Based on the way you've been holding your ribs, it appears not." Her curt, almost satisfied-looking nod had me smiling wider. "Glad to see your training is paying off."

I slapped my palms together. "So, Ferris wheel, then?" Or chestnuts first? Decisions, decisions.

Noticing a shiver that she tried to hide, I reached for her

and guided her to one of the firepits nearby, where a few kids roasted marshmallows. The air was cooler than normal, even for this time of year, plus we'd been outside for most of the day.

"I'm fine." But the stubborn woman held her gloved hands above the flickering flame and that small victory had me feeling triumphant.

I couldn't take my eyes off her. Emilia took gorgeous to an all-new level. Black spandex paired with dark knee-high boots, a bright red turtleneck beneath her coat, with her long, wavy hair down and ruby studs in her ears. And when she turned toward me, her cheeks flushed from the heat of the fire, her deep brown eyes colliding with mine, I just wanted to sweep my tongue along her plump bottom lip and lick away the gloss.

"I think I have a better idea," she said a moment later when her attention caught on something beyond my shoulder. Before I could say a word, she headed in that direction.

I followed her, still not quite sure where she was leading us, but she was clearly claiming the victory now.

We moved alongside busy vendors dealing with the rush of last-minute holiday shoppers as she led me to our destination.

"We had a deal. Ferris wheel," I insisted as we passed a couple, arm in arm, gazing at each other all lovey-dovey. A sudden punch of jealousy struck me at the sight, and I had to push it aside because I was too sore for any more blows.

But damn, they looked like a normal couple, free to live normal lives. And . . .

Did I want to be normal? Ordinary?

I glimpsed at Emilia, her long hair gently swaying as she walked in front of me. *No, I want extraordinary.*

Emilia shot me a look from over her shoulder, her bright

smile like a spotlight on my soul. That smile made me forget Luca, and Bridgette, and all the others. They were all history in my mind. "Mm. Make me."

Oh, if we weren't in the thick of a crowd right now, I certainly would make her. I'd put her over my shoulder and carry her to the Ferris wheel, even slap her arse a few times as we walked.

The woman wouldn't kill me for it.

Probably not.

Maybe a little.

"How about this?" She stopped in front of a booth made to look like Santa's workshop and pointed to a desk set up for writing letters to Santa. There was even a little red and white post box in which to "mail" the letters.

"Write Santa a letter or take a romantic ride on a Ferris wheel?" I closed one eye as if the decision were a hard one. "Shite, that's a tough choice. Not on your nelly will I be swapping—"

"Not on my what?" She laughed and shook her head.

I hadn't seen this woman so light and carefree in . . . maybe ever.

We hadn't discussed The League, Luca, or The Alliance once. It'd been a grand day. More than just grand. Pure bliss. Seeing her happy, her eyes sparkling like this, made me wish to relive this day over and over again. Even if it meant getting the shite knocked out of me by Adam every morning.

"Why are you smiling?" She strode closer, grabbed hold of the lapels of my jacket and tilted her chin up to meet my eyes.

I was on the verge of stealing a kiss, the only thing we hadn't done today that would have made it that much more perfect. But she really would kill me if I attempted any PDA. "Just looking at you."

Her eyes teasingly narrowed with suspicion, letting me know she was onto me and my wicked thoughts.

Oh yeah, my thoughts were getting naughtier by the minute. Emilia in sheer white lingerie. A semi see-through bra with lacy snowflakes covering her nipples to make for a little peep show before the bra came off. It would be like unwrapping a sexy present, and feck if that image didn't get me a little hard.

Emilia's gaze left mine and swiveled to the post box. "My father had me write a letter to Santa when I was growing up. I wrote faithfully every year until I turned twelve."

Her quietly spoken words zipped me back to the present. "What'd you ask for?"

"A mom." She blinked rapidly, appearing stunned she'd answered so candidly.

After that heartbreaking confession, I knew I was about two seconds away from losing the fun and carefree Emilia, and I wasn't ready for her to leave me just yet. "I never wrote to Santa, so let's do it. This can be my first time."

"Really?" She set her bag on the old-fashioned-looking desk and reached for a clipboard that held a blank sheet of green paper, then handed it to me along with a pencil topped with a red Santa hat eraser. "I love first times. I've had so many with you, so . . ." More blinking, then she lowered her eyes and reached for another clipboard.

I knew exactly what I was going to write. I scribbled it down and tucked the paper inside an envelope from a stack lying next to the post box, already addressed to Santa at the North Pole. "Ready?" I asked once she had her red envelope in hand. "Together?"

She nodded, and we stuck our envelopes in the thin rectangular slot at the same time as if magic might really carry our letters to the North Pole and make our dreams come true.

"Adults who write letters to Santa are really wishing for miracles," she said once we were on our way. I hid my gloved hands in my coat pockets, resisting the urge to link our arms or clasp her hand.

"Mistletoe. You have to kiss," someone called out in our direction. Both Emilia and I stopped in our tracks and looked up, carrying our focus to the bunches of mistletoe tied with red ribbons and strung overhead by a street vendor. "Bad luck if you don't."

I gave her my most charming smile in hopes of wiping the indecisive look from her face. A rarity for Emilia.

"We don't want bad luck to cancel out our wishes, do we?" I proposed, lifting my hands from my pockets to capture her waist and draw her closer to me.

"We're in public," she whispered.

"No one aside from a bunch of strangers will see us." I brought a gloved hand to the back of her head.

She reluctantly but surprisingly nodded, so I dipped her back like we were in a romance movie. The Ferris wheel from *Grease* was our backdrop, so it worked.

And somewhere, I overheard those same carolers singing *O Holy Night* as I set a kiss to her mouth. We may have been surrounded by the smell of gingerbread and hot chocolate, but the only scent striking me was Emilia's.

I'd meant for our kiss to be quick, considering we had an audience. But when she lightly moaned in response, I lost myself in her. The kiss deepened, our tongues tangled, and I barely heard the applause erupting around us.

My mind flashed back to our first kiss at the club in Vegas. Then breezed on to the one by the lion statue at the MGM. I could feel those kisses wrapped up in this one, strange as it sounded. A fusion of the moments we'd shared as if signaling the beginning of something else.

I righted her a few seconds later, my lips still lingering close to hers, hungry for more. She kept hold of my eyes, her hands still resting on my chest. Her purse was the barrier between our bodies, preventing us from fully touching.

"*Amore prohibito*," she said, her lips hovering near mine.

I may have failed out of Italian at Trinity, but those words weren't hard to figure out. *Amore* was love. *Prohibito* meant forbidden.

It was either a warning to herself or to me. I wasn't sure. Maybe both.

Nevertheless, I caressed her jaw and slanted my mouth over hers again anyway. And damn, did she respond.

"Oh my," I heard someone say. "It's snowing. Like in a fairy tale."

Emilia and I pulled back at the same time and looked heavenward. Not ready for this moment to end, I tightened my hold of her as a flurry of snowflakes fell around us.

I returned my focus to her face as a single flake caught on the long, dark lashes above her right eye.

My chest grew tight with emotion as I stared into her beautiful eyes. "A fairy tale, indeed."

CHAPTER SIXTEEN

SEAN

"WE SHOULDN'T HAVE KISSED IN PUBLIC," EMILIA SAID AS WE started for the hotel, our hands full of shopping bags.

"Yeah, but it was mistletoe. And who could've possibly seen us?" I retorted.

"You're a McGregor. Practically a celebrity in this city. Any number of people with a mobile could have taken the shot and hashtagged it on Instagram. We could be trending. Couple in love at the Christmas market."

"Couple in love, huh?" I asked once we'd piled the shopping bags and ourselves inside the lift. "Was it that hot of a kiss we'd really light up people's newsfeeds and trend?"

Her mouth parted to protest, but she huffed out a breath instead.

"You plan on telling me what you asked Santa for?" I asked when she didn't say more.

"And are *you* going to tell me what you asked the big guy for?" Was she toying with me, skirting her tongue between her teeth?

"There's a rule, right? It won't happen if we share. Or maybe that's a birthday wish. I can't remember." And

Emilia's birthday was coming up. I needed to shop for that, too. She'd shoot me with an arrow if I celebrated her birthday, but the pain would be worth it if I could somehow produce one of her killer smiles. "So, we don't tell each other unless we get what we asked for. Agreed?" I set the bags down and removed my gloves, shoved them in my pockets, then offered her my hand.

She eyed my palm suspiciously before finally clasping my hand, her black leather glove preventing me from feeling any of her soft skin. I wanted to feel a lot more than her hand, though. And she had to know that. One look in my eyes told that story. "Agreed."

When the doors chimed, she reached for a few of her bags she'd collected while shopping, and I picked up the rest. "You're full of surprises, McGregor," she tossed out before exiting the lift.

I tried to shake off the fact this was the second time she'd called me by my last name today. We may have needed to keep distance between us because of rules and promises, but that not-so-small issue of her fear of commitment . . . well, I just hoped she wasn't attempting to build a new wall to replace the one I was fairly certain our time together had begun to knock down.

Once in the hotel room, Emilia removed her gloves and coat, then sat on the stool at the breakfast counter and removed her boots, leaving her in only the spandex and red turtleneck. So breathtaking. "I'm worried. Still no update from Roman on Luca. The idea Luca's pulling our strings infuriates me."

That idea is also why I look like my brother took a bat to my ribs. Luca was a bloody mood killer.

And now that she officially brought up work, it had me

remembering Cole's words before we started sparring. Well, before Adam and I knocked the shite out of each other.

The German is being transferred to a League prison for interrogation. We can't get him to talk. I'm sorry, Cole had quickly announced in the locker room before joining the others. I'd chalked up his hurried statement and quick exit to him being angry at himself for not getting anything out of the guy.

"I assume Cole or Sebastian updated you on that German guy."

Emilia visibly tensed. "You mean that he's being transferred to a League prison since he won't talk?"

I nodded. "Maybe you should have spoken to him. You're good at getting people to open up." *You're just not great at opening up about yourself.*

Her face fell. And hell, she was looking at me with the same sad eyes as Cole had this morning. "Something wrong?"

"No." She scrunched her brow. "But you're right, I should have questioned him, but he's already in transit now. Too bad no one has gone for the money yet," she said, then nearly gave me whiplash with a subject change by adding, "Anyway, I'm hoping to hear from Roman soon."

"Didn't Roman say his girlfriend—"

"Harper's not his girlfriend," she interrupted. "He's got issues like me."

I blinked in surprise at her shocking and out-of-nowhere confession, and her eyes widened as if she couldn't believe what she'd just said. "What kind of issues?" *Emotional? Fear of intimacy? Commitment?* I could keep going with the running list I'd been compiling in my head, but I'd prefer to hear her answer.

"I didn't mean . . ."

To say that?

"But yes, Roman said Harper is designing some special software program that will be able to triangulate Luca's previous whereabouts using data from the tracker"—Emilia sped right ahead into business-mode—"when he was apparently without it and in disguise," she said as if her confession hadn't shaken the room.

"Sounds technical and impossible." I frowned. "But after seeing Harper's cyber magic in October, I'm confident she'll come through for us."

"Right." Standing again, her eyes worked over me. Starting at my chest and then sliding down to my trousers. "Show me."

"Show you what?" This time, I was certain she was purposely trying to give me whiplash. My palm went to the breakfast counter as I stood in front of her, and I'd swear this unflappable woman was growing flustered before my eyes.

"The damage. I want to see where it hurts."

In my heart mostly. "Everywhere. But don't worry, if you're thinking about a repeat of Scotland, I can handle the pain." And I just couldn't help myself. After the fun and playful day we'd had, why not?

She brought her hands to the buttons of my shirt and began working them free. "I have some cream that will help. A special blend from Tibet."

I snatched her wrist and stopped her from inspecting the bruises on my sides once my shirt was open. Those lips of hers were still glossy despite our passionate mistletoe kiss.

I wanted the arsehole Luca out of my head, and only this woman in my mind.

"A bath, then? It should relax your body. I'll run you one." The woman was stubborn, nothing new, but I wouldn't object to getting naked in her bath, so I nodded and followed her into the bedroom.

"You joining me?" I asked while discarding everything except for my boxers. Not that the thin material could hide the hard-on I was sporting at the sight of Emilia bent over the tub, the black stretch material showing off her incredible assets. "It's big enough for the two of us."

She righted herself as the water ran, added some lavender-scented bubbles, and studied me. "What do you think, McGregor?"

I closed the space between us and circled her waist. "Why do you keep calling me that?"

"It's your name." A defiant lift of her chin had me wanting to tease my lips along her neck before taking her lower lip between my teeth and lightly biting.

"Using my surname won't make you feel less for me, you know that, right?" I pushed back while guiding one hand up her silhouette to her cheek. "No one can see us here." Her body was tense, a rigid and defensive line. She was keeping something from me. Maybe something new. I could feel it. But knowing this woman, she wouldn't share until she was damn good and ready. If ever.

"I'll get in with you," was all she said before sidestepping my touch.

Tossing aside my boxers, I stepped into the water and did my best to act like a man and not yank my foot out at the feel of the heat shocking my body.

I sank into the Jacuzzi-style tub, and bubbles began rising over me, hiding my body. I bent my knees and set my hands on the edges of the tub, watching Emilia go through the motions of stripping. I did my best not to allow my gaze to lock on to the scar by her breast when she faced me.

But my fingers curled inward on reflex. Too bad the arsehole from South America was already dead.

"How does the water feel?" she asked while striding naked toward the tub.

"Good," I managed to croak out while all my blood rushed south.

Those dark, luminous eyes of hers peering at me with what I wanted to believe was longing was all it took for me to lose control. I sat up and reached out to secure my hands around her hips. "Get in here," I commanded, not giving two fecks about my bruises. The sight of her naked body had all worries about what she might be keeping from me fleeing my mind.

Emilia joined me in the water and nestled herself between my legs, her back to my chest. When she pressed her arse against my cock and turned her head, I couldn't resist pressing my lips to the soft, warm skin of her cheek, now slightly flushed. She sighed and angled her head back farther, offering me her mouth, delivering what felt like sweet surrender.

But sweet wouldn't last long. My hunger for her had been boiling all day. The Irish were known for boiling everything, and bloody hell, my desire had been simmering for too long.

"Sean," she moaned. *Sean*, not McGregor. Good.

I cupped her breast, dragging suds over her hard nipple, and my other hand ran between her legs to part her sex as I deepened our kiss. Still soft, languorous pecks. Teases of her tongue into my mouth every so often but never fully giving it to me.

The dull, achy throb that existed in my chest was a distant memory with her this close.

My warm breath hit the shell of her ear as I told her she was beautiful in English and then in Italian, "*Sei bellissima.*"

My mouth joined hers again as I pushed one, then two fingers inside her tight pussy. Each thrust of my hand had her clenching around my fingers and moaning against my lips.

"How is it you have no tan lines?" I asked when she shimmied on my lap a few moments later, our mouths breaking apart.

The jet streams vibrated against my skin, little massages on my back as I held her.

She began to shift around, so I withdrew my fingers, and she carefully straddled me. "I sunbathe in the nude on my terrace back home."

The idea of her guards possibly seeing her made me crazy, but I ignored the thought because Emilia was mine. Well, right now for the holidays, but maybe . . .

"Does this hurt?" She swept her fingers over my skin where bruises were slowly beginning to show up. My muscles jumped at her touch, and I couldn't help but wince in pain. But with her sitting on top of me like this, all I could think about was repositioning my body and slamming my cock inside her.

"I'm good. How's your side?" I asked, realizing her bandage was gone.

"Don't worry about me." She set her palms on top of my pecs and lightly scraped her short nails down my chest, one of the few places missed by Adam's right hook.

"Not possible," I answered honestly and leaned closer to capture her lips. I wanted to bury myself balls-deep inside her. Have my thoughts forever painted with sounds of her whimpers and cries in ecstasy as she writhed, grinding against my cock. As if reading my thoughts, she placed her hands on my shoulders and lifted her hips. "Can I—?"

"Please." She reached between us, set my tip to her

center, and sank onto me, her mouth a rounded O from the movement.

Emilia moved slowly. Considerate of my injuries even though I didn't give a shite about them. "Harder," I told her, holding her one hip, my hand nearly slipping on her sudsy skin.

I palmed her cheek with my free hand and kissed her again as she shifted up and down on my cock, the water splashing violently out of the tub. She'd been tight at first from being in the water, but her desire had slicked her sex, and I was fighting to hang on as she rode me.

"Sean, oh yes." Her words echoed in my ears as I stretched her tight walls, feeling them close around my stiff cock. I resisted the impulse to groan and close my eyes, not wanting to lose sight of this woman.

Her back bowed and her soapy tits lifted, and my jaw tightened as I bit down on my back teeth. I brought my palms to her breasts and swept the pads of my thumbs over her tight nipples, giving them a pinch that had her throwing her head back in ecstasy.

A few minutes later, she stilled her hips and leaned forward to catch my gaze, and I was struck by the emotion in those big, brown eyes of hers. I'd swear she looked at me as if she could see past my flaws but managed to love me anyway.

Fuck. No amore. She didn't love me.

But I'd pretend for tonight. Because I knew what I felt for her was *amore* all the way. Maybe it wasn't an obsession. It was love. And twenty months of pretending it was anything else was absurd.

CHAPTER SEVENTEEN

SEAN

"The room and your flat are secure, sir."

"Good. Thank you." I ended the call and pocketed my mobile. Emilia and I had discreetly sent in a League team to sweep her hotel suite, as well as my flat, to do a thorough check for any listening devices, malware in our computers, and so forth. We couldn't be too careful with Luca out there scheming.

I set a palm to the glass, looking out at the busy club Sebastian and Alessia owned. I was on the second level in a private, soundproof room. The wall of glass offered me a view, but no one down below could see me.

There was a Christmas party theme happening tonight, and the dancers were all in red and green. The DJ dressed like Santa kept throwing out candy canes to the crowd, and the bar had "Nice" and "Naughty" signs posted on either end.

Two years ago, I would have been down on that floor, pulling a scantily clad blonde into my arms to dance. Take her back to her place and ride her like a racehorse. Then slip out after without remembering her name. Without ever thinking about her again.

Now, I wanted what Adam and Anna had. They weren't at the club tonight. Instead, they were comfortable on their couch at home watching a marathon of holiday movies at Anna's insistence while their son slept.

I'd rather be on a couch, with my wife in my arms, my child asleep, than at a club. And I would give anything for that woman to be Emilia.

"Brought you something stiff. Thought you might need it."

I turned at the sound of my sister's voice and thanked her for the scotch. I did need something strong. The special Tibetan cream Emilia had provided me for my bruises had helped, but the scotch would hopefully help me with the anger. I'd managed to push thoughts of Luca out of my head while Emilia and I shopped yesterday and made love after. But we were without new leads, and I was growing beyond edgy.

"The others will be up soon. Just waiting on Emilia to finish her call." Holly joined me at the window to view the crowd.

Emilia was talking to her friend Roman in Alessia's office, looking for an update on our Luca problem.

"Still radio silence on the listening devices?" Holly didn't normally involve herself in League business, so I wasn't expecting her to bring that up.

I set my free hand into my pocket while stealing a sip of the scotch, and that quick sip turned into me throwing back the entire drink. "Bridgette must be using a new purse instead of the one she normally carries. The signal from the tracker shows it hasn't left her home since she arrived back in Germany on Sunday. I'm getting the feeling that's Luca's doing. He probably followed us or predicted our next move would be to target Bridgette in Scotland."

"Knowing Luca, I'm surprised Bridgette didn't keep using that purse to feed you fake intel. Let you believe her conversations with her husband were legitimate to throw you off even more." Her brow tightened as if mulling over her words. "Maybe Luca knew you guys would be able to see through it. Who knows with that crazy son of a bitch?"

"I feel like we're at square fecking one," I admitted and set the glass on the table in front of the lone leather couch in the small space.

"He's a psychopath," Holly murmured, "which makes it hard to predict his next moves or know his endgame."

I went back to the window and set a hand to the glass, my gaze immediately settled on Emilia, who was entering the main floor of the club from the back hallway. My breath froze at the sight of her in a red sequin wrap dress with a plunging neckline so deep that I wondered what kind of magic she used to keep her breasts from tumbling out. Then again, her tits were magical, so I shouldn't have been surprised.

I'd seen her in the dress earlier that evening. In fact, I'd shoved it up to her waist, dropped to my knees just inside the hotel room, and sucked her sweet pussy before we came here tonight. And yet, my breath was still gone at the sight of her striding through the club. A powerhouse of a woman moving like she owned it, and she drew every straight man's eyes, but she intimidated the hell out of them.

Emilia lifted her gaze to the window. She couldn't see me, but she knew I was there, and I was certain by the way my pulse jumped she knew I was watching her. She stopped to talk to Alessia, who had come around from the bar, and I focused back on my sister. She was in a similar dress to Emilia but in green.

I hadn't felt as festive today and went for all black instead: black trousers, black button-down, black belt.

I'd suggested Emilia use my belt to stifle her moans earlier today, to keep my younger brother from hearing her with his bedroom right up against hers. But Emilia flipped the script and fucked me even harder.

Hearing him and Sara having sex should have been a mood killer. Ethan's loud grunts and Sara's yelling out how "godly" my brother's cock was should have been like a bucket of cold water. But I was too far gone to care, and Emilia kept on riding my dick like it was her job and more than likely gave them something to listen to as well.

How we even heard them in the first place, I'll never know. A headboard, sure. But you'd think that a swanky hotel would have been designed so that the master bedrooms of neighboring suites didn't share a wall. I couldn't even give Sebastian shite for it since he'd bought the hotel after it'd been built.

"So." I smiled at my sister. "Know any psychopaths I could go to for some advice on how to better understand Luca?" I was only partially teasing.

"Sebastian has been particularly broody today. Maybe he can help." She scowled.

"He's always broody."

"Not with me." She sucked her lip between her teeth. "I made a decision. Tell me if I'm wrong, okay?" Her eyes focused on mine, a plea there. But I wasn't sure if she wanted me to agree or disagree with her. "I know what I'm giving Sebastian for Christmas."

"If it involves sex, please spare me the details." I rolled my eyes. "Will it make him less moody, yeah, but—"

"Killing. I'm going to tell him it's okay."

My head jerked back in surprise. "You're giving the gift of killing, huh? That's, uh, special." I shot her a puzzled expression and made it overly dramatic.

"You know what I mean." She slapped my chest, managing to miraculously miss one of my bruises. "I want him to do what he needs to do to stay safe and keep people safe without feeling guilty anymore. No more angry make-up sex needed." Her lips twitched. "Well, for that reason, at least."

"Never thought I'd have this kind of conversation with my sister, but yeah, I think you're doing the right thing. He's out of sorts about it."

Her shoulders fell with guilt. "So, what are you getting Emilia?"

"Still working on it. I might sneak out tomorrow or before we do the Twelve Pubs of Christmas thing on Thursday." What do you get a woman who has everything but the one thing she keeps rejecting—her own happiness?

I spotted Alessia and Emilia walking up the stairs with Cole and Sebastian right behind them. Protective, even though they didn't need to be.

"Do you think it's wrong we're keeping the truth from Ethan?" Holly asked softly.

"Yes," I blurted, turning my focus back on her. "But I'm worried the more he knows, the more danger he'll be in. And we still don't know to what extent Sara is involved. Is Luca forcing her to help him? Is she voluntarily doing it? Or is she totally clueless and a pawn in his game?" I shook my head. "Or that cocksucker could have put her in our path just to throw us off. A red herring. When it comes to that man—"

"Anything is possible," Holly finished for me.

"Started the meeting without us, I see," Sebastian said, and Holly and I faced him and the others filtering into the room. He shut the door behind them and went to stand by his wife. "You want to stay or go?"

"Stay," Holly said with a firm nod, one that seemed to

surprise Sebastian.

Emilia sat on the couch next to Cole and Alessia. I felt her eyes on me, but damn it, I couldn't seem to rip my focus off her crossed legs. To stop thinking about how heavenly her pussy tasted. She always came so hard for my tongue, and I loved it.

"Ahem," Emilia admonished, slightly clearing her throat to draw my attention.

I slowly worked my eyes up to her face, probably a dark, lust-driven smile on my lips reflecting the thoughts swirling around in my head, all of which involved Emilia naked and none of which included discussing Luca.

"What'd Roman have to say?" I asked, still unable to wipe away my naughty smirk. I also needed to find a way to adjust my crotch without my family noticing.

Emilia swept her tongue between her lips like a tease, slowly uncrossed her legs, and parted her knees ever so slightly. Oh, she knew what she was doing to me, but I kind of loved the fact we both were kicking thoughts of Luca to the curb in favor of more lustful ones.

"You two need a room?" I looked to my cousin who'd spoken, a devil of a smile on his face. The fecker.

"We're in one, thanks." Emilia didn't miss a beat. "And no updates from Roman. We need to be patient. Luca is a master at fooling cameras, so we're lucky to have Roman's assist to even track down what he's been up to."

"No complaining. Appreciative," Cole noted with a nod, then directed his focus to me. "But we do need to address the elephant in the room, and I'm not talking about that bulge you got in your trousers."

"Cole." Alessia playfully smacked her husband's arm and blushed. Oh, I'd be going against my cousin in the ring after my body recovered. I cocked my head, turned to the side, and adjusted myself, to hell with everyone in the room. When facing them again, I glanced at my sister to find her fighting a laugh. They were all loving this pain I was in, so it seemed.

"You talk to Luca's uncle? You know Luca better than anyone. What is Luca up to?" I asked Sebastian, hoping to get back on the right track and pull my head out from between Emilia's legs where my mind had taken it.

Sebastian set his back to the window and deposited his hands into his pockets. "Luca has always wanted the power he feels he was denied. He also knows if he doesn't provide us with credible and valuable intel, he's done. I think he's feeding us enough information to keep himself alive while he plots a way to take a leadership position to try and safeguard himself from death."

"No way does The League let him back in," Cole hissed.

Sebastian's jaw clenched. "I'm not talking about The League."

My dick was officially down. "He's making a play for an Alliance position, and he's going to deliver us to get it?" I spoke my theory aloud as it came to me.

"They don't operate that way." Sebastian's gaze took a slow tour around the room before landing on Emilia last.

"Oh my God." Emilia abruptly rose to her feet. A hand banding over her abdomen. "That's it." Emilia circled the table and stood before us, her gaze moving back and forth. "Luca knows us, knows how we operate. He calculatingly pointed our focus onto Atlas. We discovered Bridgette's affair, and he fed us Atlas's travel dates to confirm the affair without actually telling us about it. He knew exactly what we'd do. If Luca's working with Peter, it's possible he promised Peter a way to deal with both Atlas and The League. Help Peter become the most powerful Alliance leader."

"And in return, Luca earns himself a high-level position, possibly assuming control of France. And France has always been the country Luca wanted when in The League," Sebastian added on.

I balled my hands into fists and slammed them into the window, which had it vibrating. I ignored the pain since my hand was already achy from the fight with Adam yesterday morning.

"Somehow, Sara is Luca's avenue to try and take us down. He's even got her under League protection. That attack was most likely fake. He expected Ethan to show that night and then call me for help." How could I let Sara share a bed with my brother knowing this? Well, it was still a theory but a damn good one. I needed facts first. Proof, I reminded myself. Ethan was blinded by his feelings for her, and he'd only hate me if I suggested a hint of the truth without anything to back it up.

How the hell were we supposed to resume our holiday fun knowing this?

My spine straightened at the realization that we actually could, and quite easily.

We knew the bastard's plan. And he didn't know we knew, which meant we could finally have the upper hand.

A slow smirk touched my lips. "The plan needs to be changed, but I say we take this son of a bitch down in Monaco," I said in a low, deep voice. "It ends there." I looked to my cousin and then on to everyone before meeting Emilia's eyes. This holiday might be the only time I had with Emilia. I refused to let Luca take that from me. "Luca may have thrown us a curveball or two"—I stared deep into Emilia's brown eyes—"but this fecker is not going to ruin our Christmas."

CHAPTER EIGHTEEN

EMILIA

"Damn him." I switched the mobile to FaceTime and leaned it against the glass mirror above the vanity in the bathroom so Roman could see why I was cursing. "Look what he sent me to wear tonight."

Roman cupped a hand over his mouth. "It's, uh, not that bad." His mumbled words had me rolling my eyes.

"Hiding the quiver of your lip won't erase the smile I can hear in your voice." I shook my head and glared at the hideous green V-neck jumper staring back at me from the mirror's reflection. "I look like a gaudy Christmas tree." I flicked one of the little red balls hanging beneath a swag of glittery gold garland. One row of garland would have been bad enough, but there were four of the dreadful things cutting across the front, each one embellished with little red and green balls that swung when I moved. *Let's just see how a certain someone likes blue balls instead of red and green.* But the *pièce de résistance* were the five gold jingle bells representing buttons that ran down the middle. Great. Everyone within a kilometer would hear me approaching like

I was a damn cow. "Guess he chose this one because he knew he'd get an eyeful of my boobs."

I momentarily shifted the camera so Roman wouldn't see me shoving and adjusting my bra from the outside of my jumper, trying to keep my breasts from escaping the deep V-neck of the ridiculous thing.

"There's some statistic out there about Christmas sweaters being the key to happiness. Look it up."

"You may be the smartest guy I know, but you're full of shit on that one." And Roman really did have a genius-level IQ. In fact, he was almost too smart. His superior reasoning ability was most likely the culprit in preventing him from pursuing the woman I knew he was in love with. The dangers of overthinking. I knew all about that.

Roman was one of the few people I let my guard down around, and it was nice having him in my corner. He wasn't quite as broody as Sebastian, but he had his moments.

I snatched the phone and went into my bedroom, holding it at arm's length to peer at him. Sean would be here soon to pick me up, and then I'd have my chance to flip him to his back as punishment for this jumper. Of course, the idea of straddling him and taking him on the floor, riding the hell out of him before we went out tonight sounded rather appealing.

It was hard to believe tomorrow was Christmas Eve. The week had flown by. We'd been wrapped up in holiday activities with his family, and we'd spent every free moment having sex.

Sean convinced everyone at the club Tuesday night to carry on with our lives this week despite what we guessed was Luca's plan. We had League members doing the legwork and the preparations for Monaco. And we had eyes on Luca every second of the day.

So, Sean won. We chose not to let Luca ruin Christmas.

Plus, Sean took every opportunity to distract me by using his tongue and his impressive cock to get me off, which had done wonders for my psyche as well.

He was right, though. This week was our chance to experience a little semblance of normalcy, a normal I was chasing like an elusive dream because I knew what Sean and I had would come to an end soon. This relationship had an expiration date that was fast approaching.

He was a strong man, but he wasn't raised to be a warrior like me. He didn't have a steel cage around his heart to keep it from breaking. So, it was important I still tried to maintain some sort of distance between us, which I'd done by slipping out of his bed every night and even slipping out of my own bed when he fell asleep at the hotel this week. The only time I'd allowed myself to sleep in his arms was in Scotland. I couldn't bring myself to do it again.

But no matter how much sex we had, how many times he brought me to climax, I couldn't get enough of him. I only wanted more. More of everything he had to give to me in our short time together.

I frowned, my stomach hurting at the idea things would truly end between us. Luca aside, this week had been magical with him.

The only hard part was plastering on a fake smile whenever Sara was around. We'd decided to hold off on interrogating her for information like I wanted to do. For one, her disappearance would tip off Luca we were onto him, and also, Sean had a soft spot for his kid brother. He didn't want to devastate him before Christmas, especially without proof. But Sean had to know Ethan would be out for blood, all of ours, when he learned we'd kept the truth from him.

I gulped at the realization Sean might feel the same toward me, Cole, and Sebastian when he learned we'd lied about the German thug. I needed to be straight with Sean soon, didn't I? We agreed not to tell him that the German had died until after the holidays. But we hadn't defined which holiday—Christmas or New Year's. I was hoping for the latter.

"Emilia? Where are you?" Roman snapped his fingers in front of the screen and set his back to the dark green wall. "I lost you for a second. But hey, I thought you called for an update, not to complain about your holiday getup."

"Ah, snarky on me tonight, aren't you? That's new," I teased. "Well, we've talked every day this week, and you've yet to discover Luca's evil plan, so I'm assuming you're about to let me down again?"

"Well, damn," he said around a chuckle. "Tell me how you really feel."

"I trust Harper's computer program is working overtime to figure out this problem. Which is mine, by the way, and not yours, but—"

"Bad guys are bad guys, Emilia. You don't own them. They're our problem as much as yours." Roman was pretty straightforward, which I respected.

"You on your childhood bed?" I asked, deflecting his question once again.

"The only room where I can escape my sisters." He smirked, his white teeth showing.

"Not spending Christmas with your friends this year? Harper?" I shouldn't push him because what if he pressed about Sean? But this jumper had me acting a fool already.

His shoulders lifted and fell with a deep, drawn-out sigh. That wasn't a good sign.

"Did you make it clear to Harper that you and I are only friends?" And there I went again. Two for two. "I saw the way she looked at me at my place in October. We've known each other since—"

"I saved you from some creepy assassins who dropped down out of the sky at that wedding years ago," he cut me off because, of course, he'd rather talk about that than Harper.

"By the way, you got Sebastian in a lot of trouble with his wife," I scolded, but in this jumper, I probably didn't come across all that serious.

"Bad guys don't count." He lifted his shoulders as if that were answer enough.

"Not everyone feels that way. Besides, what you do is nowhere near what we do. You're military."

He worked his jaw a little as if he wanted to say more but wasn't capable of getting "more" out. I could relate.

"Roman."

"Emilia," he countered in a dramatic voice like a big brother would respond if I'd been lucky enough to have one. He could be my adopted brother, like Sebastian, I supposed.

"How's Sean? Break his heart yet?" And I had that coming.

Roman's brows rose, warning me to quit while I was ahead and not poke the bear.

"Wait, aren't we supposed to be talking about what you *didn't* find out yet?"

"You're making the assumption today was another unsuccessful day."

"Yeah, because you wouldn't have been sitting on your thumbs waiting for me to call if you had some intel."

He laughed. "Touché, but I should have something for you soon. Luca isn't stupid enough to use the same disguise every time he removed his tracker and traveled without wanting you to know about it."

"I know, but you also promised me you have the best

cyber minds in the world working with you," I jested, reminding him of our last call, and the one before that, and so on. In all fairness, I'd asked my contacts at MI6 to help, and they were coming up empty, too. "I really appreciate all your help. You know that, right?"

"Hey, we pretty much got your castle in Sicily blown to hell in October, so we owe you. Plus—"

"Bad guys are bad guys," I repeated his earlier words. "And it's not a castle."

"Harper's tinkering with her program as we speak. Adding more data to the algorithm to give the software an assist in recognizing Luca and seeing beyond his disguises so we can find where he went when he was without his tracker."

My shoulders sagged with guilt. "You know what, enjoy your holiday." That's what we were all trying to do here, so why shouldn't he? "Tell Harper to do the same. We can regroup after Christmas."

"Harper's program will still be working even if we're not behind a laptop." He tipped his chin. "And maybe take your own advice and relax for the holidays."

"Have you seen me?" I pointed to my jumper. "I'm wearing a Christmas tree. You can't get more holiday spirit than that." I gave him a nod and said, "Okay, so we're agreed. Don't call me until after Christmas. You still think your team can make it over for an assist during the final takedown? I originally thought you could help virtually, but I think I need extra boots on the ground. People I can trust without question. Our plan also requires the assistance of someone with better cyber skills than mine."

"You sure you still want our help? I mean, it's taking us soooo long," he joked.

I shook my head and laughed. "Of course. We need all the

help we can get. We have people set up all over the world, but I'd like you by my side if possible."

"You know I'll be there," he said with a tight nod. "Well, as long as I'm not jumping out of a plane or hiking through a jungle hunting down some other bad guy," he added in a serious tone.

"In that case, can you pencil me in for New Year's Eve? Maybe New Year's Day, too?"

"See, I can't tell if you're kidding or not." He smiled.

"Regardless of any intel you find, we're going to make a play in Monaco." I paused. "Just think about it. Talk to your people. Sean is going to be here any second, though. I should get going." I left the bedroom, walking with the mobile held out in front of me.

"Have fun. Oh, and before I forget, did you get the care package I overnighted you?"

I went into the kitchen and eyed the open box on the counter. "Your definition of care package could use some work." I poked around the bubble wrap to look at the electronics.

"You rather I send you chocolate and fuzzy socks?"

I picked up one of the small black electronic boxes and examined it with my free hand. "No, these spy gadgets are more my speed. But I do have my own. We just had the place swept for bugs, so you didn't need to go to the trouble. I have contacts at MI6 who provide me with the latest and greatest."

He guffawed. "Yeah, our stuff will make theirs look like it's from the Stone Age. Those black boxes I sent you can pick up any and all signals. If it's streaming a signal or connected to Wi-Fi, no matter how great their tech is, you'll pick up on it."

I frowned and set one of the small squares back inside the box. I'd position them around my hotel room later. Maybe

Sean's flat, too. Then we wouldn't need to have my place checked for spyware and listening devices as frequently as we were.

We couldn't be too careful, I supposed. I had my own countermeasures to prevent anyone from monitoring my conversations, but Roman was right. Their tech was probably superior to what MI6 gave me. "Thank you. And, Roman, have a merry Christmas. I hope you get everything you wished for."

"Not possible," he replied in a low voice, his light mood quickly changing, "but you too." He ended the call, and I tucked the burner into my purse and went to the door.

I mentally prepared myself for the smirk on Sean's face when he saw me in this jumper, then swung open the door.

But it was me that nearly died laughing instead.

Sean opened his palms. "What?"

He had on a red jumper with an upside-down snowman on the front. But the icing on the cake was the orange carrot nose poking straight out from the jumper and strategically located close to the bottom, with two green balls hanging beneath it. "Not blue balls, huh?"

He stepped forward and pulled me into an embrace like I was his. Like I'd always belonged to him and always would. "You took care of that for me this week," he said in a teasing tone before sweeping an index finger from my collarbone down to my cleavage.

"They might go back to that color since you're making me wear this hideous thing," I teased.

"Are you kidding? You look phenomenal." His husky tone was hypnotizing as he dragged his palm back up until I lost sight of his hand. He tugged at my hair, fisting it into a ponytail to pull me in for a heated kiss as he walked me backward and into the hotel room.

The door swiftly shut, and he gently took hold of either side of the V at the neck of the jumper and pulled the sides down my arms. "Maybe I'll be turning blue after all. Thinking about you in this white lacy bra while we're out all night," he said after exposing my bra and seeing the surprise I'd picked out earlier at a store. Not Sara's place, of course.

His thumb dipped beneath the cup of my bra and teased my nipple, which had my sex thrumming with excitement.

When I stepped out of his reach and cupped both my breasts, he brought a hand over his trousers, along the hard ridge of his erection as he observed me.

Starting at the tall, black boots I was wearing with my black skinny jeans, his eyes slowly climbed up my body to my hands covering my breasts.

"All good things come to those who wait." I seductively wet my lips. "Also, payback for this jumper." I winked and fixed my jumper back in place. Sean groaned and kept a hand to his crotch.

"And . . . blue." He quickly captured my waist and brought me flush with his chest. Hands on my body. Lips tight to my mouth. Desire pouring out of the both of us and mingling in the air. "You're mine later." He slapped my ass while still holding on to me, and it took all my strength not to rip his jumper over his head and go down on him. Alleviate the pain between his legs so then he'd help me release the tension between mine.

"I talked to Roman. Still no updates. And silence continues to be the theme on the listening devices." *And oh, by the way, the German died. Internal bleeding.* But I kept that update to myself.

Sean loosened his grip on me. His lust dialing down at the mention of work but not enough to send the message to his hard length still pressed to my body.

"That means we can keep enjoying the holidays, I suppose. Reality can wait." He brought his mouth to my ear. "So, you think you're ready for this night?"

His warm breath tickled my ear and sent shivers over my skin—every part of me pebbling, including my nipples. I looked into his eyes and hooked my arms behind his neck. "I can handle almost anything you throw at me." *Just not love.* I couldn't handle that.

Sean gently released me, and I was certain he was reading my thoughts. He remained quiet as we made our way to the street. We weren't taking our cars since we'd be getting drunk, and the pubs were only a short walk away.

His Maserati probably still smelled like sex. We'd had brunch at his parents' house with everyone earlier, and he'd pulled off the road a few kilometers away after we'd left, unable to wait until we reached the hotel or his flat.

The car hadn't been designed for sex, but somehow, we made it work. That red leather interior had matched my dress, and he had the seat heaters on, so it'd been warm against my skin when he fully reclined the passenger seat and climbed on top of me.

Thinking about those strong hands firmly on my thighs as he shoved with purposeful intent the material of my dress up my legs, shifted my panties aside to bury himself inside me . . .

Yeah, it was probably a good thing we were walking. Ugly Christmas jumper or not, I was in the mood for him to ravage me again. To make me feel things that went beyond the physical I'd never known existed before him.

"I'm going to miss us," I confessed, halting on the footpath at the realization of what I'd said.

He stilled, too.

But I didn't look at him, so I had no idea if he was eyeing me or stroking that new beard he was growing.

I cleared my throat, attempting to also somehow clear the air. The crisp, December air.

I started to move, but Sean reached for my wrist and hurriedly guided me to an alley between two buildings.

He had my back to the brick wall within seconds. Palms over my shoulders as he leaned into me, pinning me with his gaze.

"McGregor," I whispered, my defenses flimsy and full of shit.

"Shhh," he commanded, and I was too weak with those vivid blues of his pointed at me not to obey.

His mouth brushed over mine, and I surrendered. Gave him my tongue. My full attention. And, at least for this moment, I gave him my heart.

CHAPTER NINETEEN

EMILIA

"So, why in the hell doesn't he have to wear a ridiculous jumper?" Sean asked, eyes on Sebastian sitting alongside Holly at the first pub. I happened to like Sean's ridiculous jumper. Maybe it'd bring out the playful side in him I knew he'd been suppressing for the most part now as a League leader.

I elbowed Sean and tilted my chin toward Sebastian since the first pub's rule was *No Pointing*. That rule was going to be hard for me. I talked with my hands, and so did most Irish people I knew.

From the sounds of it, we were going to be going along with the same set of silly rules as the rest of the city tonight for the 12 Pubs of Christmas.

Sean followed my gaze and smiled. "Ah." Upon closer inspection, the red reindeers lined up on Sebastian's cream-colored jumper were humping.

Sebastian hooked his arm around Holly, a pint in hand, as we waited for everyone else to show up. Whenever his eyes cut to me, I saw the concern there. Worry about how Sean would take the news once he learned the truth about the

German. How his wife would handle the news that he'd harbored a secret from her. But we had our reasons for withholding the truth, and hopefully, both Sean and Holly would forgive us.

"Trust me, I'm not happy about this," Sebastian grumbled darkly.

"Penance," Sean muttered as he slapped a hand over Sebastian's shoulder twice.

Penance for breaking his promise to Holly, and ouch, I could actually feel the heat of the angry stare Sebastian sent my way at Sean's words.

"Anna picked out our jumpers. Decided we ought to match." Holly quickly dropped her hand to her lap, catching herself just in time before pointing at my jumper to highlight the fact we matched.

"But not us, huh?" Sean asked. "No humping reindeers for me."

Sebastian grimaced. "I'm way too old to be pub hopping."

Holly lightly laughed and placated him by stroking his back. "Not that much older than us." She brought her free hand to the side of her mouth as if hiding her words from him. "He has a reputation to protect."

But maybe Sebastian had a point. Our wealth and surnames meant something in the cities in which we lived.

I rarely traveled with security anymore, hating to draw attention. That and I could handle myself. And the McGregors lived on the edge—opting to be free from bodyguards as well. Honestly, we could protect ourselves, but not everyone knew that, and anyone who tried to test us would quickly find out.

"Maybe we ought to keep a low profile," I suggested, eyeing Sebastian in agreement just as Holly covered her face when the flash from a camera suddenly lit up the room.

Two guys a few meters away were calling out Holly's name. She'd been recognized. And Holly wasted her efforts by tugging at the back of Sebastian's jumper to try and stop him from going toward the men who snagged her photo.

"Not even five minutes in, and he's looking for trouble," Sean laughingly said, watching as Sebastian snatched one of the guys' mobiles and appeared to be deleting whatever photo he'd taken. Better than him stepping on it and crushing the mobile with the heel of his boot. The guys should consider themselves lucky.

The two men scurried off, and Sebastian rotated his neck, irritation punctuating each step he took toward where we remained amused at the bar. "Bloody idiots," he hissed and grabbed his beer. "They zoomed in on your cleavage." He guzzled down the pint. "Why'd Anna have to pick a sexy jumper for you?"

"Sexy?" Holly and I blurted in shock at the same time.

"Yes," Sean and Sebastian both quickly responded, which had Holly and me chuckling.

Sean pointed to the door a moment later. "There's Anna and Adam now. And the others."

"Oh, you pointed," Holly exclaimed. "Gotta take a shot."

"Shite. I'm gonna be piss drunk by the end of this night," Sean replied as Adam neared us.

"Kind of the point." Adam slapped hold of Sean's hand to pull him in for a quick hug. "Not still sore, are ya?"

Sean jerked a thumb at me. "Nah, miracle Tibetan cream."

"Is that what we're calling it?" Adam mused, barely hiding his amusement.

"I think that counted as pointing too, Sean." Well, Holly was going to get her brother too drunk to even make love to me tonight. Where would the fun be in that?

. . . *Make love?* I stole the shot Holly had handed Sean and tossed it back instead. "I was mentally pointing. Promise." I set the little glass down and stole a look at Sara hanging on to Ethan, giving off the clear vibe to everyone at the pub he was a taken man. They'd only just arrived after Adam and Anna and already Sara was getting on my nerves.

"Of course, that's what you're wearing," Cole said, lightly tapping Ethan on the shoulder and drawing my attention his way. Ethan's red and green jumper read, *Santa's Coming,* and had a photo of Santa whispering, *That's what she said.*

Ethan's eyes twinkled as he shrugged and reached for one of the newly poured pints. "What?" he asked nonchalantly. "It's more festive than either of yours." He pointed to Adam and then Cole. Cole's jumper was the simplest of everyone's: *Naughty Until Proven Nice.* And Adam had a boxing Santa on his jumper. Probably custom made.

Holly abruptly replaced Ethan's beer with a shot at the sight of his pointing. "Damn, I could do this all night." Holly eyed the bartender. "Better keep them coming."

Sean wrapped an arm around my waist, then immediately retracted his hand as if remembering no PDA. Too many cameras, as Sebastian clearly proved.

But his gesture had been spotted by Sara, and her lips twitched into a brief frown.

Yeah, the McGregor she wanted was Sean. And I wanted to take revenge on Ethan's behalf for the future heartbreak she was going to cause. Her dramatic and over-the-top moaning during sex was probably her sick way of trying to put on a show for Sean. I'd need to chat with Sebastian about making a few penthouse upgrades, the first of which needed to be soundproofing the damn rooms. I was surprised Sebastian hadn't received noise complaints from the neighboring suite when he was living there and dating Holly.

"So, what's the rule at the next pub?" Alessia spoke up for the first time, her dark eyes searching the crowd of patrons as if trying to find somewhere we could all relocate but failing. It was far too packed.

"No killing." Cole blinked quickly, then swiped a palm down his face.

Shit.

"I meant no swearing," Cole corrected, and Alessia's gaze fell knowingly to the ground. The lie was on his mind. It was hurting him to keep what he knew from Sean. But Christmas Eve was tomorrow.

"Well, feck." Sean grinned, which distracted my dark thoughts. "We better drink our pints fast there. I won't last a bloody minute."

I really did love the Irish accent, always had. And Sean only made me appreciate it that much more. I loved the way he said *shite* instead of *shit*. *Feck* instead of *fuck*. Well, unless he was referring to sex with me and then . . .

I wet my lips, the memory of his mouth between my thighs that morning as he got me off springing to mind. How he'd tossed my legs over his shoulders and devoured me. The way his beard had simultaneously tickled me and driven me absolutely mad.

I needed to stop thinking about my morning wake-up call before Holly noticed my pointed nipples and made me take a couple of shots.

"Agreed." Ethan stepped in front of Adam and Sean, bringing a hand to both of their shoulders, which forced Sara to back up a little. Lose her claim of him.

The brothers probably missed each other since we basically forced Ethan to live in New York until we took down The Alliance. Little did we know that even 5,000 kilometers away, he was still getting pulled into the middle of it all.

We quickly finished our beers and ducked out of the pub without Sebastian finding a reason to beat anyone to a pulp. We lasted all of seven minutes at the second pub because the McGregors cursed like sailors and were going to get too drunk before we made it to the third pub.

We survived the next few places without drawing too much attention. I was starting to think the jumpers were like disguises for our identities. That or everyone else at the pubs was too drunk to notice. But it worked.

"That wasn't hard," Anna said once we left the next pub twenty minutes later. That rule had been to drink only using our non-dominant hand, so we probably lasted the longest there of all of the places so far. Anna and Adam even stole an impromptu dance in front of an Irish band, and Cole and Alessia joined them. Sean and I had watched and clapped along, same as the others.

"Why didn't I remember to take a piss in the last pub?" Ethan groaned as we hurriedly drank our beers in the next bar since the rule was no using the lavatory.

"Because once you break the seal, you're done," Anna said with a laugh, and I could tell she was getting pretty tipsy. It had Adam growing a bit more protective of her, keeping a watchful eye on strangers. A possessive hand around her at all times.

"Finally," Holly exclaimed once we were in the next pub. She crossed one ankle over the other as we stood in the women's lavatory line. "Having fun?"

"Yes," I confessed. The alcohol helped loosen me up, that was for sure.

"You look surprised you're having a good time." She

pushed her dark locks to her back, her cheeks a softer red than normal from all the drinking.

"Well, I'm not used to bouncing from one jam-packed pub to another while dressed like a Christmas tree." I swept my long hair up and fanned my face. It may have been cool outside, but it was damn hot in there.

I caught sight of Sean talking to Adam, clutching his abdomen as he laughed at something Adam was saying to him, and I'd swear, he must have felt my eyes from across the room because it was as if the sea of people parted so he could take one long look at me.

Our eyes met, and everyone and all the noise fell away.

"He's really into you," Holly announced, and I tore my focus from Sean to look at her. Her eyes were set Sean's way. "My brother has never been in love." Her forehead tightened, and she hiccupped. Oh boy, Holly was in the throes of alcohol-induced oversharing. I'd done the same thing at the after-party in Scotland. "I'm honestly not sure if he thought he was capable, and then you came along and bam." She slapped a hand to her mouth and closed her eyes. "Just kill me now. I'm drunk blabbering. I never drink this much, especially not since Siobhan was born."

I wrapped a hand over her wrist, and she slowly lowered her palm to her side. The bathroom was now empty, but neither of us moved. "I don't want to hurt him, you know. He's an amazing man, and I think the world of him." I needed her to hear my truth. I was feeling a bit emotional. Damn the Christmas cheer and ugly jumper for making me feel this way. "And I . . . I . . . ." The words were stuck, not because I couldn't get them out, but because I honestly didn't know what I wanted to say.

I needed a moment.

Forget peeing.

"Bathroom is free," I said, motioning to the door before scurrying away, dodging drunk and happy people to get outside.

"Hey, you good?" I sucked in the cool, refreshing air, then pivoted to find Sebastian outside. "I asked Sean to let me check on you instead." He tapped a closed hand to his lips. "More like insisted."

"It's hard to talk to you while reindeer are humping on your jumper," I deflected and smiled.

He lowered his focus to his jumper before pulling his eyes back up to mine. "Emilia."

"You don't need to big brother me." I held a palm between us, and he reached for my arm, guiding me away from foot traffic and off to the side of pub number . . . *number what?* I had no clue.

"This isn't just about my promise to your father to watch out for you. This is about me caring." He released my arm and set a hand to the brick at his side, angling his head to get a read on me. And after all the beer I'd consumed, he might even succeed. "You're falling in love with Sean, aren't you?"

"Love?" I sputtered the ridiculous word, then looked away from his dark eyes. Once upon a time, those eyes were haunted and sad. But now, the only time I saw a shadow of the man he used to be was when he and Holly were in the thick of a disagreement, usually about The League. The other night at Sean's parents' place, when Holly abruptly left the dinner table, his fear of losing her had filled his gaze. And it loomed in his eyes this week after we'd chosen to lie to her and Sean about the German dying. "How are you and Holly? Did you make up?" I'd rather turn the tables and make him uncomfortable than be put on the spot to share my feelings. As evidenced moments ago, I became a deer in the headlights, unable to speak.

"You don't have to do that." His brow scrunched. "You can talk to me. You need someone to talk to."

"I have plenty of people to talk to. Talked to Roman just tonight."

He glared at me.

"And you're some open book now, huh?" I scoffed. "Don't be a hypocrite."

"I know what your father asked of you. He told me what he wanted." His hands dove into his pockets. "I didn't want to bring it up, but now I'm feeling the need to."

"He told you?" My stomach was queasy, and despite the cool air, my skin was growing flush and warm.

"And I told him he was wrong. He shouldn't ask you to marry anyone other than someone you love. Look what marrying Sophia did to him."

"Look what loving Penelope did, too," I whispered. "He died sad and alone."

"She was married to the enemy." Sebastian issued the reminder in a deep, solemn voice. "Sean's not married, nor is he the enemy. And it'd be insane to throw away love because of a rule or a promise."

I gave him my back, unable to have this conversation with him. He may have moved mountains to be with Holly, but only because Holly loved him fiercely and refused to allow him to push her away.

I couldn't keep my shoulders pinned back, not even if the ancient Roman gods willed it to happen. "I'm not in love. There's no point having this conversation. I can't change," I cried out, willing the angry tears forming in my eyes not to fall. "I'll never be able to love him." I knew it was a lie before I'd spoken the words, but I let it sail free anyway.

When I turned around, my stomach dropped like lead at

the sight of Sean standing behind Sebastian, holding open the front door just as everyone began to pour out of the pub.

A look of hurt flashed across his face before he turned away, and my body trembled while guilt burned hot and heavy inside me.

Sebastian hung his head for a moment before giving me a tight, disappointed nod. I was certain I was far more disappointed in myself than he could ever be.

"Next pub rule sucks," Sara said, feigning disappointment as Ethan hooked an arm around her waist. "Kiss someone you didn't come with."

Yeah, if she set her mouth on Sean, I'd whack her in the head with a shovel and then use it to bury her body.

Killer, my subconscious, now named Chanel, whispered in my head.

I had no right to be jealous of Sara, or anyone, for that matter. I'd witnessed the pain in Sean's eyes at the words he'd overheard.

"Not gonna bloody happen." Sebastian twisted back to peer at Sara, his jaw working overtime. Sean, on the other hand, kept walking as if oblivious or uninterested in Sara's comment. In a daze or something.

"It was a joke," Ethan clarified, yelling a little to try and get Sebastian's attention. "Although, I overheard others discuss that they were modifying the rules and following that one in the next pub. So, watch out for random lips."

I trailed behind everyone, keeping my arms tight across my chest since we didn't have our jackets tonight.

Alessia had slowed, waiting for me to catch up with her. "You okay? Is this about the thing we're not telling Sean yet?" she whispered.

Sean had already swung open the door to the next pub and entered on his own, ahead of everyone else.

Damn it. I seriously messed up.

"No," I told her. "I screwed up, is all," I added before we went inside. The real rule for this pub was no talking to anyone you knew. So, we grabbed our pints and scattered about.

A band played traditional Irish folk music, so I pinned my back to one of the columns in the small space and watched them perform. I was anxious to get on to the next place. But maybe it was better I couldn't talk to Sean right now. Or to anyone in our group. What would I possibly say?

"Hi, love." I didn't bother to look at the man at my side, attempting to gain my attention. My focus was solely on the woman who was striking up a conversation with Sean by the bar.

"Back off if you don't want to drink your beer through your nose," I told the man whose breath was too close to my face as I studied the gorgeous woman with Sean.

I had to get used to this sight. Get used to him moving on. It was bound to happen. Destined to, I supposed. But it didn't change the fact that it felt like my heart was breaking.

Sean casually scanned the crowd, seemingly disinterested in whatever she was saying. When he made eye contact with me, there was such a hollow, empty look in his blue eyes that I wanted to drop to my knees and beg him to forgive me. Forgive my walls. My fears. Even the rules and promises that kept us apart.

But I remained frozen in place and all alone, as usual. His focus left the woman, and I followed his gaze to find Sebastian attempting to peel a blonde's hands off his arms.

What on earth? Oh shit, she was trying to kiss him. The fake rule.

Sebastian was carefully trying to rid himself of the clingy woman without accidentally harming her.

Sean was on his way for an assist, but he stopped when Holly beat him to it.

I found myself moving through the crowd to get to them in case extra help was needed since the blonde was drunk and out of her mind.

"You need to get your hands off my husband," I overheard Holly tell the woman.

The blonde faced Holly and lifted her hand as if she might strike Holly, but Holly shifted to the side and clocked the girl across the jaw.

Well, that was unexpected.

"Oh man," someone yelled, and I realized we were two seconds away from a wild bar fight breaking out, and with our names and faces, we'd wind up on the cover of a tabloid for sure.

Sebastian snatched hold of Holly's hand and hurried her to the street before the bartender called the police.

I exited the pub, deciding maybe this night ought to be over, but stopped short at the sight of Holly with her back pinned to the side of the building and Sebastian kissing the hell out of her. Watching his woman fight for him had clearly turned him on.

They were oblivious to everyone around them, and I decided this would be a good time to make my escape.

"I'll walk you back to the hotel." I turned around to see Sean striding behind me.

Maybe he hadn't heard what I said to Sebastian after all? But no, the look in his eyes was one of betrayal.

He'd known what he was getting into with me, though. And yet, I also knew he was falling. Falling hard. Holly saw it happening, too.

And I'd done nothing to stop it. So no, I couldn't dodge blame. This was my doing.

"That's up to you," I said softly before continuing to walk.

I took the long route back to the hotel, deciding I wasn't ready for whatever conversation surely would happen once we arrived.

He kept silent the whole time, as did I.

Thirty minutes later, I opened the door to my suite, but Sean stayed in the hall. One hand on the doorframe, indecision in his eyes. As if he were in the midst of an internal battle . . . follow his dick or listen to his heart.

A heart I'd just broken into a million pieces from the looks of it.

"See you tomorrow." He frowned, his blue eyes combing over me. The indecision was still there. Clear as day. He wanted to keep up the charade. The illusion of Sean and Emilia behind closed doors. Avoid reality. But he was also hurt. *I* hurt him. So, he would leave. Shove off the door and turn away.

"You still want me to come to Christmas Eve dinner?"

"Of course," he said in a deep but low tone. "Goodnight, Calibrisi."

Calibrisi? Shit. That hurt. I clutched my chest, each step he took away from me a crushing blow. "Wait." I joined him in the hall, unable to watch him leave like this. "Please," I whispered.

"What is it?" He slowly turned, giving me only his profile.

"You don't have to go."

"I think I do." His chest rose and fell with slow, deep breaths.

"About what you heard, I didn't mean . . ." I closed my eyes. "I'm sorry."

"You don't need to apologize. You were always upfront with me," he returned, being far more kind than I deserved.

I opened my eyes to see him stepping into the lift. A hand balled at his side, the other diving through his hair. His back ramrod straight.

"I'm sorry," I repeated, my words strained, the guilt refusing to let go of my vocal cords. He lifted a hand and pressed the button for the lobby. "Don't leave. Stay."

His gaze slowly traveled up to my face. A hard clench of his jaw as he worked to contain whatever emotions were vying to get free. "I would," he said with a slight nod as the doors began to close, "but what's the point?"

Once the doors had closed, I dropped to my knees. I felt as though all the air had been sucked from my lungs—like I was truly drowning. I couldn't breathe. And an all-consuming pain I had no idea how to handle gathered like a storm inside me.

And then the tears fell. Tears of a coward. A liar.

The ugly tears streamed down my face like an unstoppable force. I raised my fist and pounded on the lift doors, then walked my hands up the shiny surface, trying to get back to my feet. But my knees buckled as another deep, ugly sob worked loose, and I caught sight of my distorted reflection in the shiny, gold doors. "What the hell is wrong with me?"

CHAPTER TWENTY

SEAN

I SWAPPED THE RIDICULOUS SNOWMAN JUMPER FOR A BLACK long-sleeved shirt from the overnight bag in my Maserati, then put on my knee-length coat. I'd been planning to spend the night with Emilia, but that had abruptly changed, and I was in no condition to drive. My flat wasn't too far, so I'd be walking.

The valet who'd brought my car around looked a bit taken aback when I peeled off my jumper right then and there. Honestly, I couldn't have cared less.

I shut the door to the vehicle and returned the keys to the valet. "I'll be back for it in the morning."

"Where are you going?" Sara. Exactly what I didn't need. And where was Ethan? "Something wrong with you and Emilia?"

What the feck? "I'm not in the best mood, Sara. If I were you, I'd head upstairs to the suite you're sharing with my brother," I warned as I turned away from the hotel, not bothering to button up my coat.

Sara had changed as well, and her white peacoat hung open to show a red wrap dress beneath. Was she going clubbing without my brother? "Wait up." Her heels clicked on the path as she attempted to keep up with me.

"Go back to Ethan," I hissed. She didn't deserve my anger, but I had the distinct feeling she was going to feck over my brother soon enough. I'd hate to see him brokenhearted, too. I was in a foul mood, and if she pushed me, I'd snap and question her loyalties. And the last thing I wanted to do was clue her in on our suspicions about her.

"Sean, please." She grabbed my arm, and I whirled around on the footpath like a rabid dog. "Ethan is . . . well, he's not you. I thought I could do this, but . . ."

Do what? Date my brother as a substitute for me or use him to betray us all?

I leaned in closer to her and gritted out, "What in the bloody hell is that supposed to mean?"

When her lips abruptly crushed against mine, I blinked in shock, snatched hold of her arms, and ripped her away from me. "What the hell, Sara?"

"I-I can't stop thinking about you." She attempted to get closer, but I held her firmly and kept her at arm's length. "I think fate brought you back into my life."

She called it fate. I called it Luca. The Alliance.

"You need to end things with Ethan, and now. Stay away from my family. And don't think for one fecking second you ever have the right to kiss me." I let go of her and tried to walk away, but the woman was relentless.

I almost laughed at the irony—the woman I wanted had pushed me away, and the woman I had no interest in was falling at my feet.

Emilia had been upfront and honest with me from the start. I'd known the truth but hearing her declare that truth so profoundly to Sebastian earlier had hurt so much I couldn't begin to put it into words. In her mind, she was incapable of loving me. I'd been such a fool.

"Wait, don't tell Ethan, please." There was a tremble to her voice, but for all I knew, she was acting.

I stopped walking and faced her. "I'm not. *You're* going to tell him it's over."

She chewed on her lip, batting her eyelashes and stroking the belt of her coat as though certain I'd change my mind in a few minutes. Not gonna happen. Her plan had gone to hell, whatever it may have been.

"I'm drunk. I didn't mean to kiss you or say those things. I got confused." She tried to bring her hand to my chest, but I grabbed her wrist before she got the chance. I dropped it quickly and pinned her with a glare that warned her not to try it again. Thankfully, she seemed to understand my silent command. "Ethan was flirting with someone, and I got pissed because I-I am in love with him. I went to the hotel to change to go out dancing on my own to make him jealous. I saw you and . . ."

Damn it, Ethan. He was smashed at the last pub, and I could see him doing just that. Not because he wasn't committed to Sara, which right now had me seriously questioning his judgment, but because he was a natural flirt, a player. Learned his habits from me. But chances are, he didn't have a clue what the feck he was doing. And regardless, it shouldn't have driven his *girlfriend* to kiss me. I didn't trust her, not after learning she'd met with Luca, and I knew there was something she was leaving out.

"Goodnight, Sara. And don't follow me again." I didn't bother to look back.

I slowed down at the sight of Sebastian and Alessia's nightclub. Had he and Holly ended up here after my sister surprised the hell out of all of us by punching that woman who was trying to kiss her husband? Even if they were here, did I want to face my family again tonight?

Feck it. I didn't feel like being alone the night before Christmas Eve. I went into the club, said hello to the staff on duty, and went in search of my sister. The bouncer outside had said Sebastian was there, as well as Cole and Alessia. My guess was that Adam and Anna had gone home.

I swung open the door to Sebastian's office and stopped dead in my tracks. Then cursed, quickly turned my back to the room and mumbled, "Maybe lock the door next time?"

Holly's back had been to me, and thank God for that since she was topless, as she sat astride Sebastian in his desk chair. But it was the moaning that did me in. I did not need to hear that from my little sister, and it would require something strong to rid it from my memory.

Since neither had acknowledged my presence, too wrapped up in each other, I quickly and quietly shut the door and cringed as I left the hall and went back into the club.

"Oh shite, you weren't just back there, were you?" Cole stepped in front of me as I exited the back hallway.

I grimaced. "Yup. Where were you to warn me to not go in?"

Cole motioned to the dance floor and slapped a hand on my back. "Sorry, you slipped past me. Alessia and I were dancing."

Cole had also changed. Must have had spare clothes at the club. We'd all been itching to get out of those festive jumpers, so it seemed.

"I need something strong to unsee my sister like that." I covered a hand over my eyes once we reached the bar top.

"Ohh, you didn't warn him?" I lowered my hand at the sound of Alessia's voice to find her rounding the bar.

"He blew past us while we were dancing." Cole sat next to me as Alessia whipped us all up some drinks.

"Where's Emilia?" Alessia looked around the club while pouring some sort of new concoction she'd probably dreamed up into three glasses.

"Tired and at the hotel," I quickly answered. "But I saw Sara on my way here, and she was acting strange."

"Ah, well, some girl Ethan used to sleep with started talking to him at the last pub we were at while Sebastian was nearly getting kissed, and Ethan being Ethan—"

"Got it," I cut off Cole. "I'd thought Ethan had changed, but maybe I was wrong."

"He has some growing up to do," Cole said with a nod. "He'll get there."

Hopefully. Of course, maybe "there" wasn't such a great place to be. I was "there," and it felt shitty.

"Not that I feel bad for that woman since she's most likely using Ethan to get to us," Cole added. "Hopefully, that friend of Emilia's finds something soon to confirm our suspicions about Sara."

"Is that her sexy Navy SEAL friend?" Alessia playfully waggled her brows a few times, and I was certain she was purposely trying to get a rise out of her husband.

"Who said he's sexy? You didn't meet him," Cole growled out, playing into her hands.

"I don't know. A rough and tough SEAL. Sounds hot." Alessia was tipsy and clearly jonesing for some make-up sex from the looks of it. And I'd bet that was what was happening between Holly and Sebastian, given all the tension between them this week.

"Still can't believe Holly punched someone tonight," I said, trying to distract Cole from Alessia's teasing. "And Ma was worried it'd be Sebastian doing the fighting."

"Right?" Alessia grinned, then handed us our drinks. "I call it, 'Christmas Surprise.'"

I eyed the red and green drink with suspicion, sniffed it, then took a sip. I had no clue what was in it, but it was pretty good. A bit sugary for me, but as long as there was alcohol in it, I was happy.

"I think I need a moment with my wife." Cole cleared his throat and stood. "Excuse us."

Alessia circled the bar, and he took her hand and led her upstairs. Most likely to one of the soundproof private rooms we'd been in on Tuesday night, feeling the need to put some Irish in his American wife.

Maybe coming to the club had been a bad idea. I was surrounded by family members getting laid. Enjoying life. Loving each other. That was how this week was supposed to go. I wasn't supposed to be sitting at a bar alone.

So what if Emilia couldn't love me? I'd always known that.

And before I knew it, I was on my feet.

Heading back to the hotel.

It wasn't long before I was standing in her hallway, breathlessly pounding on the suite door.

Emilia opened up a minute later, her hair wet and lying like dark silk against her white robe. Her face was once again void of makeup, and she was stunning.

"What are you doing here?" she asked, a worried expression on her face as I sidestepped her to get inside without an invitation.

The door shut behind us, and I whirled to face her. God, she looked so sad and vulnerable. I wanted to make all the bad stuff disappear—The Alliance, Luca, her guilt about Chanel. But I wasn't a miracle worker, and she wouldn't have accepted it anyway. Instead, I framed her face between my palms. "Sex," I murmured darkly. I didn't know what in the hell I was doing, but feck it. I'd take whatever she was willing to give me. Screw my feelings.

I set my mouth to hers and kissed her hard. I hated that my kiss was laced with desperation, but I felt her begin to wilt. To melt right into my arms.

I swiped my tongue over her lips before pushing into her mouth.

She clung to me. Kissed me back as fiercely as I kissed her.

Was I there to have make-up sex for a fight that never really happened between us, hoping it'd heal the friction? Bandage the wounds between us? Maybe. But my efforts would most likely be temporary because I knew she couldn't love me.

"Sean," she whispered between frenzied kisses. My hands moved over her body, and I untied the belt of her robe.

"No talking. No feelings. Just fucking," I ordered, taking her face in my palms once again to look into her eyes. "Can you do that?" One night with her would be better than a lifetime of being with anyone else.

"I can't." She pulled out of my arms, knotted her belt, and crossed the room to stand next to the Christmas tree.

"Why the hell not? This is what you've wanted the entire time," I roared, frustration curling around my words.

"Because I do have feelings for you," she cried, her shoulders drooping. "I-I have feelings for you, Sean," she repeated, this time softer.

She afforded me the chance to look into her eyes again, and the sight of tears slowly spilling down her cheeks had me stalking toward her with hurried steps.

This strong woman was coming undone. I tried to hold her, but she found the fight inside her again. She resisted and struggled, tried to shove me out of the way. And when that didn't work, her open hands turned to fists, and she gently struck my chest, more tears crashing down like a broken dam, a decade's worth or more of pent-up emotions flooding out.

I would let her hit me if it helped, but I wouldn't let her go. I held on to her arms as her shoulders slumped ever so slightly. "Stop fighting me," I said softly. "Let me hold you." *Let me in.*

"I thought I was done crying." Her voice was still not quite right. Pained. "I'm not supposed to cry."

Had she been crying since I left? *Damn.*

When she stopped striking me, I pulled her tight to my chest and set my chin on top of her head. My body relaxed once she fit perfectly into my arms. "It's okay to cry." I cupped the back of her head with one hand and held on to her waist with my other.

Emilia remained still. Motionless. The silence had me wondering if she'd rebottled the tears and shielded herself from her own feelings again.

"I know you have feelings, Emilia," I admitted. "You express them in the way you look at me, the way you kiss me." I swallowed. "I feel them. I feel them the strongest when we make love."

She gently pulled away, and I repositioned my hands on her hip bones over the plush fabric, then locked on to her glistening eyes.

"You know I'd never ask you to choose between me and the promise you made to your father. You must know that. If that's what you're afraid—"

"What if you leave me someday? Or I leave you?" Her lower lip trembled, fresh tears falling. "What if you die? Or I die." She sniffled. "What then?"

"What if I don't?" I carried my palms up to gently squeeze her upper arms. "And what if you don't?"

She closed her eyes. The tears cut off, at least for now. "I'm scared," she whispered. "I'm not used to being scared."

She'd admitted her fears before but never so candidly. Never with such raw, unchecked emotion.

"Of what?" *Please tell me the truth this time.* I brought a hand beneath her chin, wishing she'd look at me. I needed to see her big, brown eyes.

"Being with you and getting hurt." Her lids finally parted. "And also, not being with you and spending a lonely life full of regret." It was this path I was worried she'd take.

She swept her tongue along the seam of her mouth, catching the last remaining tear lingering there.

"You know as well as I do the only guarantee in life is—"

"That everyone dies?" she offered bluntly.

"Well, yeah, but that wasn't what I was going to say," I responded, my insides feeling a bit mangled at the idea of anything ever happening to her. "I just know with absolute certainty that not being with you would be a tragedy. That's a fact."

"I hate tragedies." She drew her hands to my chest before sliding them up the sides of my neck. "Why can't fairy tales be real?" Her dark brows lifted, her lips a pale pink from the lipstick she must have smeared off before her shower.

"Who says they can't be?"

"What about the rule? My promise?" Her mouth close to mine. So close.

"We'll figure it out." I dipped down, doing my best to restrain myself until she was ready. "If you're in," I began, my voice rough as emotion choked me up, "I'm in."

Contemplative eyes narrowed on me, and her lips rolled inward.

"You don't have to make a decision now," I reminded her.

As long as I knew that she was finally letting me in, letting her walls down, well, I could wait.

She peered up at me, and I was going to get lost in her bottomless brown eyes. "Make love to me."

I didn't hesitate, not after she'd used the word "love" for the first time. I lifted her into my arms and carried her into the bedroom, shouldering open the door without losing hold of her. Her robe slid open slightly, revealing her long, sexy legs draped over my arm. She looked at me differently somehow. She was softer, more open to me. Open to the possibilities of *us*.

I set her on the bed and removed my clothes as she untied the robe, allowing it to open all the way and expose her golden skin and toned body.

I peeled off my clothes and climbed on top of her, holding myself over her with my forearms.

"Be with me," she whispered, and that was all I needed to hear. I pushed my cock into her warm, wet sex and filled her to the hilt.

Her brown eyes were heavy-lidded as we gazed at each other, sharing a moment of stunned silence at how perfect it felt to be connected without any walls between us.

She clutched hold of my arms as we slowly made love.

A moment later, she closed her eyes. "What's wrong?" I froze even though my body begged to keep moving.

"There's something you need to know, but I . . ." The forlorn look on her face was going to break me in two.

"Shhh, it's okay," I promised as her lids parted.

"I think I might cry again, which is crazy, especially because us like this—it makes me happy. A kind of happiness I didn't believe was possible for me."

I shut my eyes for only a second to recall an expression

I'd once heard years ago, but it had always stuck with me. "'If you have not cried, your eyes cannot be beautiful.'"

The side of her lip went between her teeth. "That's Italian, you know. Sophia Loren said it," she whispered. "'*Se non hai pianto, i tuoi occhi non possono essere belli.*'"

"Yeah, sounds much better when you say it." I caught the single tear that rolled down her cheek with the tip of my finger.

"See." I swallowed the knot in my throat, mesmerized by her glimmering eyes. "Beautiful."

CHAPTER TWENTY-ONE

SEAN

"WHERE IS HE?"

I jumped out of bed when I heard my brother's angry bellow from the living room and grabbed the shirt and jeans I'd worn last night from the floor. Unable to find my boxers, I hastily put on my jeans without them.

What time is it? I checked the clock on the nightstand as I tossed the shirt on the bed, deciding not to wear it. I hadn't even heard Emilia get out of bed this morning. Maybe Ethan had woken her up, no doubt pounding on the door, but I'd been too deep asleep to hear it.

It was the first full night we'd spent together since Scotland, and I hadn't wanted to get out of bed, worried it was a dream.

"What's going on?" I barked out, flinging open the bedroom door to find Emilia in black sweats and a dark tee, hands on her hips and standing before Ethan like a gatekeeper.

Ethan's dark brows lifted, and he pushed past Emilia, accidentally knocking her arm with an elbow in his haste. He strode toward me, hands clenched into fists and jaw tight, his

269

face and neck flushed with anger. *Great. What the feck did I do?*

He came at me swinging, and I caught his punch mid-air just before it connected with my jaw. He'd been working out based on the fact it was taking a lot of my energy to keep his fist from slamming into my face.

"What's wrong with you?" Emilia set a hand to Ethan's shoulder, attempting to get him to back down.

And then it dawned on me. Sara. Of course. "You really want to hit me?"

"Yes," he seethed, retracting his fist but leaning his face closer to mine.

I took a step back and held both palms up, hoping he wouldn't come at me again. I didn't want to flip my brother to the ground, but I would.

"I was worried dating your ex was a bad idea, but I never thought you'd betray me." He stabbed the air, which was the more intelligent thing to do than try and hit me again. "How could you make a move on her like that, especially when she's vulnerable? After what she went through being attacked and—"

"I didn't make a move on Sara," I said calmly, "and the fact you'd even think that means you need to grow up." I caught Emilia's curious eyes. My run-in with Sara last night had completely slipped my mind once I'd arrived at Emilia's suite. Emilia had, in her own way, given herself to me. Part of herself, at least. And we'd had the best sex of my life after she'd opened up.

"She said you came onto her. What? Did Emilia turn you down, so you hit on my girlfriend? Kissed her? What, did you fall onto her lips?" Ethan folded his arms and jutted his chin, his square jaw just begging for my fist. And I'd deck him if he continued to believe Sara over his own flesh and blood.

I scratched my neck, the scruff there from my week-old beard starting to grow itchy.

"She rejected you, so you came back to Emilia, is that it?" And my brother was officially going to need to walk himself right the feck out. Now.

"Get out," I snarled. "You have no bloody clue what you're talking about." I set a palm on my chest. "Sara chased *me* down. *She* threw herself at me, and when I pulled her off me, she was apologetic, said she was confused because she saw you flirting with *your* ex. I told her to tell you what she did and stay the hell away from my family." I turned my back, unable to face my kid brother. "I need you to leave. I can't even look at you right now."

"Ethan." Emilia's soft tone immediately eased my tension. "We didn't want to ruin your Christmas, but we've had concerns about Sara ever since she was 'attacked.' A friend of mine did some digging, and we have footage of Sara meeting with Luca Moreau in New York."

"Luca? *The* Luca?" Ethan asked, clearly shocked by the news. "No, that can't be right."

Yup, he was blinded by love, or more likely lust. During the short time I'd been with Sara years ago, she'd struck me as the gold-digger type. Always playing her sex kitten games and pouting when she didn't get her way. And based on last night, she hadn't changed. He needed to move on, and I didn't want to hurt him, especially not right before Christmas, but if he had the nerve to accuse me of hitting on her, then so be it.

"There's a chance The Alliance targeted her as a way to gain access to our family because you two are dating," I explained.

"What proof do you have?" Ethan asked defiantly.

I slowly faced him, doing my best to keep my twitchy

palms—feck, did I need to hit something—at my sides. "We know she wasn't desperate for that loan. Did she need help to keep living the lifestyle she wanted? Yes. But she didn't need almost a million dollars to save her business, and she never applied for a bank loan. She lied, Ethan. And Luca was one of the men who met with her before The Alliance deposited cash into her account."

"She probably knew she couldn't get a bank loan. No big deal," Ethan defended her.

"The money she wired to pay back The Alliance, the money I transferred into her account, hasn't been touched. Doesn't that seem a bit suspicious to you? If they went to the trouble of sending some goon to her shop to threaten her, then why haven't they done anything with the money now that they have it? Why is it sitting in an unnamed account in Germany?" I added.

"You're spying on her? What the feck?" Ethan shook his head. "And what if Luca's using *her* without her even knowing it? Did you even think about that option? From what I understand about that lunatic, it's more than possible." He approached me, lifting his strong, stubborn chin. Why was he provoking me?

"Yeah, it's possible," Emilia replied. "But not probable. She's involved herself with some very sordid people. Even if she were clueless about The Alliance, she's certainly not acting like a woman who was threatened with violence last weekend if she didn't hand over her loan payment to Krause." Emilia stood before him, confident in her convictions. This was the Emilia I had come to know. A fierce leader. "I've watched her, Ethan. She has her eyes set on Sean."

So, she'd noticed, too. Prior to the kiss on the street last night, from the sounds of it.

"I need to think." Ethan started for the door.

"Maybe don't bring her to dinner tonight," I warned. "Not unless you're absolutely sure you can trust her."

He shot one quick, angry look at me from over his shoulder, then took off. The door slammed shut behind him, and I found myself alone with Emilia. Her arms were crossed over her chest, the tight material of her T-shirt emphasizing her breasts. I couldn't make out her nipples, so she must have put on a bra before opening the door for Ethan. And that reminded me of her confession that she sunbathed in the nude at home in Sicily. I wanted to talk to her about that, but baby steps.

Emilia had cried. Admitted that she had feelings for me. We'd made love. That was a big deal for her, and I wouldn't be pushing my luck again. Not yet.

"I was going to tell you." I strode her way and set my hands on her shoulders. "After I dropped you off last night, Sara followed me out of the hotel and then threw herself at me."

"Unfortunately for your brother, I'm not surprised." She walked her fingers up my chest, and my muscles twitched at her touch.

Would I ever get enough of this woman? *Nope.*

"Dinner and Mass tonight are going to be awkward whether he brings Sara or not." I huffed out a frustrated breath. Maybe we should have warned Ethan sooner?

"You think he'll come?" Emilia looped her arms around my waist and tipped her chin up.

I combed my fingers through her long, dark hair, some of the strands tangled from last night's sex marathon. God, the heated look in her eyes and the way she gave herself over to me when I'd wrapped her hair around my fist . . .

She'd mentioned she had something to tell me last night, but then her eyes glistened with tears, and she never shared.

I'd asked her later what she'd wanted to say, but she changed the topic like a pro, and I couldn't seem to get myself to press, worried she'd leave the bed and walk away from me again.

"Ma's heart will break if he doesn't, and then I'll feel like an arse."

"Maybe let him cool off and talk to him before tonight?" she suggested.

"I suppose. I might need Adam and Cole as reinforcements."

She moved to the window, shifted the floor-to-ceiling drapes off to the side, and looked out at the city. Instead of a normal overcast day, morning sunlight poured into the room, shining on her, making this fierce and beautiful warrior look like an angel.

"I've always loved Ireland." Her lips crooked into a small smile when she turned her head to seek me out. "You know, that night in Vegas when you sat next to me at the fight . . ." She slowly shook her head. "When I heard your deep voice and Irish accent, I was afraid to look over at you. Afraid to match that incredible voice to a face, thinking there was no way you'd be as sexy and handsome as you sounded."

I shifted the material of her shirt slightly off her shoulder and bent to kiss her soft skin, then held her hair out of the way and planted kisses up the side of her neck. Just being close to her, touching her, listening to her soothing voice as she recalled the night we met so long ago calmed my tension and stress about Ethan.

"But then I finally looked at you, I felt as if I'd been KO'd in that Octagon. Now that I remember the rest of that night"—she kept her cheek turned to view me—"it's like every single moment has been painted and is hanging in my head like an art exhibit."

I pressed my lips to hers for a brief kiss before she returned her focus to the city.

"When I dropped my clutch, and you handed it back to me, I felt—"

"Electricity?" I finished for her because that was exactly what happened to me.

She nodded, still looking out the window. I lifted my gaze to see her reflection in the glass.

"I'd never seen anyone so beautiful in all of my life."

"And now?" Emilia turned into me, bringing the back of her hand to my cheek.

"You're even more beautiful than you were then." My cock strained inside my jeans, the need for her taking over. Something primal happened whenever we were near each other.

We were two seconds away from making love when her burner began to ring. Shitty timing.

"That must be Roman. He's only supposed to call if he has news." Emilia hurried to the mobile and placed the call on speaker.

"Hey, do I have both of you?" Roman asked.

"Yeah," I confirmed.

"Good. Open your email," he instructed. "Sent you some video footage."

Emilia worked her fingers quickly over the screen to access her email account.

"Harper's talented, but your pal Luca has an extraordinary ability for becoming invisible when he wants to. So, we went a different route. We checked Sara's personal calendar and work itinerary and did the same for Bridgette. Then we compared them to see if the two had come in contact with each other after the loan was deposited into Sara's account. Turns out it was quite a few times since they work in the same industry. We canvassed CCTV footage and discovered Sara with what appears to be the same two men she'd met with in New York. Bridgette was with them as well. We've identified Hans. The other man is obviously in disguise, but can you identify him as Luca?"

Emilia opened the footage, froze the frame, and zoomed in on the face. "Yes, that's him. When and where was this taken?"

"Milan, three weeks ago. It shows Luca and Hans exiting Bridgette's hotel room, which confirms she's most likely aware of, if not in on, her husband's plans. Sara was in the room as well," Roman explained. "It also proves this was one of the occasions when Luca removed his tracker because the data you gave me from the device indicates he was in Paris at that time."

Emilia resumed the video and watched the scene play out. "Bridgette, Sara, the German, and Luca," she mused, "but no Peter. Do you think it's possible that Peter wasn't the one who gave Sara the money?"

"I had those same thoughts," Roman began, "so, I looked into Peter Krause. I didn't have time to widen my search beyond the last few months, but he's never been near Luca or Hans from what I can tell. Not on camera, at least."

And there went our damn theory. We'd have to rethink things and rework the puzzle. But there was no doubt in my mind Luca was still making a play for power within The Alliance, which also included taking us down.

"Thank you, Roman. This may change things," Emilia said.

"I thought it might. Be in touch if I learn more," he replied. "By the way, I have four other guys, as well as Harper, who can come with me to Monaco on New Year's Eve. We'll be there."

"Thank you. That means a lot." Emilia exchanged a few more words with him, then ended the call.

Once Emilia's eyes were on me, I began to work through my thoughts out loud. "Bridgette's father handed over his Alliance leader position to Peter Krause when Peter married Bridgette. The leader position rightfully belonged to Bridgette as heir, but her old-school father refused to give it to her." Emilia nodded. "Peter may be the acting leader of Germany, but the power still lies with Bridgette's family."

"What if Luca is taking a page from his old playbook?" She set her burner down and folded her arms. "Think about how he tore apart the Petrovs. Maxim Petrov's daughter, Ivana, was denied a leadership position in the family business because she was a woman as well. Luca turned Ivana Petrov against her brother, Dimitri, and he ended up in a League prison. The same League prison Luca held Alessia captive all those years. Then, when the time was right, he gave Alessia no choice but to kill Dimitri."

Emilia reminded me just how much of a sick bastard we were dealing with. Luca had tried and almost succeeded in turning the most powerful Russian crime family on The League by disrupting the Petrovs from the inside. He'd seduced Ivana with ideas of power, made her feel wronged for not taking over instead of her brother because she was a woman. Then Ivana teamed up with her cousin, Adrian, to have Dimitri killed. Only Luca, being Luca, faked Dimitri's death and hid him away in his League-controlled prison where Dimitri met Alessia.

"And you think Luca is doing the same thing with Bridgette?" My jaw began to ache as if Ethan had actually punched me. How hard was I clenching my teeth? "But how does Atlas fit into all of this?"

"What if we've had it wrong? What if it was *Luca* who

persuaded Bridgette to start an affair with Atlas in hopes he'd turn on Peter? Atlas falls in love with Bridgette and then . . ."

"Takes out her husband for her, freeing her from the marriage to Peter," I finished for her in agreement. "But wouldn't she wind up bound to yet another man? What would the play be there? Maybe Luca convinced her that she was being cheated out of her rightful position of power just as he did with Ivana? But they must know her father would never let her run Germany, even if Peter died."

Emilia's eyes narrowed, a determined expression on her face to figure this all out. And I was certain she was seconds away. "Bridgette was forced to marry Peter. No choice in the matter. But what if Luca seduced her? Tricked her into falling in love with him? Promised her they'd rule Germany together, as equal partners, once Peter was out of the picture. No more runway shows. Ultimate power."

"And neither Atlas nor Peter has any clue they're pawns in Luca's game. She and Luca are the ones pulling the strings. And I'm assuming Sara gave Bridgette the heads-up I was coming to Scotland. Or Luca assumed it would happen because of the intel he handed to you. It's also why she stopped using that purse."

"Luca had no choice but to provide us with credible intel so we wouldn't end our deal with him. But what if the intel he gave us was to serve his own purposes somehow?" she asked. "And how does Sara fit into all of this? We're still missing pieces to this puzzle, and it's pissing me off."

"Hard to think like a psychopath," I repeated what I'd said to my sister at the club Tuesday night.

"Luca's managed to not only worm his way into The Alliance once again, but he's in their good graces. And all while he was under *our* protection." Emilia shook her head, clearly having a hard time accepting the fact Luca was playing us. "We didn't know he'd aligned himself with The Alliance in the past until we discovered his betrayal to Sebastian."

How could I forget that part? Luca had not only kidnapped Alessia and faked her death, but he'd targeted my family after learning Sebastian's feelings for my sister.

"I had my doubts he'd be able to get The Alliance to trust him again, but I should have suspected he was up to something more devious when he first told me he was working on getting close to the Laurents."

"What if Luca's play is to have Peter killed somehow? Encourage Atlas to offer to step in to marry Bridgette. Unite their families, thereby joining all three countries."

Emilia set a hand to my forearm, eyes sweeping to mine. "At that point, someone will surely invoke The Final Hour ritual. I would assume Atlas will make his move within days after Peter dies out of fear Bridgette's father will find a replacement for Peter, or even resume control of Germany himself until Bridgette remarries."

"So, that's how Luca plans to do it," I said, shocked by how purely evil but also kind of genius Luca truly was. "Once Atlas enters that fighting ring for that hour-long ritual to prove himself worthy to control all three countries, Luca will declare himself one of the challengers and join the ring. He'll make his claim for Bridgette."

"And per the rules, if Luca defeats Atlas, he has a shot at taking everything from him. He'll kill Atlas and marry Bridgette himself."

"He's been planning this since last year. We have to assume every step he's made since Simon and Milo's plane went down was for this moment."

Emilia's grip on my arm tightened. "Or before then . . . I wouldn't put it past Luca to be the reason that plane went down." Her skin blanched, and I knew deep down that she was right.

Luca, the master manipulator, always thinking three moves ahead. I blinked a few times, trying to wrap my head around this new theory. It was right in front of us the whole time, but somehow, we'd missed it. "Luca needs us taken down, so we're not a threat to him. That will also help prove his worth to The Alliance if anyone challenges him after The Final Hour ritual." My body tensed, anger tightening my muscles. "He'll be unstoppable."

My brows lifted in surprise when a beautiful but wicked smirk cut across Emilia's lips. "Well, fortunately, I have just the idea of how to stop him."

CHAPTER TWENTY-TWO

EMILIA

"It doesn't feel right. We can't eat Christmas Eve dinner without Ethan here." I watched with sympathy as Sean's mother, Cara, paced in front of the large brick fireplace in the living room, the soothing crackle of the roaring fire obscured by the distressing sound of her heels hitting the hardwood floor with each step. Despite her anguish, she looked like an angel, dressed in a cream-colored cashmere dress. She wore her dark hair down this evening, which made her look younger, less like the mother of four adult children. But the worry on her face and her nervous pacing were decidedly that of a concerned mother.

"Maybe he'll show up in time for Mass," I offered.

Cara turned out to be different than I expected based on what I knew about her. We'd spent limited time together before the holidays, and my opinion of her hadn't been great considering I knew what she and Ronan had done to Adam when he was younger. They'd lied to him. Told him he'd paralyzed a guy in a fight to try and scare him into never fighting again, which had devastated Adam for years.

The two loving and concerned parents I saw surely would

never purposely hurt their son like that. But I supposed they'd only been trying to protect Adam and worried fighting might get him killed. Everyone had their reasons for doing things, and sometimes the only sense it made was to themselves.

Like my lying to Sean, telling him the German thug he'd fought in Sara's store was in a League prison rather than dead from internal injuries sustained during that fight.

After realizing Luca's true intentions regarding Bridgette that morning, I should have told Sean the truth of what had happened. But whenever I opened my mouth to do so, the words just got stuck. I was terrified of how he'd look at me.

And then we'd spent the rest of today with Sebastian and the others to fill them in on what Roman had told us, which then led to devising a new plan to destroy Luca and The Alliance.

And on top of all that, I finally took the awkward step and admitted my connection to Chanel. It shocked them all, well, except for Sean and Sebastian. I could see sympathy as well as curiosity on their faces, but they'd kept their questions to a minimum.

As for Ethan, he'd been MIA since he left my suite this morning. Sean hadn't been able to track him down or locate Sara. Ethan had texted his parents to let them know he was busy and that he may or may not show up tonight. We didn't believe he was in actual danger, though. Luca's big plan wouldn't include kidnapping Ethan. Well, I hoped not, and I certainly didn't want to utter that possibility to Sean, or he'd lose his mind.

It was so hard to sit there and go through the motions of the holiday festivities, knowing what we did, though. But Sean and his siblings didn't want to set off any red flags to whoever may be watching us, including Sara. They also didn't want to ruin the children's Christmas. Or Cara and

Ronan's holiday. So, for the time being, we were putting on a show of being a normal and happy family. The plan we'd devised didn't go into motion until New Year's Eve anyway.

I glimpsed at Sean, where he sat on the brown leather couch with Siobhan on his lap, and I couldn't help but let out a quiet sigh.

Now that was a sight to see. Sean had been distracting himself about Ethan by focusing on his niece and nephew since we arrived at his parents' estate an hour ago.

Siobhan had cute little red ribbons in her dark hair. A bright red matching dress with white stockings and the cutest little doll-like shoes on her feet. Sean bounced her on his strong thigh with her arms stretched out as he held her hands. He had a loving smile on his face whenever she laughed, but I knew he was hiding his mood—for her, for his parents.

Beneath the black trousers and the white button-down shirt was a taut, distressed body. We had a plan, but that didn't change the fact he was agitated and irritable.

"And the youngest is supposed to light the candle." Cara's pacing stopped when her husband blocked her path near the huge and beautifully decorated Christmas tree in front of two windows overlooking the back. "Braden and Siobhan can't do it yet. Ethan always lights the candle."

Apparently, a candle was to be lit on Christmas Eve and put in the window as a symbolic welcome to Mary and Joseph on their travels. The milk and bread, not cookies, were set out by the fireplace for St. Nick already. The sacks, not stockings, were laid out for Santa to fill tomorrow for Braden and Siobhan. Dozens and dozens of gifts wrapped in shiny paper circled the bottom of the tree.

The McGregor tradition dictated that we have dinner, open one gift each, and then make our way to St. Patrick's Cathedral for Midnight Mass. Instead, we were anxiously awaiting the arrival of the last McGregor, no idea if he'd show up.

"Cara, my love, he'll come. He won't miss tonight. Ethan texted, remember? There's been no accident. He's fine." Ronan massaged the sides of her arms, trying to help her calm down.

Sean peered my way, a dark gleam in his eyes.

The rest of the McGregor family had scattered about the house. I wasn't sure what they were doing, but Holly had passed Siobhan over to Sean before disappearing from the room ten minutes ago.

I crossed the space, which should have been full of animated conversation and laughter rather than tension, and headed for the fireplace, my gaze settling on the flickering flames that danced around the real logs.

"Ma, drink this."

I pivoted to see Holly entering the room, a small tray of drinks in hand, and Sebastian trailing behind her. She looked lovely in a similar cream-colored cashmere dress as her mother's, her dark hair in a chignon at the nape of her neck. My wardrobe was a bit bolder by comparison—a green wrap dress with black stockings and black knee-length boots.

"Hot toddy?" Holly asked me after handing a drink to her mother. "Hot whiskey," she added when I looked at her in confusion.

"Thanks," I said as Sebastian sat alongside Sean and took Siobhan from him to hold on his lap.

"Adam and Anna are finishing Braden's bath, and they'll be down soon," she added.

We were all supposed to spend the night so that we'd already be together for Christmas morning. Instead of staying in Sean's old bedroom, his mother gave us one of the guest rooms with a larger bed. I guess she assumed we were together, but I doubted any of us would be getting any sleep if Ethan didn't make an appearance tonight.

Maybe it would have been better if Roman had called on December 26th with the news of the surveillance footage, but then again, Sara already messed up the holiday by kissing Sean and lying to Ethan about it.

I was still bitter about that. The idea that she set her mouth on my man, and damn it, he was mine—to hell with my issues.

Sara was lucky I didn't hit women. Well, not unless they tried to kill me. That was a deal breaker.

Sean stood, a plea in his eyes, and walked toward his mother. "Maybe we ought to go ahead with the evening."

His mother lowered the glass of hot whiskey from her lips, appearing to be mortified at the notion.

"We could read *The Dead*," Holly said, a smile crossing her face.

"The what?" I asked in surprise.

Cara's facial expression changed quickly, her eyes lighting up, and when she began to describe the short story by James Joyce, which was the Irish version of *A Christmas Carol*, I realized her love of literature had momentarily eclipsed her worries.

Good call, I thought while tipping my head at Holly.

"It's a tale about the magic of life. Of death." Cara moved to one of the red velvet armchairs near the fireplace. She set her glass on her thigh, her eyes darting around the room as she told the story in her own words.

Every so often, I saw Sean peering my way. Becoming a bit less intense with every line his mother shared. The flames danced off his blue eyes as he stood next to the fireplace, one hand on the mantel, the other holding his drink. He'd rolled his sleeves to the elbows, showcasing his strong forearms and the titanium Tag Heuer watch he usually wore.

His piercing eyes met mine and managed to soothe me. His gaze had softened, less broody now. He wasn't undressing me with his eyes, but it was as if he were envisioning a future between us now. A big family. Christmas stories by *our* fire. Laughter and love.

Or maybe it was me imagining all of those things with him.

I could see my life in Dublin.

I set the whiskey on the mantel and drew a palm down the column of my neck as those beautiful ideas worked through my mind, and Cara wrapped up the story.

"Your gift. The one you get to open tonight," Sean announced when his mother finished, and Adam, Anna, and Braden, as well as Cole and Alessia, had now joined us in the living room. "I'd like to give it to you now."

"Maybe we should wait for Ethan?" Cole spoke up, standing by his wife where she sat in another one of the red armchairs opposite Cara.

"You know how Ethan is," Sean said, sounding angrier with Ethan than at the situation that possibly endangered him. "And he doesn't need to be here while I give Emilia a gift." He reached into his pocket, and I heard a startled gasp from Cara.

When did he have time to sneak out and shop for me? We'd been together almost every minute this week.

I followed the line of muscle along his forearm toward his hand, which held a small blue box.

There was no way in the world Sean would propose to me. I knew that, and yet, I couldn't wrap my head around what could be inside that box. I was certain it was Cara's engagement ring assumption that had propelled me three steps back, nearly bumping into Alessia where she sat.

I couldn't let him give me a gift when there was a lie between us. A big, big lie. He deserved more from me.

Sean met my eyes, then focused on the box in his hand before returning his gaze on me, a painful expression crossing his face, the same one I'd witnessed when he overheard me tell Sebastian earlier in the week I could never love him.

He was breathing slowly, evenly. Eyes tight, brows slanted. Disappointment in my response flashing across his face, and it had my stomach turning. "Emilia, I—"

My hand lifted as if to part the seas, to stop this handsome man from saying more. "I lied," I whispered, and this was a moment I knew I'd never forget. Never forgive myself for, either. Because the uncomfortable truth I kept putting off telling him, the truth I never wanted to share with him, spilled from my lips like a dying confession, "The German. He's not in prison. He died."

I felt Cole's eyes on me. Sebastian's, too. Their heated looks burned through me.

But it was Sean's gaze that turned dark as his hand dropped to his side that gutted me. That look would be forever etched into my mind. This moment would go down as one of the worst in my life.

I turned and hurried out of the living room, uttering my apologies to everyone on the way out.

"What on earth is going on?" I heard Cara say.

"Adam and Ethan aren't the sons you need to pray so hard for, Ma." I stopped in my tracks just outside the room at Sean's murmured statement.

I shook off the hurt in his voice and the painful meaning in his words, then started moving again. We weren't in a fairy tale, after all, were we? I was ignorant to believe it could be different. That *I* could be different.

Within a few seconds, Sean grabbed hold of my arm and urged me into the closest room. He spun me around before slamming the door shut behind him.

The angry mood he'd been in earlier had nothing on this moment.

He held the box between us, biting down on his teeth. "*Not* a ring," he hissed. "Do you think I'm an idiot to propose to you when I don't even know what you want for us?"

My back went to the wall inside the office as if somehow a wall could not only hold me up but also stop the feelings pushing through me with such intensity.

Sean angrily shoved the box back into his pocket. "I knew something was up. I knew it, damn it. You were lying to me. And I'm guessing Cole, too. And no way does Sebastian not know this." He lowered his head, his palm meeting his forehead as he walked the length of the room, cursing under his breath. "When were you planning on telling me? The third Tuesday from never?" He stopped walking and whirled around to face me with fire in his eyes.

"I didn't want to ruin your Christmas. I asked Cole and Sebastian to lie. Don't be mad at them."

He dragged his gaze along the length of my body as if he wanted to punish me. Hurt me for what I did to him. I knew he'd never do that, but he could easily bruise my heart. I'd never known it was possible to feel so emotionally banged up but seeing this man I cared about angry with me . . . well, it was possible. Painfully possible.

"You lied to me. Straight-up lied. That's one thing I never expected from you, Emilia. I knew you were a lot of things, but I didn't think liar was one of them. And don't you dare tell me this is the same thing as what we've done by withholding the truth from Ethan about Sara."

The tic in his jaw became more prominent even though the ice in his blue eyes softened, but not by much.

He was in pain and lashing out. Rightfully so, I was on the receiving end. Damn my backbone that shouldn't be so erect after everything I'd done to him. Pushing him away. Hiding my feelings. The lying. Plus, the ruining of his family's Christmas.

"If it were up to me, I might never have told you," I admitted, probably making things worse.

"And that's why you panicked at the sight of what you thought was a damn engagement ring and told me the truth in front of my mother?" He pulled back, adding more space between us. Maybe he didn't trust himself not to kiss me, because honestly, the way he kept eyeing my mouth, it looked like he was seriously considering it. Or maybe bite my lip and draw blood.

"It was an accident. You didn't mean to kill him. He bled internally and died in his sleep. I don't think you should consider this—"

"Murder?" he spat out.

I pushed off the wall and advanced toward him, trying to fight the urge to challenge the man I cared about, especially since this was all my fault. But it was my nature to go to battle. To fight and win. "So, it's murder when you kill but not when I do it?" I glared at him. "I knew you'd feel this way. I knew you'd never be able to live with taking a life." Anger rose inside my body and had my limbs trembling. "Nor can you love someone like me, either. A murderer. And despite what you say about wanting Luca dead, you don't believe in killing even in the name of justice." I pressed up on my toes to be almost nose to nose with him.

He caught me off guard by spinning me around to the closest wall. He trapped me with his hands over my shoulders and my back to the floral wallpaper. "I don't love a murderer. I love you," he rushed out, the deep timbre of his voice stealing the meaning of his words for a moment.

Sean reached for my hands and threaded our fingers together, sliding our united palms up the wall at my sides. He gripped tighter and held us in place. I had no idea what to say, and this was certainly not how I'd expected Christmas Eve to go.

"I was trying to protect you from my world," I said softly, the typical stubborn fight inside me dying in this position, with his body pressed up against mine. His conflicted gaze on me. But it was his words that had my body going lax.

"I'm already in your world, Emilia. I've been living in it for a long time." He released my hands and backed up, and the chilling effect from the loss of his touch had me clutching my chest. "But you're never going to make room for me in it, are you? At every turn, you'll push away when things get too heavy for you." He reached into his pocket, pulled out the box, and placed it in my hand. He leaned forward and brought his mouth to my ear. "It's a diamond necklace of a lion's head. For the MGM where we first met. For courage to be together. And for Chanel. It was designed by that company." And then he pulled away and started for the door. Each step a shard of glass in my heart.

"Sean, wait. Where are you going?" I tightened my hand around the box, fighting tears. Why did it feel like goodbye? The real goodbye?

"I need to find my brother. Make sure he's okay. He's family, after all. Someone who will still be here tomorrow, who won't push me away no matter how scared he is," he said from over his shoulder without meeting my eyes.

"Don't get behind a wheel. Please." I moved toward him in quick steps, but he refused to look at me. "What if I can make room for you?" I cried, and his body tensed.

Before he had a chance to respond, there was a knock at the office door, followed by Ethan saying in a grave voice, "We need to talk."

CHAPTER TWENTY-THREE

SEAN

"Sara has some things she needs to tell you," Ethan said tersely. He poured a generous amount of whiskey from a decanter into a cut crystal tumbler as he stood inside the office, looking extremely uncomfortable. My brother looked even more on edge than I felt, which I didn't think was bloody possible.

Not five minutes ago, I'd been so mad I could swear I saw red. The color of blood had painted my vision like the falling curtain in a theater performance. And then Emilia, like she had a habit of doing, pulled me from the cliff's edge and away from crazy. I had no idea how I'd gone from being mad at her to confessing I loved her.

But the fact of the matter was I'd killed a man with my bare hands. Punched him to death. My brother, the life-long fighter, had never done that. But *I* had. Emilia had been wrong to lie to me. I could handle it. I'd known the day would eventually come when I'd have to take a life, but I'd wanted that life to be Luca's, not that of some stranger. Was killing in the name of justice wrong? Probably yes. But would I ever look at Emilia or my cousin or anyone else in my family, including myself, differently for having done it? Feck no.

I could own up to my actions. I'd find a way to deal with this too. I didn't need Emilia coddling me. To learn Cole and Sebastian knew what I'd done as well made me want to snatch the bottle of whiskey from Ethan and drink it dry. I'd be having a word with them after Sara enlightened us with whatever she had to say, assuming she didn't change her mind and clam up. If she put on her victim act like she'd done with Ethan the other night and accused me of kissing her, I'd see red again.

At least Ethan was here, alive and okay. Thank God this devil-woman hadn't slipped something into his drink and hand-delivered him to The Alliance or Luca, a thought that had only occurred to me while Ma recited her version of *The Dead* earlier.

When Ethan had arrived, he requested I be the only one present when Sara spoke. She refused to talk in front of anyone else. I'd been on the verge of arguing, but I was worried my brother would sweep her away from me before she divulged whatever truth she had to share. But how much of what she had to say could I trust? What if this was part two of Luca's evil plan?

"What is it?" I barked out at Sara, my arms folded across my chest. I had my back to Da's desk, which sat at the center of the room. It'd been my great-grandfather's desk, passed down over the years. One day, Adam or I would inherit it. Most likely me since Adam left the family business and only oversaw work with the McGregor Youth Foundation.

When I'd been mad at Emilia, I'd pictured setting her on that very desk and fucking her hard. Taking her with everything I had. I was pissed the German died. Angry at Luca and The Alliance. But mostly, seething mad at the fact I was so in love with her, and I was afraid I'd never be able to knock down her walls and make her mine forever. Every time I witnessed a glimmer of hope, she pulled back. That moment tonight, when she saw what she thought was an engagement ring . . . holy hell, the fear in her eyes had been a dagger to my heart.

Ethan was already on drink number three. Still nothing from Sara.

She was wringing her hands together in front of her pale pink blouse. Her hair was messy as if she'd been tearing at it, not the perfectly posh image she usually portrayed.

"I don't have all night. It's Christmas Eve," I reminded them, agitation deepening my tone.

To hell with this. I braced my hands on the desk at my sides. "You didn't apply for a loan. Bridgette approached *you*, right? Offered you a cash infusion to help you out? Said her husband does that sort of thing all the time," I rattled off the facts, assuming I was right, and Sara's eyes opened wide in shock. She took one hesitant step closer. "But two creeps showed up, and when they discussed the terms of the loan, there was an unusual stipulation. Let's just say it was unconventional when it comes to loans. Even off-the-books loans. How am I doing?" I asked smugly, unable to stop myself.

This woman was most likely sent to spy on my family. She not only used my brother, but she put him in danger. And I'd kill anyone who hurt my family. I shook my head and winced at the dark thoughts.

"Talk. Now," I snapped when Sara still hadn't opened that mouth of hers to reveal the bloody truth we were waiting to hear. Or whatever version Luca wanted her to hand over to us.

My nerves were strung tight, and she had no idea the kind of night I'd already had, so she needed to stop further pissing me off.

Ethan didn't intervene in her defense. He just kept refilling his drink.

Yeah, he was furious, that was for sure.

She didn't bother to search his eyes for help, either.

Burned some feckin' bridges, did ya?

"Were you spying on me?" Sara's indignant question initially took me by surprise. And didn't she have some damn nerve asking that?

I pushed away from the desk and cocked my head, moving like a lion, the one inked on my body. *Prey, meet your predator.* That was me right now. I was sick of Luca and his games. Sick of The Alliance.

"Okay, you don't need to answer that." She held up a hand when I edged within two quick strides of her.

I planted my feet, focusing on this woman Ethan claimed to be in love with, and I couldn't believe I'd ever slept with her. She was too soft for me. Too weak. Nothing like the strong woman who made me insane, but that I still didn't want to live without.

"Yes to everything you said," Sara admitted. "No names from the men. One was French because he called me *ma chérie.*"

Yeah, that was Luca, for sure.

"They said they'd hurt me if I told anyone the details of our conversation." Sara chewed on her lip.

Ethan didn't react to her sloped shoulders or soft tone. He just kept tossing back shots of whiskey like his entire world was crumbling before his eyes.

"Be afraid of *me*, Sara." I leaned in closer, showing my teeth like the wolf I felt like now. Lion. Wolf. Didn't matter to me. They both had a strong bite. "Fear me." I pointed to my chest. "Not them."

"Sara, just tell him. I'm losing my patience," Ethan snapped, drawing both of our eyes his way. "Tell him how they asked you to keep dating me. To make me fall in love with you. Spend the holidays with me." He swiped a drop of whiskey from his bottom lip.

This wasn't terribly shocking. I needed to hear more.

"The attack at her store. It was a setup. A damsel-in-distress thing, isn't that what you called it, *babe*?" Ethan snickered, anger flaring his nostrils. "To see how far I'd go for you. Pay off some bullshite debt of yours." Ethan flung the glass against the wall, but the crystal was too strong to break. Instead, it bounced to the floor, and I followed the gold liquid streak down the wallpaper.

"The German guy. You knew he was coming." It wasn't a question. It was confirmation we'd been right. "You were expecting my brother to show, but I came instead and killed him."

"He's dead?" Sara backed up a step, and I turned to Ethan to gauge his surprise, but his eyes had a glazed-over look from all the shots.

"Why'd he instruct you to tell me Krause gave you the loan?" That part still didn't make sense. Why would Luca want us suspicious of Sara? Wouldn't he worry we'd dig deeper and discover his involvement?

"I-I wasn't supposed to tell you that story. But I got nervous when I found out you knew Bridgette's name, and I just went with it, which is why I asked you not to say anything to her in Scotland. I was worried they'd kill me if they knew I told you who really gave me the money. I was supposed to lie and say it was some New York criminal married to a model I'd met at a fashion show." Her eyes were puffy from crying. "You weren't supposed to be there that night at my store, though. Just Ethan." She sniffled, then said quietly, "And it would have been easier to lie to him than you."

"What the hell does that mean?" Ethan hissed in anger, burned by this woman again.

Sara looked back at me, ignoring my brother. "Bridgette said she could help me out with a loan. Make my dreams come true. I could expand and have stores in every major city. I-I didn't expect two thugs to show up to explain the strings attached to the money."

"Those strings, they involved my family," I said bitterly, still not sure if I could trust whatever she had to say.

"I refused. Ethan and I had only been dating for a few weeks, and it wasn't serious. But they expected me to turn a notorious playboy into a committed man. They said I needed to spend the holidays with him in Dublin."

This part, I did believe. "They threatened you?"

She nodded meekly. No backbone at all.

"But that's all they said I had to do at the time. Well, not until they showed up again at an event in Milan three weeks ago." Maybe she was telling us the truth. She got in over her head and was looking for a way out. "They said I needed to play the damsel in distress. Beg you for help and protection."

"Why?" I hissed through my teeth.

"They knew you'd fall for it, I guess. Put me in Sebastian's hotel to keep me safe. Preferably the second penthouse, but that wasn't a deal breaker. But it's like they could predict what you'd do since I didn't even have to ask.

There was a backup plan if everything didn't fall into place, though."

I didn't even want to know the alternative plan. Or any of this, for that matter. I lunged forward, nearly grabbing hold of her. But I didn't shove her against the wall like I would have if she were a man. "What the feck did you do?" I asked despite how much I didn't want to hear the answer because I knew in my gut what she was about to say.

We'd had the place swept for bugs. It couldn't be possible, but somehow . . .

"I thought they wanted me to, um, tap your room or something, but no, they wanted me to . . . to get proof you and Emilia were a couple."

My skin grew tingly and hot at her words. Not what I expected at all.

"The Frenchman had me download an app on my mobile. Something he created because when I googled the app, I couldn't find anything about it. But he said there was a camera in Emilia's room, and I-I just needed to hit a button on my mobile to start recording footage. The problem was I had to be at the hotel for the signal to pick up, so we only managed to record whenever I was in the hotel."

"What?" I asked in astonishment. "How the hell did you get a camera in my room?"

She held up a defensive hand, eyes wide. "I didn't. Based on the camera angle, it looks like it's in the light over your bed. Maybe he wired it there somehow? I didn't ask, and he didn't tell me. My job was simply to press a button when I was at the hotel and hope you were screwing each other."

Ethan dug his hands into his pocket. "Her mobile. Here." He typed in the passcode she must have provided and handed it to me with the app open.

It was official.

I saw red again.

A dark crimson.

And now I really did feel like killing someone.

"I'm so sorry, Sean. I should never have agreed. But I was scared. You have to help me, though. Please," she pleaded, and her tears looked real, but for all I knew, she was playing me just like Bridgette had back in Scotland since she'd clearly known I wasn't my cousin.

"How could you do this to me? To my brother?" Ethan yelled and turned his back to her, the fighter coming out of him. I could see it in the rigid lines of his body. And before I knew it, he was punching his fist through the wall.

I pocketed her mobile, unable to check for sex videos on it, or *I'd* be punching the wall after seeing them. "Damn it, Ethan." I checked his hand, blood streaking down onto the floor near where the drops of whiskey had pooled. Whiskey and blood. Perfect.

"I'm sorry. About this morning." He looked at me with apologetic eyes.

"This is my fault. The League. They used you to get to me. To us. I should have told you sooner." I let go of his hand and turned back toward Sara. "When did you send the recordings?"

"Sent them to him this morning. And then I told him I was done. No more helping him," she whispered, regret in the lines of her face.

Luca saw Emilia naked. Saw her having sex with me. He'd tainted my most memorable moments, and he would pay dearly for that.

God, the things I was going to do to that man. He'd have me begging to kill him. Emilia would need to adjust our plans so I could murder him myself. No other outcome was acceptable.

"You're going to kill him, aren't you?" Sara's eyes crinkled as she observed me. "You really are dangerous, aren't you?"

I slanted closer to her, bringing my face near hers. "You have no idea."

CHAPTER TWENTY-FOUR

EMILIA

I CLUTCHED SARA'S MOBILE IN MY HAND, MY BODY trembling from shock. Cole had locked her in the guest room with Ethan for the time being. She'd probably rather be in jail than alone with Ethan and his anger, but we were all too furious to care about what she wanted.

I'd been worried about our mistletoe kiss being plastered all over Instagram when Sean and I were at the Dun Laoghaire Christmas Market, and all this time, the real danger had come from behind closed doors—*my* closed doors.

My stomach clenched as I watched erotic images of myself, naked and straddling Sean, play out in more than one scene. His hard glutes squeezing as he pounded into me from behind in others. The low light did nothing to disguise who the "actors" were. And the director of my sex tape was Luca Moreau. How fucking insane was this?

I wanted to punch Sara in the throat, for starters. She must have watched the videos, probably imagining it was her with Sean. I felt violated on a whole new level.

I had always planned for Luca to die—I didn't give a

damn who his uncle was. But now I would thoroughly enjoy it. Relish in his final gasps for air. I could taste revenge on my tongue. In my fingertips as my free hand curled into a fist at my side.

Sean's poor parents were beside themselves with worry. Clueless as to what was going on, but they knew Christmas Eve dinner wasn't going to happen. And forget Midnight Mass.

"Emilia." I looked up to see Sebastian entering with my tablet in his hand. I was behind Sean's dad's desk in the office where I'd remained parked for a good twenty minutes, staring at our most intimate moments on Sara's mobile.

Sean and I agreed she was telling the truth after Sebastian called security at his hotel. He also had his staff do a quick check of the hotel records and discovered a service order to an outside company had been placed to repair supposed faulty electrical wiring in the penthouses two weeks before I even arrived.

Sebastian's name must have been forged on the order, and knowing Sebastian, he'd be chewing out his staff for not double-checking with the on-site maintenance crew to confirm there was an actual issue in the penthouses first.

But when he had his security man text him a clip of footage from the day the electrician had arrived—Sebastian was able to confirm the electrician was Luca in disguise. Yet another time he'd ditched his tracker and had been bold enough to walk through the front door of Sebastian's hotel.

Only a man like Luca, who'd been best friends with Sebastian and knew the ins and outs of the hotel, could have come up with such a devious idea. And he'd clearly known I always stayed at Sebastian's hotel when in Dublin.

The security guard found a wireless endoscope snake

camera hidden inside the chandelier over not just my bed but the one in the other penthouse. Luca must not have known which suite I'd stay in.

Those types of cameras could be bought online for cheap, but Luca must've modified and rigged it to bypass our counter security measures. I regretted the fact I never got around to setting up the devices Roman had sent me. Surely those would've picked up the signal.

But I had to assume that due to Luca's mods, he could only transmit the footage to a nearby device. So, he needed someone inside one of the two suites, which was where Sara came in. With a click of a button, she was able to send the footage to the app he'd had her download on her mobile.

Sara was naïve for someone capable of managing three international stores. Then again, Luca had also fooled Sebastian for years, which was no easy feat. So, anyone was fair game to fall victim to that man. And once he'd ensnared her, she was stuck whether she wanted to be there or not. A mouse with her tail trapped and nowhere to go. Luca's mistake was not killing Sara before she owned her shitty decisions and told Ethan the truth.

Luca had sent me to London to discover Atlas's affair, then worked Sara into our lives and into the bedroom next door, and now the video footage. What had been the purpose of that? Why would he need to prove Sean and I were sneaking around together?

My stomach plummeted, and my skin grew clammy when realization dawned on me.

"I know why Luca did it," I murmured.

Sean had his back to the wall, near where Ethan had punched a hole into it. Plaster particles lay on the floor next to spilled whiskey and an empty glass.

Sean looked to Sebastian and back at me, waiting for the revelation to spill from my lips.

"Rule one." I stood, my legs shaky, and Sean's face went ghost-white at my quick words. "He's going to turn the other League leaders against us with the proof we were ignoring League rules. They won't trust us. He wants to weaken me. Us. And The League by tearing us apart."

"Damn it," Sebastian said under his breath, but Sean remained pale, most likely in shock. I was in denial, too. And yet, some strange part of me felt almost free. If they kicked me out of The League . . . "We'll deal with that soon. First"—he set the tablet in front of me—"we need to listen in on this conversation. I got an alert there's activity on Atlas's listening device."

I set the mobile face down on the desk and eyed my iPad.

Sebastian leaned forward and turned on the app. "And the good news, this device is something Luca doesn't know about."

Sean circled the desk to stand beside me as we listened. Two people were talking, and they were speaking Greek. We'd need to translate since my Greek was sorely lacking.

"I think that's Penelope talking with Atlas." I sat taller and clutched the chair arms.

"Speak English," Atlas hissed a moment later, clearly angry about something Penelope was saying. "I have men out in the hall, and I don't need them overhearing you mother me."

"Atlas, I am your mother. What do you expect?" Penelope's voice was softer. "You're packing up and leaving on Christmas Eve. We've never spent a holiday away from each other. Where could you possibly be going? Why would you leave me alone?"

Now it made sense as to why we were finally picking up conversation. He was traveling.

"You're not alone. You have ten guards here." The sound of a zipper followed Atlas's words.

"Please, son. You've been acting so strange lately. I'm worried. And now this," Penelope went on.

Penelope was a beautiful woman, and I could see why my father had been physically attracted to her. Tall, curvaceous, with long black hair and striking brown eyes. She spoke five languages from what I'd learned. Brilliant and kind. And when Chanel died, I was certain a part of her died, too. She stopped seeing Papà after that, and it broke his heart.

"You have been spending hours at the gym every day. Theo says you've been training. Fighting, I mean."

"Theo ought to mind his own business and not run to my mother to report my daily activities," Atlas grumbled in response.

Please give us something useful. I didn't want to listen in on a mother and son argue on Christmas Eve.

"You're going to do it, aren't you? The Final Hour. That's why you're fighting, is it not? You're in love with a married woman. Bridgette Krause. Theo says—"

"Are you sleeping with him?" Atlas barked out. "He's my right-hand man, as he was Father's, but the way you constantly go on and on about him, it has me wondering who I can trust in my circle if he's going to be screwing you."

"Atlas, how dare you speak to me like that." Penelope's voice dropped to a whisper.

"No, that's right. You're still mourning *him*, aren't you?" Atlas bit out as if he were chewing on words that gave him a bad taste in his mouth.

Sean and I quickly glanced at each other, then lowered

our eyes back to the iPad as if we could see Penelope and Atlas displayed there as Atlas continued talking.

"Father suspected the affair. I overheard him talking in his office to Theo. Years before he died. He figured there was only one reason why you were so adamant he didn't have Calibrisi or his only daughter killed over the years—because you loved the man."

A tight fist-like pain formed in my stomach, and I closed my eyes. This was not the conversation I expected to overhear. It was too much. Too painful. The memories were choking the air from my lungs.

"So, who do you love? Your new man, Theo? Your old lover, Calibrisi? Or Father? Did you ever even love Father?" A loud puff of air as if he'd expelled a deep breath came over the line. "Arranged marriage, I know. But was I a product of a loveless marriage? Were you forced to have me? Because I have no intention of marrying a woman I don't love. I won't wind up like my father. Or you."

"You, my son, were a product of love." Her tone trembled when she spoke. I could visualize her hand going to his shoulder, her brown eyes glistening as she eyed her only son.

He was quiet for a moment. "I love Bridgette, yes. And I will marry her."

"You want the power. The coveted German position that marrying her will bring you," she said softly as if it broke her heart.

"No, Mother, I'm not like Father. I just told you. I love her. I'd give up everything to be with her. The Alliance. All of it."

What? My pulse ratcheted higher at his words.

"But she won't, am I right? And so, the only way you can have her is to fight. Go into the cage for an hour against the strongest fighters in The Alliance. You will risk death for this woman?" Penelope's voice cracked.

My eyes flew open. Atlas was truly in love, and he had no idea he was walking into a trap laid out by Luca and the woman who would soon break his heart when he found out the truth.

"I never wanted this life," Atlas roared. "Maybe Chanel was the lucky one. She got to escape."

Penelope's gasp was audible. "She died! How could you say that?"

Oh God, my stomach. I was going to be sick.

"There's something you should know now. It will give you time to prepare for what is inevitable," Atlas said, his tone low. "To be with Bridgette, I'll have to—"

"Kill her husband," Penelope finished for him. "I'm well aware of the ways of The Alliance. But, Atlas, my son, you've never taken a life. Your men have done it and made it look as though it was by your hand. I don't believe you can commit murder. You're right. You're not Simon. Not cold-blooded and ruthless." She was weeping, and I was, well, shocked.

This Atlas was who Chanel described to me when we were younger. A lover, not a fighter. How much about Atlas were rumors to help him look strong? Undefeatable?

"Krause is a bad man, Mother. *He* is a ruthless killer. The world will not miss him. And I can't tolerate the woman I love being forced to be with that old man."

"The Alliance leaders will never let you get away with—"

"I didn't say I'd personally kill the man. But yes, he will die. Per my order."

Luca's plan. Our theory so far was right.

"But there's more," Penelope said a few moments later. "Oh, I can see the pain in your eyes. There's someone else you have to hurt, isn't there? Who? Why?" Penelope's words were muffled as if holding a hand to her mouth.

"A man I'm working with, he used to be League, but we trust him now, well, he believes there's only one way Bridgette and I will ever be safe, and that's to . . ." He let his words trail off, and I had to assume it was because of the audible crying we heard from Penelope.

"Luca. He's the trusted source," Sebastian said in a low voice, his palms snapping into fists.

"You-you can't kill Emilia." Penelope had stopped crying, but her voice was weak. "She was Chanel's best friend. You never knew. They kept their friendship a secret. The two of them had a special bond. That's one reason I never wanted Simon to hurt her."

"What?" Atlas was taking deep breaths between beats of silence. "Why? How?"

"They met when I was—"

"Sleeping with Emilia's father?" he asked in a deep, angry voice.

"You can't harm her. You can't. Please." Desperation that stunned me to my very core bled through her words. "I've never asked anything of you, son, but I am asking you this."

"Emilia is a threat to Bridgette. Luca has proof she's going after her. Emilia was at Bridgette's fashion show in Scotland, wearing a disguise. She has a friend of Bridgette's practically imprisoned in a hotel owned by the Irish leader, Sebastian Renaud. The League is looking to hurt Bridgette, and I won't let anyone harm the woman I love. I'll end Emilia's life to protect Bridgette, to send a message no one messes with the woman I love."

Oh, that motherfucking Luca Moreau. The depths to which he planned and plotted behind our backs was almost impressive on a twisted, horrific level.

Sean began cursing in what sounded like his own language because the anger had his words all mangled up. He tossed a hand in the air and turned his back to us.

"You'll also start a war," Penelope whispered and then added in a sharper voice, "And I'm sorry, but I don't care if Emilia were to target the Pope in Rome. She's off-limits. Do you hear me?" Penelope's words had Sean spinning around, a look of surprise on his face as he observed me.

I knew she and Papà loved each other and would have lived their lives together had it been possible, but this felt . . . like more.

My pulse continued to race. Breathing uneven. Eyes glued to the app once again.

"You know, Father did try to kill her." Atlas's deep voice was weaker this time, less volatility there. "That's what I overheard him discussing with Theo. He'd mentioned trying a few times. He said he had to make it look like someone outside of The Alliance killed her. He wanted to punish Calibrisi for loving you like he believed he did. And he didn't want Grandfather to know about it, because for some reason, you managed to convince your father to leave the Calibrisis unharmed as well."

"When? Tell me what you know." Penelope was rattled by this new information, and hell, so was I.

When did Simon Laurent try to have me killed?

And, oh God, if the bastard accidentally murdered his own daughter ten years ago . . . I'd bring him back from the dead to kill him again.

"He said something about South America. I don't know, but that obviously failed. And then he was going to try a wedding in Spain. But I think there was another time."

The assassins the night I met Roman.

Paulo in Brazil.

. . . But first, Vegas?

"Another time." The words snapped out of her mouth in heartbreak.

Was Simon responsible? Did he frame the crime family in Naples for Chanel's murder when he'd meant to have me killed instead? How could Simon have lived with himself knowing he'd killed his daughter?

My head was spinning. Or was it the room? I needed to sit.

I am sitting.

I blinked rapidly, my body shivering.

Sean came behind me and set both hands to my shoulders for support, but I barely felt him.

"I think . . . I think Simon killed Chanel," Penelope said, her meek, saddened tone cutting into me. "She was with Emilia that night, and oh God, I think he sent someone to murder Emilia but failed."

"No. Impossible," Atlas yelled, then he began cursing in French and Greek. *Freek.*

My stomach fluttered as nervous anticipation coiled tight inside my chest.

"We can't know that for certain since Father is dead. Theo is still too loyal to Father to share what happened. But I do know the woman I love will also die if I don't protect her from Emilia. From The League. You can support your only living child, or you can choose to warn the daughter of a deceased lover. That's your choice." There was a distinct shake to the listening device as if he'd snatched the bag and was starting to move.

"Please, wait," Penelope called out to him. She switched back to Greek and began frantically pleading. I had no idea what she was saying, but she was most likely begging him to save me, which felt insane since she'd never seen my father again after Chanel died. And since Penelope knew the truth behind Chanel's murder, Papà must have told her what really happened that night in Vegas. Oh God, she must have blamed him. Blamed herself even. For not finding a way to stop our friendship.

"No, that can't be true," Atlas said a moment later. "I-I don't believe you," he hissed, and the door slammed. He began issuing commands to someone in the hall, most likely his guards, and then from the sounds of it, he passed the bag off to someone. A driver, maybe.

"That's it," Sebastian said. "Well, for now. If he meets with Bridgette to discuss his plan, we'll be listening."

"I want to know what she was saying to him in Greek. Can you run it through my translator app?" I slowly rose and turned to find Sean moving the chair out of the way to drag me into his embrace.

I let him hold me, let my guard down in front of Sebastian because I needed Sean's strength right now.

I could barely speak or think.

"Atlas is walking into a trap," Sean said darkly. "How the hell does Luca think he'll get Emilia alone and away from us for Atlas to try and kill her?"

"The videos," I said into his chest, finally pulling away. "Turn The League against me for breaking rule one. That's how."

A string of curses ripped free from Sean's mouth again, and he left my side, went to the wall near where Ethan slammed his fist, and bowed his head. Both hands were knotted, pressed to the wall as he tried to calm himself down. To keep from going after Luca now and killing him like I wanted to do.

But me? I was reeling after learning the truth about Atlas. Hearing Penelope plead to save me. Knowing The League may soon turn on me, and everything Papà ever wanted for me would be over. No more legacy left to carry on. It was overwhelming.

"I think I have it," Sebastian said. "One second, and I'll read it."

Sean backed away from the already damaged wall to join us. Eyes dark, his expression intense.

"Penelope said," Sebastian started, "you already lost one sister. I won't let you kill your other one."

"What?" Sean eyed the tablet in confusion. "Bad translation, I assume. Try it again."

"Yeah, it must be wrong." Sebastian began working at the screen again, his fingers moving fast. A slight tremble in his large hand that I had to be imagining.

A shiver rolled down my spine, and goose bumps scattered over my skin beneath my clothes. Every part of me was frozen with the truth I knew was to come. The truth he'd already spoken.

I'd spent years ignoring the gnawing feeling in my gut Papà had lied to me about my mother. I'd even wondered about Penelope since I'd felt so drawn to Chanel. She used to joke we could pass for sisters with the same coloring, hair, and physique. But I'd blindly obeyed and trusted Papà because he was my family. He was everything to me and all I had. I never had any reason to think he would lie to me.

To protect you, a voice whispered inside my head. Not Chanel's this time but Papà's.

I snapped my eyes shut when a memory pulled to mind. Penelope and Papà talking in bed while we were in Bali. I'd been so shocked to discover Papà sleeping with the enemy that I'd barely clung to the words I heard them say to each other.

"I hate that you can't see her grow up. I know there was

no other way, but it kills me, my love. It kills me." Papà had said something like that to Penelope as I'd approached the bedroom from what I could remember now. Maybe not word for word, surely my memory had distorted it, but what if . . .?

"I never saw any pictures of Sophia, my mother, while she was pregnant," I said softly, my eyes flicking open. "Father said she thought of herself as fat and wouldn't go in front of a camera, but what pregnant woman doesn't want a photo? I hated her for leaving, so I never pressed. Never asked questions about her. But what if Sophia wasn't my mother?" My eyes widened. "What if Sophia left because my father had a child with another woman?"

"But why would Penelope give you to your father instead of raising you? You were born before she married Simon, but she couldn't hide her pregnancy from her father. And still, how would she have hidden that from Simon?" Sebastian looked up from the iPad, a frustrated look on his face.

I took the tablet and saw he'd tried three more translator sites, and they all turned up the same results.

The meaning was clear.

I was Penelope's daughter.

My mother is Alliance.

It felt like I was losing Chanel all over again, this time as a sister.

"Romeo and Juliet," I mumbled, hating that play even more now. "Lovers who couldn't be together but also had a child." Bile worked into my throat, and my insides quivered as if I might throw up. "Atlas is my half brother."

"Emilia." Sean swooped by my side in an instant as if realizing I was about to fall.

I'm a Calibrisi. I don't fucking faint. Don't do it. But . . .

"He lied to me. He lied," I kept saying, over and over again, my vision clouding from anger. "He told me to marry an Italian. Preserve the bloodline. Our family heritage. The legacy." I was visibly shaking as my shock turned into something ugly and painful. "And all of this time, I'm the daughter of a Greek woman. The daughter of a Castellanos." I swallowed. "The daughter of the enemy."

CHAPTER TWENTY-FIVE

SEAN

EMILIA HADN'T SPOKEN A WORD SINCE WE PACKED OUR BAGS and left my parents' home last night. Not a single syllable as she stared out the window while I tore down the roads to get to my flat. Going to the hotel had been out of the question. I couldn't stomach the thought that Luca had watched us making love in that bedroom. I wanted to set the fecking suite on fire.

Sebastian discovered the video cameras exactly where Sara had said they would be in the penthouses. He also tasked League guards to discreetly watch over Sara, as well as Ethan. And as much as Ethan hated it, he had to stay by her side so as not to draw suspicion in case Luca had eyes on Sara.

I couldn't believe Atlas, Alliance leader of Greece and France, had never taken a life, but *I* had. I shoved the thought from my mind. I didn't need to go to a dark place, not when I needed to do my absolute best to be the light for this woman before me.

It was Christmas morning, and for the first time in my

life, I wasn't celebrating with my family. I couldn't possibly leave Emilia's side after everything we'd learned last night.

I tucked my hands into the pockets of my black sweats and went into my ensuite to find Emilia soaking in the tub, still wearing the pajamas I'd changed her into when we arrived at my flat.

She'd had a traumatic night. One shocking blow after another, rendering her speechless. And I didn't blame her.

So much of what she'd been told and grew up believing had been a lie. The most important person in her life, her father, had not only hidden the truth from her, he'd forced her to make a promise to him that was downright insulting since he not only loved a Greek woman, but he'd had a child with her.

This was a side of Emilia I'd never seen. Vulnerable didn't even come close to describing it, and it killed me to watch her. To see her suffering. And I didn't know how to fix it.

Before Ethan and Sara had shown up last night, I'd been on the verge of walking away from Emilia, worried she'd never be able to give me her heart, even though she held mine. But now, I didn't know if the truth she'd learned, as well as her fate with The League, would tip the scales for better, or for worse, between us.

I leaned into the doorjamb and watched her, not quite ready to enter the bathroom. Not sure what to say. She'd slept in my arms last night. Quiet. Not even crying. I think her silence scared me more than anything. I knew how to work with anger or tears, but the quiet felt oddly loud.

I still couldn't grasp how the hell her father, and not Penelope, had ended up being the one to raise her. I was curious who knew the truth about Emilia aside from Penelope

—and now Atlas. Of course, Atlas didn't believe his mother. Would he ever? Would the fact Emilia was his half sister change his plans, which involved killing his own flesh and blood in the name of a woman he loved?

The sins of the father. Wasn't that a cornerstone for most tragedies, damn it?

"Merry Christmas," I said softly. I honestly didn't expect a reaction given the strange state she was in—sitting in the tub wearing pink pajama shorts and a camisole. I knew if I looked, I'd be able to see her nipples poking through the wet fabric, but not from arousal, and that knowledge only added to my sex drive being buried six meters beneath a boulder of holy shite news.

"You should be with your family." Her sad brown eyes slowly moved to my face. "I'm sorry I ruined your Christmas."

I pushed away from the door, thankful to hear her voice again. I knelt next to her and reached for her hand draped over the side of the tub. She didn't resist, and I laced our fingers together.

"I, um." Her lower lip began to wobble, and I saw what was finally coming.

The tears.

Not wanting to waste any time, I quickly climbed into the tub, sweats and all, sending water sloshing over the sides, then pulled her into my arms as she cried, her emotions shifting from stunned and into grief.

I didn't shush her, just held her tight to my frame and let her sob. Weep for every lie she'd been told. Every year she'd lost out with her mother. For the sister mistakenly murdered, possibly by Simon for wanting vengeance for his wife's affair with the enemy. Simon had clearly known killing his wife would have resulted in his own death at the hand of Milos, Penelope's father, so he had to go after Emilia instead. It really was a Shakespearean tragedy.

"This isn't me," she mumbled into my chest. "But I'm afraid I have no idea who I am anymore."

"I know who you are," I whispered into her ear as I cradled her head against my body. "A strong and intelligent woman. With a kind heart. A beautiful soul." I inhaled when she pulled back and found my eyes. "The woman I love." I'd fight for her. I'd been crazy to think for one second I could have ever truly walked away last night and not found myself coming back again. I kept coming back no matter how many times she pushed, didn't I? Drawn to her for all of time, like two star-crossed lovers, our fates intertwined. But the difference was our story would not end tragically.

Her glossy eyes held mine, and I knew she wanted to say more. To share her feelings, but her mouth tightened instead, and she set her forehead to mine. Her hands wandered over the sides of my arms, scraping her short nails lightly over my skin.

She was searching for something in her touch. Seeking comfort, maybe. I'd give her whatever she needed. However she needed it.

"Make love to me, Sean." Her eyes found mine again. "You're the only thing I know is real in my life. The only part of me untainted by lies and deceit." She spun around and set her mouth to mine, and I growled out a husky sound of approval when our tongues twined together. My chest grew tight as emotions warred inside me. "Love me, please. Love me, Sean."

"Always." I held the sides of her face as I kissed her tenderly, but when she shifted on top of my lap, even with those thin shorts on, hell, all bets were off. It was hard to be gentle when she was grinding against my cock. "I feckin' love the hell out of you, woman. So. Damn. Much." My deep voice punctuated the air with each word as I kept her face framed between my palms and stared deep into her eyes.

She rolled her lips inward for a brief moment and then nodded as if she accepted my words as the truth. Finally accepted my love.

A few minutes later, I stood and peeled off our wet clothes, then carried her to my bed. She was all I wanted for Christmas, but damn, I wanted her to be happy. She deserved it.

"My letter to Santa, my wish," I rasped against her ear, our bodies still damp from the bath, "was to be with you," I confessed.

She clutched my arms as I held myself over her and buried my cock deep inside her warm sex, then pulled almost all the way out before plunging in again. "In some strange way, I guess I got my wish, too," she responded.

I lowered myself closer to her and swept my tongue along the seam of her lips, brushing our noses together. "And what was your wish?"

I felt her breath fan out on my mouth before she slanted her lips to mine, stealing another kiss. "That I'd be able to break my promise to Papà without feeling guilty. That I'd be able to be with whoever I wanted without that burden weighing me down. Live my life how I want with whom I want," she whispered.

I lifted myself up enough to look into her eyes. Hearing her wish shouldn't make me feel this amazing, especially after everything we'd learned since yesterday, but today, on Christmas, I had Emilia in my arms. And she was returning my love in maybe the only way she knew how to right now, with her touch. With her eyes. With the way that she let me in when we were together like this. "And what does that mean?"

She swallowed, a sheen of emotion covering her big, brown eyes again. "That means I'm yours."

I smiled and pressed a gentle kiss to her lips. "Don't you know you've been mine since Vegas?"

* * *

"An emergency virtual meeting has been called for tonight, Christmas, and we're not included? Are you serious?" I snaked a hand around the nape of my neck and squeezed. "We're League leaders, for feck's sake."

Sebastian's shoulders fell, no doubt weighed down by a shite ton of guilt. He'd spoken to Édouard Moreau, the French League leader and Luca's uncle earlier in the day. Moreau had the most pull in The League, but based on the devastated look on Sebastian's face, he already knew the outcome of the upcoming meeting.

Emilia came out of my bedroom wearing one of my Trinity tees that went to her mid-thighs. Her long legs carried her our way, and I had to pull my focus up to her beautiful face, once again without any makeup.

"Anything new from Atlas and the listening device?" she asked, ignoring the fact she must have overheard Sebastian's announcement of The League's emergency meeting to discuss a matter of utmost importance. The fact that none of us were included meant they had received the video footage of Emilia and me, and we were the subject of their discussion.

"No. But the tracker shows Atlas in Monaco. I sent someone to his location late last night who informed me Atlas has been training at a gym since before the sun came up,"

Sebastian answered her. "He's prepping for The Final Hour. And he must be worried if he's spending his Christmas in the gym."

I dropped down on the sofa in my living room. The bubble of bliss Emilia and I had trapped ourselves in all day by making love had burst, and we'd been pushed into reality with a harsh shove.

"How is everyone? How was Christmas?" Emilia asked cheerily, clearly avoiding mentioning The League as she joined me on the couch.

Sebastian frowned and set his back to one of the columns in the living room, quietly observing us. His jaw clenched, worry in his eyes. "Not the same without you," he finally said. "But Adam managed to keep Cara and Ronan calm."

The conversation with my parents as to why Emilia and I had abruptly left last night wasn't one I was looking forward to having.

"The League will terminate both of your positions. Possibly mine, as well as Cole's and Alessia's, if they believe we kept your relationship a secret." Sebastian dropped the news on us, news that I had a feeling was coming but wasn't prepared for Emilia to hear yet.

She didn't need any more heartache. Any more pain. Writing down a Christmas wish and hoping it came true was one thing. Having her entire life altered and her fate out of her hands was quite another.

"I won't let you go down with me." Emilia rose, her back going ramrod straight. "Ireland needs you. This city needs you all." She went to the kitchen, grabbed her mobile, then came back into the room.

"What are you doing?" I stood, nerves tightening my vocal cords as she brought the mobile to her ear.

She ignored me. Probably afraid I'd challenge her decision.

"Moreau, it's me. Emilia," she said into the mobile a moment later. "I will resign as League leader of Italy. I will not put up a fight." She was quiet, and I had to assume Moreau was speaking.

My pulse was racing as I studied her, her gaze focused on the floor. I glanced at Sebastian, but he was unreadable.

"I won't have your nephew ripping The League apart over me. I know the decision will be split. There will not be the votes needed to kick Sean and me out," Emilia went on. "And this will cause problems, problems I don't want for The League. Let me help you take down The Alliance as promised, and then you have my word I will quit. Regardless of your decision, though, Sean and his family, as well as Sebastian, stay on as League leaders after The Alliance has been taken down if they so choose."

I took a quick step toward her, but she lifted a hand in protest. No, I couldn't possibly let her do this. The League was her life. It was never mine. I only wanted her. Her safety. My family's safety. Not this. She might resent me for it, and I could never live with that.

"We both quit," I said, a firm grit to my voice. This was not happening. She'd already broken her promise to her father, although after his lie about the identity of her mother, I wasn't sure that promise still held any weight. But I couldn't have her throw away everything she'd worked for, not for me.

Emilia looked away, not repeating my words to Moreau. "This is the only way, Moreau, and you know that. You don't want to go to war with me." Her voice was steady as she maintained her resolve. Not an ounce of regret in her voice as she spoke, but I could see it in the way she refused to meet my eyes.

"I have a plan, one that I believe will finally end The Alliance once and for all. A different plan than originally discussed, but if you cared for my father, you will trust me. Let me do this. And then you can elect someone of your choice to take over Italy, and you'll have my support, which you know you'll need."

Damn, this woman was strong. Tough. But why was she giving up without a fight? We could get the rule changed. Fight for her position.

. . . And what was that about a new plan?

"Yes, okay." Emilia handed the mobile to Sebastian. "He wants a word with you."

Sebastian hesitantly took the mobile. "Alright." He was quiet as Moreau spoke. "Consider it done." He ended the call and handed Emilia her mobile back. "Why'd you do that?" he scolded, the same question on my mind.

"I can no longer lead Italy, knowing what I do now about my mother, about my half brother. I'm a Castellanos by blood. I-I cannot possibly stay on. It wouldn't be right." She set her mobile on the coffee table, and her eyes went to the window. We never did get around to putting up a tree in my flat together like I'd wanted to do, and right now, this room was in desperate need of holiday cheer.

"Emilia, are you sure? No one has to know about your mother," Sebastian spoke up, catching my eyes and lifting his chin, silently urging me to talk some sense into her.

"But I'll know," she whispered without turning. "And that's a secret I refuse to carry."

"Emilia," I said softly, approaching her as if she were an injured animal.

"What'd Moreau want from you?" she asked Sebastian instead.

I stood behind her, wanting to touch her, to do something,

but she was slipping into her suit of armor, preparing herself for a battle on all fronts.

"He asked me for a favor," Sebastian started in a deep voice. "To let you be the one to finally end things." His words had me looking back at him in shock. "He wants Emilia to be the one to kill Luca Moreau."

CHAPTER TWENTY-SIX

EMILIA

MONTE CARLO, MONACO (FIVE DAYS LATER)

"Close your eyes," Sean commanded.

"No." I tipped my chin in defiance. "When I turn thirty-one, I want to look at you as you lean in to kiss me. I want to see the man who stepped in to be my prince that night ten years ago here tonight, doing it again."

Sean's brilliant blue eyes studied me for a moment before diverting to his watch. "Ten seconds."

All I'd wanted for my birthday was to be alone with him in our hotel room. To make love the night before the New Year's Eve event when our carefully crafted plan went into effect. To forget my father's lies and the fact I was leaving The League, the only real life I'd ever known.

"Happy birthday." His husky voice had my body tightening with need as he dipped in and slanted his mouth over mine, gingerly touching my lips. Soft and sweet. No tongue. The same way I now remembered he'd done in Vegas for our first kiss.

Kneeling on our hotel bed, I clutched his biceps and

offered the line I said to him a decade ago. "Do it again but put your tongue in my mouth and taste me this time."

"I'll need a name for that, love." He nipped my lip, pulling it between his teeth, and I groaned in anticipation of what I knew was to come.

I was wearing the beautiful lion pendant he'd given me on Christmas Eve and nothing else. He'd refused to let me give him anything other than myself after our disastrous Christmas. But I had the perfect gift and was just waiting for us both to come out of this mess alive.

"Julia," I said against his mouth.

"Mm. No, beautiful." He took a fistful of my hair and gently tugged. "You. The real you. That's who I want tonight and every night after."

His words stole my breath. Sean's love once scared me, but now I couldn't imagine life without it. To be loved by this man was a privilege I almost lost. But I was lucky he was strong enough not to let me push him away.

When our heated confrontation in the office of his parents' home on Christmas Eve had him turning away from me, I realized how he must have felt each time I rejected or denied the truth of his feelings. It was as if my world was suddenly crumbling and falling apart right before my eyes. That was the moment I knew I would do everything in my power not to lose him.

"Forever," I whispered, and that one word had his tongue working my lips open for a hot and passionate kiss. The kind that made my knees weak and my core clench.

My nails bit into his biceps and then raked over his chest.

Maybe, oh God, maybe I ought to tell him my true feelings now. Give him my gift. What if I died without him knowing he opened my heart up to not just the possibility of us but to loving him like I'd never known I was capable?

Fate brought Sean into my life ten years ago, and he was back here with me now. I finally believed doors had been opened for us, but it was up to me to walk through the right one.

"Where are you?" Sean whispered, stroking my cheek with his thumb in small circles. "You're not here with me. Thinking about tomorrow? Well, technically today."

"Thinking about us," I admitted.

"I know you said no gifts for your birthday," he said a moment later, "but I couldn't help myself. I'd like for you to wear it now." He let me go and was off the bed and digging into his suitcase a moment later. He presented me with a medium-sized box wrapped in red paper, a nervous smile parked on his lips. And now he had me nervous.

"Never opened a birthday gift in the nude," I said with a laugh and rested my back against the headboard, stretching my legs out in front of me.

Sean hopped back on the bed and knelt between my feet, then slid his hands up my legs. He took a moment to appreciate my center, a hungry look in his eyes, before swiping a thick finger along the seam of my sex and then bringing it to his mouth.

"You taste so damn good," he groaned.

I felt intoxicated by the sheer eroticism of it all. The sight of his masculine hands on my body, the seductive way he moaned as he licked me from his finger had me bending my legs at the knees and parting my thighs, ready for him to have another taste. "Your gift first, love." He lightly swept his palm over my abdomen, caressed my breast, all the while I held the box off to my side on the bed.

What gift? I just wanted this man to devour me multiple times over.

Sean shifted to sit alongside me, his back to the

headboard. He stroked his hard length, precum glistening the tip, distracting me from the box. "Open. It." The command sent shivers up my spine and had me bringing my thighs tight together once more when need strummed between my legs.

We hadn't made love all week. Sean felt the need to give me time to come to terms with the fact Papà had withheld the truth about my real mother even to his dying day.

But when we arrived at the hotel ten minutes ago, Sean and I had stumbled around the room ripping each other's clothes off like lust-thirsty teenagers. Well, after we did a thorough check of the room first. No way would we let another camera wind up watching us have sex.

"Sweetheart, I've lost you again." He tucked my hair behind my ear, his warm skin sending shivers down my body.

"I usually don't like endearments," I confessed, "but . . . say it again." I gripped hold of the wrapped present, my lust squeezing through me.

He gathered my face in both palms. "Sweetheart," he repeated before licking my lips open and pushing his skilled tongue into my mouth. "I've missed you," he said a moment later. "Please open the gift, so I know whether or not you hate it, and then we can either have passionate sex or angry sex."

"Oh." I kind of liked both options. Angry sex with this man, when he lost control and let the dominant alpha out to play, was so freaking hot. But sweet lovemaking was on another level as well. That kind of love lasted a lifetime, and no one had ever been able to give me that before him. "Regardless," I said with a sultry smile, "I want angry sex followed by love sex."

"Present." He pulled away and pointed to the gift, and I swear, if I didn't love this man so much, I would smack him for making me wait so long to have him inside me again.

I bit into my lip as I eyed the box. Too big for a ring. I

wouldn't ever make the mistake of having such a disastrous reaction to his gift as I did to the necklace. I was still angry at myself for ruining that moment and right in front of his family.

I slowly removed the paper and stared at the square box in surprise. It was a glass bottle with the line, *For the woman I love, and for the friend and sister she lost that will never be forgotten*, printed in italics on a soft yellow label. And in smaller black print beneath those words was the Coco Chanel quote, *In order to be irreplaceable, one must always be different.*

"Chanel loved that quote," I whispered. "How'd you know?" Tears filled my eyes, and judging by his narrowed eyes, that wasn't the reaction he'd hoped for.

"I looked up Coco, and that one stuck with me. Reminded me of you. Irreplaceable. Different than anyone I've ever met." His lips tipped into a small smile, and he removed the silver top. "I called up someone I know that works at Chanel, and I asked if they'd make a special one-of-a-kind bottle for you. I told them about you. Your strength. Courage. Determination and bravery. Your beauty." He nudged the glass bottle closer to my nose, and I inhaled the heavenly scent. "What do you smell?"

"Love," I mouthed, choking up with emotion. I lost hold of the bottle to loop my arms around his neck. "Love sex first. I changed my mind." I set a kiss to this thoughtful and amazing man, and before I knew it, he had me flat on my back and straddling me.

He gently stroked my cheek, and he leaned closer, but I stopped him from kissing me again. A firm hand to his chest as he held my eyes.

"Sean McGregor," I said in a shaky voice, "I fucking love you." I blinked, startled by how that came out, and a slow smirk spread across his face. "I mean I love to . . ." Screw it. I couldn't lie. My only gift to give was this. "I love you. And *you're* irreplaceable and so, so different." I sniffled. "And I'm so thankful to have someone love me as much as I love them."

Tears filled this strong man's eyes, and I guided my hand around the nape of his neck and pulled his mouth back to mine. Taking everything I wanted, everything I never knew I needed.

CHAPTER TWENTY-SEVEN

EMILIA

NEW YEAR'S EVE

PENELOPE CASTELLANOS-LAURENT WAS STUNNING IN AN elegant, Mediterranean-blue evening dress that skimmed the floor and sparkled as if it were sprinkled with diamonds. Her long dark hair flowed over her shoulders, the front pinned back from her face and held with a glittering clip. She looked like a Greek goddess. And she was my *mother*.

She hadn't noticed me as I stood on the edge of the thick crowd of wealthy guests in the massive ballroom of the hotel, but I hadn't been able to take my eyes off her since Sean and I arrived thirty minutes ago.

"Sure you don't want anything to drink?" Sean asked.

I stole my focus away from Penelope to behold the handsome man I loved. He looked brilliant in a black jacket with a crisp white shirt and black bow tie. And any other night, I'd be imagining slowly stripping him out of all of it at the end of the night, but I needed to keep my focus.

My floor-length gown was plainer than Penelope's but no less eye-catching, at least according to Sean. Blood red silk and clean lines hugged my body, the only enhancement a deep V cut out of the back that ended just above my ass. And right now, Sean's free hand rested on the small of my back, dangerously close to dipping below the line of fabric to touch my nude panties.

I love you. I'd actually said it. And not because I was worried I might die tonight—well, maybe a little worried—but it was the truth, and he deserved to know.

Unlike Papà and Penelope, I would no longer let people or their rules dictate who I could love or with whom I was allowed to spend my life. I would do better. Be better.

"No, I shouldn't drink." I was far too nervous just being in the same room with Penelope and Atlas, never mind the rest of tonight's agenda. There was too much on the line to risk clouding my senses with even a sip of champagne.

Sean held a tumbler of bourbon in his hand, keeping up the appearance of enjoying the party by taking a casual sip every few minutes.

I doubted Sean would be drinking if he knew the real plan, the one I forced Sebastian to keep from him. The one Roman helped prepare. Sean would be part furious and part terrified when I put all the cards on the table.

My stomach clenched with anticipation as I waited for Peter's arrival. Still a no-show, but he'd be there at some point.

I surveyed the room and spotted Atlas conversing with an older gentleman. The man seemed to be doing all the talking while Atlas stood there looking bored, which gave me a chance to take in Atlas's features. He was built similarly to Sean and was also in a tux. His dark hair was tapered at the sides and purposefully unruly at the top. Tall, broad shoulders, square jaw with a beard. Dark eyes like Chanel's. Like mine.

My brother.

No, half brother, I reminded myself. He still had Simon's blood in him. But he also had Penelope's, and that part had me shaky and confused whenever I considered the plan. The plan Sean would be furious about once he saw the pieces falling into place.

I stole a look at another man and woman in the room who were pivotal to tonight's plans. Roman and Harper. Roman's family in Spain were rich and powerful, so he'd used his connection to them to gain access to the event tonight. I envied Roman's parents giving up tradition to move to America and raise their kids differently.

Harper looked beautiful in a navy-blue gown that wrapped around her curves and crisscrossed just above her breasts. Roman was in a black dress shirt and trousers instead of a tux, and he seemed more interested in Harper than surveilling the room. Of course, he had a comm in his ear and a team he'd brought with him standing in the wings watching over all of our moves. Until Peter arrived and the signal was given, Roman and Harper were simply a wealthy powerhouse couple partying on New Year's Eve.

I'd felt a little guilty asking Roman to bring Harper to Monaco to assist us, especially after he told me she'd been left for dead years ago while on a job in Monte Carlo. But her cyber skills surpassed those of anyone we knew. I supposed if she were like me, that experience would have made her stronger and more resolved to maintain her calm while here.

"Hey," Sebastian said on approach a few minutes later, his large frame blocking my view of Atlas. "You good?"

"As good as can be," I responded while doing another survey of the room, spying Cole and Alessia in position near the terrace doors.

"While you're here, I'm going to go have a quick word

with my cousin." Sean rested his hand on my back, his warm palm comforting against my chilled skin. He guided me to face him and gently brought his lips to mine.

Longing to continue the kiss, I pushed up on my toes and leaned in closer, but I was worried Sean might somehow sense my anxiety if I lingered, so I stepped back.

His forehead creased as he studied me, a conflicted look moving across his face, and his hand on my back tensed up as if he was having second thoughts about leaving.

"I'm fine," I told him, then lifted my chin, motioning for him to go. He hesitantly nodded but left to speak with Cole.

"I'm worried," Sebastian announced as soon as Sean was out of earshot.

"About the plan?" I side-eyed him discreetly.

"No, your plan may be dangerous, but it's genius." He set a hand on a small bar-top table off to his left. "I'm worried Sean will punch me as soon as he discovers we lied to him. If someone put Holly in danger—"

"I'm not Holly," I reminded him, but my heart sank at the sight of Sean talking to Cole, his back stiff. "He's definitely going to want to hit you, though."

Sebastian faced me, hands diving into his pockets. "You sure this is what you want to do? We could still go with the original plan?" His eyes moved to Atlas for a brief moment before landing on my face.

"As we've discussed, Luca might see through that plan, and we can't take that risk. You and I know him better than anyone else. *This* he won't expect." When I fully faced Sebastian, I saw the internal battle he was fighting playing out in his dark brown eyes. "Ah, the promise you made to Papà."

"Forget the promise. I want to keep you safe because you're like a sister to me. I care about you." That had to be hard for him to say because he really wasn't great at expressing his emotions with anyone other than Holly.

I reached for the necklace Sean gave me, then realized it wasn't there. I hadn't wanted to risk losing it, and I was worried Sean's feelings had been hurt when he watched me set the lion necklace aside instead of putting it on. "I'll be fine." I almost added *I promise*, but promises felt so meaningless after Papà's lies. "Maybe let Sean get in one good punch."

"I'll try," Sebastian answered with something of a growl, then touched his ear a second later. "Luca's here," he informed me.

"And Peter and Bridgette just arrived," I said while spotting the couple entering through the double doors from the hall.

Sean had a comm in his ear as well, which explained his abrupt glance our way.

"I'll move into position and alert our two men outside." Sebastian set a hand to my shoulder, his brows tightening, then gave me a squeeze and walked away.

My gaze shot to Atlas, and I noticed an immediate shift in his posture when his eyes caught sight of the newest attendees.

The German model's entry into the ballroom elicited quite a few audible gasps and murmuring erupted throughout the room. She moved gracefully in a sheer silvery gown, which had sequins artfully pieced together over her feminine areas. Her breasts, ass, and the V between her legs were concealed but not by much.

Judging by his glacial stare, the gown didn't seem to impress Atlas as much as it angered him. He ignored the gentleman talking to him and cut across the room toward Bridgette, completely forgetting himself. Forgetting she wasn't his, not yet. Nor would she ever be if Luca had his way.

"Well, someone is jealous and possessive," Sean spoke up now that he was at my side again.

"Looks that way." I briefly closed my eyes at the thought that my half brother was about to throw his plan to have Peter killed out the window all because of a sexy dress. He was out for blood now. "Devil incoming," I whispered when Luca materialized to serve as a blockade to Atlas in his path of destruction.

It was hard to be in the same room as that bastard. Even harder to have Sean at my side, knowing it was brutal for him to remain fixed in place when he wanted to throttle the life out of him.

Luca wore all black, and his longish brown hair flipped at the collar of his shirt. His beard was thicker than he'd ever worn it in the past, most likely to hide the evil grin always on his face.

"I want to kill the fecker," Sean said out of the corner of his mouth as he reached for my hand.

My grip went lax at the realization Atlas had found a new target to stare at—me. His jaw hung open, brows slanting inward as if he were seeing me for the first time.

Luca followed his eyes to me, and he dared to smile before walking away.

I was fairly certain someone else was watching me now, too. I felt her watching me before I turned to confirm she was there.

My mother.

Standing less than ten meters away was the woman who abandoned me. Penelope's glass fell from her hand as she looked back and forth between Atlas and me, likely in shock at seeing her children in the same room. Knowing her son was planning to kill her only living daughter.

Atlas stalked across the room with purposeful strides, moving past me without stealing another glance, and headed straight for his mother as one of the servers cleaned up the drink she'd spilled and the broken glass.

"Where'd Luca go?" Sean asked as he scanned the room.

"Shit, I don't see him." I'd been distracted. "I don't see Peter now, either. I think it's time. We need to make our move soon, so they don't beat us to it." I'd worked the words loose from my tightened throat, regretting I was about to deviate from what he thought was the plan.

Penelope remained frozen in place while someone replaced her drink as Atlas talked to her, his back to me.

"I need to go." I ripped my focus from my mother and half brother to peer at Sean. I pushed up on my toes and set a kiss to his full lips. "I love you," I murmured before he captured my mouth again, this time in a hot and searing kiss, one that left a mark on my heart.

"This isn't goodbye," he said as if reading my thoughts. "Just get it done quickly. Promise me."

"I promise," I said in a shaky voice. *Another broken promise.* "But I still want to tell you that I love you." I stepped out of his reach, which was harder to do than I'd expected.

He nodded, his mouth tight, then he touched his ear. "You've got the perfect chance to make your move now. Peter's alone in the men's room down the hall," he relayed the information that had come over his comm as I didn't have one.

Four of Roman's SEAL buddies were in position as our eyes for tonight. And Peter in the bathroom alone was almost too good. Could I get that lucky?

Maybe one last kiss, though.

Sean snatched my arms and crushed his mouth to mine as if he'd heard my thoughts. His tongue parted my lips, offering me what felt like an intimate moment in the midst of a crowd.

"Love you," I said once again, softer this time, then abruptly turned and left.

Once out of the ballroom, I went straight for the men's room, hoping Peter was still inside alone. I casually slipped my hand down to my ankle beneath the dress and retrieved the syringe.

I pushed open the door without hesitation and found Peter at the sink, washing his hands.

Peter turned off the faucet and carried his eyes to meet mine in the mirror. "Emilia Calibrisi," he whispered, his voice laced with a faint German accent. "You're even more beautiful in person than in your photos." He tossed a paper towel in the rubbish bin and faced me. There were no lines of distress on his forehead or around his eyes, clearly not threatened by a woman.

Lifting a hand, he ran his fingers through his wavy black hair threaded with silver and pushed it off his forehead.

I ignored him and ducked my head to ensure the private stalls were empty.

"What? Looking for a good time?" he asked, his tone crass and bullish.

"We don't have much time, Krause."

"Oh, time for what?" He smirked as his eyes lazily descended my body in appreciation.

"Soon, most likely tonight, someone will try to murder you. I'm here to keep that from happening." I returned to the door and set my back to it in case anyone tried to come inside. Of course, Roman's teammates would most likely run interference were that to happen.

I only had two minutes, though.

Peter laughed, his coal-colored eyes flitting over my body again. "I have heard you're dangerous, and I am intrigued to see what you're truly capable of. But savior? No, you wouldn't save your enemy." He pocketed his hands—an insulting gesture meant to show how little he thought of my abilities.

"There's a plot to unseat you from your leadership role. You need to die for that to happen." My stomach knotted. I wanted to keep Atlas out of this as much as possible. "We have a common enemy at the moment, Luca Moreau. He and your wife are scheming together."

He frowned at the mention of Luca's name. It was the first sign of worry I'd seen so far.

"I have a plan. Work with me and stick to it, or you will die, simple as that."

"I don't believe you." He closed the space between us but remained out of arm's reach. Maybe he did know what was good for him.

"I'm going to fake your death, Krause." I showed him the syringe containing a solution that would put him into a deep sleep and slow his heart rate to the point that it would be virtually undetectable. "My men will pronounce you dead, then load you into an ambulance where they'll revive you. But the public must believe you've died. At least for a few days." Faking a death, a page from Luca's playbook.

"Ha." He pointed to the syringe. "You think I'll let you stab me with that thing?"

I never really believed he'd willingly allow it, but a woman had to try, right?

Before he knew it, I lunged his way, brought an elbow to

his face, and kneed him in the balls. A cheap shot, but I was short on time.

Before he had a chance to comprehend what happened, I injected the solution into his neck. In a desperate attempt to stop me, he shot his hand out around my throat, but it was too late. His grip quickly weakened as the drugs worked through his system.

He slid down the wall to the ground, legs outstretched in front of him. His head tipped down, and his arms hung uselessly at his sides.

"Well, you look dead," I said under my breath just as there was a knock at the door.

"Peter, are you in there? What is taking so long?" Bridgette asked after first saying something in German.

I buried the syringe in the rubbish bin just in time before the door flung open. My two minutes must've been up, and the SEALs knew they had the go-ahead to let Bridgette discover a lifeless Peter *with* me by his side—the part of the plan Sean knew nothing about.

It took a moment for Bridgette to comprehend the sight of me standing in front of her husband's lifeless body. She blinked repeatedly, the door nearly swinging back in her face. "What did you do? This wasn't—"

"The plan?" As soon as I cut her off, she began screaming in panic as she backed up out of the bathroom.

I exited the bathroom, dropped to my knees, and brought my hands behind my head at the sight of two security personnel hurrying to respond to her frantic calls.

"The man in the restroom . . . he's dead," I told the men on approach, my eyes never leaving Bridgette's. "And I killed him."

"What have you done?" she cried, eyes going to me as one of the guards grabbed hold of my arms and twisted them behind my back. "You-you . . ." Speechless wasn't a good look on her, and as much as I wanted to clue her in on the fact she was now the one being played, I bit my tongue.

The guard yanked me to my feet as his partner propped open the restroom door and rushed over to Peter. Bridgette took that as her cue to begin crying, giving everyone an award-worthy performance as the other man announced he was struggling to find a pulse.

I had to give her credit for keeping up the act. She'd wanted her husband dead. And she got what she'd wanted. Not the way she'd intended, but it'd still work for her plan. By the time she found out my true intentions, it would be too late.

I glimpsed at The League members dressed in medic uniforms advancing quickly toward us as the two guards escorted me in the opposite direction, past the entrance to the ballroom where dozens of shocked guests began pouring out.

My gaze cut to Roman, who appeared with Harper, and I gave him a tight nod, letting him know everything went according to plan.

"Wait." Sean's voice carried through the crowd, and I instinctively turned my head his way.

As soon as our gazes connected, I saw awareness in his eyes. His nostrils flared, and his blue eyes grew darker. He realized I'd done this behind his back, that I hadn't let him in on the change in plans.

Pain and sadness cut through my heart like knives, overwhelming me as I witnessed his disappointment and the fear swirling in his irises.

The guard first yelled in French, but when Sean didn't budge, he yelled in English to back off.

"Emilia," Sean mouthed, agony written across his beautiful face.

I closed my eyes as we sidestepped him, unable to meet his tortured gaze. The pain I knew I'd caused him tonight was far too much for me to handle, and I was worried Sean wouldn't be able to look past it.

I didn't glance back as the guards hustled me forward, but I dared to hope Sean loved me enough to forgive one more lie. And that I survived to see it happen.

CHAPTER TWENTY-EIGHT

SEAN

My fist slammed into Sebastian's jaw with a jarring thud, drawing startled looks from the few guests still lingering in front of the hotel as if they were waiting for more excitement. Well, I supposed I just gave it to them.

"Back off," I hollered in their direction before reeling my hand back, itching to strike Sebastian again. Based on my throbbing knuckles and the red mark blooming on Sebastian's cheek, I was certain I hit him harder than I'd meant to.

Anger burned my lungs as I hissed, "You son of a—"

But I dropped my words, along with my fist, at the look of sadness and hurt in his eyes. This man was my friend as well as part of our family and hitting him again wouldn't undo the fact Emilia had just been hauled away by the police. Nor would it magically bring her back.

I stumbled away from him and reached up to claw my fingers through my hair.

Sebastian placed a hand on my shoulder and moved me farther away from the hotel entrance. There were still a few uniformed officers on-site speaking to two plainclothes men who I assumed were detectives. I knew as soon as the front desk informed them Emilia and I were sharing a room, they'd be bringing me in for questioning.

Maybe that wouldn't be such a bad thing if it meant I'd get a chance to confirm her location and that she was okay.

But what the actual feck happened tonight?

"The plan was for Emilia to drug Peter, then for Roman to stumble upon him in the restroom afterward and alert hotel security." I heaved out a deep, worried breath. "Why was she taken away in cuffs? Why did you two change the plan, and why wasn't I included?"

Sebastian remained quiet. Calm. Allowing me to come to my senses, but I was out of bloody sorts with Emilia gone.

Now I understood her passionate goodbye kiss and the *I love you* before leaving to confront Peter in the restroom. She'd known exactly what was going to happen. How she'd break my heart with worry. And that she might not survive.

I pulled at my hair and paced the footpath near where Sebastian stood, and then it came to me. The truth hit me so damn hard I nearly struck Sebastian again.

"She thinks Luca will come for her," I rasped, the idea sending chills every which way beneath my tux jacket. "She wants Luca to think he has the upper hand."

"We're controlling the narrative," Sebastian said, confirming I was on the right track. "We couldn't anticipate when or how Luca would try and lure us to him, but we knew he wanted us in Monaco based on all of his recent antics. Emilia sitting in a jail cell was not what he planned for, however."

"So instead of waiting for him to come to us, she set the trap." *Damn it.* That very idea had lurked in the back of my mind, but I hadn't dared suggest it when we devised our plan of attack for Monte Carlo. "You think Luca will take her to the location of The Final Hour?" I went on when he remained silent.

Part of our original plan was to keep tabs on Atlas to discover the location, but we'd only had theories as to how Luca would draw us out.

"Why didn't she tell me?"

Sebastian's lips flattened into a firm line as he extended his arm and held out his hand, gesturing to me as the obvious reason.

Because I'd say no. I'd refuse to put her in harm's way. "Where is Luca now? I assume our people have him in their sights?"

"Luca left the hotel the second he heard about Peter's 'death' and Emilia's arrest. We're following him," Roman announced over comms. Shite, my head was such a mess I'd forgotten I was wearing the damn thing. "It'll take him time to scramble together a plan to get Emilia out of jail. I'm going to guess he has someone on the inside at the local precinct, though, in the event something went wrong with his original plan to have Peter killed."

Luca always had a plan, as well as multiple backup plans, so Roman was most likely right. And it was why Emilia had decided to beat him at his own game and throw Luca a curveball. She was brave, but I was still mad at her for keeping me in the dark.

"Tell me you planted one of those undetectable trackers under Emilia's skin." I set my hands to my hips and bowed my head.

"The same kind we used on Luca, yes," Sebastian answered, but there was a break in his voice, which had me lifting my eyes to his face. He was worried, wasn't he? And that had me on edge even more.

"And Luca will be expecting that," I said with a shake of

my head. "You want him to find it, don't you? He'll think he outsmarted us." Images of that cocksucker cutting into Emilia to remove the tracker had my palms twitching with the need to hit someone or something. I was my twin brother right now, ready to lose myself in a fight to alleviate my anger.

But this was the greatest fight of my life—bringing Emilia back home safely.

"We have Roman and his teammates with us, and Luca will never anticipate their assistance. We're not the type of people to have drones in the sky, but they are, and they've got Emilia's every move covered. Wherever Luca goes—we'll be going, too." Sebastian turned to the side, his gaze moving to the hotel entrance just as Atlas exited. "But there's one more piece of the plan that I'm a bit more uncertain about."

Sebastian looked back at me, then tipped his head toward where Atlas was talking to the valet.

"You can't be serious." I dropped my head in shock when I realized what Sebastian was implying. "Atlas won't—"

"He's her brother," Sebastian cut me off.

"Atlas only just learned Emilia is his sister. They've been on opposing sides their entire lives. Atlas is one of the bad guys, and he can't be trusted."

"Bad guy is a relative term. Depends on who you're talking to." Sebastian was already on the move, heading for the enemy.

I ignored whatever the hell that was supposed to mean and caught up with him.

We were about to find out if Atlas would choose his sister over his lover.

And feck if I felt the odds weren't in our favor.

* * *

WE WERE STILL IN MONTE CARLO, AND IT'D BEEN ALMOST seventy-two hours since Emilia's arrest.

I was thoroughly exhausted. Mostly from fear and worry for Emilia, but also because I hadn't slept since she'd been arrested, and it was taking its toll. The eyes staring back at me in the mirror of my ensuite were bloodshot. I hadn't bothered to shave, and my clothes were a wrinkled mess.

As I'd assumed, I was brought in for questioning by the detectives, and I'd nearly broken down and blurted out that Emilia couldn't be a murderer because our people were holding a very much alive Peter Krause in an American safe house fifteen kilometers away. I would've done almost anything to see her while I was at the police station. To save her.

But this was what Emilia wanted, and I forced myself to cooperate, to try and accept her decision to risk herself as a means to end Luca and The Alliance.

I'd repeated the story Sebastian rehearsed with me, and the detective seemed to buy it. Of course, I had to believe there were unmarked units outside the hotel watching me now that Emilia had "escaped" custody. She was a fugitive. Most likely, not something on her bucket list. And did she have a list?

God, the things you thought about when you were worried.

Like the fact I understood why she hadn't worn the necklace I bought her to the New Year's Eve party, and yet it still kind of hurt my feelings.

I splashed cold water on my face and tried to conjure up some sort of switch inside my head to turn off the *code red* signal that had been blaring for three days.

Last night, the police station had received orders to transfer Emilia—most likely Luca had pulled some Alliance strings—and not even ten minutes into the drive, the unit had been ambushed. Roman watched the scene unfold via drone, so we now knew her location. A heavily guarded estate ten minutes from the hotel, owned by The Alliance leader of Monaco. The man looked like a young Christian Bale, the *American Psycho* movie version, from what Roman's teammate, Finn, had said. I had no clue what that meant, but the idea Emilia was in the presence of Luca, and now another psycho, made me want to puke.

"If he touches her . . ." I began as I caught sight of Alessia through the open ensuite door as she strode my way.

"I don't think Luca will harm her in the way you may be fearing. He never did any of those things to me. Yes, he forced me to fight for my life. And even kill." Alessia's voice was soft, not as bitter as I expected considering what the bastard had put her through.

Of all the things that'd gone through my mind since Emilia was abducted by Luca's men last night, torture hadn't been one of them. That thought I refused to accept as a possibility.

"The intel Roman picked up suggests we'll be getting her back tonight." Alessia squeezed my bicep. "The Final Hour is sure to be happening soon since Atlas announced his desire to be with Bridgette now that they believe Peter is dead."

And if whatever "chatter" Roman heard is wrong, what then?

"Atlas said none of that, and he blew us the feck off when we tried talking to him." The conversation with him had lasted less than a minute.

We'd explained Luca's true intentions with Bridgette. Begged him to save his sister and choose the right side in this fight, and then he turned and left us without a word.

"If he tells Luca we approached him—"

"Luca will assume we're desperate. That we know he kidnapped her, and he'll think he won since he was smart enough to remove the tracker." She let go of my arm, her big brown eyes, similar to Emilia's, tightening on me in the mirror. "Blood will prove stronger than you think. Sebastian wasn't exactly jumping with excitement to let me into his life when he discovered I existed."

"Yeah, but you weren't facing an upside-down hourglass with the sands of time running out," I grumbled and faced her, crossing my arms.

"Well, we have a backup plan if Atlas doesn't reach out before The Final Hour."

I hated relying on hopes and maybes.

"You really love her, don't you?" She gave me an uneasy smile. "I'm glad she found someone. I wasn't sure if she'd ever be able to open her heart, but I'm so happy it was to you."

"I'm going to marry her. Have kids. A life." Screw The League and anyone who tried to stop me. And the promise to her father was blown to hell now that we knew she was Penelope's daughter. So, what was left to stand in our way but Luca and The Alliance? And they were on the verge of going down. I had to remain strong. Believe everything would work out.

Alessia's expression softened, but before she could speak again, Roman appeared in the doorway.

"Got a second?" he asked.

Alessia gave my shoulder a quick squeeze, and then we left the ensuite.

Roman was tall, broad-shouldered with dark hair and eyes. His father was from Spain, and his mother from Brazil. Emilia told me his parents had fallen in love and chose to leave behind a life of wealth to raise him and his sisters in the U.S.

Roman's attention veered to the open doorway through which I saw his colleague, Harper Brooks, sitting at the kitchen counter and typing away at the laptop in front of her. I'd worked with Harper and Roman before, back in October, and there was an obvious connection between them now as well as then. But from what I could tell, they were exes who still had feelings for each other, or they were afraid to take the plunge and be together. *Why am I even thinking about this?*

"How are you holding up?" Roman asked quietly.

I dragged my hands through my hair, then sat on the bed where Emilia and I had made love countless times between when she'd turned thirty-one and when she'd shown up at the ball in that red silk dress. "I'm not holding up. Not at all."

Roman set his back to the wall by the open door and propped a black-booted foot to the wall. We hadn't addressed the fact Emilia had discussed her plan with him instead of me. It would only stir up feelings of jealousy, which was not the emotion I wanted to be dealing with right now. Not when Emilia was in danger.

"We got word that Atlas announced his desire to marry Bridgette now that Peter is gone."

"Did anyone invoke The Final Hour?"

"Yes, as expected. And the leaders are opting not to travel here with it being short notice. They'll be streaming the event. The only leader aside from Atlas that'll be there is—"

"The Christian Bale lookalike?"

He nodded. "And we'll handle him directly."

"So, when the rest of the leaders join the call to watch the fighting take place, you really don't think Harper will have a problem hacking their servers?"

"No, but she's got an assist on standby Stateside if needed." Roman glanced at her through the open doorway again. "We'll make sure to get enough evidence to take them down."

"Well, we have teams in a few locations keeping an eye on the most dangerous of the leaders."

"Wait until those bastards see all of their dirty secrets being broadcast all over the internet. On every social media site in the world. There'll be nowhere for them to hide." The sound of a Southern drawl similar to Anna's caught my attention.

Roman's teammate, A.J., stood in the doorway wearing a black ball cap with dark cargo trousers, boots, and a black long-sleeved tee.

"A world of warriors fighting for us by dispersing the truth," A.J. went on, his arms across his chest as he casually leaned into the interior doorframe.

I stroked my jaw in thought. "Guess that's one way to look at it. And Atlas? Penelope? Did you talk to your government about a solution for them?"

"We'll do our best to honor the favor Emilia requested, but it depends on their sins." Roman nodded and dropped his boot to the floor.

"Any updates before we head out?" I asked.

"Wyatt is on overwatch," A.J. answered. "He's one of the best snipers in the world, and he's got eyes on the estate where Emilia's at. And Chris is with him as a spotter."

Chris's fiancée, Rory, was how I'd first met Roman and the others back in October. A.J.'s friend, Rory, met and fell in love with his teammate, Chris, which led them all to meeting Emilia and myself when Rory got into trouble taking down a trafficker. Roman had called Emilia for an assist, and that was when her mansion became the site of a *Die Hard* movie.

A.J. motioned for me to follow him, so I stood, and we all went into the living room.

Sebastian was talking to Harper and their other teammate, Finn. Cole and Alessia must've been getting ready in their room, and I assumed Cole was pleading with Alessia to stay behind with Harper.

I peeked at the hotel phone on an end table next to the couch, hoping Atlas would call and prove to be a better man than I thought he might be, but we were running short on time.

"Based on our eyes in the sky, there are ten armed guards outside the perimeter of the estate, and we've got thermal imaging picking up six heat signatures inside the home," Harper said upon noticing we'd joined her and Sebastian.

Unlike A.J. and the others, Sebastian was in a suit. The thought of him decked out in the same getup as the SEALs almost made me laugh.

"We've prepped a breach strategy whether Atlas calls or not. But we have confirmation Atlas left the hotel with Bridgette five minutes ago," Roman said, standing off to the side of Harper's chair.

I had to assume Atlas wouldn't be calling, then.

"You still on your killing diet?" Roman asked as he directed the question to Sebastian.

If Emilia weren't in trouble, I'd grin right about now.

"Emilia's being held inside that estate," Sebastian said through gritted teeth, "so, yeah, anyone who tries to stop us gets a bullet."

I thought back to Holly's words to me that night at the club, which now felt like decades ago, that she'd planned to give her husband the "gift of killing" for Christmas. Good thing, too, or he'd be sleeping at the hotel again.

We exchanged a few more words, discussing strategy, and then I went back to my room to change.

Suit or SEAL? I opted for neither. Loose-fitting black sweats and a long-sleeved dark shirt in case I needed to use my fists.

"Hey," I said to Roman twenty minutes later when we were all gathered in the living room, my eyes moving back to the hotel phone that'd yet to ring. "What would you do if the woman you loved was in danger?"

Roman swallowed, and his eyes flicked to Harper, her back to us as she worked on her laptop. I wasn't sure if she heard me, but she'd stopped typing.

"I'd cut down anyone that stood in my way to get to her. No lines I wouldn't cross," he answered without hesitation.

And I believed that, but . . . "If push comes to shove, and you can let the guy who hurt her live—would you?"

Now it was Sebastian studying me, and my fingers curled inward at my sides as I thought about what might happen when I came face to face with Luca again.

When I focused back on Roman, there was a dark look in his eyes, and he said, "I think you know the answer to that."

CHAPTER TWENTY-NINE

EMILIA

FORTY-FIVE MINUTES LATER

Luca's calloused palm scraped along my cheek, a testament to the fact he'd been fighting. Training for this moment. He remained crouched in front of where I was bound and gagged to a chair. "In another life, maybe we would have ruled together, *mon amour.*"

Yeah, the one time we had sex a lifetime ago would still go down as my greatest drunken mistake.

I kept still, my chin tilted defiantly. I wouldn't give this bastard the luxury of watching me squirm or resist the zip ties locking my hands at the back of the chair. Nor did I try to free my ankles from the ropes tied to the chair legs, either. The khaki trousers and long-sleeved shirt provided by the jail kept the ropes from burning into my skin, at least.

But it wasn't time to make a move yet.

Obedience wasn't my MO, but in this case, allowing Luca to feel as though he had the upper hand was exactly what I was after.

His lips curled into a smirk. "Who will rule Italy now that

you're gone?" he asked, slowly dragging his hand down my neck as if we were lovers. His touch made me cringe, and if I weren't already gagged, I would, well, gag. His fingers skated across the wound on the back of my shoulder where he'd carved out the tracker. He pushed his thumb into raw flesh, his body far too close as he leaned in to inflict pain, trying to get me to cry out.

I bit down on the gag in my mouth, but I wouldn't give the bastard what he wanted.

His shoulders fell, feigning disappointment, but I knew better than to believe his act. He pulled his hand back and stood. "I like keeping that wicked tongue of yours in check."

They hadn't blindfolded me or covered my head when the police car was "ambushed" and they brought me to my current location. The two officers in the squad car hadn't put up a fight at all, and the men who came for me only roughed them up a bit. Luca must've paid the officers a premium price for faking my escape.

But the fact the men didn't bother to shield my vision from the location meant they were confident I'd never leave. I'd recognized the owner of the home as Arnaud Dupont, Alliance leader of Monaco. He was a horrible human being from what I knew about him, and I could only hope I'd be the one to take him down when this was over. When I had arrived, Luca actually intervened to stop the man from making me his "plaything" while we waited for The Final Hour to begin.

Luca hadn't stopped Arnaud for my benefit, though. He'd warned Arnaud not to be fooled by my looks and assured him I'd find a way to kill him, regardless of restraints if he touched me.

"Be a good girl and look sad, or maybe I'll let Arnaud

have his way with you." Luca's sinister voice dropped a few octaves.

Despite Luca distracting me with his bullshit, I kept my wits about me, cataloging every detail in the room as well as the men who came and went and what I could understand from their comments. I'd just overheard one of them say Atlas had arrived and the fight would be starting soon.

We were beneath the first floor, in a large unfinished space. Maybe it was Arnaud's torture chamber because the stains on the concrete under my feet appeared to be dried blood, and there was a faint, metallic smell in the air.

A makeshift cage stood in the center of the room with a spotlight overhead, and one of Luca's men, or maybe Arnaud's, had just positioned a wide-lens camera on the room and set up some sort of display projector to mirror his laptop. Multiple screens appeared on one of the white-painted concrete walls.

Luca set his hands into the pockets of his crisp black trousers. Was he attending a board meeting or a fight to the death?

"I've been preparing for this night for a long time, *mon amour.*" His eyes were so vacant and void of emotion. Had he always been so dead on the inside? Such a monster?

If you can stop calling me your love, that'd be great. Dark thoughts of how I would kill this prick and the asshole Arnaud circled my mind like a carousel, each option more vivid than the last.

"Did you know I arranged for Simon and Milos's plane to go down?" he whispered so the other man in the room didn't overhear. "The affair between Bridgette and Atlas was my idea, too."

I knew Luca wouldn't be able to resist sharing what he considered clever triumphs. *Keep talking, asshole.*

"Bridgette fell in love with me, though. I can't wait to see the look on Atlas's face when he learns the truth. You're all a bunch of fools. Playing into my hands." His devious grin grew wider. "I have another dirty little secret, which I'm betting you already know since I heard The League got my little package."

The video footage.

"Those videos have provided me so much pleasure. I particularly like the ones of you after a shower, walking around naked and carefree, bending every which way to get dressed. But the ones of you fucking McGregor while you're on top . . ." He lifted a hand from his pocket and adjusted his crotch.

I clenched my jaw, trying to maintain a steady sense of control, knowing he was doing his best to rile me up.

"You know, Emilia, I'm rather disappointed in you." Luca slowly shook his head as if he were dealing with a naughty child. "I thought you were much smarter than you've shown me lately. First, you completely missed my video cameras in your room"—he smirked and began pacing in front of me —"and then you killed Peter. I should have left you in prison and killed your lover and his buddies." Luca brushed his hands together like he was removing dirt. "But that wouldn't have been much fun." He turned his back to me and looked at the fighting ring for a few quiet moments. The man really loved to hear himself talk, didn't he? Always so insecure and needing to flaunt his power.

Luca swung back around to face me. "You knew how badly I wanted to kill you myself, so you figured I'd use my powerful influence and get you released, bring you here. And then your buddies would show up for a surprise attack. Really, Emilia, you think I'd do that without checking for a tracker first? Shame on you." He shifted the bulge in his trousers again, clearly loving every second of this. "Ah, *chérie,* but The League has banished you. The only friends you have are the Irish," he gloated. "Oh, I would have loved to have seen your face when you learned why Sara was really in your life." He snickered. "Did she confess her sins to you before or after you heard from my uncle?"

He must've tried to have Sara killed last week only to discover she was being guarded, and therefore we knew her involvement in his scheme. At least Luca received the intel we wanted him to hear, that The League turned on me. Refused to come to Monaco and help us. He had no idea of the deal I made with his uncle.

"I'd love to take the gag out and hear what you have to say, but—"

"Luca, what are you doing?" I looked around Luca to see Atlas coming down the spiral stairs.

"Just talking to my pet," Luca smugly stated.

Atlas strode our direction, crossing the room in only a fitted pair of shorts, the kind UFC fighters wore in the cage.

"You ready for this? Ready to be more powerful than any leader in history?" Luca smiled.

"I'm ready. Bridgette is speaking with Arnaud. They'll be down soon to watch." Atlas stood beside Luca, observing me with a frown on his face.

There was a softness to his eyes I hadn't expected. Pity? Or had the plan worked? Had Sebastian and Sean convinced him to help tonight?

"Take out her gag," Atlas instructed.

"I don't think that's a good idea." Luca held a hand up. "The leaders are all joining soon. We don't need her running her mouth." He lifted his wrist and checked his watch. "Five minutes until the feed goes live, and we'll be broadcasting to every Alliance leader in the world. The fighters just arrived."

"Fighters?" Atlas scoffed. "More like assassins." He squatted in front of me, head tipped to the side. "You look like her." His dark eyes narrowed. "Like both of them."

Chanel and Penelope?

"Who?" Luca asked.

"She's not to be harmed until the end." Atlas ignored Luca's question and rose to his feet. "I sent word to my men ten minutes ago to collect her lover and friends. We'll be taking them down tonight instead of tomorrow."

My pulse fluttered at his words. I wanted to be hopeful, but I couldn't be certain if that statement meant he was on our side or that he'd twisted the plan to benefit himself, knowing our intentions.

"That wasn't our agreement and for good reason. Do you have any idea what they're capable of? You can't bring them into this house." Luca began pacing off to my side, his forehead tight, eyes downcast.

"Call your men and tell them to hold off. Trust me when I say you don't want them here, subdued or not, and especially not Sebastian." Luca came to a halt and stabbed a finger toward Atlas.

"What's done is done." Atlas nodded. "And you're not a leader. You don't call the shots, Moreau." He leaned in closer to his face in a challenge, his muscular body dominating Luca's leaner frame.

"This was my damn plan," Luca hissed. "You wouldn't be here if it weren't for me."

Well, these two turning on each other wasn't what I'd expected.

"If your men can capture Sebastian and the others, it's because they want to be caught. They want to be brought to Emilia." His voice grew louder during his rant, the veins in his neck on display. He squatted before me and circled a hand around my throat. "You little bitch."

"Let. Her. Go." Atlas grabbed Luca's shoulder and yanked him back, but Luca only gripped tighter.

I kept my eyes open, refusing to surrender to him, but his grip was cutting off my air, and my vision was growing hazy. But before I knew it, Luca's hand was gone from my neck. My eyes watered, and I saw that he was now lying on his back on the cement floor.

"You've made a mistake," Luca warned, pushing up off the ground and wiping his hands along the sides of his trousers.

"You challenging me is the only mistake I see." Atlas turned toward the stairs and yelled something in Greek, which was followed a few seconds later by two men hurrying down the steps. Atlas jerked his head and motioned for his men to take Luca away. "I want him out of my sight."

"You'll regret this, Laurent. You'll fucking regret this." Luca looked at me, rage burning in his eyes before the two men escorted him out. "She killed Peter so I'd bring her here. They're scheming. I can assure you of that," Luca tossed out at the last second before he disappeared.

Atlas turned and squatted in front of me. "Emilia," he said softly.

"Sir, we're going live now," the man who'd been working the projector announced, interrupting whatever Atlas was about to say.

He bowed his head for a brief second, then released a breath and rose.

I carried my focus to the wall where the faces of at least fifty men were now displayed as if the wall was one giant split-screen TV.

Arnaud, The Asshole of Monaco, came down the stairs a

moment later, Bridgette trailing behind him in a flashy gold dress with stilettos.

"It's time," Arnaud said when Atlas had yet to leave my side.

Atlas peered at Bridgette, then back at me, and his shoulders sloped as if he were unsure of what to do or who to choose. He turned and crossed the room to greet Bridgette and Arnaud, both now settled alongside the other guard who'd set up the screens.

Bridgette smiled and took the hand Atlas offered. She linked her fingers with his, and they stood before the wall of leaders.

"As you have heard," Atlas began, his voice full of confidence, "I would like to step in for Peter Krause and marry Bridgette." He raised their clasped palms. "Unite our families and our countries." He looked back over his shoulder at Arnaud. "Arnaud Dupont invoked The Final Hour, and since we were still in Monte Carlo, it made sense to move forward sooner rather than later with this ritual."

Ah, of course. Arnaud was working with Luca, and he'd made sure he'd be the one to invoke the challenge.

"And how do I know you didn't have my son killed for this very reason?" someone spoke up from one of the screens, and I recognized him as Peter's father. He'd be relieved to learn his son was alive after this was over. He'd be arrested soon after, though, so a family reunion would be short-lived.

"The murderer is here with us tonight. Our men took her from police custody. She confessed to killing your son," Atlas said while motioning my way. "I plan on seeking vengeance for that act against her and The League."

Murmurs from the many screens had the room buzzing with noise and static.

"We have a pact in place with The League and do not

wish to risk our business operations to avenge your would-be wife's late husband. We're not looking for a war," another man said, and I recognized him as the leader from Romania.

"*They* broke the pact and declared war by killing my son," Peter's father protested and banged his fist to his desk. Other leaders followed in agreement.

"It's time we end The League," Arnaud said, stepping forward. "It's open season on every one of them after tonight."

"Then let us begin." Atlas turned to Bridgette, set a kiss on her cheek, then left her side and entered the cage.

Bridgette went to stand by Arnaud, arrogance in every line of her body, as the first fighter in similar shorts to Atlas descended the stairs.

Arnaud gave a short introduction and went over the rules of the fight. A large clock on the opposite wall, similar to a stopwatch and set for sixty minutes, would begin once the fighter entered the cage, and it would be paused between fights. Atlas had to survive the hour with some of The Alliance's best fighters. Only then would he be permitted to marry Bridgette and amass even more power.

My stomach was in knots as I watched the first fight begin.

Atlas handled himself well. Impressive strikes. Devastating blows to his opponent's midsection. Brutal leg kicks. He was a superior fighter to this man. But how would he stand up to the other fighters? Would he survive?

I had no clue when Sean and the others would arrive, but I didn't want to sit here and helplessly watch my brother die.

My shoulders flinched when the blond fighter went flying a few minutes later from a kick to the chin.

Atlas walked up to him, and instead of finishing him, he extended a hand.

He's not a killer. Not yet, I reminded myself as I watched the next fights progress in a blur.

My hands grew numb from the zip ties, my head throbbed, and my throat was sore from Luca's earlier attempt to strangle me.

The sounds of bone and the hard smacks of flesh connecting had my abdomen tightening with every punch and kick.

The coppery smell of blood hit my nose and had me wanting to cough, but the gag prevented that from happening.

By the fifth fight, and thirty minutes later, Bridgette strode across the room my way, the sound of her heels on the floor subdued by the fighting inside the ring.

Bridgette crouched next to me but kept her eyes trained on Atlas. "Sean would've fucked me if Atlas hadn't shown up that night," she whispered. "I saw the desire in his eyes when he held my naked body. You can't fake the kind of lust he had for me."

It was the first time since being held captive I resisted my restraints. This woman had a way of getting under my skin even more than Luca.

Sean was clearly a trigger for me.

Bridgette tried to come across as confident and casual in her conviction that Atlas would prevail as the victor at the end of The Final Hour, but she failed. There was a tremble in her voice, and her hands shook slightly. She was nervous and afraid. Atlas dismissing Luca was unexpected, and I could tell she was anxious about the prospect of being bound to marry another man she didn't love.

"Luca wants you to die first, but oh, I would love to watch the look on Sean's face if it's me who gets to slit your throat while you sit helpless in this chair." She pushed up off her thighs and applauded Atlas when he defeated another fighter.

Atlas turned toward the stairs, panting and breathless from exertion. But instead of the next Alliance challenger, Luca emerged along with Atlas's two guards.

Luca had Atlas's men in his pocket, too, didn't he?

"What are you doing?" Atlas called out, stepping out of the ring.

"Your next fighter," Luca announced.

I bit down on my gag at the sight of Sean being nudged down the steps by another man.

"This man helped Emilia arrange Peter's death," Luca announced, giving me a smug look. "I suggest Sean McGregor, Irish League leader, die inside of the ring tonight as penance for his sins."

Sean's gaze flew to me once he'd descended the stairs, relief in his eyes to see I was still alive.

"That isn't how The Final Hour works, Moreau," Atlas snapped. "I'm fighting the best of the best from The Alliance. If I wanted to fight a spineless McGregor, I'd go to Dublin." His eyes flicked to Sean for the briefest of moments, then back to Luca. "Get out of my sight."

"If Atlas doesn't want to fight him, I can." Luca reached for a knife from the back of his trousers beneath his dress shirt and pointed it Sean's way.

Atlas spoke to his guards in Greek, but they didn't budge, which had him growling out more words that they continued to ignore. "You work for Luca now, is that it?" Atlas spun around to face Bridgette. "And you?" He stalked toward her, eyeing her with fierce intensity. "You're with him as well?"

Bridgette's hand went to her chest as if she were about to feign shock at such an accusation, but then Luca spoke up. "Yes, she's with me. And I'm challenging you for her hand in marriage, Laurent." His focus moved to the wall of men. "And I'll kill Sean McGregor and Emilia Calibrisi to prove my worth to The Alliance."

Atlas charged Luca like an angry bull, and Bridgette screamed when Arnaud pulled out a gun.

"Back off, or you get a bullet to the head," Arnaud hollered toward Atlas.

I didn't need anyone getting caught in the crossfire tonight. *That* wasn't part of the plan, damn it. Well, not unless it was Luca, and I'd prefer he die a different death.

Atlas clutched hold of Luca and looked back at Arnaud. "You, too?"

"Afraid so," Arnaud stated unapologetically, gaze cutting to me as if he had every intention of making me his plaything at some point regardless of Luca's warnings.

Oh, I'd be more than happy to end this fucker. But first, Luca needed to be dealt with.

What was Sean's play? What had he and Roman planned? And had they managed to get Atlas on our side?

"No guns," Peter's father announced loudly. "That is in violation of the tradition."

"Put it down," another leader shouted. "Now."

I spied Arnaud slowly lowering his sidearm out of the corner of my eye, then watched as Sean removed his black pullover and tossed it. "Fight me, Moreau. If you survive, then you go up against Laurent," he said in a steady voice.

"If you can't beat The League, you have no business stepping into that ring with Laurent," Peter's father spoke up.

Bridgette stood by watching, her face scrunched in part fear, as well as excitement.

Atlas released hold of Luca with a shove, then said, "I want you out of here, Arnaud. And my guards who betrayed me. I don't need to be stabbed in the back anymore tonight."

Atlas's eyes went to the blade Luca had dropped when he'd charged him.

"Fine. Agreed." What sounded like a unanimous decision came from the leaders on screen.

Surprisingly, Arnaud left without argument, taking the guards with him.

Bridgette backed up to the wall closest to me, gaze intently focused on Sean and Luca now squaring off outside the cage.

You've got this, Sean. Acid burned and rolled around my stomach, but I believed in him.

Sean glanced at the screens on the wall as he snapped his fists. "Just an FYI, I'd open a new tab on your laptops and check the news. You might find it interesting. I'd bet you're trending now that your dirty laundry is being broadcast all over the world."

Relief poured through me. *Harper did it!*

"What'd you do?" Luca hollered, his eyes wide and frantic as the men on video began cursing, and before I knew it, the wall was one blank screen.

Bridgette ran across the room, rushing for the stairs—the only sensible thing that woman had ever done.

"You betrayed me," Atlas said, closing the space between him and Luca. "Used me. Manipulated me. You belong in Hell," Atlas seethed at Luca, who stood frozen in shock at how his plan had gone south. "But I promised McGregor he'd have his chance with you, and unlike you, I'm a man of my word."

My stomach clenched into a knot, and hot tears filled my eyes.

Oh my God.

Without warning, Sean charged Luca. A flying leg kick I hadn't expected sent Luca backward and onto his ass.

At the sound of my feeble cries for help, Atlas hurried to my side and removed the gag, allowing me to suck in a deep breath.

"Hi," Atlas said in a low voice, a half smile, half frown forming on his lips.

"The knife," I told him. "Can you cut me free?"

His brows drew inward as if he had a lifetime of words to say and no time to say them, then went for Luca's knife.

My focus remained glued to Sean and Luca fighting even when gunfire erupted from somewhere outside.

"I'm gonna assume that's your people taking out any resistant guards," Atlas said while cutting my ankles free from the chair legs. "I need to stop Bridgette from getting away. She belongs in prison." He crouched in front of me and placed a gentle hand on my knee. "But I promised Sean I wouldn't let you get hurt, and if I untie your hands and you step in to help him, you might."

"Atlas, no. You can't leave me like this." My nostrils flared, and my heart pounded fiercely. "Please."

"I'll be right back." He set the knife on my lap, gave me one tight nod, then took off for the stairs.

"No," I cried, which had Sean swinging his gaze my way, a distraction he couldn't afford while going up against Luca.

And it cost him.

Luca sent an elbow strike to the back of his head, then did a double-leg takedown.

I squirmed and tried to get free as Luca straddled Sean, smashing his face with punch after punch.

No, no, no. I had to do something.

My eyes fell to the knife.

Throwing my weight backward and leaning to the right, I tipped the chair over in one hard movement and landed on my side, but now the knife was out of reach. I bent my knees and set the balls of my feet to the floor, using all my strength to rotate my body into position to snatch the knife with my still bound hands.

Sean was upright again, blood dripping from a cut above his eye. He trapped Luca up against the exterior cage wall, too close for Luca to defend himself as Sean dominated him with elbows to the face.

I stilled, completely engrossed in the fight. Terrified of any other outcome than Sean defeating Luca.

Luca headbutted Sean, which had Sean stumbling a step, losing his grip on Luca while he shook off the dizzying effects.

I felt around, searching for the knife, my hands opening and closing like a struggling clam to grasp it with the zip ties around my wrists.

The cool metal felt like heaven when I secured it in my hands. Now the hard part, cutting through the ties blind.

I lifted my eyes, on the brink of panicking that I was running out of time when I saw that Sean appeared to have the upper hand at the moment. Luca's elbow was bent in an unnatural position as Sean applied pressure on the joint causing Luca to cry out in pain.

Forced to hold the knife at an awkward angle, I sawed at the zip ties using one hand to create friction between the plastic while I watched the two men brawl like an old-school street fight. Sean stood above Luca now, and in one quick motion, he lifted his leg and brought his foot straight down onto Luca's chest.

"You deserve to die," I heard Sean rasp. And it was Sean's turn to bloody up Luca, raining punches that sent Luca's face flying to the side with every jab. The look in Sean's eyes told me he was right on the edge, a punch or two away from finishing it.

The shooting had died down except for a few sporadic shots outside and maybe upstairs. Precision shots taken from a distance by Roman and his team, most likely.

Sean held on to Luca's shirt with both hands and lifted his torso off the ground, drawing him closer. Luca's blood covered Sean's hands and spattered his face. "Death is too easy for you," he said with disgust, then shoved Luca back down.

He set a hand to the floor and rolled to his back. He was out of breath, and he probably had trouble seeing with the cut over his eye.

Sean wasn't a killer. Ultimately, he couldn't do it. The German was an accident.

"Sean," I whispered, and he slowly sat up to view me.

I finally managed to cut the zip ties free, but I caught Luca stirring as I started to stand. He'd been faking being down and out. And he was going for something at his ankle.

"Sean!" I screamed at the realization Luca was in the process of sitting up and had secured a gun.

Without hesitating, I reeled my arm back and threw the knife across the room as Sean had begun to face Luca.

The blade landed directly in the center of Luca's throat. He dropped the gun, his eyes and mouth opening wide in stunned silence as blood sputtered and gurgled from his mouth. Luca clutched his throat below the knife in a vain attempt to save himself, but then he fell backward in one loud thud.

The devil was finally dead.

"Emilia." Sean captured me in his embrace. "Are you okay?" he asked, but at the sounds of heavy footsteps and familiar voices, we slowly walked toward the stairs.

It was Roman and two of his Navy SEAL friends, A.J. and Chris. And behind them, Sebastian and Cole.

"Everything okay?" Roman asked, lowering his rifle, allowing the sling to catch it. He looked at Luca's bloody and lifeless body on the ground, then back to me.

"It's over," I cried with relief as Sean hooked an arm around me, drawing me tight to his side when Sebastian and Cole walked up to Luca.

"Did you get Arnaud?" *Please say yes.*

"The psycho with the bad toupee?" Chris asked. "He resisted. Shot the fucker between the eyes. That ugly rug slipped right off."

"Music to my ears," I whispered as Sebastian crouched next to Luca, cocking his head as if he was struggling to believe it was finally over.

"I had no choice," I said to Sebastian for some strange reason, despite the fact we all knew Luca was not leaving Arnaud's house alive tonight.

"May the devil torment you with horrible carnival music nonstop until the end of time," Chris said while standing over Luca next to Cole.

"Carnival music?" Cole stroked his jaw, his eyes dark and focused on Luca. He wanted him dead as much as we all did.

"Haven't you ever heard that carnival game music? Damn, trust me, it's torture. That music is more effective torture than waterboarding. Play it on repeat, and you'll have terrorists giving up their enemies quicker than you can say 'clown,'" A.J. spoke up, his Southern accent thick and filled with humor.

"Ah, yeah, that does sound painful." Cole's voice was flat as if still in shock.

"Where's Bridgette? Atlas?" I asked and finally left Sean's comforting embrace.

"They're okay. Upstairs," Sebastian said with a nod.

"Harper hacked the signals of everyone who logged in to

view the fight," Chris answered. "She pulled a Black Widow and shared their crimes with the world."

Black Widow, huh?

"They have nowhere to hide," Roman confirmed.

Was it really over?

For real, for real?

For once, had my life not ended in tragedy?

I turned back into Sean's arms, and unexpected emotions poured out of me.

An ugly, broken sob tore from my chest. Sean was bruised and cut and bleeding all over me, but he held me tight all the same. He soothed me. Gave me his love and let me know I hadn't lost him.

This man was my equal. My other half. My absolute everything.

CHAPTER THIRTY

EMILIA

THREE HOURS LATER

"You're in the clear," Sebastian said once we were safely inside the hotel suite. It was after midnight, and we were all exhausted.

I'd had to sneak into the hotel without being recognized, which was why I'd ditched the prison clothes to blend in with guests, wearing jeans, brown boots, and a wool peacoat. The short blonde wig was the final piece of my disguise.

Once in the suite, I quickly discarded the wig and the pins that'd held my long locks in place beneath it.

"The authorities will be seeking you out for your statement," Sebastian said inside the living room, "but they won't bother you until tomorrow morning. Luca's not the only one with contacts here."

Sebastian had used a burner phone to make an anonymous call informing the police he'd heard gunshots coming from Arnaud's estate. We'd had to beat it out of there before they showed up because I was not going back to jail. But we left them a belated Christmas present—a bunch of bad guys all tied up with a laundry list of their sins attached to their chests.

Thankfully, Sebastian had doctors on standby as well, paid for by The League, and they met us at the hotel to patch up the cut above Sean's eye and give me a once-over, despite me insisting I was fine.

"Can't be charged for murder if the man didn't really die," Sebastian went on. "And we have Luca and his people pinned for your kidnapping."

Good. This is all good. I stole a look at Sean sitting close by chatting with Harper and Roman in the living room. They'd come through for us, thank God.

Sean told me he hadn't been sure which side Atlas would choose until he was literally walking out of the hotel room and received the phone call.

Atlas had arranged for some of the guards he trusted with his life to come to the hotel and "escort" Cole, Sebastian, and Sean to Arnaud's estate. Roman and his teammates had spared those two men during the fighting.

"I can't thank you enough." Sean directed his words to Roman and his team of SEALs, the same team we met back at my house in Sicily in October. Tonight, they had come through for us and returned the favor. "Sorry about your holiday."

"Nah, taking down baddies is fun to me, don't sweat it." Finn, who I heard the others refer to as Echo Five, slapped Sean on the back and quickly retracted his hand with a *Sorry, man* when Sean winced.

He'd be black and blue for at least a week.

"He didn't hurt you, right?" Roman asked me a moment later, his voice soft. "Luca?"

"If he did, we'll find some voodoo spell to bring him back to life so we can torture him a bit more before ending him again," Wyatt, Roman's British teammate, offered as if he did that sort of thing every day.

And how exactly was a Brit an American SEAL? I never bothered to ask before, but I made a mental note to ask Roman when all this craziness finally died down.

"No, but that Arnaud jerk wanted to." I grimaced. "Surprisingly, Luca stopped him."

Sean shook his head, still angry at the idea I'd been alone with any of those guys. He held on to his side and moved around the crowded group to stand next to me.

"Is it really over?" I swiped at a tear that broke free and pulled my attention to Sebastian. Cole and Alessia were off to his right.

Sebastian turned to Harper for an answer since she pretty much ran the show for us digitally.

Harper nodded. "There's no way any of those men will be able to escape conviction, not with the intel we shared all over the internet. And I 'personally' sent it to every major agency, from Interpol to MI6." Her smile was big and bright, but her eyes looked tired—no doubt from being up for days as well as being glued to a computer screen. "Bridgette will be trading in her couture for khakis. We have enough incriminating evidence to prove she was complicit in her father's and her husband's businesses."

"And what about Sara?" We had yet to discuss an outcome for her.

"We'll make sure Sara gets slapped with an ankle bracelet and does at least a thousand hours of community service in a bright orange jumpsuit, of course," A.J. said with a smile.

I wished worse for her, but the orange outfit while picking up rubbish was a nice visual and justice enough.

"What about Atlas and Penelope?" I asked, my heart beating faster.

Sean reached for my hand and laced our fingers together while we waited for an answer. My nerves tangled at the idea I only just discovered I had a mother and brother and might already have them taken away.

Roman shoved his hands into the pockets of his cargo trousers. "Our government managed to cut a deal with the French and Greeks to keep them in U.S. custody. Neither country wants to be involved in the shit show Harper unleashed. So, the Castellanoses will be under electronic monitoring without jail time, as long as they fully cooperate and turn over everything they have on The Alliance. When the time comes, they'll also need to be placed in WITSEC. The Feds recommend they assume new identities after the trial."

Sean squeezed my hand, a silent question wondering if the outcome was acceptable for me. And it was better than I'd hoped for. I wasn't sure how Atlas and Penelope would feel about going into hiding, but it was better than jail or being taken out by former Alliance members.

"Can you put in one more request?" I stepped forward, bringing Sean with me since I'd kept our hands united. "I'd like a chance to speak to them before the authorities take them away."

Roman looked at Wyatt and the others.

"I'll see where they're being held. Find out what I can do." Wyatt left the suite, and a few other SEALs began packing up their gear.

I hadn't seen Atlas since he'd left the knife on my lap to search for Bridgette. I was still a bit peeved he'd chosen to listen to Sean and leave me tied up. Also, angry at Sean for that, too. But Sean and I were even since I lied to him about the actual plan, and those were the last lies I wanted between us.

"Can I have a second alone?" I tipped my head toward the bedroom, eyes on Harper.

Harper exchanged a quick look with Roman, then nodded, and I let go of Sean's hand, and she followed me into the bedroom. The room still smelled like the custom perfume Sean had given me for my birthday. Had he sprayed it while I was gone?

I shut the door behind us, and Harper peered at me, a confused expression in her eyes. "We couldn't have done this without you." I sat on the bed, my legs unsteady after everything that had happened.

She remained by the door, still guarded. "Team effort."

Humble. I liked that. "Listen, these last few weeks have made me realize some things," I began, my voice a little shaky. "I'd always believed I would be less strong or that I'd become more vulnerable if I let my defenses down and allowed myself to fall in love. To be loved in return." I swallowed, not sure what in the hell I was doing. Roman was going to kill me. "And I can see a lot of myself in you." I released a deep breath when she repositioned her stance as if uncomfortable with the direction of the conversation. "Roman and I are only friends. We've only ever been friends."

Her eyes lifted to mine in a flash, narrowing on me.

"But I really care about him, and I can tell he's hurting. I don't know if he's got his head in his ass or if it's—"

"Me?" She frowned. "Maybe it's both of us for different reasons." She took a small step closer. "I think we're better suited as friends."

"Hm." My shoulders dropped. "But you must know the chemistry between you two is phenomenal. It's a tangible thing when I'm in the same room with you both, and I'm guessing I'm not the only one who notices. That kind of connection doesn't just go away."

Why was I pushing the woman? Right, I cared about Roman. He was my friend, and I wanted him to have what I had. Love and happiness. A future with someone he couldn't imagine himself without. The old Emilia would never, not in a million years, be having this talk with anyone, but love had a funny way of opening my eyes.

Harper glanced toward the window, but her body language told me she was ready to bolt for the door. "I'll care about that man until the day I die," she said softly before bringing her gaze back to me. I saw the unshed tears in her eyes as she gave me a small nod and opened the door.

I wanted to stop her, but I wasn't sure what else to say. I didn't know their full story, and I had to hope they'd both come to their senses before it was too late.

"Looks like Wyatt came through," Harper said, motioning toward the living room. "Want me to send them in?"

My heart jumped into my throat, so I only nodded.

Atlas and Penelope walked through the doorway a moment later. Sean was behind them as if not trusting them enough to leave me alone.

"Hi," I managed, rising from the bed and wringing my hands as a myriad of emotions threatened to drown me.

Penelope was staring at me as if she were standing before a ghost. Did Chanel and I look that similar, and I'd subconsciously ignored that truth? Or did seeing me remind her of Papà? I didn't know the woman well enough to discern her expression, and it hit me hard that I'd likely not have that chance anytime soon.

Atlas's hands were stuffed into his trouser pockets, clearly unsure how to act in this situation as well. We were on the same page there. What to say? What to do?

"You know the truth," Penelope said softly and made the first move, appearing to glide across the room in her wide-legged flowy black trousers and blue silk top. She was a stunning woman who had great style, just like her daughter Chanel—my sister.

"I know part of the truth," I confessed, anxious to learn what I didn't. I hated that my father wasn't alive to share their story, and pained by the fact this woman was my mother and couldn't be in my life. "You're my mother. Papà loved you," I rushed out the quick facts. "But how'd I come to live with him?"

Penelope motioned for Atlas to sit alongside me. A parent about to speak to her children. Enlighten them with a story about her past.

Atlas hesitantly strode closer and sat on the bed, leaving a few meters of space between us.

I looked to Sean, who was leaning against the interior doorframe. I needed to find his eyes for support, and he lightly nodded, letting me know he was there for me and wasn't going anywhere.

"Your father and I were in love for a long time. We met at eighteen when our parents were both vacationing in the same location. When we discovered we were from rival families, we made every effort to stay away from each other, but the connection was too strong." She paused and took a breath. "Years later, our parents found out we snuck away to see each other whenever possible. Your grandfather was still in charge of the family at the time, and he ordered your father to marry an Italian. And my father threatened to kill him if we kept sneaking around."

"And what happened?" I whispered, barely able to utter the words.

"I made him marry Sophia, worried about what my

ruthless father would do. But then I discovered I was pregnant." She set her back to the wall opposite us. Tears filled her eyes but refused to fall. "My father hid me away while I was pregnant to keep anyone from finding out and said I had to give you up for adoption."

My world was spinning, but I tried to take slow, calming breaths.

"I begged and pleaded to let your father raise you instead. We promised not to tell anyone the truth, and my father surprised me by agreeing once you were born. Of course, he viewed it as a smart business move, not the loving act of a grandfather. He said it'd keep your father off his back, keep him from attacking us since he not only loved me but had our child."

Atlas's head had bowed forward, his focus on his hands in his lap. Purple bruises had begun to take the place of the redness where he'd been hit and punched. He and Sean were equally banged up in that regard, though I imagined hearing his, *our* mother's revelation was adding an entirely new level of pain.

I looked back to Penelope, waiting for her to continue, to give us more.

"I chose your names, though. Emilia, which is Latin for rival and excel. I knew no one would ever rival your beauty. And your middle name, Tessa, meaning huntress. A strong and independent woman like I wished I could have been," she explained sadly.

I gripped my chest at her words, emotion threatening to overwhelm me.

"Sophia left him not too long after he brought you into his home as a baby." Penelope's lower lip quivered. "We tried to stop seeing each other, especially after I was forced to marry Simon and Chanel was born."

"But you didn't," Atlas said in a low voice, his eyes on the floor.

"No, we didn't. We continued to see each other until your sister was taken from all of us." She sniffled. "I couldn't bear to face him again after that. It was too painful."

I slowly stood, wanting so much to reach out for her. Hug her. Comfort her. But she was still a stranger to me.

"We did what we could to protect you, Emilia. Being stricken from your life was so painful that I couldn't possibly let your father endure that hardship, so I never told him the truth about Atlas."

My entire body went weak, and if I weren't sitting, I would have collapsed.

I stole a look at Atlas, who was now on his feet, his gaze pinned to Penelope, her hand outstretched as if begging for forgiveness.

"You're a Calibrisi, my son. Not a Laurent. And I didn't tell your father, Emilia, because I knew the pain of not being allowed to raise you," she quickly explained.

You, my son, were a product of love, Penelope's words from the listening device Christmas Eve came back to me.

Atlas peered at me as if searching for even more of a resemblance.

Papà had a son. Oh my God.

I wasn't the last living Calibrisi.

Atlas turned from us, went over to the window, and moved the curtains aside to set both palms to the glass.

"I'm so sorry to the both of you." Tears fell more steadily down her cheeks now, which finally brought me to my feet. "I hope one day you can forgive me. Maybe once it's safe, we can be a family? Start fresh?"

"Family," I whispered, not sure what to make of that word. I looked to Sean, his expressive eyes full of so much love. He was my family. Could I make more room in my heart? I hadn't wanted Atlas and Penelope sent to prison because part of me hoped . . . "A fresh start sounds nice," I said softly, gently wiping away a tear.

Atlas slowly turned toward us. "We're from two different worlds. I was raised as a criminal." His husky voice bled with sadness and pain. But maybe also hope.

"Chanel used to always tell me you were a kind man with a big heart. Not like your father. And now it makes sense because you're not Simon's blood." I couldn't hold back my tears any longer, and Sean came to my side when Penelope had yet to budge. Possibly worried I'd reject her. "You're not a bad man, Atlas. You were just raised by one. There's a difference."

Sean circled an arm around my side, holding me tight.

I glanced back and forth between my brother and mother, wondering what the future held for us.

"You, my son, made the right choice tonight. Like I said, you're a Calibrisi. You have his strength and passion inside you." She strode closer and set the back of her hand to my cheek. "And the woman you became would make both your Papà and Chanel proud."

I fought the heavy sob that tried to escape, trying desperately to not completely lose control.

But I couldn't stop myself. I pulled free from Sean's hold and buried my face in Penelope's chest and sobbed. She wrapped her arms around my trembling body and held me tight.

"My daughter. My beautiful daughter." Penelope gently smoothed her hand down the back of my head like I'd always envisioned a mother would do to comfort her child, and Atlas surprised me with a tissue once I was safely back in Sean's arms.

"I could've killed you," Atlas said, his tone tortured. Eyes dark. "I-I could've killed my own sister."

"But you didn't," Sean spoke up for the first time.

Atlas stole a look his way. "You love her?"

Sean lowered his chin to peer at me, then focused back on Atlas. "Hell yes, I do."

Atlas came closer and brought his hands to his hips. "I'll do better. For you and Chanel." He reached forward and set a hand on my shoulder. "I'll need time to forgive your lie, Mother." He looked her way. "But I'll get there."

Penelope pulled him in for a hug, and I turned to see Roman standing in the doorway.

"I'm sorry. It's time for them to go," Roman said with regret.

"Okay," I mouthed. We said a few awkward goodbyes, but I knew I'd be seeing them again.

Sean held me in his arms once we were alone.

"Well, this is about as fairy tale as it gets, right?" My attempt at a joke sounded more like a strangled cry. I had decades' worth of tears escaping tonight.

He stepped back to cup my cheeks and brought his mouth close to mine. "Pretty sure fairy tales end in a kiss."

"Won't that hurt?" I winced at the sight of his bruised face and swollen lips.

"Mm." He smiled. "Not as much as it will if I don't kiss you." He seized my mouth a moment later, and I wilted in his arms.

I had my life back.

The life I never knew I'd lost.

And the one I never knew I wanted.

"I love you, Sean," I said against his lips. "And if you'll let me . . . I want to move to Ireland to be with you."

CHAPTER THIRTY-ONE

EMILIA

PARIS, FRANCE (THREE DAYS LATER)

"I brought you something." I sat on the blanket I'd laid out in front of Chanel's headstone and reached into the bag for a bottle of champagne and two flutes I'd brought from my house in Italy.

After we'd tied up all the loose ends in Monaco, I'd gone home with Sean to say goodbye to the place where I grew up. To say goodbye to Papà and tell him I forgave him for lying. To tell him about his son.

I'd stood in his study and breathed in the familiar smells of earthy leather, sweet cigar, and musty books one last time. And then I'd smoked one of his vanilla cigars and drank some of his whiskey.

I apologized for the promise I was going to break by being with Sean, but I was certain Papà would forgive me now that I knew the truth about the woman he'd spent a lifetime loving. He'd never want that life for me if he knew how much I loved Sean.

I popped the champagne's cork and filled both glasses, then set one on the edge of the stone and raised my glass.

It was a cold day. Snow covered the ground, and the tree branches were bare. But it felt perfect to me.

"This time, sister, I'm drinking champagne because I'm in love." Tears welled in my eyes, and I let go of a deep breath before sipping the gold liquid. "I hope wherever you are, you can see me. And that you know the truth. We're sisters." I swallowed more of the champagne, trying to maintain my resolve. "Fate brought us together, but I'm so sorry you died because of it."

I could feel her there, the same way I'd felt Papà in his study just yesterday.

It may have been freezing outside, but a sudden blanket of warmth wrapped around my shoulders, sending goose bumps scattering beneath my clothes.

Simon Laurent's right-hand man, Theo—now Atlas's right-hand man—told us Simon wasn't the one who'd ordered the hit on me ten years ago in Vegas. I supposed I believed him because I couldn't fathom how Simon would have been able to live with himself knowing he'd accidentally had his own daughter killed. Not that it made him any better of a man, considering he did try to kill me two other times.

"Remember the man from the fight that night? The Irish guy?" I asked her, reaching forward to set a hand to her headstone. "I'm going to marry him someday. Have kids. Maybe even a big family. He has two brothers and a sister. That sounds like the perfect size for a family."

I looked down as a tear fell into my flute.

"I bet I'll be a hormonal grump while I'm pregnant," I said around a half sob, half chuckle. "But, Chanel, he's made me a better person. The kind of woman I know you'd respect." I finished the champagne and refilled the glass.

"The League offered to let me keep my role as leader now that The Alliance is dismantling all around the world." I sniffled. "But I don't want it. They can find someone else to rule Italy." My chest constricted briefly, knowing I was closing another chapter of my life by stepping down as leader. "You know that cliché saying . . . home is where the heart is? Well, I finally realized it's true. My place is in Ireland with Sean."

I let those words sink in for a minute. With me. With my sister. And as I sat in silence, I felt no protest inside me. No fears or objections over my words. It was truly what I wanted.

"Maybe I'll help out The League in Ireland since Sean and the others have agreed to stay on even though The Alliance has met its end." A world without that evil group sounded sublime, but I also knew it was only a matter of time before a new criminal society rose from the ashes and took its place. And someone had to be there to stop them.

I finished my drink, then polished off the one I poured for Chanel.

"I wish I had known the truth while you were alive, but in my heart, I think we both always knew." I recorked the bottle and placed it and the flutes back in my bag.

I kissed my first two fingers, then set them to her name on the headstone.

"Goodbye, sister. I know you're watching out for me like you've been doing for years."

I slowly stood and folded up the blanket after a few more quiet minutes alone with her.

"I bet it was you, right?" I tipped my chin to the clear blue sky and closed my eyes. "You brought Sean back into my life when I needed him, didn't you?"

A break in the clouds sent a bright ray of sunshine down

on us, covering me with warmth, and I chose to believe it was Chanel answering me.

I smiled and turned around to see my man waiting for me off in the distance, his back to the limo in his long, dark coat. Respecting my time.

I picked up the bag and blanket and headed toward my future.

"You okay?" He brought his gloved hands to my cheeks.

"I had a lot of champagne in that short time," I said around a hiccup, which had him smiling.

"Mm. You and champagne . . ."

I pressed up in my brown boots and set a gentle kiss to his lips, then whispered, "Take me home."

CHAPTER THIRTY-TWO

SEAN

DUBLIN, IRELAND (TWO WEEKS LATER)

"HOW'S HE HOLDING UP?" EMILIA ASKED, LYING NAKED beneath me in the bedroom of my flat. "Ethan, I mean."

"I'm still inside you, love. Maybe ask about my brother after I pull out," I said with a laugh, then rolled off her. She shifted to her side and set the back of her hand to my cheek.

I reached for her hardened nipple and smoothed it between my thumb and index finger before settling my hand on her hip, scooching her closer to me.

"So?" Emilia arched a brow, waiting for an answer. "You dropped him off at the airport this morning. How was he?"

Ethan would spend six more months wrapping up his work in New York before returning to Dublin for good. With The Alliance crumbling day by day, it'd finally be safe for him to come home where he belonged.

Cole and Alessia had no intention of returning to New York, so we'd need to find a replacement for Ethan to help my uncle head up our offices in the U.S. before the summer.

"He'll have a lot of song material to work with after this

trip, that's for sure," I joked, and she playfully whacked my chest.

"Not funny."

"What?" I asked innocently. "If he ever wants to follow his dreams, he needs some good songs."

She was quiet for a moment. "You think he's over Sara?"

"I doubt he was ever really under Sara." It was easier to tease than talk about my brother being miserable because his evil ex had aligned with the devil. Even if she'd been provoked and coerced, she should have known to go for help instead.

"Sara's stores closed down in all three locations." She frowned. "Why does that make me feel bad when I can't stand her?"

I smirked. That was easy. "You've got a bigger heart than you let on, Emilia. And she was a female entrepreneur, so maybe you—"

"I don't sympathize with her just because she's a woman. She used her sexuality to bait your brother into a trap that could have gotten a lot of us killed." She blew a strand of hair from her face. "But she did have great pieces, perhaps that's why," she reasoned as if trying to convince herself she didn't pity Sara. "Maybe I need to open a few boutiques. Get into the lingerie business," she added in a provocative voice this time.

"Only if you model everything for me, and only me." I lifted my brows up and down, and then a thought struck me. "Maybe we need to make our own sex tape to erase the memory of—"

"Not gonna happen." She reached between us and fisted my cock, giving it a firm tug. "I can't risk the footage getting leaked. I find myself curiously jealous when it comes to you," she said in a sultry tone, and I felt myself growing hard again with her holding me. "The idea of another woman getting to see you naked makes me crazy."

I fecking loved hearing her say that.

This confident, badass woman was protective of our love.

"Have I ever told you how happy I am that you're here with me?" We planned on building a house together not far from where Holly and Sebastian lived, and Adam and Anna, as well.

Emilia gifted her mansion to her staff back in Sicily to let them sell or keep. She said they'd lived there all of their lives, that it was their home as much as hers. And that made me love her even more, which I didn't think was possible.

Her father's associates still handled the day-to-day business for all her companies worldwide, but she was considering becoming more involved in the British, Irish, and Scottish locations.

"I know you're happy." She released her hold of my cock and placed her hand lovingly on my chest, then said, "Because I'm happy."

She had a mother now. A brother. It was surreal.

Of course, she'd had limited verbal contact with them since Monaco for their safety, but Emilia had said if she'd learned of her family before she fell in love with me, she most likely wouldn't have given Penelope and Atlas a chance. *I* opened her up to all the possibilities life had to offer. To love. To be able to forgive, as well.

"I'm looking forward to this weekend," she said. "Since we never did get to have Women's Christmas, I love that we girls are going away for a few days. It'll be nice."

The idea of Emilia in a tiny string bikini, soaking in the rays on a beach in Bora Bora while men who weren't me had a front-row seat to the view . . . well, let's just say my jealousy was rearing its ugly head.

But after everything we'd all been through, the women deserved a weekend off. Plus, I knew my sister hadn't had a vacation since her daughter was born.

They'd have guards whether they wanted them or not in case any remaining Alliance members attempted to put a hit out on them, but we had our ears to the ground, listening for any potential chatter. Roman and his men were doing the same. So far, nothing. They were all too busy trying to handle the collapse of their empires while wearing handcuffs.

"So, I guess you need to buy a bikini since I didn't see one in the bags you brought from your place in Italy."

She smiled. "Are there nude beaches in Bora Bora? I'll have to check."

"Hell no." I pinned her beneath me in one quick movement and stared into her eyes. I was utterly mesmerized by this woman who made me crazy, in a good way, and my need for her was insatiable.

"I'm still mad at you for putting your life in danger back in Monaco, by the way," I said when the thought struck me. I could have lost her, and I never wanted to consider the idea it could happen again.

I trapped her arms over her head with one hand, linking her wrists together, and she arched her back, offering me her tits like a temptress.

"And I'm mad you told Atlas to keep me restrained."

I winked and lowered myself to kiss her before murmuring, "A guy's gotta do what a guy's gotta do."

When I lifted my head, I discovered a cute scowl on my fierce woman, and I couldn't help but let out a laugh.

"Are you looking to have some angry sex?" She hid a smile by tucking her lips inward. "I might have another idea, actually, but you might not want angry sex afterward."

"Oh? A different kind of sex, then?"

She chuckled, then tipped her head, motioning for me to let her up.

"Where are you going?" I called after her, watching her hips sway from side to side. My attention fixed next on that beautiful, bitable arse of hers as she walked toward the dresser we now shared.

She shifted her long, dark hair over her shoulder and to her back, and I sat up to enjoy the view. I wanted to kiss the small dimples in her lower back above her arse, then work my way south and around to that delicious pussy.

Lowering my hand to my lap, I reached for my cock and stroked myself.

Emilia opened the top drawer, shuffled a few undergarments around, then turned toward me with a hand behind her back. And what was she up to now?

I released my shaft and let go of a deep breath at the same time. Why the hell was I so nervous?

Emilia's dark eyes captivated me as she crossed the room to stand alongside the bed, and I dropped my feet to the floor in anticipation of whatever she planned on sharing with me.

Different sex? Kink? Did she finally want to give me that arse of hers?

And damn, was I painfully rock hard at the thought.

Emilia's lips twitched, and when I looked back to her eyes, I found them glossy.

Okay, maybe not kinky sex.

I stood, nerves getting the better of me and causing my dick to die a quick death.

"What is it?" I reached for her arm and pulled her closer to me, but she kept her other hand locked behind her back.

I tried to turn her to see what she was hiding, but she wouldn't let me. "You bought two boxes. One for Christmas, one for later, right?" she asked in a soft voice. "Well, I found the other one."

Ohhhh.

She found the ring?

Was she not ready for that level of commitment even though we were meeting with an architect next week to discuss the plans for our house?

I waited for the alarm, the fear in her eyes to show up. But it didn't come, so I took a relaxed breath when she moved back to showcase the blue Tiffany's box.

"Give it to me now," she urged, a single tear falling down her delicate cheek.

I took the box from her, my heart thumping wildly. Was this happening? Was this woman about to make my Christmas wish come true? I'd left that part out when I'd shared my wish, not wanting to scare her, but . . .

"I want my gift, Sean." She caught her tear with her tongue when it reached the corner of her mouth. "Give it to me."

Without hesitation, I fell to one knee, still living in a world of total shock but so damn happy. "Emilia Tessa Calibrisi, will you marry me?" I opened the box to show a two-carat round diamond set in white gold with small diamonds wrapped around the band to represent infinity.

She chewed on her lip as tears overwhelmed her eyes and ran down her cheeks. "Yes." She lowered to her knees, placed her hands to my cheeks, and kissed me.

I deepened our kiss, nearly dropping the ring box. Chills coasted over my naked body.

A naked proposal. Of course.

"Forever sex," I whispered against her lips. "I want forever sex now."

EPILOGUE

SEAN

BORA BORA (A FEW DAYS LATER)

"You think they'll kill us for crashing their trip?" Adam asked as we searched out the girls at the luxurious hotel, which was set not far from Mount Otemanu, the tallest remnant of the Bora Bora volcano that formed the island nation millions of years ago. The skies were as clear as the crystal blue water, aside from one lonely cloud looming over the peak of the volcano behind us.

"Probably," I said while nudging Adam in the side before pushing my hands into the pockets of my khaki linen trousers.

We were walking along the sandy path that led to a network of docks extending out over the stunning lagoons where the bungalows sat atop thick, chunky stilts. Before the girls left, they told us they'd reserved two neighboring bungalows over the turquoise water. When we arrived, Sebastian had immediately snuck off to reserve a few more so each couple would have some privacy at night.

Cole and Sebastian walked ahead of us as if on the

lookout for imminent danger. The only danger I worried about was Emilia or Holly shoving me fully clothed into the ocean as punishment for showing up uninvited to their girls' trip.

Were we going to be on thin ice? Yes.

Were we most likely certifiable for showing up? More than likely.

But love made you do crazy things, so I've been told, and not to sound like lovestruck fools, but we missed them. You know, the whole twenty-six hours they'd been away.

Plus, what about their safety? That should have been reason enough for us to fly there. We hadn't caught wind of any potential threats, but we couldn't be too careful.

Sebastian decided it'd be better if we were their bodyguards in addition to the men we assigned to discreetly keep an eye out from afar, especially after he'd seen the first report, which included photos of the women we loved scantily clad in barely there bikinis. He got it in his head that the guards would be beating off to those images, and a couple of fingers of Proper Twelve later, we found ourselves packing our bags. Sebastian grumbled incessantly about the inconvenience of flying commercial but nevertheless booked our flights on one since the women had taken our private jet.

We'd been forced to sit in economy since first-class and business were full, and no amount of wooing managed to get us out of the back row. The *very* back row. Our heads had nearly brushed the ceiling, and there hadn't been enough fecking legroom. We kept elbowing each other to try and get more space, but there was none to be found. Emilia was going to get a laugh out of that for sure.

"Up ahead," Cole said as we passed an infinity-edged pool surrounded by gardens. The panoramic views of the crystal clear ocean and the lush greenery along the shores of Bora Bora would make for a great honeymoon, I noted.

Honestly, if Ethan and the rest of my family were somehow magically down here, I'd ask Emilia to marry me on the beach this weekend. To not wait until the summer as we discussed after she'd surprised me by demanding I pop the big question.

From the moment I dropped to one knee in front of Emilia, I'd been living in an unbreakable bubble of bliss. According to my colleagues, my head had been in the clouds all week at work. And I was still reeling with happiness. But when Emilia boarded the plane with Holly, Anna, and Alessia, that bubble damn near exploded.

I needed her in my arms ASAP.

Her body writhing beneath me.

I needed to trail my lips up her smooth, golden skin before burying my face between her legs.

"They're not in here," Sebastian announced, and I'd barely registered that we'd made our way to the door of the first bungalow.

"Not here either," Cole said, walking away from the bungalow next door.

"They weren't in the pool we passed by. Maybe scuba diving? Or at another pool? Another part of the beach?" Adam proposed, stroking the scruff on his jaw.

"You know how many things can go wrong scuba diving?" Sebastian removed his shades, his eyes thinning with worry.

"What if they trusted some gobshite to take them sailing, and he tries to—"

"Emilia and Alessia won't let some arsehat hurt them," Cole interrupted Adam's comically terror-stricken voice.

What is wrong with us? "What are we really doing here?"

I asked with a laugh, suddenly feeling a bit stupid for how hastily we'd left Dublin as if the world was on fire, and we had to put out the flames.

"Well, we're here now," Sebastian grumbled and put his glasses back on. "Maybe they'll be happy to see us."

I followed my brother's gaze toward a beach off in the distance to a group of people sunbathing. I didn't see Emilia or the others, and there was no way I'd miss them.

"Maybe we're thinking about this the wrong way. How about we head to the rooms we reserved, wash up, then go down to the beachside bar, and we'll just happen to run into them like it's a coincidence." Adam shrugged.

"You're hilarious," Cole said. "What'd you drink on the plane? That cheap whiskey go to your head?"

"It might work," I said with a smile. "They'll be drinking, maybe dancing, and then we'll—"

"Break the legs of any man that gets within breathing distance of them," Sebastian suggested in a calm voice.

"No." I laughed. "Our presence will go over a lot better if they're relaxed from a day doing whatever they did, and they've got a few drinks in them. Let *them* come to *us* like flies to honey. Then we'll pull them in to dance."

"I'm telling Emilia you likened her to a fly," my brother said, laughing at his own terrible joke. I gave Adam the finger, which only made him howl even louder.

"What are you, some Casanova now?" Cole interrupted, pushing his sunglasses into his thick dark hair so I could see him rolling his eyes.

"Ah hem."

We all turned at the sound of a woman clearing her throat. Well, too late for the bar-side surprise. Holly was standing behind us with a less than amused look on her face.

She had a black . . . *something* wrapped around her hips

and a black triangle bikini top, with arms pinned to her chest. "And what are you all doing here?"

Sebastian stepped out of our line to try and pull her to him, but she held up a hand, stopping him in his tracks.

"Did someone die?" Holly asked.

"No," Sebastian answered.

"Is Siobhan sick?"

He shook his head.

I fought an amused smile, not wanting my sister to reach over and smack it off my face. And believe me, she would.

"Are we in danger?" She looked around Sebastian to find our gazes before resetting her focus on her husband. "Because we better be in danger for you four to be here. I mean, we're talking nuclear-launch-codes-stolen-by-a-madman kind of danger." Holly's tone wavered a bit in the middle while she'd tried to pull off angry, but she should have kept her sunglasses on because I could tell by her eyes she was dying to fling her arms around her husband's neck and kiss him.

"Looks like we're the only ones in danger," Adam said while turning to the side to see Anna, Alessia, and Emilia now heading down the path our way.

The women stopped for a brief moment once they'd spotted us before resuming their journey. They were all in their bikinis and cover-ups. A stack of magazines in Anna's arms—oh, wedding magazines for Emilia. Anna loved planning events.

When Emilia's eyes met mine, I immediately knew I wasn't in trouble. She wet her glossy lips and raked her brown eyes over my body in a sensual gaze that promised hours upon hours of wickedly delicious vacation sex.

She was dressed similarly to Holly, but in red, which I liked to consider her signature color. She looked absolutely breathtaking. And I wanted to rip off every scrap of fabric with my teeth.

I stole a look back at my sister to see her already making out with her husband, her tote bag forgotten on the pathway, her belongings carelessly spilled about.

Adam pulled his wife into his arms as soon as she reached him and gave her a sad puppy dog face, after which she broke into giggles. "We missed you," he admitted, really hamming up his performance.

"He said you reminded him of a fly, Anna. One of those big ones *y'all get on horses*," I said, pretending that Adam had actually said such a thing. But she smacked him in the chest after giving him a shocked look, and I laughed at my brother's expense.

"Do you hate us for crashing the party?" I heard Cole ask Alessia before kissing her again.

"I mean, I'm only disappointed I lost the bet," Emilia answered for the group. Her voice was husky, a tone I'd come to know meant she was about to rip my clothes off. I wrapped my arms around her waist and buried my face against her neck as if it was just us.

"Bet, huh?" I whispered into her ear. Ah, she was wearing the perfume I had bottled for her.

"Yeah, Emilia thought y'all would have been here by noon today." Anna chuckled. "I was thinking more like last night. Alessia said by dinner."

"And Holly?" Sebastian asked, letting out a slight groan that told me he had gone back to ravishing his wife. But he and my sister were behind me now and thank God it wasn't Holly moaning. I fought off a shiver and fixed my eyes on my fiancée.

I brushed the hair off Emilia's face and cupped her sun-kissed cheeks.

"Holly thought you'd never even let our plane take off out of Dublin." Emilia shot me a wicked, sexy grin.

Kinky sex with an ocean view it is, then. When in Bora Bora, right?

"Yeah, well, Sebastian did try to bribe the pilot to say there was an issue with an engine and that the flight had to be grounded," Cole announced.

"Yeah, I figured, so I paid the pilot even more," Holly responded, and I could hear the smile in my sister's voice.

"Well, this is going to be a problem," Emilia said, bringing her arms over my shoulders and linking her wrists casually behind my neck. "We don't have enough bedrooms for you boys. I hope you all got your own places."

I lowered my hand and pinched her arse, which drew her closer to me. "I need to get you naked. Check to make sure you have tan lines and haven't been bad." I winked. "Otherwise, we might be trying out discipline sex tonight," I said into her ear, remembering her story about sunbathing in the nude back in Italy.

"You better do a very thorough check," she murmured, and her breath in my ear had my pulse skyrocketing and my cock going painfully stiff.

"Sorry, boys, but we have plans. Some hot former military guy is taking us sailing beneath the moonlight later," Alessia announced.

I caught her turning away from Cole only to be yanked back into his arms in response to her attempt to get a rise out of him like she loved to do. Guess she liked angry sex, too.

"Woman," Cole said gruffly, then scooped her into his arms and began carrying her toward the bungalows while she playfully squealed and laughed.

"Dinner and dancing later, everyone," Alessia called out over Cole's shoulder with a wave.

"Make that much, much later," I said, eyes back on Emilia, my thoughts drifting to all of the naughty things I planned to do with my fiancée.

"I got pregnant with Braden in a setting like this," Anna hollered at Alessia.

Now that The Alliance was practically a thing of the past, Cole and Alessia planned to ditch the birth control and start a family. And someday, hopefully not too far into the future, I'd see Emilia's belly round with my child.

Before I knew it, we'd all split up for privacy. Ravenous for the women we loved.

"Strip," I commanded while peeling off my black tee and untying the drawstring of my casual linen trousers. I kicked off my loafers and let the fabric fall to my feet.

Emilia walked backward toward the living room of the bungalow, slowly removing the red see-through wrap from her hips to reveal the tiny scarlet bikini. Her breasts spilled out of the top, and when she turned around and shimmied her hips, I gasped at the lack of material covering her perfect ass.

"Remind me again what happens if you discover I don't have any tan lines?" She peeked back at me from over her shoulder, tossing me a seductive look. Her lips poised as if ready to take my cock in her mouth.

I shoved down my boxers and fisted my cock. "Woman," I said with a laugh while stepping out of my boxers, "you don't want to find out."

I hurried toward her, and she surprised me by saying, "Maybe I do," then let out an excited yelp and took off running toward the bedroom.

Ah, she wanted a chase.

Yeah, I could do this.

She jumped onto the bed in one quick movement, then bounced off in a flash, like the time she'd been hunting bad guys in the park back home, and I'd shown up on my bike for an assist. God, that felt like forever ago. Back then, I'd been tormented by my inability to have her, and now we were in Bora Bora. Engaged to be married.

Maybe fairy tales really did exist.

I caught up with her on the terrace overlooking our private pool—not giving a damn I was standing outside in the nude. I grasped her by the waist and spun her around, crushing her against my body.

"The only thing I want you wearing while we make love is your engagement ring and your perfume," I said between hungry, heated kisses.

"Mm." She teased her tongue between her white teeth. And then the little sneak escaped from my arms, bolted back into the bungalow, and tossed out from over her shoulder, "Well, you gotta catch me first."

***

Continue for bonus scenes between Sebastian and Holly.

BONUS SCENES

SEBASTIAN - OCTOBER 2021

"You sure you're okay?" my driver asked over his shoulder.

We'd been sitting in the driveway of my home for about fifteen minutes. After the first five, he'd lowered the privacy glass, and we chatted about a lot of nothing as I sat in the back of the limo, a drink on my thigh, eyes cast on the charming home Holly had bought before we were together.

"I have a feeling I'll be sleeping on the couch or worse shortly after I walk through the door," I said in a low voice, thinking back to what happened two nights ago in Sicily.

In the midst of what felt like WWIII, I'd flung a man across the foyer of Emilia's home, then lifted him by the shirt, and smashed an elbow into his face. It wasn't like he didn't deserve it. The arsehole worked for a man who bought and sold people like cattle and treated them even worse.

"My wife may not want me killing anyone, but that doesn't mean this won't hurt," I'd seethed in anger, the

violent part of my past willing the man to give me a reason to end his life.

"I have no problem killing him." Roman had shot the guy twice in the chest in one fast move. *"Maybe call your wife and get permission?"*

I realized he hadn't been kidding when his buddy Chris suggested, *"Or ask forgiveness after?"*

They had no idea what it was like to be married to a strong, stubborn Irish woman. I loved that woman more than anything in the world, and yet . . . I sputtered, *"Yeah, okay,"* as if someone else had spoken for me and accepted the gun Roman had provided.

So, so easily, too.

What kind of person did that make me? All the lives I'd taken in the past had been warranted, right?

I wasn't . . . a bad man. No, Holly wouldn't love that man.

But how could I walk through that door and face her after breaking my promise?

I gathered another large gulp of liquid courage and manned the feck up. "I'll get my things," I told my driver when he tried to help me.

"Good luck," he said once we were both outside the house, the sky dark and bleak. Ominous and foreboding.

"Thanks, I'll need it." I sighed, then went inside to face the music. Happy to be home to see my wife and child but worried about the fallout.

I set my bag down and worked the top two buttons of my black dress shirt open as I searched for my family in the quiet house.

The light in the kitchen was on, and the sweet smell of something baking wafted to my nose.

I stopped inside the doorframe of the kitchen to find my beautiful wife standing at the counter wearing a pink apron, her hair in a messy bun. Her back was to me, and she was shaking her hips, most likely mouthing the words to a song playing from her mobile on the counter. The music was playing softly, which meant Siobhan was probably already asleep.

I crossed my arms, enjoying the sight of our messy kitchen while my wife danced around, oblivious to my presence. And then a thought struck me—the front door had been unlocked, it was nighttime, and I hadn't been home.

What the hell was she thinking? I pushed myself away from the doorframe just as Holly turned to find me closing the space between us. She gasped and dropped the spatula covered in what looked like dough as I pulled her to me.

I licked her pouty lips clean of the evidence that she'd tasted her creation before putting it in the oven—something chocolatey.

She gripped my biceps when my tongue sought hers, and we shared an intense, chocolate-flavored kiss. And I knew once I laid the truth on her, I might not get another one anytime soon.

I moved the apron out of the way and dipped my hand between our bodies as she moaned and arched her back, drawing herself nearer. Slipping my hand into the waistband of her pink silk pajama bottoms, I spread my palm over her center, a thin piece of lace the only thing keeping me from fingering her.

I desperately needed to make love to Holly, but as long as I held on to my secret, how could I?

"Take me," she cried into my mouth, and damn, did I ever want to.

I deepened our kiss and traced my index finger over the lace while using my free hand to unleash her dark locks from the bun. I grabbed hold of her hair and wrapped it around my fist, backing her up to the counter in the process.

I was sure whatever chocolate creation she was baking was tasty, but my wife was the only thing I wanted to eat.

"Where's Siobhan?" I asked between kisses.

"Asleep," she returned before I drew her chin up by gently yanking on her hair to gain better access to her delicious mouth.

I lightly bit her lip, then released her hair and sank to my knees to worship at the altar of my wife.

"Why was the door unlocked?"

"Because I knew you were on your way home."

"Don't do it again," I ordered as she untied her apron and flung it to the floor in a hurry.

"Yes, sir," she whispered in a sexy voice.

I removed her bottoms, my mouth trailing from her abdomen and down as I took them off.

Her nude-colored thong came off next.

"Oh, I like this coming-home greeting," she cried when I licked her clit, my tongue dragging along her seam in one hard stroke from bottom to top.

Her short nails clawed at the sides of my head, holding me in place.

"Come for me, my love," I said before taking her into my mouth again, delirious with the desire to pleasure her.

"Sebastian," she rasped as if biting down on her back teeth when I sucked and licked, then thrust two fingers inside her and crooked one to hit the sensitive spot that made her wild.

"No, too soon."

Fine with me. I could do this all day. Eat her pussy forever. My cock swelled, and I felt the tip becoming slick from precum. Heaven help me because I was going to blow a load going down on my gorgeous wife. This upcoming Christmas marked our second anniversary, and my desire for her only intensified—never weakened.

"Ohhhhhh." She couldn't stop the orgasm even if she wanted to, and I added more pressure, which had her grabbing hold of my shoulders and stifling a yell to prevent waking Siobhan.

When I knew she was fully satisfied, I slowly rose, and she surprised me by going in for a kiss. A deep, erotic one that'd keep me warm for the few nights I anticipated I'd be sleeping on the couch.

"Since when do you listen to country music?" I asked once our lips broke apart, just now noticing what sounded like American country. "Anna?"

"She's got me hooked. Luke Bryan's voice is heaven." She went for her pajamas and pulled them on without her thong. Because, well, it was now dangling from my finger.

"Heaven, huh?" I closed one eye, and she laughed and snatched her thong from me.

"His music puts me in the mood."

"Oh, really?" I folded my arms. "So, it was him that got you off just now, was it?" I teased, pretending to be jealous of some country music star. But if he really did get her horny, then country music would end up on my "Feck That" list where Luca Moreau ranked at number one. *This* Luke guy might be a close third, ranking beneath Holly's arsehole high school boyfriend.

"No, only *you* get me off." She smiled while opening the oven to check on whatever she was baking. "But music is romantic. And sexy. Don't you think?" She closed the oven, still clutching her thong in one hand, then came around and stood before me.

My back to the counter, I set my hands on either side of me, observing this woman I loved, and realized I was avoiding telling her the truth by talking about country music.

"I killed a few people." And . . . I just ripped the Band-Aid right the feck off.

Maybe that was too abrupt of an approach because she dropped her thong and backed up with a furrowed brow as if I'd suddenly become a threat.

I held both hands in front of me, half-expecting to see blood there. "They were all bad people, Holly," I rushed out as her back hit the kitchen island. "And they could have easily hurt me or someone else if I didn't shoot them." God, that sounded pathetic. If I wasn't able to convince myself, how would I convince her?

Her gaze fell to the floor and losing sight of her big green eyes was a knife to the heart.

"If you can look me in the eyes and tell me you would have died if you hadn't taken their lives, I'll understand."

I swallowed the hard knot in my throat. Fecking hell. I couldn't do that.

The first guy had rounded the corner, and I popped off two headshots without a second thought. Surely, he'd been armed. When I squeezed my eyes closed to try and remember, though, I wasn't sure.

Like riding a bike, Chris had said jokingly, and I'd hated to admit pulling that trigger had felt good. Chris and his teammates were military, though. Well, they used to be. I wasn't so sure who they actually worked for now because I doubted their government knew about their clandestine trip to Emilia's home.

I'm a fecking killer. I don't deserve your forgiveness. My shoulders slumped, but I forced my gaze up to see if she was looking at me.

"It's not about those men who died. I know they were all evil. You wouldn't pull the trigger if they weren't the worst of the worst." She took two steps closer but kept herself out of arm's reach. "I'm worried about what killing them will do to you. Deep down, I think it hurts you. Makes you feel as though you're bad and destined for Hell." Her eyes filled with tears. "And I love you so much that I can't stand to see you in pain." She swiped at a tear that escaped down her cheek, and that one tear nearly broke me. "I-I need space. A day or two. I'm just . . . hormonal. I'm weaning Siobhan off breastfeeding, and then you drop this bomb on me after going down on me, and—"

"I understand," I said with a tight nod. But my stomach was knotted, and I wanted to hold her in my arms and not walk out that door.

"I'm sorry." Her voice sounded hoarse like she was forcing the words out.

"Don't. This is my fault." I stiffened. "I was in the middle of what felt like a war," I admitted. "Surrounded by gunfire, we were trying to help two people get to safety, but I think I could have taken them down without killing them. I'm so sorry."

I turned and left her alone in the kitchen, said goodbye to my sweet baby sleeping in her bedroom, then grabbed my bag still by the door and left.

HOLLY

My man had to be hurting. Not only because of his actions but because of mine as well. I kicked him out.

I'd messaged him not even an hour after he left and told him that I'd made a mistake and to please come home. But he decided it'd be best if he stayed at the hotel for a few days. To get his head together and give me some space, too. And then I went and drank a bottle of wine.

And the next night, I'd cried into my glass of whiskey.

I hated fighting with him. And this felt like a huge fight. But I really was hormonal.

Two nights without him, knowing he was choosing to be away, and it wasn't for work, had me going stir crazy.

And God, sitting through a board meeting yesterday at work had been HELL. I'd stared at my husband's empty black leather chair, all the while fighting back tears.

Sean kept kicking me under the table like we were teenagers picking on each other during Ma's Sunday family dinners.

And now, I was standing outside the hotel, frozen in place as I stared up at the building, clutching my keys like they were a lifeline. The valet probably thought I'd lost my mind.

I'd dropped Siobhan off with Anna and Adam before heading to the hotel to get my man back. Sean and Cole hadn't seen him since he'd returned from Italy, and normally my husband buried himself in League matters to relieve his stress. Well, sex was often his preferred stress reliever, but that wasn't an option right now.

I finally handed the valet my keys, pulled in a deep breath of air, then walked through the lobby as if I owned the place. Okay, so I kind of did own it since Sebastian was my husband.

I greeted the familiar staff and hurried to the lift, not bothering to ask if he was upstairs because I was his wife, and shouldn't I know where my husband was?

The ride to the penthouse went way too fast, just like my pulse.

In his original text, he'd said he was in "his penthouse," the one he lived in before moving in with me. I didn't want it to be "his" anymore, damn it. Not ever again. His place was next to me.

Did I approve of him taking a life? No. I believed that decision rested on the shoulders of law enforcement and the military.

I loved him, though. Until death do us part. I wanted to die before him—gray and old with lots of wrinkles from decades of laughter. Sebastian would never let that happen, though. No, the man was a deal maker, and he'd arrange with fate to take him first. He'd make a deal.

I knocked on the door and took one giant, nervous step back as I waited.

Please be here.

A few seconds later, the door swung inward, and I blinked in surprise to see a pretty brunette standing there.

Little fluttery wings worked up a storm in my abdomen as I stared at her in the hotel robe, her hair wet from a shower.

"Can I help you?" she asked, her accent French from the sounds of it.

"Is Sebastian here?" I asked around the knot in my throat.

"Renaud?" She arched a brow before a man came up behind her and circled his arms around her waist possessively. *Not* my man.

And how could I ever think such a horrible thought?

"He checked out an hour ago when I called to let him know my husband and I were coming into town. This is my favorite room in the place." She scrunched her brow. "And you are?"

"His wife," I blurted.

"Ah." She grinned and offered her hand. "*Enchanté.* I work out of the Renaud Industries office in Paris. Pretty much run it since he's in Dublin all of the time. That man hates being away from you."

Oh. You're Cecilia. Of course.

"Why was he staying here?" she asked, taking me by surprise.

"Oh. I had a bit of a cold, and I didn't want him getting sick," I lied through my teeth, and the woman and her husband backed up as if I had the plague. "He must have decided to surprise me and went home when I told him I wasn't contagious anymore." They took another step back.

Please have surprised me and be home now.

I quickly said goodbye, then made my way home as fast as possible, only breaking the speed limit a tiny bit.

When I arrived, the house was dark, and my shoulders fell in disappointment.

I went to the door but . . . it was unlocked.

I was certain I'd locked it when I left, and Sebastian would never leave it unlocked unless he was home.

I pulled myself together and went inside.

My heart sank at the sight of him sitting on the floor next to the fireplace. One leg stretched out, the other bent, a glass resting on top of his knee.

His gaze swiveled my way, and his lips parted, but he didn't speak.

"I was at the hotel looking for you." I dropped my purse and hurried to him.

He raised the glass to his lips and finished what was left of his drink. "I missed you."

I fell to my knees at his side, ignoring the pain that quick movement caused on wooden floors. "I missed you, too." I reached for him and palmed his cheek. "Don't ever leave me again."

"You sure?" he asked, his voice husky and deep. "I don't want you to hate me for—"

I silenced him with my finger. "I could never hate you." I chewed on my lip. "But I would love to have make-up sex with my husband. A lot of it." I wanted to be wrapped in his arms. To feel our bodies joined as they should be. He was mine forever and always. "I love you so much."

He set down his drink, relaxed his bent leg, and urged me to straddle him. "You forgive me for breaking my promise?"

I nodded, my emotions stealing my voice.

He raced the pad of his thumb along my bottom lip and pulled it down. "I'll do better. For you. For our family," he said before crushing his mouth over mine.

* * *

SEBASTIAN - DECEMBER 2021 (2 MONTHS LATER)

"Well, just no punching anyone for looking at your wife the wrong way, okay?" Holly's mother said while focusing her gaze on Adam, and then she plopped more food onto his plate.

"I've only done that once. Or twice," Adam said with a sheepish grin.

Ethan mumbled, "Bullshite."

"I wasn't referring to you." Holly's mother sent Adam a stern but loving look.

Oh, she was talking about me, wasn't she? *Shite.*

"He'll be on his best behavior." Holly pinned me with a hard stare, demanding I behave for the 12 Pubs of Christmas.

"I don't make promises I can't keep." And feck if that was the wrong thing for me to say. Holly had forgiven me for my broken promise in October, and she'd even laughed a little at some of the SEAL humor I'd told her about when it came to Roman and the others.

But the daggers she was shooting me now . . . did she forget how sorry I'd been?

"If you'll excuse me." Holly set her red linen napkin on her plate and stood in a hurry. Even the legs of her chair sounded angry with me as they scraped across the floors.

I abruptly rose and ran after her, my jaw clenched with worry.

Frantically sorting through my mind for different ways to apologize, I hurriedly followed Holly up the stairs, down the hall, and to her childhood bedroom.

As soon as I crossed the threshold, she announced, "We need to have sex. Now."

Reaching behind me, I shut the door, then scratched the back of my head, wondering if this was some big joke.

"Babe." I approached her slowly, like I was confronting a wild animal, as she began stripping out of her clothes.

Okay, so we're doing this now? I turned around and locked the door.

"Aren't you mad at me?" Why wasn't I just going with it? Yeah, her hormones were still a bit off now that she'd stopped breastfeeding, but . . . I doubted pissing her off made her horny.

But before I knew it, my wife was standing before me in nothing but a very tiny thong.

"I am mad, but I don't want you sleeping at the hotel ever again," she quickly rushed out. "So, I need you to screw the anger out of me. I-I don't want to be upset with you for only doing your, um, job, for protecting people."

Oh damn. I was such a bloody idiot for putting her through this. Especially when I didn't know if I'd be able to keep myself from killing once we reached the final takedown of The Alliance.

She didn't need to worry about me, though. I could handle the consequences of my actions as long as I had her and Siobhan in my life. What I couldn't handle was losing them.

"Sebastian, this isn't a request," she demanded, her spine straightening, and her eyes intently focused on mine. "I want it hard, rough, and dirty. Now. Here, in my old bedroom."

I searched her face, needing to be confident this was what she truly wanted. And what I saw was anguish, not because I'd killed against her wishes, but because she was frightened of losing me. I needed to ease that pain, release that anger, and show her by taking her fast and hard, just like she wanted, that she was mine forever.

So, I did it. I hoisted her into my arms, and she hooked her ankles around my back as I walked us to the bed.

God, did I love my wife.

And like hell would I lose her.

But thoughts of Luca crowded my mind and it had me biting down on my back teeth like some blood-thirsty beast.

"Hey, get out of your head. I need you to be *here* with me," she said, placing my hand on her chest just above her heart. She cupped my cheeks and locked her focus on my eyes, bringing me back to her. Back to the bright light of her world. The world I couldn't live without.

Crossover Information

ROMAN, HARPER, AND THE REST OF ECHO TEAM CAN BE found in the Stealth Ops Navy SEAL Series. Roman and Harper's book, *Chasing Shadows*, releases March 25, 2021.

VISIT MY WEBSITE TO DOWNLOAD A FREE BONUS SCENE starring Harper and Roman, *A Stealth Ops Holiday*.

PLAYLIST

Be Kind (with Halsey) - Marshmallo, Halsey

Love Looks Better - Alicia Keys

Too Much To Ask - Niall Horan

Wonder - Shawn Mendes

Ask Me How I Know - Garth Brooks

What Ifs (feat. Lauren Alaina) - Kane Brown

Take You Dancing - Jason Derulo

Without You (feat. Usher) - David Guetta, Usher

Dynamite - BTS

Blinding Lights - The Weekend

Levitating (feat. DeBaby) - Dua Lipa, DaBaby

Relation, Remix - Sech, Daddy Yankee

Spotify: The Final Hour

READING GUIDE

Get the latest news from my newsletter/website and/or Brittney's Book Babes / the Stealth Ops Spoiler Room /Dublin Nights Spoiler Room.

A Stealth Ops World Guide is available on my website, which features more information about the team, character muses, and SEAL lingo.

Publication Order
Pinterest Muse/Inspiration Board
Bonus Scenes

* * *

Stealth Ops Series: Bravo Team

Finding His Mark - Book 1 - Luke & Eva
Finding Justice - Book 2 - Owen & Samantha
Finding the Fight - Book 3 - Asher & Jessica
Finding Her Chance - Book 4 - Liam & Emily

Finding the Way Back - Book 5 -Knox & Adriana

Stealth Ops Series: Echo Team

Chasing the Knight - Book 6 -Wyatt & Natasha
Chasing Daylight - Book 7 - A.J. & Ana
Chasing Fortune - Book 8 - Chris & Rory
Chasing Shadows - Book 9 -Harper & Roman (3/25/21)
Book 10 - Finn (2021)

Becoming Us: *connection to the Stealth Ops Series (books take place between the prologue and chapter 1 of Finding His Mark)*

Someone Like You - A former Navy SEAL. A father. And off-limits. (Noah Dalton)

My Every Breath - A sizzling and suspenseful romance. Businessman Cade King has fallen for the wrong woman. She's the daughter of a hitman - and he's the target.

Dublin Nights

On the Edge - Travel to Dublin and get swept up in this romantic suspense starring an Irish businessman by day…and fighter by night.
On the Line - novella
The Real Deal - This mysterious billionaire businessman has finally met his match.
The Inside Man - Cole McGregor & Alessia Romano
The Final Hour - Sean and Emilia

Stand-alone (with a connection to *On the Edge*):

The Story of Us– Sports columnist Maggie Lane has 1 rule: never fall for a player. One mistaken kiss with Italian soccer star Marco Valenti changes everything…

Hidden Truths

The Safe Bet – Begin the series with the Man-of-Steel lookalike Michael Maddox.

Beyond the Chase - Fall for the sexy Irishman, Aiden O'Connor, in this romantic suspense.

The Hard Truth – Read Connor Matthews' story in this second-chance romantic suspense novel.

Surviving the Fall – Jake Summers loses the last 12 years of his life in this action-packed romantic thriller.

The Final Goodbye - Friends-to-lovers romantic mystery

WHERE ELSE TO FIND ME

Thank you for reading Sean and Emilia's story. If you don't mind taking a minute to leave a short review, I would greatly appreciate it. Reviews are incredibly helpful to keeping the series going. Thank you!

www.brittneysahin.com
brittneysahin@emkomedia.net
FB Reader Group - Brittney's Book Babes
/ Stealth Ops Spoiler Room
Pinterest Muse/Inspiration Board

Printed in Great Britain
by Amazon

54592383R00255